MARY

OF

NAZARETH

MARY

OF

NAZARETH

A NOVEL

MAREK HALTER

Translated by Howard Curtis

CROWN PUBLISHERS NEW YORK

Translation copyright © 2008 by Crown Publishers, a division of Random House, Inc.

Originally published in France as *Marie* by Éditions Robert Laffont, Paris, in 2006. Copyright © 2006 by Éditions Robert Laffont, S.A., Paris.

Library of Congress Cataloging-in-Publication Data
Halter, Marek
    [Marie. English]
    Mary of Nazareth : a novel / Marek Halter ; translated by Howard Curtis.
        p. cm.
    I. Curtis, Howard, 1949–   II. Title.
PQ2668.A434M3713   2008
843'.914—dc22   2007041790

ISBN 978-0-307-39483-5

Printed in the United States of America

DESIGN BY BARBARA STURMAN

10 9 8 7 6 5 4 3 2 1

First American Edition

Do not be afraid, Mary, for you have found favor with God. You will be with child and give birth to a son, and you will name him Jesus . . . The Lord God will give him the throne of his father David, and he will reign over the house of Jacob forever, and his kingdom will never end.

—LUKE 1:30–33

Who then is the parent?
The mother and the child.

—AVADANAS, Indian tales and fables

Jesus is the most radiant figure in History. But although everyone now knows that he was a Jew, no one knows that his mother Mary was also a Jew.

—DAVID BEN-GURION

Historians now believe that the birth of Jesus may well date to the year 4 B.C., in other words, four years before the official calendar of the Christian era begins. The error has been attributed to a monk in the eleventh century.

MARY

OF

NAZARETH

PROLOGUE

Night had fallen. All the doors and shutters in the village were closed, the noises of day swallowed by the darkness.

Joachim the carpenter was sitting on his wool-padded stool, gripping the burrs wrapped in cloth with which he polished one delicately veined piece of wood after another. Once each piece was finished, he placed it carefully in a basket.

These were gestures to which he was accustomed, made heavier now by sleepiness. From time to time he stopped, his eyelids closed, and his head drooped.

On the other side of the hearth, his wife, Hannah, her face pink in the light from the dying embers, threw him a tender look, a smile crinkling her cheeks. She winked at her daughter Miriam, who was holding up a skein of wool for her. The child made a knowing face in response. Hannah's agile fingers resumed pulling on the strands of wool, crossing them and twisting them at such a regular rhythm that they formed a single thread.

They were startled to hear yells from outside, close to the house.

Joachim stood up, neck and shoulders tensed, all sleepiness gone.

They heard more yells, voices sharper than the clanking of metal, a sudden incongruous burst of laughter, a woman's moan that ended in sobs.

Miriam studied her mother's face. Hannah, her fingers tight on the wool, turned to Joachim. Mother and daughter watched him as he put the piece of wood he had been working on into the basket, with a precise, careful gesture, and threw over it the handful of cloth-wrapped burrs.

Outside, the cries grew in volume and intensity. The village's one street was in an uproar. Oaths and curses could clearly be heard now through the doors and walls.

Hannah put away her work in the cloth laid out on her lap and looked at Miriam. "Go upstairs," she said in a low voice and, without further ado, took the skein from the girl's outstretched arms. "Go upstairs," she said again, her voice harsher now. "Hurry up!"

Miriam walked from the hearth to the curtain that concealed a shadowy staircase. She pulled back the curtain, then stopped, unable to take her eyes off her father.

Joachim was on his feet now, walking toward the door. He, too, stopped. The bar was down across the door and the single shutter. He had placed it there himself. The door was well blocked, he knew.

But he also knew it was useless. It would not protect them. The people who were coming were not deterred by doors and shutters.

The shouts were closer now, echoing between the walls of the storerooms and workshops.

"Open up! Open up in the name of Herod, your king!"

The words were uttered in bad Latin, and repeated in bad Hebrew. The voices, the accent, the way they yelled—it was all like a foreign language to the inhabitants of the village.

It was always like this when Herod's mercenaries arrived to spread terror and calamity through Nazareth. They preferred to come at night; nobody knew why.

Sometimes they stayed for days on end. In summer, they would camp just outside the village. In winter, as the whim took them, they would throw whole families out of their houses and settle in. They would not leave until they had stolen, burned, destroyed, and killed. They would take their time, savoring the harm and suffering they caused.

Occasionally, they would take prisoners away with them. Men, women, even children, who were seldom seen again, and after a while were assumed dead.

Sometimes, the mercenaries left the village alone for months. A whole season. The youngest, the most carefree, almost forgot that they existed.

The cries were echoing all around the house now. Miriam could hear the scraping of soles on the cobbles.

Joachim felt his daughter's eyes on his back. He turned and peered into the shadows. He was not angry to see that she was still there, but waved his hand urgently. "Quick, Miriam, upstairs! Be careful!"

He made a face at her that might have been a smile. Miriam saw her mother press her hands to her mouth and look at her in dread. This time, she turned and set off up the stairs.

She had to keep close to the wall to find her way in the dark, and made no attempt to avoid the steps that creaked. The soldiers were shouting so much, there was no risk they would hear her.

They were banging so hard on the main door that the walls shook beneath Miriam's hand as she opened the door leading out onto the terrace.

From here, the hubbub of cries, commands, and moans melted into the darkness. Down below, in the main room, Joachim's voice seemed surprisingly calm as he raised the bar and the door swung open on its hinges.

T H E soldiers' torches were like a red wave in the darkness. Heart pounding, Miriam resisted the desire to approach the low wall and watch the scene. It was easy enough to guess what was happening. Cries echoed through the house below her. She heard her father's protests, her mother's moans, the mercenaries ordering them to be quiet.

She ran to the other end of the long terrace overlooking the workshop, avoiding the jumble of objects that cluttered it: baskets, sacks containing old pieces of wood, sawdust, badly baked bricks, jars, logs, and sheepskins. Her father had thrown all these things here, due to lack of space in the storeroom.

In a corner was a heap of rough-hewn logs that seemed to have been thrown there so casually that they were in danger of collapsing. But the heap was there for show only. The hiding place Joachim had built for his daughter was surely the finest, the cleverest thing he had ever constructed in his life.

In among the heaped logs, which were so heavy they needed at least two men to lift them, were a number of thin planks of carob wood, made to look as if they had been jammed there when the logs had subsided.

But the plank at the side of the pile could be pushed to open a trapdoor, cleverly camouflaged to look like a normal piece of wood, gouged by tools and eroded by bad weather.

Beneath it, skillfully dug within the heap of logs, which had in fact been carefully fixed into place, was a hollow big enough for an adult to lie down in it.

Only Miriam, her mother, and Joachim knew about this hiding place. None of their friends or neighbors was aware of its existence. It would have been too risky. Herod's mercenaries had ways to make men and women confess what they thought they could always keep silent.

Her hand on the plank, Miriam was about to work the mechanism when she froze. Despite the growing din in the street and the house, she sensed a presence close to her.

She turned her head sharply. There was a flash of something

light, a piece of fabric, which then vanished. She peered into the shadows behind the barrels of brine where olives were left to soak, aware that she could not stand here for too long.

"Who's there?" she whispered.

No answer. From below came Joachim's muted voice, stating, in response to the angry cries of one of the soldiers, that there had never been any boys in this house. The Almighty had never given him any.

"Don't lie!" the mercenary screamed, his accent making the syllables seem to tumble over one another. "There are always boys in a Jewish house."

Miriam had to hurry. They would be coming up before long.

Had she really seen something or was it her imagination?

Holding her breath, she walked forward. And bumped into him. He jumped like a cat pouncing.

A tall thin boy, from what she could see in the dim torchlight filtering up from the street. Bright eyes, skin taut over the bones of his face.

"Who are you?" she whispered in surprise.

If he was afraid, he did not show it. He grabbed hold of Miriam's tunic by the sleeve and, without a word, dragged her to where the darkness was at its thickest. The tunic ripped. Miriam let herself be drawn down into a crouching position next to him.

"You fool!" he said, in a curt, serious voice. "You'll get me caught!"

"Let go, you're hurting me."

"You idiot!" he growled.

But he let go of her arm, and huddled against the low wall.

Miriam half stood up and moved away. If he thought he could escape the soldiers by hiding here, he was as stupid as he was rough.

"Is it you they're looking for?" she asked.

He did not reply. There was no point.

"It's because of you they're destroying everything," she said.

This time it was not a question. But he still said nothing. Miriam peered over the barrels. The mercenaries would come up here and find him. They would not listen to reason. They would think her parents had been trying to hide this idiot, and the family would be doomed. She already saw Herod's soldiers beating her mother and father.

"So you think they won't see you behind there! You're going to get us all arrested!"

"Be quiet! Get out of here, damn it!"

This was no time to argue. "Don't be so stupid. Come on, quick! There's just time before they come up!"

She hoped he would not be too obstinate. Without waiting for him, she ran to the heap of logs. Of course, he did not follow her. She looked toward the door of the terrace. Below, her mother's protests could be heard above the noise of objects being smashed.

"Hurry up! I beg you!"

She pushed the plank and the trapdoor opened. At last he had understood and was standing behind her, although still inclined to argue.

"What is this?"

"What do you think? Get in, it'll be big enough."

"But you—"

Without answering, she pushed him with all her strength into the hiding place. With a certain satisfaction, she heard him bang his head and curse. Then she lowered the trapdoor, taking care not to make any noise. She tilted the plank to block the mechanism that would have made it possible to open the door from the inside. "This way, we won't run any risk because of him!" She did not know him, did not even know his name. But she did not need to know any more to guess that he was someone who did exactly what he wanted.

She crouched behind the barrels just as the mercenaries came up onto the terrace, waving their torches.

———

———

THEY were pushing Joachim before them. Four soldiers in leather breastplates, carrying swords. The plumes on their helmets shook each time they moved.

They moved their torches about to throw light on the clutter of the terrace. One of them hit Joachim on the back with the pommel of his sword, forcing him to bend. It was a pointless gesture, more humiliating than painful. But the mercenaries liked to show how cruel they were.

"Now this is what I call a good place to hide!" their leader cried in bad Hebrew.

Surprised, Joachim did not reply. He looked embarrassed.

The officer, who was watching his reaction closely, laughed. "Yes, of course! Someone's hiding here!"

He barked out orders, and his men set about searching the place, overturning everything. Again, Joachim assured them that there was no one hiding in his house.

The officer laughed again. "Yes, someone came into your house! You're lying, but for a Jew you're a bad liar."

Suddenly, there were two almost simultaneous cries. A cry of surprise from one of the soldiers, and a cry of pain as the soldier pulled Miriam out by her hair.

Joachim also cried out, and tried to move forward to protect his daughter. The officer grabbed his tunic and pulled him back.

"That's my daughter!" Joachim protested. "My daughter, Miriam!"

The soldiers shone their torches in Miriam's eyes, blinding her. Her chin was quivering with fear. Everyone was looking at her, including her father, who was furious that she was not in the hiding place. Jaws clenched, she pushed away the hand holding her hair. To her surprise, the soldier relaxed his fingers with a certain gentleness.

"That's my daughter," Joachim said again, imploringly.

"Be silent!" the officer screamed. He turned to Miriam. "What were you doing there?"

"Hiding," Miriam said, her voice shaking more than she would have liked.

The officer was pleased to see her fear. "Why hide?" he asked.

She glanced over to where they were holding her father. "My parents make me. They're afraid of you."

The soldiers laughed.

"Did you think we wouldn't find you behind those barrels?" the officer said mockingly.

Miriam shrugged.

"She's a child, officer," Joachim cried, his voice firmer now. "She hasn't done anything."

"If she hasn't done anything, why were you so afraid we'd find her?"

There was an embarrassed silence.

Then Miriam replied, "My father was afraid because he's heard that Herod's soldiers kill even women and children. He's also heard that you take them away to the king's palace and they're never seen again."

The officer laughed, startling Miriam, and the mercenaries laughed in imitation. Then the officer grew serious again. He seized Miriam by the shoulder and stared at her intensely.

"You may be right, little girl. But we only touch those who disobey the will of the king. Are you quite sure you haven't done anything wrong?"

Miriam held his gaze, her features motionless, her eyebrows raised uncomprehendingly, as if the mercenary had said something absurd.

"How could I do anything to the king? I'm only a child. He doesn't even know I exist."

Again, the soldiers laughed. The officer pushed Miriam so that she fell into her father's arms. Joachim hugged her so tightly she could hardly breathe.

"Your daughter is a crafty little devil, carpenter," the officer said.

"You should keep an eye on her. Hiding her on the terrace isn't such a good idea. The boys we're chasing are dangerous. They even kill your people when they're afraid."

H ANNAH, guarded by some of the mercenaries, was waiting at the foot of the staircase as they came down. She hugged her daughter and stammered a prayer to the Almighty.

The officer issued a warning. A gang of young brigands had tried to seize the tax collector's villa, looking, once again, to rob the king. They would be caught and punished. Everyone knew how. And all those who helped them would suffer the same fate. No mercy would be shown.

When the soldiers had finally gone, Joachim hastened to bar the door. There was a loud crackling from the hearth. The mercenaries had not merely overturned the furniture, they had also thrown Joachim's work on the fire. The pieces of wood he had fashioned so carefully now burned brightly, adding to the dim light from the oil lamps.

Miriam ran to the fire, crouched, and tried to remove the pieces of wood with the help of an iron poker. It was too late.

Her father put his hand on her shoulder. "There's nothing there to save," he said softly. "It doesn't matter. What I made once, I can make again."

Miriam's face was blurred with tears.

"At least they didn't touch the workshop," Joachim sighed. "I don't know what held them back."

As Miriam was getting to her feet, her mother asked, "How did they manage to find you? God Almighty, did they discover the hiding place?"

"No," Joachim said. "She wasn't there, she was behind the barrels."

"Why?"

Miriam looked at them. Their faces were still gray with fear, their eyes overbright, their features drawn at the thought of what might have happened. She thought of the boy hiding upstairs, in her place. She could have told her father about him. But not her mother.

"I thought they were going to hurt you," she murmured, "and I didn't want to stay up there all alone while they did that."

It was only a half lie. Hannah drew her close, wetting her temples with her tears and kisses. "Oh, my poor girl! You're mad."

Joachim set one of the stools on its legs and smiled slightly. "She stood up well to the officer. Our daughter is a brave girl, and that's a fact."

Miriam moved away from her mother, her cheeks flushing pink from the compliment. Joachim's eyes were full of pride, and almost happy.

"Help us to tidy up," he said, "and then go to bed. We shan't have any more trouble tonight."

T H E yells of the mercenaries did in fact cease. They had not found what they were looking for. In fact, they very rarely did, and this frustration often drove them as crazy as wild animals. When that happened, they slaughtered and destroyed without discrimination or pity. That night, however, they simply left the village, exhausted and sleepy, and went back to the legion's camp two miles from Nazareth.

As usually happened in cases like this, each household closed in on itself. The villagers bandaged their wounds, dried their tears, calmed their fears. It was only at dawn that they ventured out and spoke to each other about the terror they had been through.

Miriam had to wait for quite a while before she could slip out of bed. Hannah and Joachim, still shaking with fear, took a long time to fall sleep.

When she finally heard their regular breathing through the thin wooden partition separating her bedroom from theirs, she got up and, wrapped in a thick shawl, climbed the stairs to the terrace, taking care this time that no step creaked.

A crescent moon, veiled in mist, lacquered everything in a pale light. Miriam advanced confidently. She could have found her way in pitch darkness.

She easily found the plank that kept the hiding place closed. As she moved it, the trapdoor was pushed violently from the inside, and she just had time to step aside and avoid it hitting her. The boy was already on his feet.

"Don't be afraid," she whispered. "It's only me."

He was not afraid. Cursing, he shook himself like an animal to get the straw and wool from the bottom of the hiding place out of his hair.

"Not so loud," Miriam whispered. "You're going to wake my parents—"

"Couldn't you have come earlier? A person could suffocate in there. And there was no way to open the damned box!"

Miriam chuckled.

"You locked me in, didn't you?" the boy growled. "You did it on purpose!"

"I was in a hurry."

The young man merely snorted.

To placate him, Miriam showed him the mechanism that opened the trapdoor from the inside, a piece of wood that just had to be pushed hard. "It isn't complicated."

"If you know how it works."

"Don't complain. The soldiers didn't find you, did they? If you'd been hiding behind the barrels, you wouldn't have stood a chance."

The boy was starting to calm down. In the gloom, Miriam could see his bright eyes. He might even have been smiling.

"What's your name?" he asked.

"Miriam. My father is Joachim, the carpenter."

"For a girl your age, you're brave," he admitted. "I heard you with the soldiers; you handled them well." The boy rubbed his cheeks and neck energetically, to wipe off the wisps of straw that still clung to them. "I suppose I have to thank you. My name's Barabbas."

Miriam could not help laughing. Because his name wasn't a real name; all it meant was "son of the father." Because of his serious tone, too, and because she was pleased that he had complimented her.

Barabbas sat down on the logs. "I don't see what's so funny," he said grouchily.

"It's your name."

"You may be brave, but you're still as silly as a little girl."

The barb displeased Miriam more than hurt her. She knew boys' minds. This one was trying to make himself seem interesting. There was no need. He was interesting without having to make an effort. He was a pleasant combination of strength and gentleness, violence and fairness, and did not seem overconscious of the fact. Alas, boys of his kind always thought that girls were children, whereas they, of course, were already men.

Intriguing as he was, though, he had brought the soldiers down on their house and the whole village.

"Why were the Romans looking for you?" she asked.

"They aren't Romans! They're barbarians. No one even knows where Herod buys them! In Gaul or Thracia. Perhaps from among the Goths. Herod isn't capable of maintaining real legions. He needs slaves and mercenaries."

He spat in disgust over the low wall. Miriam said nothing, waiting for him to answer her question.

Barabbas peered into the dense shadows of the surrounding houses, as if to assure himself that no one could see or hear them. In the weak light of the moon, his mouth was handsome, his profile fine. His cheeks and chin were covered with a curly beard as thin as down. An adolescent's beard, which probably did not make him look all that much older in the full light of day.

Suddenly, he opened his hand. In his palm, a gold escutcheon glittered in the moonlight. It was instantly recognizable: an eagle with outspread wings, a tilted head, and a powerful, threatening beak. The Roman eagle. The gold eagle fixed to the tops of the ensigns carried by the legions.

"I took it from one of their storehouses," Barabbas whispered, and laughed proudly. "We set fire to the rest before those stupid mercenaries even woke up. We also had time to pick up two or three bushels of grain. It's only fair."

Miriam looked curiously at the escutcheon. She had never seen one so close. She had never even seen so much gold in her life.

Barabbas closed his hand again and slipped the escutcheon into the inside pocket of his tunic. "It's worth a lot of money," he muttered.

"What are you going to do with it?"

"I know someone who can melt it down and turn it into gold we can use," he said, mysteriously.

Miriam took a step away from him, torn between conflicting feelings. She liked this boy. She sensed in him a simplicity, a frankness, and an anger that appealed to her. Courage, too, because you needed courage to confront Herod's mercenaries. But she did not know if she was right. She did not know enough about the world, about what was just and what unjust, to be certain.

Her emotions drew her naturally to Barabbas's enthusiasm, his anger at the horrors and humiliations that even young children suffered daily in Herod's kingdom. But she could also hear her father's wise, patient voice, and his unswerving condemnation of violence.

Somewhat provocatively, she said, "You're a thief, then?"

Offended, Barabbas stood up. "Certainly not! It's Herod's people who call us thieves. But everything we take from the Romans, the mercenaries and those who wallow in the king's sheets, we redistribute to the poorest among us. To the people!" Underlining his words with a gesture, he went on, his voice full of barely contained anger. "We aren't thieves, we're rebels. And I'm not alone, believe me. I'm one rebel among many. The soldiers weren't only after me tonight. When we attacked those storehouses, there were at least thirty or forty of us."

She had suspected as much even before he admitted it.

Rebels! Yes, that was what people called them—usually not approvingly. Her father and his fellow carpenters in Nazareth often complained about them. They were reckless, dangerous young men their parents should have kept locked up at home. What did they gain by provoking Herod's mercenaries? One day, because of them, every village in the region would be wiped out. A rebellion! A rebellion of the weak and the powerless, which the king and the Romans could put down whenever they chose!

Not that there weren't plenty of reasons to rebel. The kingdom of Israel was drowning in blood, tears, and shame. Herod was the cruelest, most unjust of kings. Now that he was old and nearing death, his cruelty was compounded by his madness. Even the Romans, soulless pagans that they were, were not as bad as Herod at his worst.

As for the Pharisees and Sadducees, the custodians of the Temple in Jerusalem and its wealth, they were not much better. They shamelessly submitted to the king's every whim. The laws they made were not there to promote justice, merely to help them hold on to the trappings of power and increase their wealth.

Galilee, far to the north of Jerusalem, had been ruined by the taxes that enriched Herod and his sons and all those who shared in their shameless ways.

Yes, Yahweh, as he had done more than once since he had made his covenant with Abraham, had turned his back on his people and his kingdom. But was that a reason to answer violence with violence? Was it wise, when you were weak, to provoke the strong and risk unleashing widespread carnage?

"My father says you rebels are stupid," Miriam said, trying to make her voice sound as reproving as possible. "You're going to get us all killed."

Barabbas laughed. "I know. A lot of people say that. They complain about us as if we were the cause of their misfortunes. They're scared, that's all. They prefer to sit on their backsides and wait. And what are they waiting for? Who knows? The Messiah, perhaps?"

Barabbas dismissed the word with a gesture of his hand, as if to scatter the syllables into the night.

"The kingdom is full of messiahs, fools, and weaklings, men, every one of them. You don't need to have studied with the rabbis to know that we can't expect anything good from Herod and the Romans. Your father is deceiving you. Herod was slaughtering, raping, and stealing long before we came on the scene. That's what keeps him and his children going. They're only rich and powerful thanks to our poverty! Well, I'm not the kind of person who waits. They won't find me cowering in my hole."

He fell silent, choked with anger. Miriam did not say a word.

"If we don't rebel, who will?" he went on, his voice even harder. "Your father and all the old men like him are wrong. They'll die whatever happens. And they'll die as slaves. But I'll die as a Jew, a son of the great people of Israel. My death will be better than theirs."

"My father is neither a slave nor a coward. He's as brave as you are. . . ."

"What good did his bravery do him just now? He had to beg when the mercenaries found you hiding on the terrace!"

"I was only there because you needed saving! They broke everything in our house and our neighbor's houses, my father's work, our furniture. All that, just so that you could show off!"

"Oh, be quiet! I've already told you, you talk like a child. Such matters are not for children!"

They had tried to talk quietly, but had both been carried away by the argument. Miriam ignored the insult. She turned to the staircase, her ears pricked, to make sure that there was no noise inside the house. Whenever her father got out of bed, the bed emitted a particular creak that she always recognized.

Reassured, she turned to face Barabbas again. He had walked

away from the logs and was now leaning over the low wall, looking for a way to get down from the terrace.

"What are you doing?" she asked.

"Leaving. I don't suppose you want me to go out through your father's precious house. I'd rather leave the way I came."

"Barabbas, wait!"

They were both wrong and both right, Miriam knew. So did Barabbas. That was what made him angry.

She went close enough to him to put her hand on his arm. He shuddered as if she had stung him.

"Where do you live?" she asked.

"Not here."

What an irritating habit that was, of never answering questions directly! All part of being a thief, she supposed.

"I know you don't live here, or I would have seen you before."

"In Sepphoris . . ."

A sizable town, an hour and a half's walk to the north. You had to go through a dense forest to get there. No one would ever dare venture into it at night.

"Don't be silly," she said gently. "You can't go back now." She took off her woolen shawl and handed it to him. "You can sleep in the hiding place . . . Leave the trapdoor open. That way, you won't suffocate. And if you put this shawl around you, you won't feel too cold."

His only response was to shrug and look away. But he did not refuse the shawl, and he abandoned his attempt to escape over the wall of the terrace.

"Tomorrow," Miriam said, with a smile in her voice, "as early as I can, I'll bring you some bread and milk. But when it gets light, it's best if you close the trapdoor. Sometimes, my father comes up here as soon as he rises."

———

———

By dawn, a thin, cold rain was falling, and everything felt damp. Unseen and unheard by anyone in the house, Miriam took a little pot of milk and a hunk of bread from her mother's reserves, and climbed to the terrace.

The trapdoor was closed. The wood glistened with rain. Making sure that no one could see her, she pulled on the plank. The panel tipped just enough to show her that the hiding place was empty inside. Barabbas was gone.

He had not been gone for long. She could still feel his warmth in the woolen shawl, which he had left behind, carefully folded. So carefully that Miriam smiled. It was as if he had left her a sign. A sign of gratitude, perhaps.

Miriam was not surprised that Barabbas had vanished like this, without waiting for her. It went well with the image she had of him. Restless, foolhardy, unable to settle. Besides, it was raining, and he must have been afraid of being seen by the people of Nazareth. If anyone had discovered him in the village, they would have been sure to connect him with the young men who were being hunted by Herod's mercenaries and might have been tempted to take revenge on him for the fear they had felt.

All the same, as she closed the trapdoor again, Miriam could not help feeling slightly disappointed. She would have liked to see Barabbas again, to talk to him at greater length, to see his face in the full light of day.

It was highly unlikely their paths would ever cross again. Barabbas would most likely want to avoid Nazareth in the future.

She turned away to go back down to the house, and as she did so she shivered. The cold, the rain, her fear and anger—it all came together within her at the same time. In turning, she had caught sight of the three wooden crosses that stood on the hill overlooking the village, and although she was accustomed to the sight by now, it never failed to arouse a sense of horror.

Six months earlier, Herod's mercenaries had hanged three men there, three "thieves" captured in the area. By now, the three corpses were nothing but shriveled, putrefied, shapeless masses half-eaten by birds.

That was what awaited Barabbas if he got caught. It was also what justified his rebellion.

PART ONE

THE YEAR 6 B.C.

CHAPTER 1

Tʜᴇ torpor of early morning was shattered by the cries of children.
"They're here! They're here!"

In his workshop, Joachim was already at work. He exchanged glances with his assistant, Lysanias, but did not let himself be distracted by the noise. In a single movement, they lifted the cedar beam and placed it on the workbench.

Groaning, Lysanias massaged his lower back. He was too old for this heavy work, so old that no one, not even he himself, could remember when exactly he had been born, in a village somewhere far away in Samaria. But Joachim had been working with him forever, and could not imagine replacing him with a young apprentice. It was Lysanias, as much as his own father, who had taught him the trade of carpentry. Together, they had made more than a hundred roofs in the villages around Nazareth. Several times, their skills had been demanded from as far away as Sepphoris.

They heard footsteps in the courtyard as the cries of the children still echoed around the walls of the village. Hannah stopped in the doorway of the workshop. The morning sun cast her shadow across the floor as far as their feet.

"They've arrived," she said.

The words were unnecessary, she knew. But she had to say them, to give an outlet to her fear and anger.

Joachim sighed. "I heard."

There was no need to say more. Everyone in the village knew what was happening: The tax collectors of the Sanhedrin had entered Nazareth.

For days now, they had been going from village to village in Galilee, and the news of their coming had preceded them like the rumor of a plague. Each time they left a village, the rumor grew. It was as if they were devouring everything in their path, like the locusts inflicted on Pharaoh's Egypt by the wrath of Yahweh.

Old Lysanias sat down on a wooden block and shook his head. "We should stop yielding to those vultures! We must let God decide who to punish: them or us."

Joachim ran his hand over his chin and scratched his short beard. The previous evening, the men of the village had gathered to give vent to their fury. Like Lysanias, several of them had decided they would give nothing more to the tax collectors. No grain, no money, no objects. Let each person step forward empty-handed and say, "Go away!" But Joachim knew these were just words, the hopeless dreams of angry men. The dreams would fade, and so would their courage, as soon as they had to face reality.

The tax collectors never came to plunder the villages without the help of Herod's mercenaries. You might be able to present yourself to the tax collectors empty-handed, but anger could do nothing against spears and swords. It would simply provoke a massacre. Or drive home your own powerlessness and humiliation.

The neighborhood children stopped outside the workshop and surrounded Hannah, their eyes bright with excitement.

"They're in old Houlda's house!" they cried.

Lysanias stood up, his lips trembling. "What can they possibly hope to find at Houlda's? She doesn't have anything!"

Everyone in Nazareth knew how close Houlda and Lysanias were. If it had not been for tradition, which forbade Samaritan men to marry Galilean women, or even to live under the same roof, they would have become husband and wife a long time ago.

Joachim stood up and carefully tucked the ends of his tunic into his belt. "I'll go," he said to Lysanias. "You stay here with Hannah."

Hannah and the children stood aside to let him pass. No sooner was he outside than he was startled to hear Miriam's clear voice. "I'll go with you, Father."

Hannah immediately protested. This was no place for a young girl. Joachim was about to agree with her, but Miriam's determined expression dissuaded him. His daughter was not like other girls. There was something stronger, more mature about her. Braver and more rebellious, too.

The fact was, her presence always made him happy: a fact so obvious that Hannah never failed to make fun of him for it. Was he one of those fathers besotted with their daughters? Perhaps. If so, where was the harm in it?

He smiled at Miriam and gestured to her to walk beside him.

HOULDA'S house was one of the first you came to as you entered Nazareth from the direction of Sepphoris. By the time Miriam and Joachim arrived, half the men in the village had gathered outside it.

About twenty mercenaries in leather tunics stood a little way along the road, guarding the tax collectors' horses and the mule-drawn carts. Joachim counted four carts. These vultures from the Sanhedrin were aiming high if they hoped to fill them.

Another group of mercenaries, under a Roman officer, were lined up in front of old Houlda's house, holding spears and swords, all with an air of indifference.

Joachim and Miriam did not see the tax collectors immediately. They were inside the tiny house.

Suddenly, they heard Houlda's voice. A hoarse cry that split the air. There was a scramble in the doorway, and out they came.

There were three of them. They had hard mouths and the kind of arrogant expression in their eyes that power confers on people. Their black tunics swept the ground. The linen veils covering their skull caps were black too, and concealed most of their faces apart from their dark beards.

Joachim clenched his jaws until they hurt. Just seeing these people made him seethe with anger. With shame, too, and the desire to kill. May God forgive them all! They were vultures indeed, just like those that fed on the dead.

Guessing his thoughts, Miriam took him by the wrist and squeezed it. All her tenderness was in that gesture, but she shared too much of the father's pain to really calm him.

Again, Houlda cried out. She begged, thrusting forward her hands with their gnarled fingers. Her bun came loose, and locks of white hair fell across her face. She tried to catch hold of the tunic of one of the tax collectors, stammering, "You can't do it! You can't!"

The man broke free, and pushed her away with a grimace of disgust. The two others came to his aid. They seized old Houlda by the shoulders, making no allowances for her age and frailty.

Neither Miriam nor Joachim had yet discovered why Houlda had cried out. Then one of the tax collectors moved forward and they saw, between the tails of his black tunic, that he was holding a candlestick against his chest.

It was a bronze candlestick, older than Houlda herself, decorated with almond flowers. It had come down to her from her distant ancestors. A Hanukkah candlestick, so old that, according to her, it had belonged to the sons of Judas Maccabaeus, the first people to light candles in celebration of the miracle of eternal light. It was certainly the only thing of any value that she still possessed. Everyone

in the village knew the sacrifices Houlda had had to make in order
not to part with it. More than once, she had preferred to go without
essentials rather than sell it for a few gold coins.

At the sight of this candlestick in the tax collector's possession,
the villagers cried out in protest. In the households of Galilee and
Israel, wasn't the Hanukkah candlestick as sacred as the thought of
Yahweh? How could servants of the Temple in Jerusalem dare to rob
a house of its light?

At the first cries from the crowd, the Roman officer yelled an
order. The mercenaries brought their spears down and closed ranks.

Houlda cried out again, but no one could understand what she
was saying. One of the vultures turned, his fist raised. Without a
moment's hesitation, he hit the old woman in the face, projecting
her frail body against the wall of the house. She bounced off it, as if
she weighed no more than a feather, and collapsed in the dust.

Cries of fury went up. The soldiers took a step back, but their
spears and swords pricked the chests of those at the front of the
crowd.

Miriam had let go of her father's arm. She called out Houlda's
name. The point of a spear flashed less than a finger's distance from
her throat. Joachim saw the frightened look in the eyes of the mercenary holding the spear.

He could tell that this madman was about to strike Miriam. He
knew that even though he had been urging himself to be wise and
patient since the night before, he could no longer bear the humiliation these swine from the Sanhedrin were inflicting on old Houlda.
Nor—may God Almighty forgive him—could he ever accept a bar-
barian in Herod's pay killing his daughter. Anger was gaining the
upper hand, and he knew he would give in to it, whatever it might
cost him.

The mercenary drew back his hand to strike. Joachim leaped forward and pushed aside the spear before it could reach Miriam's
chest. The flat part of the head hit the shoulder of a young man

standing beside him, with enough force to throw him to the ground. Joachim tore the weapon from the mercenary's hand and slammed his fist, as hard as the wood he worked on every day, into the man's throat.

Something broke in the mercenary's neck, cutting off his breath. His eyes opened wide in astonishment.

Joachim pushed him away, and out of the corner of his eye saw Miriam help the young man to his feet, surrounded by the villagers who, not realizing that one of their enemies had just died, were shouting curses at the mercenaries.

He did not hesitate. Still holding the spear, he leaped toward the tax collectors. With the cries of the villagers in his ears, he aimed the spear at the stomach of the vulture holding the candlestick.

"Give that back!" he yelled.

Stunned, the other man did not move. It was possible he did not even understand what Joachim was saying. He moved back, white-faced, slavering with fear, still clutching the candlestick, and huddled against the other tax collectors behind him, as if to melt into their dark mass.

Old Houlda still lay on the ground. She had stopped moving. A little blood ran down one of her temples, blackening her white locks. Above the angry yelling, Joachim heard Miriam cry, "Father, watch out!"

The mercenaries who had been guarding the carts were running to the tax collector's rescue, brandishing their swords. Joachim realized that he was committing a folly and that his punishment would be terrible.

He thought of Yahweh. If God Almighty really was the God of Justice, as he had been taught, then he would forgive him.

He thrust in the spear. He was surprised to feel it sink so easily into the tax collector's shoulder. The man screamed in pain and at last let go of the candlestick. It dropped to the ground, tinkling slightly like a bell.

Before the mercenaries could throw themselves on him, Joachim threw down the spear, picked up the candlestick, and knelt beside Houlda. He was relieved to see that she had only fainted. He slid his arm under her shoulders, placed the candlestick on her stomach, and closed her misshapen fingers over it.

Only then did he become aware of the silence.

The cries and yells had stopped. The only sound was the moaning of the wounded tax collector.

He looked up. A dozen spears, and as many swords, were pointing directly at him. The indifference had gone from the mercenaries' faces, replaced by arrogance and hatred.

Ten paces along the road, the people of Nazareth, including Miriam, stood unable to move, held back by the mercenaries' spears.

The stunned silence lasted for another moment or two, and then there was pandemonium.

Joachim was seized, thrown to the ground, and beaten. Miriam and the villagers tried to surge forward, but the mercenaries pushed them back, cutting a swathe through the arms, legs, shoulders of the boldest until the officer in command gave the order to retreat.

Some of the mercenaries carried the wounded tax collector to his horse. Leather straps were tied around Joachim's wrists and ankles, and he was thrown unceremoniously onto one of the carts, which was already turning to leave the village. The body of the soldier he had killed was dumped next to him. Amid much yelling and cracking of whips, the carts sped away.

The horses and soldiers vanished into the darkness of the forest, and silence fell over Nazareth.

Miriam shivered. The thought of her father tied up and at the mercy of the Temple's soldiers brought a lump to her throat. Although the whole village was crowding around her, she was gripped by a boundless fear. She wondered what she was going to tell her mother.

———

———

"I SHOULD have gone with him," Lysanias said, swaying on his stool. "I stayed in the workshop like a frightened hen. It shouldn't have been Joachim defending Houlda. It should have been me."

The neighbors who had crowded into the room listened in silence to Lysanias's moans. They had told him over and over that it was not his fault and that there was nothing he could have done. But Lysanias could not get the idea out of his head. Like Miriam, he could not bear the thought that Joachim was not here with him now, and would not be with him tonight, or tomorrow.

As for Hannah, she sat there stiffly, in silence, nervously creasing the tails of her tunic.

Miriam, dry-eyed, her heart pounding, was watching her out of the corner of her eye. Her mother's mute, solitary sadness intimidated her. She did not dare make a gesture of tenderness toward her. Nor had the women neighbors taken Hannah in their arms. Joachim's wife was not an easy woman to get close to.

There was no point in crying for vengeance now. All they could do was nurse their pain and meditate on their own powerlessness.

Closing her eyes, Miriam relived the drama. She saw her father's body huddled, tied and thrown like a sack into the cart.

She kept asking herself, "What's going to happen to him now? What will they do to him?"

Lysanias was in no way responsible for what had happened. She was the one Joachim had been defending. It was because of her that he was now in the cruel hands of the Temple's tax collectors.

"We'll never see him again. He's as good as dead."

Echoing in the silence, Hannah's clear voice made them jump. No one protested. They were all thinking the same thing.

Joachim had killed a soldier and wounded a tax collector. They knew what his punishment would be. The only reason the mercenaries had not killed or crucified him on the spot was because they were in a hurry to tend to the vulture from the Sanhedrin.

They would want to make an example of him, which meant one thing: crucifixion. It was a foregone conclusion. He would hang on a cross until hunger, thirst, the cold, or the sun killed him. His death agony could last for days.

Biting her lips to hold back the tears, Miriam said in a toneless voice, "At least we should find out where they're taking him."

"Sepphoris," a neighbor said. "It's sure to be Sepphoris."

"No," someone else said. "They don't imprison people in Sepphoris anymore. They're too afraid of Barabbas's men. They've been chasing them all winter without catching them. It's said Barabbas has already plundered the tax collectors' carts twice. No, they'll be taking Joachim to Tarichea. No one has ever escaped from there."

"They might also take him to Jerusalem," a third man said. "Crucify him in front of the Temple as one more demonstration to the Judeans that we Galileans are all barbarians!"

"The best way to find out is to follow them," Lysanias said, rising from his stool. "I'll go."

Objections were raised. He was too old and tired to run after mercenaries! Lysanias insisted, assuring them that they wouldn't be suspicious of an old man, and that he was still nimble enough to get back quickly to Nazareth.

"And what then?" Hannah asked, in a restrained voice. "When you discover where my husband is, what will you do then? Go and see him on his cross? I certainly wouldn't. Why should I go and see Joachim being eaten by birds when he should be here taking care of us?"

A few voices were raised in protest, but only halfheartedly, since no one knew what was the best thing to do anymore.

"If I don't go, someone else will have to," Lysanias muttered. "We must find out where they're taking him."

After some discussion, two young shepherds were chosen. They left immediately, avoiding the Sepphoris road and cutting through the forest.

THE day brought no comfort. On the contrary, it divided Nazareth like a broken vase.

All day, the synagogue was full of men and women, praying endlessly, talking, and above all listening to the rabbi's exhortations.

God had decided on Joachim's fate, he asserted. It was wrong to kill a man, even if that man was one of Herod's mercenaries. We had to accept our path, for only the Almighty knew and could lead us to the coming of the Messiah.

They should not be too indulgent toward Joachim. Apart from putting his own life in danger, his actions had condemned the whole village in the eyes of Romans and the Sanhedrin. There would be many who would demand punishment. And the one thought of Herod's mercenaries, pagans fearing neither God nor man, would be of revenge.

There would be dark days ahead, the rabbi warned them. The wisest course was to accept Joachim's punishment, as well as praying long and hard for the Lord to forgive him.

These words of the rabbi's merely increased the villagers' confusion. Some found them full of good sense. Others recalled that the day before the coming of the tax collectors, they had been prepared to rebel. Joachim had simply taken them at their word. Now they no longer knew if they should follow his example and take action. Most were disoriented by what they had heard in the synagogue. How were they to distinguish good from evil?

Lysanias lost his temper and declared out loud that when you got down to it, he was glad he was a Samaritan rather than a Galilean.

"You're fine specimens," he cried to those supporting the rabbi. "You can't even sympathize with a man who defended an old woman against the tax collectors."

And, sure now that there was nothing to stop him, he went to live with old Houlda, who was confined to her bed with a pain in her hip.

Miriam kept silent. She had to admit that there was a degree of truth in what the rabbi said. But she could not accept it. Not only did it justify whatever Herod's mercenaries did to her father, but it also implied that the Almighty no longer showed justice toward the just. How could that be?

T H E shepherds returned before sunset, out of breath. The column had only stopped in Sepphoris long enough to tend the tax collector's wound.

"Did you see my father?" Miriam asked.

"We couldn't. We had to keep out of sight. Those mercenaries were evil. What's certain is that he stayed in the cart. The sun was beating down, so he must have been very thirsty. The people of Sepphoris couldn't approach him, either. There was no way to pass him a gourd."

Hannah moaned and whispered Joachim's name several times. The others bowed their heads.

"After that, they put the wounded tax collector in another cart and left the town. In the direction of Cana, according to the shepherds."

"They're going to Tarichea!" one of the neighbors exclaimed. "If they'd been going to Jerusalem, they would have taken the Tabor road."

Everyone knew that.

A heavy silence settled over them.

They all recalled Hannah's words. Yes, what good did it do them to know that Joachim was on his way to the fortress of Tarichea?

"At least," a woman neighbor sighed, as if in response to everyone's anxieties, "that means they won't crucify him straightaway."

"Tomorrow or the day after tomorrow, what difference does it make?" Lysanias muttered. "Joachim will have longer to suffer, that's all."

They could all picture the fortress. A stone monster dating back to the blessed days of David, which Herod had enlarged and strengthened, ostensibly to defend the people of Israel against the Nabateans, their enemies from the eastern desert.

In fact, its real purpose for some time now had been as a prison for hundreds of innocent people, rich and poor, learned and illiterate alike. Anyone who displeased the king. A rumor, a malevolent piece of gossip, a personal vendetta—anything could lead to a man being thrown in there. Most never came out again, or else ended up on the forest of crosses that surrounded it.

A visit to Tarichea was a grim experience, despite the great beauty of the shores of the Lake of Gennesaret. No one could escape the sight of the crucified. Some said that at night their moans echoed across the waters like screams from the depths of hell. It was enough to make your hair stand on end. Even the fishermen did not dare go near, despite the fact that the waters closest to the fortress were especially rich in fish.

They were all struck dumb with terror, but Miriam said in a clear, unwavering voice, "I'm going to Tarichea. I won't let my father rot in that fortress."

Everyone looked up. The deep silence of a moment earlier was replaced by a cacophony of protests.

Miriam was raving. She mustn't let herself be carried away by her grief. How could she get her father out of the fortress of Tarichea? Had she forgotten that she was only a girl? Barely fifteen, still so young she had not yet been married off. It was true that she looked older, and her father had the unfortunate habit of considering her a woman of reason and wisdom, but she was only a girl, not a miracle worker.

"I'm not planning to go to Tarichea alone," she said, when calm had returned. "I'm going to ask Barabbas for help."

"Barabbas the thief?"

Again, there was a chorus of protests.

This time, Halva, the young wife of Yossef, a carpenter friend of Joachim's, looked at Miriam and shouted over the din, "In Sepphoris, they say he doesn't steal for himself but only to give to those in need. They say he does more good than bad, and that the people he robs have deserved it."

Two men interrupted her. How could she say such things? A thief was a thief.

"The fact is, these wicked thieves draw Herod's mercenaries to our village like flies to a wound!"

Miriam shrugged. "Just as you claim the mercenaries will attack Nazareth in revenge for what my father did!" she said, harshly. "What matters is that however hard they pursue Barabbas, they never catch him. If anyone can save my father, he can."

Lysanias shook his head. "Why would he do it? We have no gold to pay him!"

"He'll do it because he owes it to me."

They all stared at her wide-eyed.

"He owes his life to my father and me. He'll listen to me, I'm sure of it."

THE debate went on endlessly, until late in the night.

Hannah moaned that she did not want to let her daughter leave. Did Miriam plan to leave her completely alone, to deprive her of her child as well as her husband? For just as surely as Joachim was already as good as dead, Miriam would be taken by the thieves or by the mercenaries. She would be violated, then murdered. That was what awaited her.

The rabbi supported Hannah. Miriam was talking with the recklessness of youth as well as the forgetfulness of her sex. It was inconceivable that a young girl could throw herself into the mouth of a wild beast, a rebel, a thief like this Barabbas. And to what purpose? To get herself killed at the earliest opportunity? To fuel the resentment of the Romans and the king's mercenaries, who would be sure to turn against all of them?

They were intoxicated with their own fearful imaginings, wallowing in their own powerlessness. Although she knew they were all fond of her and wanted what was best for her, Miriam started to feel disgusted.

She slipped out onto the terrace. Filled with all the sadness of the day, she lay down on the logs that concealed the hiding place her father had made for her when she was only a little girl. It was no use to her now. She closed her eyes and let the tears well up beneath her eyelids.

She had to weep now, for soon, without anyone noticing, she would do what she had said. She would leave Nazareth and save her father. There would be no time for weeping then.

In the darkness, Joachim's face came back to her. Gentle, friendly—and terrifying, too, the way it had been when he had struck the mercenary.

He was the gentlest of men, a man they sought out to patch up quarrels between neighbors, but he had had the courage to do what he had done. He had done it for her, for old Houlda, and for all of them, the inhabitants of Nazareth. Now she had to have the same courage. What was the point of waiting for dawn if the coming day did not see you fighting the things that humiliate and destroy you?

She opened her eyes again and forced herself to look up at the stars, trying to sense the presence of the Almighty. Oh, if only she could ask him whether he wanted her father's life!

Something brushed against her, and she jumped.

"It's me," Halva whispered. "I guessed you were here." She seized Miriam's hand, squeezed it, and kissed the fingertips. "They're afraid and they're sad, so they can't stop talking," she said, pointing downstairs, from where raised voices could still be heard.

Miriam said nothing.

"You're going to leave before dawn, aren't you?" Halva went on.

"Yes, I must."

"You're right. If you like, I can take our mule and go with you a little way."

"What will Yossef say?"

"I already talked to him. If it wasn't for the children, he'd go with you himself."

There was no need to say any more. Miriam knew that Yossef loved Joachim like a son. He owed him everything he knew about carpentry. Joachim had even given him his house, two leagues from Nazareth, the house where he had been born.

Halva laughed tenderly. "Except that Yossef is the last man I could imagine fighting mercenaries! He's so timid, he doesn't dare say what he thinks!"

She drew Miriam to her, and went with her to the stairs.

"I'll walk in front, so they don't see you leave. We'll go to my house. I'll give you a cloak; that way, your mother won't know. And you can have a few hours' rest before we set off."

CHAPTER 2

By the time they left the forest, the sun was rising above the hills. Far below, nestled deep in the valley at the foot of the path they were on, between the flowering orchards and the fields of flax, they could see the huddled roofs of Sepphoris. Halva stopped the cart.

"I'm going to leave you here. I mustn't get back to Nazareth too late." She drew Miriam to her. "Be careful with this Barabbas! After all he's still a bit of a bandit. . . ."

"If I even manage to find him." Miriam sighed.

"You will, I'm sure of it. Just as I'm sure you're going to save your father from the cross." Halva kissed her again, not a mischievous kiss this time, but a tender, solemn one. "I feel it in my heart, Miriam. I just have to look at you to feel it. You're going to save Joachim. Trust me. My intuition never lets me down!"

They had both been thinking, as they walked, about the best way to find Barabbas. Miriam had not tried to hide from Halva the fact that she was worried; she quite simply had no idea where he was hiding. She had confidently declared to the people of Nazareth that he would listen to her. Indeed he might. But first she had to get to him.

"If the Romans and Herod's mercenaries can't find him, how will I?"

Halva, always practical and trusting, had dismissed her anxieties. "That's the reason you'll find him—because you're not a Roman or a mercenary. You know the way things are. There must be people in Sepphoris who know where Barabbas is hiding. He has his followers, people who are indebted to him. They'll tell you."

"If I ask too many questions, they'll be suspicious. I'll only have to walk the streets of Sepphoris, and people will start asking who I am and where I'm going."

"People there may be curious, as they are here, but who'd go running to Herod's mercenaries to report you? You just have to say you're visiting your aunt. Say you're there to help your aunt Judith, who's expecting a child. It's not such a big lie. In fact, it's almost true, since she did have a baby last autumn. And when you see a likely looking person, tell them the truth. Someone is sure to have the answer."

"And how will I recognize a 'likely looking person'?"

"You can rule out the rich," Halva replied, impishly, "and the artisans are too serious! You must have confidence. You're perfectly capable of distinguishing a treacherous person from an honest man and a vicious shrew from a good mother."

Halva might be right. When she spoke, everything seemed simple, obvious. But now that she was nearing the gates of the town, Miriam doubted more than ever that she could extricate Barabbas from his hiding place and ask for his help.

But time was short. In two or three days, four at the most, it would be too late. Her father would die on the cross, charred by the sun, eaten by crows, jeered at by the mercenaries.

In the early morning light, Sepphoris was waking up. The shops were opening, the hangings in the doors of the houses were being drawn aside. Women were hailing each other with shrill cries, inquiring about one another's nights. Clusters of children were setting off to get water from the wells, squabbling as they went. Men with faces still creased with sleep were leaving for the fields, pushing their donkeys and mules ahead of them.

As Miriam had predicted, people cast curious glances at her, this stranger entering their town so early in the morning. Perhaps they guessed, from the slow, cautious way she was walking, that she did not know the way but did not dare ask. Nevertheless, she did not arouse as much curiosity as she had feared. People sized her up, noted that her cloak was of good quality, then looked away.

After going down several streets, she remembered Halva's advice, and began walking with a firmer stride. She turned left here, right there, as if she knew the town and had a clear idea of where she was going. She was looking for a face that inspired confidence.

In this way, she went from one quarter to another, past the stinking workshops of the furriers, and the stalls of the weavers who were spreading draperies, carpets, and tapestries over long poles, dazzling the street with a riot of color. Then came the quarter of the basket makers, the tent weavers, the moneychangers. . . .

On every face she saw, she looked for a sign that would give her the courage to utter the name of Barabbas. But, each time, she found a reason to lower her eyes and not linger. Besides the fact that she did not dare to stare at them, for fear of appearing impudent, no one looked as if they might have any idea of the whereabouts of a bandit sought by the Romans and the king's mercenaries.

There was nothing for it but to trust in the Almighty. She plunged into the increasingly noisy and populous alleyways.

Avoiding a group of men coming out of a little synagogue between two tall fig trees, she ventured into an alley just wide enough for two people to pass each other. Below the level of the pavement, a cobbler's den gaped open like a mouth. She jumped when an apprentice suddenly waved long creepers of ropes in her direction. His laughter pursued her as she ran almost to the end of the alley, which kept getting narrower as if about to close around her.

The alley led to a patch of waste ground strewn with litter and covered in weeds. There were stagnant puddles here and there. Hens and other fowl barely moved aside as she advanced. The walls of the hovels surrounding the area had not been whitewashed in a long time. Most of the windows were shutterless. A donkey with filthy fur, tied to the trunk of a dead tree, turned its big head toward her and brayed. The sound echoed, as unsettling as a trumpet raising the alarm.

Miriam cast a glance behind her. For a moment, she thought to turn around and plunge back into the alley, but she did not want to endure the apprentice's taunts again. On the other side of the waste ground, she could see two streets that might perhaps take her back to the center of the town. She moved forward, looking down at the ground to avoid the puddles and the litter. She did not see them coming. Only the sudden cackling of the disturbed hens made her look up.

They seemed to have emerged from the muddy ground. A dozen hairy, ragged boys with snotty noses and crafty eyes. The oldest could not have been more than eleven or twelve. They were all barefoot, and their hollow cheeks were as black with dirt as their hands. They were so badly nourished that, young as they were, they were already missing teeth. They were *am ha'aretz*. That was the contemptuous name the Judeans gave them. It meant morons, yokels, bumpkins, the wretched of the earth. Sons of slaves, who themselves would never be anything other than slaves in the great kingdom of Israel. *Am ha'aretz*: the poorest of the poor.

Miriam stopped dead, her face burning, her heart pounding, her head full of the monstrous stories she had heard about these children. How they attacked you like a pack of wild animals. How they stripped you naked and violated you. And even, people said with a thrill of hatred and fear, how they ate you.

This was a perfect place, she had to agree, for them to commit these horrors without fear of being disturbed.

They also slowed down. There was caution on their faces, but also the pleasure of sensing that she was afraid.

Having quickly judged that she posed no risk to them, they leaped toward her. Like cunning dogs, they surrounded her, hopping up and down, mocking her, their mouths open to show their small, hungry teeth, nudging each other with their elbows and pointing their disgusting fingers at her beautiful cloak.

Miriam felt ashamed of her own fear, her wildly beating heart, her moist palms. She remembered what her father had said to her once: "Nothing people say about the *am ha'aretz* is true. People make fun of them because they are the poorest of the poor. That is their only vice and their only wickedness." She made an effort to smile at them.

They replied with their ugliest grimaces, waved their filthy hands, and made obscene gestures.

Perhaps her father was right. But Joachim was a good man and liked to see good in everyone. And, of course, he had never been in the position she was in now: a young girl surrounded by a pack of these demons.

She couldn't just stay here and do nothing. Perhaps she could reach the nearest street, where there would be houses.

She took a few steps in the direction of the donkey, which was watching them and wagging its big ears. The boys followed her, increasing their stupid cries and threatening leaps.

The donkey brayed angrily, showing its yellow teeth. The boys were not impressed. They immediately slapped its sides and imitated its braying. Then, all at once, they were crowding around Miriam, laughing at their own antics like the children that they were, forcing her to come to a halt again.

Their laughter wiped out her fear. Yes, they were just children, amusing themselves with what they could: a scared donkey and a stupid, scared girl!

Halva's words crossed her mind. "Find likely looking people."

Well, here they were; these were likely looking people. The Almighty was offering her the opportunity she had despaired of ever getting, and if Barabbas was what they said, well, she had found the messengers she needed.

She turned suddenly, and the children leaped back, like a pack of dogs afraid of being hit.

"I mean you no harm!" Miriam cried. "I need your help!"

Ten pairs of eyes looked at her suspiciously. She looked for a face that appeared more reasonable than the others. But they all looked the same: dirty and mistrustful.

"I'm looking for a man named Barabbas," she said. "The one Herod's mercenaries call a bandit."

It was as if she had threatened them with a firebrand. They ran about, muttered inaudibly, scowled at her. Some clenched their fists and struck comic poses, like little men.

"I'm his friend," Miriam went on. "I need him. Only he can help me. I've come all the way from Nazareth and I don't know where he's hiding. I'm sure you can take me to him."

This time, their curiosity was aroused and they fell silent. She had not been mistaken. These boys would know where to find Barabbas.

"You can, I know you can. This is important. Very important."

Curiosity was followed by embarrassment. Their mistrust returned. One of them said in a harsh voice, "We don't even know who this Barabbas is!"

"You must tell him that Miriam of Nazareth is here, in Sepphoris," Miriam insisted as if she had not heard him. "The soldiers of the Sanhedrin have imprisoned my father in the fortress of Tarichea."

These last words broke what remained of their resistance. One of the boys, neither the strongest-looking nor the most violent of the gang, came up to her. His dirty face seemed prematurely aged in relation to his puny body.

"If we do it, what will you give us?" he asked.

Miriam searched in the leather lining of her cloak and took out some small brass coins: barely a quarter of a talent, the price of a morning's toil in the fields. "This is all I have."

The children's eyes shone. Their leader, though, pretended not to be excited and made a scornful face that was surprisingly convincing. "That's nothing at all. And you're asking a lot. They say this Barabbas is a really bad man. He could kill us if he doesn't like people running after him."

Miriam shook her head. "No. I know him well. He isn't a bad man, and he isn't dangerous to those he likes. I don't have any more with me, but if you take me to him, he'll reward you."

"Why?"

"I told you: He's my friend. He'll be pleased to see me."

He gave a cunning smile. His companions now crowded around him. Miriam held out her hand, offering the coins.

"Take them."

While his comrades looked on vigilantly, the boy took the coins, his fingers as light as a mouse's paws.

"Don't move from here," he ordered Miriam, his closed fist against his chest. "I'm going to see if I can take you. But until we come back, don't move, or you'd better watch out."

Miriam nodded. "Make sure you tell Barabbas my name: Miriam of Nazareth! And that my father is going to die in the fortress of Tarichea."

Without a word, he turned his back on her and set off with his gang. Before leaving the waste ground, a few of the boys shooed away the cocks and hens, which scattered in panic. Then all the boys disappeared as suddenly as they had appeared.

S H E did not have long to wait.

From time to time, a few people came along the alleys. None of them looked much more prosperous than the children. For a moment, their weary faces would light up with a hint of curiosity, and they would stare at her, before continuing on their way, indifferently.

The hens returned to pick at the ground around the donkey, which had lost all interest in Miriam. The sun was climbing in a sky studded with little clouds, heating the litter-strewn ground. The smell was increasingly sickening.

Trying to ignore it, Miriam forced herself to be patient. She wanted to believe that the children were not deceiving her and really did know where Barabbas was. She could not stay here too long; she was clearly out of place, and her presence would arouse suspicion.

Then, without warning, they were back. This time, they were not running, but walking toward her with measured steps. When they reached her, their leader said in a low voice, "Follow us. He wants to see you."

His voice was as rough as before. Miriam supposed it was always like that. But Miriam noticed a change in his companions.

Before they left the waste ground, the boy said, "Sometimes people try to follow us. We don't see them, but I can sense them. So if I say to you, 'Get out of here,' that's what you do. You don't argue. We'll meet up again later."

Miriam nodded. They plunged into a muddy alley flanked by blind walls. The boys advanced in silence, but without any fear. "What's your name?" she asked the leader.

He did not reply.

The others glanced at Miriam with what she took to be a touch of mockery, and one of them proudly struck his chest and said, "My name's David. Like the king who loved that woman who was very beautiful. . . ."

He stumbled over the name, which he could not remember. The others whispered names to him, but they could not remember Bathsheba, either.

Miriam smiled as she listened to them, but she did not take her eyes off her guide.

When the others fell silent, he shrugged nonchalantly and muttered, "Obadiah."

"Oh!" Miriam said in surprise. "That's a very nice name. Not all that common. Do you know where it comes from?"

He looked at her, and his dark eyes shone with intelligence and cunning in his strange face. "A prophet. He was like me; he didn't like the Romans, either."

"He was small, too, like you," the one called David said immediately. "And lazy. The scholars say he wrote the shortest part of the whole Book!"

The other boys chuckled. Obadiah glared at them, reducing them to silence.

How many times had they fought over the name? Miriam wondered. And how many times had Obadiah had to vanquish them with punches and kicks to impose his will?

"You know a lot," she said to David. "And you're right. The Book only contains about twenty verses of Obadiah. But they're fine verses. I remember one that goes: *The day is near when Yahweh will judge our enemies. The evil they have done will come back upon their heads. And just as you, people of Israel, have drunk on the holy mountain, so all the peoples will drink without respite until their thirst is quenched. And it will be as if there were only one people!*"

She did not mention that Obadiah had fought the Persians, long before the Romans had become the plague of the world. But she was sure that the prophet Obadiah had been just like her young guide: wild, cunning, and brave.

The children had slowed down and were looking at her in astonishment.

"Do you know everything the prophets said by heart?" Obadiah asked. "Did you read it in the Book?"

Miriam could not restrain her laughter. "No! I'm like all of you. I can't read. But my father read the Book in the Temple, and he often tells me stories from it."

Their dirty faces lit up with admiration, making them almost beautiful. What a wonder it must be, that a father should tell his daughter beautiful stories from the Book! They found it hard to imagine. Now they were dying to ask her more questions.

Miriam protested, serious again. "Let's not waste time chatting. With every hour that passes, Herod's mercenaries are making my father suffer. Later, I promise you, I'll tell you."

"And your father, too," Obadiah replied confidently. "When Barabbas has freed him, he'll have to tell us."

TURNING left and right in a zigzagging movement that did not seem to take them very far, they came to a wider street. The houses here were less dilapidated, and even had gardens. The women working in the gardens looked up, intrigued, as their group passed. Recognizing the children, they immediately went back to work.

Obadiah turned right again and plunged into an alley hemmed in by thick walls of naked brick: an old Roman building. Here and there, wild pomegranate trees and tamarisks had grown between the cracks, both widening them and concealing them. Some of the trees were so tall that they towered over the walls.

Miriam noticed that some of the boys had remained behind, at the entrance to the alley. At a sign from Obadiah, they ran forward.

"They're going to keep a lookout," he explained.

He pulled her unceremoniously toward a big tamarisk bush. The proliferating branches were supple enough to be pushed aside, and they passed through.

"Hurry up," Obadiah breathed.

Her cloak held her back, and she clumsily unfastened it. Obadiah took it from her and pushed her forward.

On the other side of the tree, to her surprise, she found herself in a field of beans, dotted with a few stunted almond trees. Obadiah leaped through the gap, followed by two of his companions.

"Run!" he ordered, stuffing the cloak into her hands.

They hurried along the outside of the field of beans until they came to a half-ruined tower. Going ahead of her, Obadiah climbed a staircase strewn with broken bricks. They entered a square room. Most of the wall at the far end had been knocked down. Through the breach, Miriam could see the back of another building. It, too, was Roman, and very old. It had a slate roof that had partly collapsed.

Obadiah pointed to a shaky wooden bridge leading from the broken wall to a skylight on the roof of the Roman building. "We have to cross. There's no danger, the bridge is solid. And there's a ladder on the other side."

Holding her breath, Miriam ventured onto the bridge. It might be solid, but it was also terribly shaky. She slipped through the skylight, let herself down gently onto a wooden floor, and stood up. The room in which she now found herself was like a small loft. Old baskets, used for carrying jars, were heaped up in a corner, eaten away by damp and insects. The floor was covered with plaited straw, broken and crumbling, which crunched beneath her feet. She caught sight of a trapdoor with its flap down just as Obadiah came through the skylight behind her.

"Go on, go down," he urged her.

The room below was dark except for the light filtering in through a narrow door. But there was just enough light to show that the flagstone floor was a long way down. The distance was at least four or five times Miriam's height.

With the tips of her toes, she groped for the rungs of the ladder. Obadiah, with a mocking smile on his lips, leaned toward her, and obligingly took hold of her wrist.

"It's not so high," he said, amused. "Sometimes, I don't even use the ladder. I just jump."

Miriam could feel the rungs wobbling beneath her weight. Without a word, and clenching her teeth, she went down. Before she had touched the ground, two powerful hands clasped her waist. She let out a cry as she was lifted and deposited on the ground.

"I was sure we'd meet again," Barabbas said, a smile in his voice.

H E was lit from behind, so dimly that she could barely make out his face.

Behind her, Obadiah slid down the ladder, as light as a feather. Barabbas tenderly ruffled his hair.

"I see you're as brave as ever," he said to Miriam. "You weren't afraid of trusting these devils with your life. Not many people in Sepphoris would have dared do that."

Obadiah was radiant with pride. "I did what you asked, Barabbas. And she obeyed."

"That's good. Now go and eat."

"I can't. The others are waiting for me on the other side."

Barabbas gave him a little slap and pushed him toward the door. "They'll wait for you. Eat first."

The boy muttered a vague protest. Before leaving the room, he unexpectedly gave Miriam a big smile. For the first time, his face really looked like a child's.

"I see you've already made a friend of him," Barabbas said, with an amused nod. "Strange-looking boy, isn't he? He's nearly fifteen and seems barely ten. It's quite a struggle getting him to eat. When I found him, he was capable of eating once every two or three days. I think his mother must have coupled with a camel to have him."

He stepped into the light from the loft, and she realized that he had changed much more than she had expected.

It was not just his curly beard, which was now thick. He seemed taller than she remembered. His shoulders were broader, his neck more powerful. Over his torso and thighs, he wore a curious white goatskin tunic, held in at the waist by a leather belt as wide as a hand.

A knife hung at his side. The straps of his sandals, good-quality Roman ankle boots, rose halfway up his calves. His head was covered with a long strip of ocher linen, held in place with red and green strips of cloth.

It was an unexpectedly conspicuous kind of costume for a man in hiding, and he had certainly not acquired it from the artisans of Sepphoris out of his own pocket.

He guessed what she was thinking, and his face lit up mischievously. "I made myself handsome to welcome you. Don't go thinking I'm always dressed like this!"

Miriam assumed he was telling the truth. He seemed more self-confident than she remembered. But there was a gentleness there, too, not entirely concealed by the curiosity and irony with which he looked at her.

He finished his scrutiny of her and remarked provocatively, "Miriam of Nazareth! It's fortunate you told Obadiah your name, or I wouldn't have recognized you," he lied. "I remembered a little girl, and here you are, a woman. A beautiful woman."

She was about to make some ironic remark in return. But this was not the moment to waste time. Barabbas seemed to be forgetting why she was here.

"I came because I need your help," she said, curtly, her voice more anxious than she would have wished.

Barabbas nodded, also serious now. "I know. Obadiah told me about your father. It's bad news." Before Miriam could say any more, he raised his hand. "Wait. Let's not discuss it here. We're not yet in my house."

They walked toward a courtyard paved with big broken flagstones. Through the cracks, Miriam glimpsed a mysterious labyrinth of narrow corridors, cisterns, fireplaces, and brick and earthenware pipes. The walls were blackened with soot and flaking in places, as if the bricks and the whitewash were only a fragile skin.

"Follow me," Barabbas said, leading her between the shattered flagstones and the gaping holes.

They came to a porch that was quite dilapidated, although the door looked as solid as if it were new. It opened without his even pushing it. Miriam followed him through it. And stopped dead in amazement.

She had never seen anything like this. The room was huge, with a long pool in the center. The roof was supported by elegant columns, but only around perimeter; in the middle, it was open to the sky. The walls were covered from top to bottom with huge painted figures, strange animals, landscapes full of flowers. The floor was composed of greenish marble slabs arranged in a geometrical pattern.

But this was only the memory of a bygone splendor. The water in the pool was so green that it barely reflected the clouds. Seaweed waved in its shadow, and water spiders scurried across its surface. The marble floor was half cracked, the paintings had flaked in places to reveal the white beneath, and the bottom part of the walls was stained with patches of damp. Some of the roof had been destroyed, perhaps by fire, but so long ago that the rains had washed away what remained of the charred structure. In the part of the room that was still sound, piles of sacks and baskets filled with grain, leather, and goatskins lay between the columns in heaps so high they almost reached the roof.

In the midst of this chaos, some fifty men and women stood or lay on woolen blankets and bundles, staring at her unwelcomingly.

"Come in," Barabbas said. "You're in no danger. We all have what we need here."

Turning to his companions, he announced with a curious pride, in a voice loud enough for everyone to hear, "This is Miriam of Nazareth. A brave girl who hid me one night when Herod's mercenaries were hot on my heels."

These words sufficed. They stopped staring at her. Impressed by this place, in spite of the disorder and the dirt, Miriam still hesitated to advance. The strange half-naked men and women on the murals, who seemed almost alive, made her uncomfortable. Sometimes only part of the body was visible—a face, a chest, limbs, the folds of a transparent dress—which seemed to make them all the more real and fascinating.

"This is the first time you've seen a Roman house, isn't it?" Barabbas said, amused.

Miriam nodded. "The rabbis say it's against our Law to live in a house where men and women are painted. . . ."

"Animals, too!" he said sardonically. "Goats! Even flowers! I long ago stopped listening to the rabbis' hypocritical ravings, Miriam of Nazareth. And this place suits me perfectly."

He indicated the surroundings with a sweeping theatrical gesture that made his goatskin tunic bob up and down comically.

"When Herod was twenty, all this was his. Just because he was his father's son and the young lord of Galilee. This is where he came to bathe. And to get drunk, of course. And to have women—women a lot more real than the ones on the walls. The Romans taught him to imitate them, to be a friendly, accommodating Jew, the way they like them. He learned his lessons so well, licked their backsides to such an extent, that they crowned him king of Israel and set him up over the rabbis of the Sanhedrin. Now Sepphoris and Galilee are much too poor for him. Only good for bleeding dry with taxes."

Barabbas's companions were listening and nodding their approval; even though they must know this story by heart, they clearly never wearied of it.

Barabbas pointed to the strange courtyard they had just crossed. "What you saw down below are the fires they used for heating the water in the pool in winter. Years ago, the slaves who were guarding it set fire to the whole system and escaped while the neighbors were putting out the fire. After that, the place was abandoned. Nobody dared enter. It was still Herod's pool, wasn't it? That's how things went on until I made it my home. And the best hiding place in Sepphoris!"

The remark was greeted with laughter. Barrabas nodded, proud of his guile.

"Herod and the Romans search for us everywhere. Do you think they'd ever think of looking for us here? Of course not! They're much too stupid."

Miriam was sure he was right. But she wasn't here to applaud him, although Barabbas did not seem to care about that.

"I know you're clever," she said coldly. "That's why I came to see you, even though everyone in Nazareth thinks you're no better than a common bandit."

The laughter died down. Barabbas smoothed his beard and shook his head, as if attempting to restrain his temper. "The people of Nazareth are cowards," he muttered. "All except your father, from what I hear."

"That's why my father is in Herod's prison, Barabbas. We're wasting time with this idle chatter."

She was afraid the harshness of her tone would make him angry. His companions lowered their eyes. Behind the group of women, Obadiah had gotten to his feet, a stuffed loaf in his hand, a frown on his face.

Barabbas hesitated. He looked them all up and down. Then he said, with surprising calm, "If your father has your character, then I'm starting to understand what happened!"

He pointed to one of the recesses in the painted walls surrounding the pool. It had been furnished as a kind of bedchamber. There was a straw mat covered with sheepskins, two chests, and a lamp. A silver pitcher and goblets stood on a large brass table framed by two wooden stools with bronze embellishments. Other furniture and luxury objects, doubtless stolen from rich merchants, had been placed around the recess.

In spite of her impatience and nervousness, Miriam noticed Barabbas's pride as he filled a glass with fermented milk mixed with honey and handed it to her.

"Now tell me everything," he said, making himself comfortable.

———

Mɪʀɪᴀᴍ spoke for a long time. She wanted Barabbas to understand how it had come about that her father, the gentlest and kindest of men, had killed a soldier and wounded a tax collector.

When she had finished, Barabbas whistled through his teeth. "There's no doubt they're going to crucify your father. Killing a soldier and sticking a spear in a tax collector's stomach . . . They won't go easy on him." He ran his fingers through his beard, in a mechanical gesture that made him seem older than he was. "And, of course, you want me to attack the fortress of Tarichea."

"My father mustn't die on the cross. We have to stop them."

"Easier said than done, my girl. You're more likely to die with him than save him." His words were ironic, but his face betrayed his discomfort.

"So be it, then," Miriam replied. "Let them kill me with him. At least I won't have bowed my head to injustice."

She had never before spoken so vehemently or so categorically. But she realized that she was telling the truth. If she had to risk death to defend her father, she would not hesitate.

Barabbas realized that, which made his own discomfort all the more intense.

"Courage isn't enough," he said. "The fortress isn't a field of beans you can just walk in and out of! You're fooling yourself. You can't get him out of there."

Miriam stiffened, and she pursed her lips.

Barabbas shook his head. "No one can do it," he insisted, striking his chest. "Not even me."

He hammered out these last words and looked her up and down with all the pride of a young rebel. She sustained his gaze, icy-faced.

Barabbas was the first to turn away his eyes. He snorted, got up nervously from his stool, and walked to the edge of the pool. Some of his companions must have heard what Miriam had said, and everyone was looking at him. He turned, his face hard, his fists clenched, his whole body taut with the strength that had made him a feared leader.

"What you ask is impossible!" he cried fiercely. "What do you think? That you can fight Herod's mercenaries the way you sew a dress? Or that attacking his fortresses is as simple as robbing a caravan of Arab merchants? You can't be serious, Miriam of Nazareth. You have no idea what you're talking about!"

A shiver of dread went through Miriam. Never for a moment had she imagined that Barabbas might refuse to help her. Never for a moment had she thought that the people of Nazareth might be right.

Was Barabbas nothing but a thief, then? Had he forgotten the fine-sounding words he had used to justify his activities? Her disappointment was replaced by contempt. Barabbas the rebel was no more. He had acquired a taste for luxury, he had become corrupted by the things he stole and had become like their original owners: a hypocrite, more interested in gold and silver than in justice. His courage amounted to nothing but easy victories.

She rose from her stool. She wasn't going to humiliate herself before Barabbas, she wasn't going to beg. She assumed a haughty smile and was about to thank him for his hospitality.

He leaped forward, his hand raised. "Stop! I know what you're thinking. I can see it in your eyes. You think I've forgotten what I owe you, that I'm only a robber of caravans. All nonsense! You're not thinking with your head, only with your heart!"

His voice throbbed with anger, and his fists were clenched. Some of his companions came closer, drawn by his raised voice.

"Barabbas hasn't changed," he went on. "I steal to live and to support those who follow me. Like those boys you saw earlier." He pointed at those who had approached. "Do you know who they are? *Am ha'aretz.* People who've lost everything because of Herod and those misers in the Sanhedrin. They no longer expect anything of anyone. Especially not from the subservient Jews of Galilee! Nor from the rabbis, who do nothing but mumble meaningless words and bore us rigid with their lessons. 'May those who come from the mud return to the mud!'—that's what they think. If we didn't steal from the rich, we'd die of starvation, that's the truth. And the people of Nazareth certainly wouldn't care."

He was shouting now, the veins standing out on his forehead, his cheeks flushed with anger. Everyone pressed behind him, facing Miriam. Obadiah pushed his way through to the front.

"I never forget my objective, Miriam of Nazareth!" Barabbas cried, beating his chest. "Never! Not even when I'm asleep. To bring down Herod and drive the Romans out of Israel, that's what I want. And to kick the asses of those bastards in the Sanhedrin who get fat off the people's misery."

Unimpressed by the ferocity of his words, Miriam shook her head. "And how do you plan to bring down Herod, if you can't even get my father out of the fortress of Tarichea?"

Barabbas slapped his thighs, his eyes screwed up with anger. "You're only a girl, you don't understand anything about war! I don't care if I die. But these people follow me because they know I wouldn't drag them into any futile adventures. The fortress of Tarichea is guarded by two Roman cohorts. Five hundred legionnaires. Plus a hundred mercenaries. How many of us are there? We'll never get to your father. What use would our deaths be? The only person who'd benefit would be Herod!"

Pale-faced, her hands shaking, Miriam nodded. "Yes. Of course you're right. I was mistaken. I thought you were stronger than you are."

Barabbas let out a cry that echoed across the pool and throbbed between the columns. Miriam was already heading for the exit, but he gripped her arm.

"You're mad, raving mad! You don't understand, do you? Even if he could get out of the fortress, your father will be like us for the rest of his life. A fugitive. He can never go back to his workshop.

The mercenaries will destroy your house. You and your mother will have to hide in Galilee all your lives. . . ."

Miriam pulled herself free. "And what *you* don't understand is that it's better to die fighting! Better to die confronting Herod's mercenaries than to be humiliated on the cross! Herod is winning, Herod is stronger than the people of Israel, because all we do is bow our heads when he tortures our loved ones in front of our eyes."

These words were followed by a stunned silence.

Obadiah was the first to break it. He went up to Miriam and Barabbas. "She's right. I'm going with her. I'll hide, and at night I'll go and take down her father from the cross."

"You keep quiet or I'll kick your backside!" Barabbas began, testily. Suddenly, he broke off, and he turned to his companions with a gleam in his eyes. "You know something? The little monkey's right! It's stupid to get ourselves slaughtered trying to enter the fortress. But once Joachim's on the cross, that's another story!"

"THEY won't let your father rot for too long in jail," Barabbas explained eagerly. "Their jail's too full. Once they've sentenced you, they can't wait to crucify you. That's when we'll be able to save him. Taking him down from that damned cross. Obadiah's right. We'll do it at night. On the quiet, if we can. I've been dreaming of pulling off a stunt like this for a long time. With a little luck, we'll even be able to save a few others with him. But we'll have to be like foxes: get in there quickly, take them by surprise, and get away even more quickly!"

His anger had passed. He was laughing like a child now, delighted to have thought up the trick he was going to play on the mercenaries of the Tarichea garrison.

"Rescuing people from the field of crosses in Tarichea! By God, if he exists, this is going to cause a stir. Herod will eat his beard! There'll be hell to pay for the mercenaries!"

They all laughed, already imagining their success.

Miriam was worried. Wouldn't it be too late? Before they tied him to the cross, her father could be beaten, badly wounded, even killed. People were often hung on the cross already dead.

"That only happens to the lucky ones. Those who've been granted a special favor to shorten their suffering. But in the case of your father, they'll want to see him suffer as long as possible. He'll hold out. They'll hit him, insult him, starve him, that's for sure. But he'll grit his teeth and survive. And we'll get him down off the cross on the first night."

Barabbas turned to his companions and informed them of what awaited them. "They won't like us saving people from the cross. The mercenaries won't leave us in peace after this. We won't be able to come back here, it won't be safe anymore, and in any case we won't be able to show our faces around town again. Once we've pulled this off, we'll have to separate for a few months and live on what we have—"

One of the older ones interrupted him, raising his knife. "Don't waste your spit, Barabbas! We know what's in store for us, and we don't mind. Anything that hurts Herod is fine by us!"

They all cheered. In an instant, Herod's former pool became the scene of intense activity, as Barabbas cried out orders and everyone prepared to depart.

Obadiah pulled Barabbas impatiently by the sleeve. "I have to go and tell the others. We'll leave without waiting for you, as usual, right?"

"But bring the mules and donkeys first. We'll need the carts."

Obadiah nodded. He walked away, turned after a few steps, pointed at Miriam, and smiled, showing his bad teeth. "I was telling the truth earlier, you know. Even if you hadn't wanted to, I'd have gone with her."

Barabbas laughed and wagged a finger at him. "You'd have obeyed me, or I'd have tanned your hide."

"Hey, don't forget I'm the one who had the idea about how to save her father, not you! You're not my leader anymore. We're partners now." His strange face lit up with pride, and for a moment it looked strangely beautiful. He added, cheekily, "And you'll see, she won't love you after this, she'll love me!"

And he strode off, his laugh echoing between the ruined walls of the baths. Out of the corner of her eye, Miriam noticed that Barabbas was blushing.

AT nightfall, a caravan, no different than all the others that circulated on the roads of Galilee on the days of the great markets in Capernaum, Tarichea, Jerusalem, or Caesarea, left Sepphoris.

There were ten carts loaded with bales of wool, hemp, and sheepskins and sacks of grain, and drawn by beasts as poor in appearance as their owners. Each of the carts had a double bottom, in which Barabbas and his companions had concealed a fine collection of swords, knives, combat axes, and even a few Roman spears stolen from the storehouses.

CHAPTER 3

Surrounded by a dozen similar boats, the small fishing boat swayed on the gentle swell of the Lake of Gennesaret. The red and blue sails had been taken down. Since morning, the fishermen had been casting their nets two leagues from the shore, just as on any other day. But today each boat was carrying four of Barabbas's companions, ready for combat. For the moment, they were enjoying helping the fishermen.

Huddled on the rough planks in the stern of the boat, Miriam watched impatiently as the sun slowly went down over Tarichea. There, beyond the horrible forest of crosses next to the fortress, her father was suffering, unaware that she was so close to him. Unaware that, when night came and if God Almighty allowed it, she would free him.

Sitting behind her on the handrail, Barabbas sensed her apprehension. He placed a hand on her shoulder. "It won't be long now," he said when she looked up at him. "You only need to be patient a little while longer."

His face was drawn with exhaustion, but his voice was still gently teasing.

Miriam would have liked to smile at him, touch his hand, tell him that she trusted him. But she could not do it. Her muscles were so taut, she had to make an effort to stop herself shaking. There was a lump in her throat, and she could hardly breathe. The previous night, overcome with anxiety, she had slept very little.

As for Barabbas, he had had hardly any rest at all, and Miriam had been amazed by his skill and efficiency.

A F T E R leaving Sepphoris, Barabbas and his band had walked all night, stopping only to let the donkeys and mules forage. By early morning, they were in the hills overlooking the shores of the Lake of Gennesaret. Tarichea was at their feet. The fortress, with its walls of hewn stones, its towers and crenellated ramparts, looked more impenetrable than ever.

In spite of the distance, Miriam immediately made out the terrible field of crosses. Situated to the right of the fortress, it extended along the shore of the lake for almost a quarter of a league. There were hundreds of crosses, like some monstrous growth of vegetation.

Indeed, nothing else grew there. There was nothing like the orchards and gardens surrounding the white walls of the town with its multitude of little alleys, which huddled cautiously on the other side of the fortress. Seen from above, the field of crosses was a long brown strip lined with a threatening black stockade, a blemish on the natural beauty of the lakeside.

Miriam bit her lips. She would have liked to rush in and make sure that her father was not yet among the black figures on the irregular crosses, although not seeing him there would have been no comfort: Might he not already have been murdered inside the fortress?

Without wasting time, Barabbas organized his troops. They were to remain in the shelter of the forest while he, Obadiah, and a few trusted companions would reconnoiter around Tarichea.

They came back grim-faced. Obadiah immediately went up to Miriam and jutted his chin toward the field of crosses. "Your father isn't there. I'm sure he isn't there."

Miriam closed her eyes and took a deep breath to calm her beating heart. Obadiah collapsed on the ground. His hollow, dirty cheeks seemed more drawn, his features more abnormally aged, than ever. The others had come closer to hear him.

"I went right up to the place, as Barabbas asked. There are lots of guards, but they're not too suspicious of kids. The stockade around the field of crosses has nails at the top. Anyone who tries to get across will be cut to shreds. There are two places where you can see inside. And what you see is no laughing matter, I can tell you."

Obadiah paused for a moment, as if he could still see these horrors in front of his eyes.

"There are dozens and dozens of them. You can't count them all. Some of them have been there so long, they're nothing but bones in bits of cloth. Others haven't been there long enough to die. You can hear them mumbling to themselves. Sometimes, some of them cry out in this weird kind of voice. As if they were already among the angels."

A long, uncontrollable shudder went through Miriam's shoulders. "If there are so many of them," she said in a hoarse, barely audible voice, "how do you know my father isn't there?"

A crafty look came back into Obadiah's eyes, and he almost smiled. "I had a chat with an old mercenary. When old-timers like him see a kid, they turn softer than a rabbi's wife. I told him my big brother was going to be crucified. First of all, he laughed and said it didn't surprise him, and I'd probably be keeping him company. So I pretended to cry, and he told me not to worry, they wouldn't do it straightaway. Then he asked me how long my 'brother' had been in the fortress, because they hadn't put anyone up on the cross in the last four days." Obadiah raised his hand, spreading the fingers. "You just have to count. Your father got to the fortress the day before yesterday. . . ."

As everyone watched, Miriam nodded and took Obadiah's hand in hers. But it was shaking so much, she let go of it after a few moments.

Addressing the company, Barabbas told them, in a haughty voice, that they should not count on getting into the field of crosses through the main gate. "It's only wide enough for a mule, and it's permanently guarded by a dozen mercenaries. If they give the alarm, it's bolted with iron bars."

"And it's closed all night, from what I've heard," one of his companions said.

In addition, the town was swarming with legionnaires—spies, too, probably. It was out of the question to find shelter there. If they walked through it in a group, they would attract far too much attention, even disguised as poor merchants, as they were. The guards were vigilant, and it was not worth taking the risk.

Everyone looked worried. "Don't make those faces," Barabbas said, mocking them. "It's going to be easier than we thought. The stockade stops at the lake. There's nothing on the shore, not even guards."

There were loud protests. How many of them could swim? No more than three or four. Apart from that, swimming with the wretches they would have just taken down from the crosses, and being shot at by Roman archers . . . It was suicide. They needed boats. And boats were something they didn't have. "And even if we had them, we wouldn't know how to use them!"

Barabbas scoffed at their pessimism. "You're not thinking any farther than your snotty noses. We don't have boats. But on the shores of the lake, there are fishermen with all the boats we need. We have grain, wool, skins, and even a few fine silver objects. Enough to persuade them to help us."

———

B y nightfall, the deal was done. The fishermen from the villages near Tarichea hated living so close to the fortress and its field of crosses. The reputation of Barabbas's band and the goods taken off the carts had done the rest.

That night, the houses on the shores of the lake had stayed open. The next day, while Obadiah and his comrades again lurked near the fortress, Barabbas had finalized his strategy, in agreement with the fishermen.

As for Miriam, she had endured hours of nightmares before Obadiah had drawn her from her restless sleep two hours after sunrise.

"I've seen your father. Don't worry: He was still walking. Not all the others were. They put fifteen men up on the cross in one go. He was one of them."

A little while later, he spoke to Barabbas. "The old mercenary's become my friend. He let me look as much as I wanted. I spotted Joachim right away because of his bald head and carpenter's tunic. I kept my eyes on him all the time. I know exactly where he is. I'd find him even in the dead of night."

Now they were waiting for darkness, their exhaustion forgotten amid the tension. Before leaving the shore, Barabbas had carefully gone over his plan and had made sure that they all knew what they had to do. Anxious as she was, Miriam had no doubt about their determination.

The sun was almost touching the hills above Tarichea. Standing out in the fading light, the fortress was a twisted mass of black. One by one, the green meadows and orchards turned gray. A strange, dull, bluish light hung in the still air, like a cloud. Soon, the field of crosses itself would disappear. From Tarichea came noises that echoed across the surface of the lake, and the last reflections of the dying sun scattered in a thousand gleams of light.

Miriam dug her nails into her palms, thinking so hard about the despair her father must be feeling that it seemed to her she could see him, praying to Yahweh with his usual gentleness. After the burning heat of the day, the cold of the coming night engulfed her.

Helped by Barabbas, the fisherman who was sailing their boat folded his net at the foot of the mast. Then he pointed to the shore. "As soon as the sun touches the crest of the hills, the wind will rise," he said. "It'll be easier to maneuver then."

Barabbas nodded. "There'll be a little moonlight. Just what we need."

While the fisherman pulled on a rope to raise the sail, Barabbas came back and sat down next to Miriam.

"Take this," he said gently. "You may need it." In his open palm was a small dagger with a red leather handle and a very thin blade. Miriam stared at it in astonishment.

"Take it," Barabbas insisted. "Use it if you have you. Don't hesitate. I want to free your father, but I also want to bring you back safe and sound."

He winked at her, then immediately turned away to help the fisherman with the raising of the sail.

All around them, on the other boats, the same silent activity was taking place. One by one, with solemn slowness, the triangular sails rose, glistening in the last light of day.

The sun set over the already dark forest, turning the surface of the lake an oily bloodred so dazzling that they had to shield their eyes.

As the fisherman had predicted, wind stirred the sail. He grabbed the helm and gave it a sudden push. The sail tipped and swelled, as if it had been punched. The boat creaked, and the stem cut through the water. Now the other boats turned. One after another, the sails flapped, the masts and ribs squeaked, and off they went across the torn surface of the lake.

Barabbas was standing beneath the sail, holding on to the mast. The stem of the boat pointed toward a vast inlet to the east of

Tarichea. "For as long as they can still see us," the fisherman said to Miriam with a smile, "we'll pretend we're on our way home."

Until it was completely dark, they had sailed southward, lowering the sail little by little in order not to be taken too far from the fortress. There was a little moonlight, but all they could make out were the nearest boats, nothing more. The lights of the palaces of Tarichea and the torches on the parapets of the fortress shone on the shore.

They sailed in silence, but the boats were so close together that the sound of the water against the hulls, the flapping of the sails, and the creaking of the masts seemed to make an almighty din that must surely have been audible from the shore.

The wind was steady, and the fishermen knew their boats as a rider knows his horse. But Miriam could sense how nervous Barabbas was. He kept looking up to make sure the sails were still swelling, clearly finding it hard to gauge their speed, fearing they would reach the fortress either too early or too late.

Suddenly, they were so close to the huge towering mass that the mercenaries could clearly be seen by the light of the torches. Almost immediately, a whistle was heard, to be answered by another. Barabbas held out his arm. "There!" he exclaimed with relief.

Miriam peered at the shore without seeing anything unusual. All at once, at the foot of the wall, a fire sprang up, so intensely that it could only have been started by a torch or an oil lamp. With each passing second, the flames grew. The fire was spreading. Cries rang out on the rampart walk, and the guards quickly left their posts.

"This is it!" Barabbas roared in delight. "They did it!"

"They" were a dozen members of his band. Their mission had been to light fires in the guards' camp and grain stores close to the market adjoining to the fortress, on the opposite side from the field of crosses. The carts they had brought from Sepphoris had been left there during the day, laden with old wood and innocent-looking fodder. The false bottoms, emptied of weapons, had been filled with pots of bitumen and jars of terebinth oil, making the vehicles highly inflammable. Barabbas's men had been ordered to set fire to them at a specific time and then escape from the town.

Clearly, they had succeeded. As if to confirm this, a muted roar echoed across the lake, and the walls of the fortress were lit up by the flames. Some distance from the first fire, more flames suddenly shot up. This second fire would confuse the mercenaries and send the villagers running from their houses.

Cries of joy rose from the boats. The flames, ever more intense, were reflected in the waters of the harbor. At last, trumpets sounded, calling the legionnaires and mercenaries to the rescue.

Barabbas turned to the fisherman. "This is the moment!" he cried, trying hard to contain his excitement. "We must charge while they're busy putting out the fires!"

H is plan worked perfectly.

Thanks to the diversion caused by the fires, there would be fewer—if any—guards watching the field of crosses and the rampart walk.

Silently, the boats drew alongside a gravel beach, and everyone came ashore. It was still pitch dark here, but in the distance the sky and the lake glowed red, and they could hear the yells of those fighting the fire.

Barabbas and his companions ran forward like shadows in the shadows, their unsheathed knives in their hands, ready to deal with any guard who might still be in the vicinity before he could raise the alarm.

A hand slipped into Miriam's. It was Obadiah.

"This way," he said, drawing her on. "Your father's up here, near the stockade."

But now Miriam, Obadiah, and his comrades hesitated, struck dumb with terror. Their eyes were accustomed enough to the darkness to make out the horror around them.

The crosses rose like a forest in hell. Some had rotted and fallen, bringing the corpses down with them. Others were so close together that, in places, the crosspieces holding the prisoners' arms overlapped.

Some crosses were still bare. But, at their feet, skeletons hung grotesquely, long since devoid of anything that could be called human.

Only then did Miriam become aware of the stench, and the bones and human carcasses that littered the ground beneath her feet.

They were startled by little growls as wild cats scattered, and a rustling in the air as night birds, carrion eaters disturbed by their sudden presence, flew off with a menacing softness.

For a moment, Miriam did not think she could go on. But Obadiah, still holding her hand, leaped forward. "Quick! We don't have any time to waste!"

They ran, which did them good. As promised, Obadiah made his way without hesitation between the crosses.

"There!" he said, pointing.

Miriam knew he was right. In spite of the darkness, she recognized Joachim.

"Father!"

Joachim did not reply.

"He's asleep," Obadiah assured her. "A whole day up there must really knock you out!"

As Miriam was still calling to her father, they heard cries and the noise of a fight from the direction of the stockade.

"Damn it!" Obadiah cursed. "They did leave some guards here after all! Quick, you others, help me."

He dragged two of his comrades to the foot of the cross and jumped nimbly onto their shoulders.

"Do the same with the other crosses close by," he ordered the rest of his band. "Some of these people must still be alive."

Miriam saw him climb the cross with the agility of a monkey, his knife between his teeth. In the blink of an eye, he reached Joachim, and gently moved his head. "Wake up, Joachim. Your daughter has come to save you!"

Joachim muttered something unintelligible.

"Wake up, Joachim!" Obadiah said again, more insistently now. "This is no time to take a nap! I'm going to cut your bonds, and if you don't help me, you're going to fall and smash your face."

Miriam could hear moans of pain from the nearest crosses, where the other boys were at work, and angry cries and the clatter of metal from the stockade, where the fight was still in progress.

"My father must be wounded," she said to Obadiah. "Cut his bonds and we'll hold him!"

"No point, he's waking up at last!"

"Miriam! Miriam, is it you I hear?" The voice was hoarse and weary.

"Yes, father, it's me . . ."

"But how can it be? And who are you?"

"Later, Joachim," Obadiah muttered, busy cutting the thick ropes. "We have to get out of here as quickly as we can, or things will take a turn for the worse. . . ."

Indeed, as Miriam and Obadiah's comrades helped Joachim down from the cross, Barabbas and his companions came running.

"The bastards!" Barabbas growled.

His tunic was ripped, and his eyes still shone from the fight. In his hand, he held not a knife, but a spatha, the much-feared long Roman sword.

"There were still four of them there, in a tent. They won't see Jerusalem again! They made us a present of their arms. But I think there was also a man at the gate of the fortress. We have to get out of here before they come back in force."

"Who are you?" Joachim muttered, in a daze.

His legs could no longer carry him, and every time he tried to move his arms he groaned. He lay now in Miriam's arms, and she was supporting his head.

Barabbas gave him a big smile. "Barabbas, at your service. Your daughter came to me and asked me to rescue you from the clutches of Herod's mercenaries. Mission accomplished."

"Not yet," Obadiah said, jumping down. "I just saw a torch at the foot of the wall."

Barabbas ordered silence and listened. He could hear the voices of the mercenaries coming closer. "They won't find it easy to spot us in the dark," he whispered. "All the same, we have to get out of here as quickly as possible."

"My father can't run," Miriam breathed.

"We'll carry him."

"The boys have taken down another four," Obadiah said. "We'll have to carry them, too."

"In that case, what are you waiting for?" Barabbas growled, and loaded Joachim over his shoulder.

THEY were in the boats, with the sails already unfurled, by the time it occurred to the mercenaries, alerted by the flapping of the sails and the creaking of the timbers, to run down to the shore.

But it was too late. They shot a few arrows and javelins at random, which vanished into the darkness. On the other side of the fortress, the fire was raging more fiercely than ever and was threatening to engulf part of the town. The mercenaries would not want to spend too much time chasing these people who, as far as they were concerned, were simply body snatchers.

The boats sped away into the night. As arranged, the fishermen burned two of them, the oldest and least maneuverable, and abandoned them to the mercy of the current, so as to make the Romans and mercenaries think they had been stolen.

As the boat sailed back northward across the lake, Joachim, his fingers numbed by the bonds that had held his wrists, could not stop rubbing Miriam's hands and stroking her face. Still confused, faint with hunger and thirst, his whole body aching, he stammered words of gratitude, mixed with prayers to Yahweh. Miriam told him how she had refused to give him up for dead, despite the opposition of their neighbors in Nazareth, apart from Yossef, the carpenter, and his wife, Halva.

"But I was the one who came up with the idea for how to save you, Joachim," Obadiah cut in. "Barabbas couldn't have managed it without me."

"In that case, I thank you, too, from the bottom of my heart. You're very brave."

"There was nothing to it, really, and, anyway, I didn't do it for free. Your daughter promised me something if I succeeded."

Joachim's laughter echoed against Miriam's breast. "Unless she's promised to marry you, I'll honor that promise."

Surprised, Obadiah fell silent for a moment. Again, Miriam felt her father's laughter as she held him close to her. It was the best proof yet that she had well and truly saved him from the horror of the field of crosses.

"Oh, it's a lot less than that," Obadiah said. "She promised me that you would tell me stories from the Book."

CHAPTER 4

Barabbas had planned their escape as carefully as the freeing of Joachim.

The band scattered. Some, accompanying the other rescued prisoners, crossed the lake with the help of the fishermen. Most quickly set out along the paths leading to the thick forests of Mount Tabor. Obadiah's young companions spread out through the villages along the shore before going back to Tarichea and Jotapata to resume their lives as vagabonds. Obadiah himself stayed with Barabbas, Miriam, and Joachim. All night, they sailed northward.

Never letting go of the helm, and using his long experience of the lake to anticipate the currents and keep the sail swelling even when the wind subsided, the fisherman kept close to the dense shadow of the shore. By dawn, they had left the gardens of Capernaum behind them. Miriam discovered a landscape that was unknown to her, even though they were still in Galilee.

It was a landscape of rolling hills covered in holm oaks, and narrow, tortuous valleys. In places, cliffs rose sheer from the waters of the lake. Between them were twisted inlets, to which clung ramshackle houses with roofs made of branches. Most of the shoreline, though, was impassable forest, with no beaches or coves for a boat to moor. A few rare villages huddled on the banks of the rivers that descended from the hills. It was to one of these hamlets that the fisherman led their boat. Five or six leagues to the north, the mouth of the Jordan was haloed in mist.

During the night, Barabbas had assured Miriam that there existed no better shelter. Herod's mercenaries rarely came to this area, which was too poor even for the vultures of the Sanhedrin, and too difficult to reach. You could only get to it by boat, which deprived any ill-intentioned visitors of the element of surprise.

It was easy to vanish into the forest, and the hills were full of hidden caves. Barabbas knew a fair number of them. More than once, he had found refuge here with his band. He had a sufficiently full purse for the fishermen to take them in without asking any questions. Miriam should not worry; they would be safe as long as it took for the Romans' anger, and perhaps even Herod's, to die down.

In truth, the choice of their hiding place was of little concern to Miriam. What did fill her with anxiety, though, as soon as the light of day revealed them, were her father's wounds.

Having spoken just a few words to his daughter in the emotion of their flight from Tarichea, Joachim had dozed off without anyone on the boat noticing. All night, Miriam had listened to his hoarse, often irregular breathing, and had forced herself not to think how painful and abnormal it was. But in the watery dawn over the lake, as he still lay fast asleep under a sheepskin, the full horror of his appearance became clear.

Joachim was unrecognizable. Not an inch of his face had been spared. His lips were swollen, and both cheekbones were open, as was the arch of one eyebrow. A blow with a spear or a sword had severed one ear and left a scar across his cheek and all the way down to his chin. Although Miriam kept dipping her veil in the water of the lake to wash the wound, it was constantly oozing blood.

She lifted the sheepskin off her father's chest. The tunic he was wearing when he had attacked the tax collectors was now no more than a scrap of cloth stained with dried blood. He was covered in purple bruises from his stomach to his throat. There were jagged cuts on his shoulders and back, also oozing blood. And, of course, the ropes with which he had been tied to the cross had cut through his wrists and ankles.

It was obvious he had been beaten—so violently, in fact, that there might well be invisible wounds, even more serious than the visible ones, that could endanger his life.

Miriam bit her lips to hold back the tears.

As the boat slowly rolled from side to side, she sensed Barabbas, Obadiah, and the fisherman turning away their eyes, horrified by what they saw. Now that day had risen, it became difficult to say if Joachim was asleep or had fainted.

"He's strong," Barabbas said at last. "He held out until he was on the cross, and he knows you're by his side. He'll live, for his daughter's sake!"

His voice was gentle, without any of his usual cocky humor, and lacked conviction.

Aware of this, Obadiah nodded in approval. "That's for sure! He knows we didn't do all this just to watch him die."

They were surprised at this point to hear from the fisherman, who had barely opened his mouth since Tarichea.

"The boy's right," he said, addressing Miriam. "Even with all his pain, your father won't want to abandon you. A man with a daughter like you doesn't let himself die. God's paradise can't compare." He paused to pull on a rope, making the sail taut again, then said angrily, "I hope the rabbis and prophets are right and the Messiah comes one day, so that we can have done once and for all with this worthless life."

Instinctively, Barabbas was about to respond with mockery. How long were the people of Israel going to believe in this nonsense that the rabbis were constantly drumming into them? How long would these poor people, who were being bled dry by Herod, wait for a Messiah to come and deliver them, instead of delivering themselves?

But the fisherman's tone, Miriam's expression, and Joachim's unconsciousness made him refrain; this was not the time to argue. It was just as well, as the fisherman was to surprise him again a little while later.

They had just pulled the boat onto shore at last. The villagers, curious to see the newcomers, had gathered to greet them. Discovering Joachim's condition, they helped to carry him and laid him on a thin straw mat. As the procession moved toward the houses, Barabbas held out the purse he had promised the fisherman, but the man pushed away his hand.

"No, there's no need."

"Please, take it. Without you, none of this would have been possible. You're going back to Tarichea. You may have problems there. What if they try to burn your boats, to force your comrades to say what they know about us?"

The fisherman shook his head. "You don't know us, son. We knew what you were going to do. I'm taking a roundabout route back to Tarichea. My comrades will do the same. By the time we get to Tarichea, our boats will be full to bursting. The best catch we've ever had. When we find out the market has been burned to the ground, obviously we'll be really angry, and we'll decide to give them our fish for free. All the housewives in the town will be overjoyed. It'll cause quite a stir."

Barabbas burst out laughing. But he still insisted. "Take it anyway. You deserve it."

"Leave it, I said. I don't want your money. I'm a Jew from Galilee. Why should I need money to save another Jew from Galilee from the cross? Only Herod's mercenaries get paid to do what they do. Don't be upset. We all know now that Barabbas is not a thief, but an honest Galilean."

———

———

ALTHOUGH Barabbas had warned him not to say anything, Obadiah was too excited to stop himself, and as soon as he could, he told everyone about the hell from which Joachim had been rescued.

This was a village outside the mercenaries' reach, and it was the first time the villagers had seen a man who had escaped from the cross. All the women in the village united to save him. They vied with each other in showing off their knowledge, unearthing the secrets of herbs, powders, potions, and soups that could reduce the bruising, close both the visible and invisible wounds, and at last give Joachim back his strength.

Miriam assisted them. Within a few days, she had learned to distinguish plants to which she had never previously paid any attention. She was shown how to grind them into powder, which they would mix with goat's fat, fine earth, seaweed, or fish bile, depending on whether they were being turned into pastes, plasters, or oils for massage. The massage was administered by big, strapping women long since accustomed to treating naked men.

A cheerful young girl made infusions and nourishing herbal teas. In his unconscious struggle against pain, Joachim kept his jaws clenched so tight, it was a wonder his teeth did not break. The young girl helped Miriam to part them with the aid of a small wooden funnel. Only then was it possible to feed the wounded man, one spoonful at a time. It was a slow, difficult, depressing task. But Miriam's young companion managed to lighten it and turn it into a very special moment, in which the daughter was able to treat the father with maternal gentleness.

Miriam watched over Joachim all night, every night. Barabbas and Obadiah tried to dissuade her, but in vain. All they could do was take turns in keeping her company, sitting beside her in the dim light of an oil lamp.

At last, one afternoon, it became clear that Obadiah and the fisherman had been right. A few hours before nightfall, Joachim opened his eyes. He had chosen his daughter over God's paradise.

H E did not seem surprised to see Miriam's face above him. He gave a slight, very pale smile. Awkwardly, he lifted his hands, the wrists still covered in plasters and bandages, and tried to touch her. Laughing and weeping at the same time, Miriam bent toward him, kissed his face, and offered her cheeks to his caress.

"My daughter, my daughter!"

Mumbling with happiness, he tried to hug her, but the pain in his shoulders was too great, and he groaned.

The women rushed out to announce the good news. The whole village came running. At last, they could see the eyes of this man who had survived the cross, hear his laughter and gentle words.

"Miriam, my angel. It's as if I've come back to life! May the Lord be thanked for giving me such a daughter."

Miriam dismissed this praise, pointing out to her father that everyone had contributed to his recovery.

Moved, Joachim looked at the rough, joyful faces around him. "You may not believe this," he stammered, "but while I was asleep, I saw Miriam by my side. I remember it very well. She was standing there, not very far from me. And I could see myself, too. I was in a terrible state, because I'd fallen off the cross and had broken in pieces. One arm here, the other there. My legs were out of reach. Only my head and heart were working as they should. And I had to keep holding the different pieces of me to stop them moving away. But I was so exhausted that all I really wanted to do was close my eyes and let my arms and legs go wherever they liked. Except that Miriam was there, behind me, stopping me from yielding to the temptation."

They were all listening, openmouthed. Joachim paused for breath, blinked, and went on. "She kept saying, 'Come on, Father, come on!

Keep your eyes wide open.' You know, in that not very pleasant tone she has sometimes, very bossy and confident for a girl of her age."

Everyone laughed, Barabbas nodded vigorously, and Miriam blushed to the roots of her hair.

"Yes, she kept telling me off," Joachim continued, his voice quivering with tenderness. " 'Come on, Father, just a little more effort! Don't give the tax collectors that pleasure! You need your arms and legs if you want to get back to Nazareth. Come on! Come on, I'm waiting!' And now, here I am, back with you and able to thank you."

THE following day at dawn, when Joachim woke after a short night's sleep, he found Barabbas and Obadiah beside him. Miriam was sleeping in the women's room.

"She looks as if she's out for a whole year," Obadiah chuckled.

Joachim nodded and looked at the boy's strange face. "Was it you who took me down from the cross? I have a vague memory of it, but it was quite dark."

"Yes, it was me."

"To tell the truth, when I saw you, I thought a demon had come to take me to hell."

"The reason you don't recognize me," Obadiah said, with a shrug, "is because the women washed me and gave me clean clothes."

Barabbas laughed heartily. "That's the greatest humiliation Obadiah's ever suffered. He misses his dirt. It's going to take him weeks and months to look like himself again."

"Cleanliness suits you, my boy," Joachim said, gently. "You ought to be pleased."

Obadiah made a face. "That's what Miriam says too. But none of you know what you're talking about. In towns, if we're like other boys, people aren't afraid of us, and they don't take pity on us either. Tomorrow, before I leave for Tarichea, I'll put on my *am ha'aretz* rags again, that's for sure."

Joachim frowned. "Tarichea? What do you want to go there for?"

"To find out what Herod's mercenaries are up to—"

"But it's much too soon!"

"No," Barabbas said. "It's been six days. I want to know what's going on in Tarichea. Obadiah will go there and keep his ears open. He's good at that kind of thing. He'll leave tomorrow with one of the fishermen."

Joachim refrained from protesting. But his stomach felt tight with fear. The violence and hatred of the mercenaries had left as indelible a mark on his mind as on his body. But Barabbas was right. He himself would have given a lot to have news of his wife, Hannah. He would also have liked to know if the tax collectors, in revenge for his escape, had inflicted on Nazareth the suffering he had just evaded.

If that was the case, he would have to give himself up and go back to prison in Tarichea. But that was something he could not tell Barabbas, let alone Miriam.

"Don't go yet," he said, squeezing Obadiah's small hands. "I think I promised you something when you were taking me away from the field of crosses, and I hate not keeping my promises."

F I V E days later, leaning on Miriam's shoulder, Joachim was trying out the use of his legs when Obadiah appeared. He leaped out of the boat before it touched shore, his face transfigured with excitement.

"We're all that people are talking about!" he cried, before he had even had time to drink a cup of grape juice. "We're the one topic of conversation. 'Barabbas saved some people from the cross.' 'Barabbas humiliated Herod's mercenaries.' 'Barabbas cocked a snook at the Romans . . .' Anyone would think you'd become the Messiah!"

There was more affection than mockery in Obadiah's laughter, but Barabbas remained serious. "What about the fishermen? Did they have any trouble?"

"Quite the contrary. They did as they said they would. They arrived in Tarichea with boats so full, the wind could hardly carry them. A truly miraculous catch. They were very angry at us for burning their boats and their market, just like the people of Tarichea. Everyone said we were ruffians, vandals, the shame of Galilee . . . Nice things like that. By the end of it, the mercenaries and the Romans were convinced we did it all by ourselves. Now, people are laughing behind their backs. Everyone's happy to have fooled them."

This time, Barabbas relaxed, and Miriam stroked Obadiah's tangled hair.

"And did you manage to restrain yourself?" Barabbas asked, gently mocking. "Or did you tell everyone that you were the best friend of the great Barabbas?"

"There was no need." Obadiah chuckled proudly. "They guessed anyway. I've never before had so much of what I wanted. I could have brought back a boatful."

"And gotten yourself denounced!" Joachim snorted.

"Don't worry, Joachim! I can spot informers a mile away. No one knew where I was sleeping or when they were going to see me. But did you know you're famous, too? Everyone knows your story. Joachim of Nazareth, the man who dared to stick a spear in the belly of a tax collector and then escaped from the cross. . . ."

"It wasn't the belly, it was the shoulder," Joachim muttered testily. "And I don't think it's such a good thing that everyone's talking about me. What about news from Nazareth? Do you have any?"

Obadiah shook his head. "No, I didn't have time to go there. . . ."

Joachim looked at Barabbas, then at Miriam. "I'm worried for them. The mercenaries don't know where to find us, but they know who to harm."

"I could go," Miriam said, "at least to see Mother and reassure her."

"No, not you," Obadiah protested. "Me. I'll go whenever you like."

"Unless we all go together," Barabbas said pensively. "Now that Joachim can walk, we can move about as we like."

They all stared at him in astonishment.

"Isn't there anywhere safe in the village where we could stay?" he asked Joachim and Miriam.

Joachim shook his head. "No, no, it would be madness—"

"Yes, Father!" Miriam exclaimed. "Yossef and Halva will take us in without hesitation!"

"You don't realize the danger, my girl."

"I'm certain Yossef will be proud to help you. He knows how much he owes you. He loves you. Their house is quite a distance from the village anyway, at the far end of the valley. We can't be taken by surprise there."

"We'll keep a lookout, Joachim," Obadiah said. "On the way, I'll round up my friends. We'll all be there. You'll see, no one will be able to approach Yossef's house without our knowing it. Ask Miriam— we're the ones who keep guard on Barabbas's hiding places, so we know what to do."

Miriam smiled at the memory of her welcome in Sepphoris, but Joachim could not be persuaded. His refusal disappointed Barabbas and marred Obadiah's joy.

I T was only in the evening, after a long silence, that Miriam said softly to her father, "I know you're very worried about Mother. You want to hold her in your arms, and so do I. Let's go to Yossef and Halva's house, even if it's only for a short time. Then we'll decide."

"Decide what, Daughter? You know perfectly well I'll never be able to go back to my workshop and build another roof with Lysanias— if he's still alive, please God!"

"That's true," Barabbas muttered. "Now you're in the same boat as me. Forget your roof, Joachim. There's something else that needs building now. The rebellion of the Galileans against Herod."

"Is that all?"

"You heard Obadiah. Everyone's happy that we got the better of Herod's mercenaries and the vultures of the Sanhedrin. Look around

you, Joachim. The inhabitants of this village all made an effort to cure
you because you'd been on the cross, and they knew how unjust that
was. The fisherman who helped us refused a gold purse. For him, it
was enough to have fought at our side. These are signs. We showed
the people of Galilee that the mercenaries are only fools. We must
continue. And on a large scale, to overcome the people's fear!"

"Hold on a second. You're going to do all that with fifty companions and a few children, are you?"

"No. We're going to do all that by drawing in all those who can't
stand it anymore. Showing them what we can do. We took you down
from the cross, you and those other poor wretches. We can do it
elsewhere, even in Jerusalem. We can harass the mercenaries. We
can fight and show that we're winning. . . ."

Joachim made a bitter grimace. "Barabbas, you're talking about a
rebellion as if it's a fit of anger. Do you think that I, or the many others who think like me, have never thought about this?"

Barabbas smiled broadly. "You see, you just said it yourself: There
are many others who can't stand Herod anymore."

"Yes, I do know some, it's true. But don't think they'll follow you.
They're wise men, not fools."

"Your daughter turned to a fool to save you, Joachim, not to
your wise friends."

Joachim was starting to get annoyed. "If a rebellion isn't supported by the whole country, it only leads to wholesale slaughter.
Herod can hit hard, and he can hit fast. The Sanhedrin is under his
thumb and has the rabbis on its side. That makes it not quite as dangerous as Herod, but just as effective."

"Always the same excuse," Barabbas grumbled. "A coward's excuse."

"Don't say such things! It takes as much courage to endure injustice as to fight in vain. And even if you managed to stir up Galilee, it
wouldn't lead anywhere. You'd have to stir up Jerusalem, Judea, the
whole of Israel."

"Let's go, then, let's not waste any more time!"

"Barabbas isn't completely wrong, Father," Miriam said calmly. "What's the point of waiting for the mercenaries to strike again? Or for the tax collectors to pay us another visit? Why always let ourselves be humiliated? What benefit can come of it?"

"Ah, so now you think like him, do you?"

"What he says is true. People are tired of submitting. And proud that you didn't let the tax collectors steal Houlda's candlestick. Your courage is an example to them."

"An example as useless as a fit of anger, you ought to say."

"Don't make yourself weaker than you are, Joachim." Barabbas grunted. "Invite your wise men to your friend Yossef's house. Obadiah can take them the message. And let me talk to them. Where's the risk in that?"

Joachim looked at Miriam, who nodded.

"What's the point of almost dying on the cross, Father, if it serves no purpose? Simply to hide in Galilee, all our lives, for nothing! It is we who decide if we are powerless before the king. To believe that his mercenaries are always stronger than us is to give him a reason to despise us."

CHAPTER 5

THEY had taken a long, roundabout route along the foot of Mount Tabor, avoiding the more frequented paths and bypassing Nazareth. Now it was agreed that Miriam would go ahead to inform Halva and Yossef.

On the winding path, lined with acacias and carob trees, leading to the crest of the hill, she walked so quickly that her feet barely touched the ground. As she approached the summit, there were more gaps in the hedges, and she saw the citron orchards, the little vineyard, and the two great plane trees surrounding Yossef's house. Without her even being aware of it, her face lit up in a broad smile.

Hearing bleating, she looked up. A flock of sheep and lambs was wandering in the field overlooking the path. She was about to turn away and run to the house when she glimpsed a figure amid the caper shrubs and the broom. She recognized the bright tunic, with its pretty blue and ocher embroidery, and the mane of wavy hair. "Halva! Halva!" she cried.

Startled, Halva stopped dead, and shaded her eyes from the sun to make out who this person could be who was running toward her.

"Miriam . . . God Almighty! Miriam!" She burst into both laughter and tears. "You're alive!"

"So is my father . . . We saved him."

"I know, Yossef told me. He heard about it in the synagogue, but I didn't dare believe it!"

"It's wonderful to see you!"

There were cries from beneath their feet. Halva broke free of Miriam. "Shimon, my little angel, you're not jealous of Miriam, are you?"

The little boy, barely two years old, fell silent and stared at Miriam openmouthed, with an extremely serious expression on his face. Suddenly, his big, sparkling brown eyes opened wide, and he held out his arms, babbling urgently.

"I think he recognizes me, don't you?" Miriam cried in delight. She laughed and bent down to pick him up. When she straightened up, she saw Halva looking pale and unsteady, with her hand over her mouth. "Halva! What's the matter?"

Breathing heavily, Halva tried to smile, and leaned on Miriam's shoulder. "It's nothing," she said in a toneless voice. "A dizzy spell. It'll pass."

"Are you ill?"

"No, no!" Halva regained her breath, and gently massaged her temples. "It's happened a few times since Libna was born. Don't worry. Come, let's go tell Yossef! He'll jump for joy when he sees you."

T H E reunion continued the rest of that beautiful day. Yossef did not have the patience to wait for Joachim. As soon as he saw his friend's tall figure coming along the path, he rushed to him, and hugged and kissed him, thanking the Almighty between his tears and laughter.

He was hardly less effusive in greeting Barabbas and Obadiah. Of course, they could all stay in his house, he cried as they came into the yard. There was plenty of room for everyone. Hadn't he followed Joachim's advice and built a secluded, almost secret room behind his workshop? They could put mats on the floor in there for Joachim and his companions. Miriam could sleep in the children's room.

They sat down around a table in the gentle shade of the plane trees that protected the house on the hottest days.

"There's no danger here," Yossef said. "No one will ever suspect you're in my house. And anyway, there are no mercenaries in Nazareth anymore."

Helped by Miriam, who swore that she was not at all tired, Halva brought drink and enough food to satisfy their appetites, which had been sharpened by the long walk. Obadiah attacked the drink eagerly but merely nibbled at the food. Knowing how impatient Joachim and Miriam were, he offered to go, as discreetly as possible, and tell Hannah that they had arrived. Joachim gave him instructions on how to get to the workshop and the house without being seen by the neighbors, and once the boy had set off, running like a fox, Yossef continued with his account of what had been happening in the village.

As was to be expected, the tax collectors had returned to Nazareth after Joachim's arrest.

"Would you believe it, Joachim? The one you wounded was there. He had his arm in a sling, but even so, it had only taken him four days to recover!"

"I'm really useless, aren't I?" Joachim said, amused. "My aim obviously wasn't as true as I thought!"

Yossef and Barabbas laughed. "That's for sure!"

This time, the tax collectors had been accompanied by three Roman officers and a cohort of mercenaries. They had behaved roughly, but no worse than usual.

"They just wanted to enjoy telling us you were going to die on the cross," Yossef said, squeezing Joachim's shoulder. "They repeated it so many times, everyone ended up believing it. Your poor Hannah was in floods of tears, moaning that the Almighty had abandoned her, that she'd lost her husband and daughter!"

He grimaced at the memory. Hannah's despair had been so extreme that Halva had stayed with her for a few days, but she had been unable to console or reassure her. They had even feared that Hannah would lose her mind.

Yossef turned to Miriam. "But I knew you'd manage somehow to prove those vultures wrong. The only thing that worried me was that the mercenaries might guess you'd left the village to rescue your father."

"Hah!" Barabbas snorted contemptuously. "The Romans and the mercenaries are so sure of their strength, they don't have any imagination. Besides, they don't even understand our language."

"That may be true of them," Yossef said. "But the tax collectors are clever. They may despise our Galilean accent, but their ears are as sharp as their hands are greedy. That's why I went to the synagogue and told everyone to keep their mouths shut. But you know how it is, Joachim. There are always people who can't be trusted."

The one good thing that had come out of this misfortune was that the tax collectors' hunger for revenge had merely increased the villagers' anger and overcome their differences of opinion.

"They bled us white," Yossef said with a sigh. "We have barely enough left to keep us going until the next harvest."

The tax collectors had taken away all they could, emptying the cellars and haylofts of all the sacks and jars they found, and ordering the mercenaries to pile the carts so high that the mules could barely pull them.

"They turned this house completely upside down, searching for money I don't have. I'd only just finished putting together two small chests for the children's clothes. So, of course, they took them. They even took the figs Halva had just picked! They were probably rotten by the time they got to Jerusalem, but they wanted to take everything. Just for the pleasure of humiliating us." Yossef sighed, but with a sardonic wink. "They didn't get our flocks, though. We'd already sent some of the boys into the forest with the animals."

"And weren't those idiots surprised to find them gone?" Barabbas asked.

"Of course they were! But we said we'd had enough and had decided not to keep livestock anymore. Since they always took it away from us, what was the point? One of the tax collectors said, 'You're lying, as usual. Your livestock's in the forest, I'm sure of it.' Someone answered, 'Well, go into the forest and find it. Be careful, though: the Almighty may have turned our animals into lions!'"

Joachim and Barabbas laughed in approval.

Yossef shook his head. "We really cursed them, I can tell you. And then imagine how happy we were when we found out that Miriam and Joachim had succeeded. Knowing you were alive and well made our hearts feel light again. Even the rabbis, who see every misfortune as a punishment from the Almighty, didn't think he'd have approved of something as horrible as that!"

Carried away by the emotion of the situation, his eyes clouded with tears, Yossef suddenly stood up and took Barabbas by the shoulders. "May the Lord bless you, my boy! You've made us happy and proud. That's something we really needed."

He was about to hug and kiss Miriam, but shyness held him back. Instead, he took her hands and kissed them tenderly.

"You, too, Miriam, you, too! How proud of you Halva and I are!"

Laughing happily, Halva took Miriam by the waist and drew her inside the house, where the two youngest children, made edgy by all this unaccustomed excitement, were starting to cry.

"You see what a state my Yossef is in?" she whispered, delighted. "Look at him; he's redder than a carob flower! When he gets emotional, he's the most tenderhearted man in God's creation. As gentle as a lamb. But so shy! So shy!"

Miriam placed her cheek against her friend's. "You don't know how good it is to see the two of you again. And I can't wait to see my mother. I didn't think I would hurt her so much when I left."

With little Shimon clutching at her tunic, Halva bent over the cradle to lift up Libna, who was crying with hunger and impatience. "Oh, as soon as she sees you and your father, she'll forget her—" She broke off abruptly. Her cheeks had turned white, her eyes closed, and she gasped for breath.

Miriam quickly took the baby from her arms. "Are you all right?"

Halva took a deep breath. "Don't worry. They're just dizzy spells. They always take me by surprise. . . ."

"Rest for a while. I'll see to the children."

"Oh, no, come on!" Halva said, making an effort to smile. "You must be a lot more tired than I am, after walking all day."

Miriam gently cradled Libna, who twisted her curls in her tiny fingers, and drew Shimon to her with a caress. "Let me help you, then," she insisted, anxiously. "Go and have a rest. You're so pale, it's frightening."

Reluctantly, Halva yielded. She went and lay down on a bed in an alcove at the far end of the room, and watched as Miriam prepared Libna's wheat cereal and made some biscuits for Shimon and Yossef, who was two years older. The oldest boy, the placid Yakov, helped as best he could. After they had eaten, she played with them, so openly and tenderly that the children, as trusting as if they had been with their mother, forgot their whims and anxieties.

Outside, Yossef was still telling Barabbas and Joachim, in his monotonous, softly passionate voice, how the news of their exploit had been brought to the synagogue by an ink merchant.

At first, many had doubted that it was true. There were so many rumors of things that people wanted to be true and that turned out to be false. But the following day, and the day after that, other merchants, coming from Cana and Sepphoris, had confirmed that the brigand Barabbas had indeed set fire to Tarichea and freed a number of prisoners from the field of crosses, including Joachim.

Everyone had sighed with relief, even those who had already started mourning for Joachim. Joy had quickly turned to a feeling of victory.

"If you entered Nazareth this evening, Joachim, the whole village would give you a hero's welcome," Yossef said. "They've forgotten how they protested when Miriam said she was going to ask for Barabbas's help in saving you!"

Joachim frowned. "We must be careful. This is when things could start getting dangerous for Nazareth."

Barabbas nodded. "That's what I find strange. It's been several days since we gave the Romans in Tarichea a kick up the backside. The mercenaries should be here by now, causing havoc in the village."

"I think there's a perfectly simple explanation for that," Yossef said. "They say Herod is so ill, he's going off his head. Apparently, his palace is worse than a nest of snakes. His sons, his sister, his brother, his mother-in-law, the servants . . . there isn't a single one of them who doesn't want to hasten his death and take his place. They're all seething with hatred. Both palaces, the Antonia palace in Jerusalem, and the one in Caesarea, are in a state of chaos. The Roman officers aren't prepared to keep backing this degenerate family. If that madman Herod survives his illness and learns that they acted without his consent, they won't be long for this world. Our king is mad, but he's the master of everything in Israel, from the smallest grain of wheat to the ungodly laws that come out of the Sanhedrin. We poor people of Galilee fear his mercenaries and his vultures. But they fear him as much as we do. So, while he's ill and can't give orders, they're all trapped in his shadow."

"That's a piece of news that does my heart good!" Barabbas cried. "And it makes me think I'm right to want—"

He could not continue, because just then loud cries and the

sound of footsteps made them all rise from the benches. It was Hannah, rushing toward them beneath the plane trees, her hands raised above her head.

"Joachim! God Almighty! Blessed is the Lord! You're there, I can see you! And to think I refused to believe this boy. . . ."

Joachim welcomed his wife into his arms. Hannah hugged him as tightly as she could, the tears streaming into her mouth. "Yes, it's really you!" she stammered. "You're not a demon. I recognize your smell! Oh, my husband, did they hurt you?"

Joachim was about to reply when Hannah broke away, her eyes and mouth wide open, her face convulsed with panic.

"Where's Miriam? Isn't she with you? Is she dead?"

"No, Mother! I'm here."

Hannah turned and saw Miriam running from the doorway of the house.

"My mad daughter!" she cried. You gave me such a fright!"

Overwhelmed by all this accumulated emotion, Hannah was having difficulty breathing, and seemed too weak to stroke their faces or touch their beloved eyes. For a moment, it looked as though she were about to faint, but then she recovered, and they all laughed.

Obadiah, who had been following her at a distance, scratched his head, ruffling his unkempt hair even more. "You know what?" he said to Barabbas. "She nearly alerted the whole village when I told her Miriam was here with Joachim. She just wouldn't believe me. She thought I was spying for the mercenaries. I was luring her into a trap, she said, things like that. Impossible to shut her up without losing my temper. What a good thing Miriam isn't like her!"

LATER, once night had fallen and the women and children were asleep, they gathered around a lamp, and Barabbas, in a low voice, revealed his great plan to Yossef. The time had come to start a rebellion that would sweep through Galilee and the whole of Israel, overthrow the ignominious rule of Herod, and free the country from the Roman yoke.

"Isn't that going a bit far?" Yossef breathed, his eyes wide.

"If what you say about Herod is right, then there's no better time than right now."

"Herod is certainly weak. But not as weak as that."

"If the whole country rises against him, who will support him? Not even the mercenaries—they'll be afraid they won't get paid."

Joachim entered the conversation. "It's a mad idea. As mad as Barabbas himself. But that's how he saved me from the cross. I think this is worth discussing with the people who hate Herod and the Sadducees as much as we do: the Zealots, the Essenes, and some of the Pharisees. There are wise men among them who'll be prepared to listen to us. If we can persuade them to bring their followers into the rebellion . . ."

"When the people see they've joined us," Barabbas said enthusiastically, "they'll know it's time to start fighting."

Yossef did not contradict them. He did not doubt either their determination or their courage. Like Joachim and Barabbas, he was convinced that passively enduring Herod's madness led only to more suffering.

"If you want to call a meeting of all these people, we can hold it here," he said. "It's not all that risky. We're quite a distance from Nazareth, and the Romans have never suspected me of anything. The people you invite will be perfectly safe. There are plenty of roundabout ways to get here. They won't even have to come through Nazareth."

Barabbas and Joachim thanked him. The real difficulty was to find men they could trust. Men of wisdom, but also men with their hearts in the right place, who had power over others. Men who were not violent by nature, but were prepared to fight. Such men were rare.

In the course of the discussion, Joachim and Yossef kept coming back to the same names. Among the Essenes, they narrowed their choice down to two men whose reputation for independence and opposition to the Temple in Jerusalem was well known: Joseph of Arimathea, surely the wisest of all the Essenes, and Giora of Gamala, who led a rebel movement based in the desert near the Dead Sea. Joachim also mentioned the name of a Zealot from Galilee whom he knew and trusted.

Barabbas grimaced, highly suspicious of men of religion. "They're even more fanatical than the Essenes."

"But they fight the Romans whenever they get the opportunity."

"They're so inflexible, the villagers are scared of them! I've heard they sometimes beat those who don't pray when they tell them to. If we have these people with us, we're never going to convince the doubters."

"We won't do it without them either. I don't believe this story of them beating peasants. The Zealots are harsh and austere, it's true, but they're brave, and they're not afraid to die fighting the mercenaries and the Romans."

"All they want is to impose their own idea of God," Barabbas insisted, raising his voice. "That's why they fight, not to help the hungry or spare them further humiliation by Herod."

"That's also why we need to convince them. I know at least two who are good men: Eleazar of Jotapata and Levi the Sicarion, from Magdala. They fight, but they're also good listeners, who respect other people's opinions. . . ."

Reluctantly, Barabbas agreed to approach the Zealots. But the argument became heated again when they touched on the subject of Nicodemus. He was the only Pharisee in the Sanhedrin who had ever shown any compassion toward the people of Galilee. Joachim was in favor of his coming, Barabbas was strongly opposed to it, and Yossef was undecided.

"How could you possibly ask a member of the Sanhedrin for help?" Barabbas cried. "They're all corrupt! You, of all people, should know that! Didn't you stick a spear into one of their tax collectors?"

"One thing has nothing to do with the other!" Joachim retorted in annoyance. "Nicodemus is against the Sadducees who bleed us dry at every opportunity. He's always responded to our grievances. Many's the time he's come to one of our synagogues to hear us."

"So what? That's hardly a great achievement. He comes, yawns through it all, and then goes back to his life of luxury in Jerusalem. . . ."

"I tell you, he's different."

"Why? Open your eyes, Joachim: They're all the same! Cowards, in the pay of Herod, that's what they are. If your Nicodemus wasn't a coward, he wouldn't still be sitting in the Sanhedrin. As soon as he finds out we're planning a rebellion, he'll denounce us—"

"Not Nicodemus. He argued with Ananias, the high priest, in the middle of a meeting in the Temple. Herod wanted to throw him in prison—"

"But he didn't get thrown in prison, did he? He didn't get hung on a cross like you! You can be sure he bowed his head and asked forgiveness . . . I tell you, he'll betray us! We don't need him!"

"No, of course not!" Joachim said, really angry now. "You don't need anyone! You can stir the people to rebellion all over the country without any support at all in Jerusalem or the Sanhedrin! If that's the case, go ahead. Why wait? Go ahead. . . ."

"Don't we just have to be a little careful?" Yossef said, in a placatory voice. "We could talk to Nicodemus without telling him what we're really thinking."

"For what purpose?" Barabbas replied obstinately. "To make sure that he's a coward like all the Pharisees?"

Joachim exploded. "What's the point of continuing with this discussion? You're talking like a child!"

The quarrel lasted awhile longer. At last Barabbas yielded, but his foul mood lasted the rest of the evening.

They still had to write and send the letters of invitation. Joachim got down to the task of writing, while Obadiah and his gang of *am ha'aretz* divided into groups of two or three, ready to scatter throughout the land.

"Aren't we giving them too much responsibility?" Yossef asked.

"Not at all!" Barabbas said, still irritable. "It's obvious you don't know them. They're more resourceful than monkeys. They could deliver messages all the way to the Negev, if they had to."

Yossef nodded, anxious not to needle Barabbas any farther. It was not until later, after a good meal, that he expressed his doubts.

"Here we are, stuck here on this hillside in Galilee," he said, broaching the subject cautiously. "I find it hard to believe that the three of us could start an uprising that would stir up the whole of Israel."

"I'm pleased to hear you say that!" Joachim cried, a hint of mockery in his voice. "I'd have doubted your intelligence if you hadn't. That's really the question: Do we have to embrace Barabbas's madness in order to counter Herod's madness?"

Barabbas glared at them, refusing to enter into the spirit of the joke. "Miriam is cleverer and braver than you carpenters," he said acidly. "She says I'm right. 'We are the ones who decide if we are powerless before the king. To think that his mercenaries are always stronger than us is to give him a good reason to despise us.' That's what she says."

"My daughter speaks well, I'll grant you that. I sometimes think she could persuade a stone to fly. But is she any less mad than you are, Barabbas? God alone knows." Joachim was smiling, affection softening his features.

Barabbas relaxed. "It may simply be that you're too old for rebellion!" he said, patting Joachim on the shoulder.

"It can't do any harm to gather the opinions of a few wise men," Yosef ventured.

"Nonsense! Who's ever seen a rebellion of 'wise men,' as you call them? It's people like me you should invite here. Thieves and scoundrels who aren't afraid to risk everything!"

———

THE next day at dawn, armed with the letters and a thousand pieces of advice from Barabbas, Obadiah and his comrades left Yossef's house.

Before leaving, Obadiah made Joachim promise that on his return he would finish telling him the story of Abraham and Sarah or the even more wonderful story of Moses and Zipporah. Joachim promised, a lot more moved by Obadiah than he admitted.

His hand resting affectionately on the back of the boy's neck, he walked along with him a little way. They parted at the edge of the forest. Obadiah said he would cut across it to gain time.

"Take good care of yourself, Joachim!" he said, making a comical face. "I don't want to find out I took you down from the cross for nothing. Take care of your daughter, too. One of these days, I may well ask you for her hand in marriage."

Joachim felt himself blushing. Obadiah was already running off through the bracken, his roguish laughter echoing among the trees. After he had gone, Joachim stood for a moment deep in thought.

Obadiah's provocative words came back to him. He saw himself in the synagogue in Nazareth, a few years earlier. It was one of those days when the rabbi had thundered at the top of his voice. For some reason, he had been inveighing against the *am ha'aretz*. They had to be cut in half, he said, just like fish. Getting carried away, he had raised a finger to heaven and cried into his beard, "A Jew must not marry an *am ha'aretz* girl! And we certainly can't let this rabble touch our daughters! They have no consciences, and to claim that they're men is ridiculous!"

Remembering these words now, surrounded by trees and undergrowth, Joachim felt ashamed, soiled even.

Could it be that the *am ha'aretz*, these paupers so despised by the doctors of the Law, were merely the victims of the age-old contempt of the rich for the poor, which even the Lord had not managed to eradicate from the hearts of men?

Nevertheless, Obadiah was the best of young men. That much was obvious. A valiant little fellow, eager to learn and affectionate to anyone who took an interest in him. Wouldn't any father dream of having such a son?

All at once, Joachim wondered if sending him as an ambassador to the haughty Essene Giora, who was constantly preaching purity, was such a good idea. In truth, neither Barabbas nor he himself had thought about that. It could well compromise the meeting before it even took place.

Nevertheless, thinking about it on his way back to Yossef's house, Joachim decided to trust in the supreme wisdom of the Almighty, to keep his worries to himself, and not to aggravate Barabbas's touchiness and impatience.

CHAPTER 6

For some weeks, they forgot the drama that had brought them together and the battle that awaited them. The days passed, gentle and calm, full of deceptive little joys, like the lull before a storm.

Miriam looked after the children. Finally able to take the rest she needed, Halva regained her color, her dizzy spells became less frequent, and, every day, her laughter rang out in the shade of the great plane trees.

Joachim spent all his time in Yossef's workshop, running his hands over the tools, lifting the shavings to his nostrils, stroking the smooth wood with the same sense of wonder as he had felt in his youth, experiencing his first amorous caresses.

Discreetly informed by Hannah, Lysanias came running to see them, babbling with happiness, blessing Miriam and kissing her forehead. He brought good news of old Houlda. She no longer felt any pain from the blows she had received and had recovered all her old energy—and her bad temper, too.

"She treats me like her husband," he chuckled delightedly. "As badly as if we'd lived together for years."

He missed the communal life of the workshop so much that he

immediately started working with Yossef and Joachim. In a few weeks, the three of them managed to do four months' work.

Every evening, putting away his tools as he had done so often before, Lysanias would declare with satisfaction, "Well, we certainly got a lot done today."

One day, Yossef, who usually responded with a grateful smile before inviting everyone to sit down to the evening meal, said, "This can't continue. I pay Lysanias what's due to him, but you, Joachim, won't accept any wages. It's unfair. I'm only getting all these orders because your workshop is closed. I feel ashamed. We have to come to an arrangement."

Joachim laughed heartily. "Nonsense! Board and lodgings, the pleasure of friendship, a quiet life . . . that's our arrangement, Yossef, and it's enough for me. Don't worry, my friend. I haven't forgotten that you're taking a big risk, having Miriam and me here."

"Miriam's another one! She works as hard as a handmaid!"

"Not at all! She's taking the strain off your wife. Pay Lysanias what he deserves, Yossef, but don't have any qualms about me. The happiness of working with you is all I need. God alone knows when I'll be able to go back to my own workshop, and nothing gives me greater satisfaction than being able to keep myself busy in yours."

Yossef protested. This was no laughing matter. Joachim wasn't being sensible. He ought to be thinking about the future. He had Miriam and Hannah to provide for.

"From now on, whether you like it or not, every time an order is paid for, I'll put some money aside for you."

Lysanias interrupted the conversation. "What you should do, Yossef, is give your customers a specific time limit, and then go over it. Otherwise, they're going to think you've made a pact with demons to be able to work so fast!"

Only Barabbas remained in somber mood. Impatient, always on the alert, he was still convinced that the mercenaries would swoop on Nazareth to take revenge for Joachim's escape. The fact that they hadn't so far done so unsettled him, and he feared they were planning something. In order not to be taken by surprise, he decided to become a shepherd.

From morning to evening, wrapped in an old tunic as brown as the earth, he would go out onto the slopes of wild grass around the house, surrounded by the sheep that Yossef had managed to hide from the greed of the tax collectors. He would get far enough away to keep an eye on the comings and goings around the village. He found this freedom, these long walks over the fragrant hills in the late spring heat, so exhilarating that more than once he slept in the open air.

His impatience, his eagerness to do battle with the mercenaries, made him less vigilant, and he did not even notice when Obadiah returned, as unobtrusive as a shadow.

I T was nearly nightfall. Miriam had told the children a last story and kissed them good night. Halva was already asleep. From the workshop behind the house, bursts of merry chatter could be heard. Joachim, Lysanias, and Yossef really enjoyed working together, Miriam thought. Soon they would be sitting around the table, as greedy for words as for food.

Their discussions could last for hours when Barabbas was present. But she was unable to take them seriously.

"They're just like children," she would say to Halva. "They want to remake the world the Almighty has created."

And they would both laugh in secret at the men's pride.

Still amused at this thought, Miriam went through into the main room of the house. It was already dark. She could smell the fragrance of a lime tree, carried on the evening breeze.

She went to look for the lamps and a jar of oil to fill them. On her return, she thought she sensed a presence behind her. She looked around, peering into the gloom. But there was no one here. No figure stood in the doorway, silhouetted against the reddening sky.

She got back to work. But when she struck a light, a hand took the stone from her. She cried out and stepped back, dropping the tinder wick.

"It's me, Obadiah," a whisper came. "No need to be afraid!"

"Obadiah! What an idiot! You scared me, creeping around like a thief!"

She laughed and drew him to her. He abandoned himself to her embrace, quivering with pleasure, then broke free, overcome with emotion.

"I didn't mean to frighten you!" he said, lighting the tinder. "It was nice to look at you, after all this time. I'm really pleased to see you."

The flames grew, dispersing the shadows. Miriam sensed how embarrassed Obadiah was after the admission he had just made. With a maternal gesture, she ruffled his unkempt hair.

"I'm pleased to see you, too, Obadiah. . . . Did you come back alone?"

"No." He pointed nonchalantly at Yossef's workshop with his thumb. "They're there. The two Essene wise men, as your father calls them. The one from Damascus, no problem. He may really be a wise man. But the other one, Giora of Gamala, is a madman. He didn't even want to see me, let alone hear what I had to say and take Joachim's letter! I was white with dust by the time I got to Gamala, and my tongue was hanging out. You'd think they'd have given me a few drops of water, wouldn't you? Not a bit of it." He growled in disgust. "My friends wanted to leave again, because there was a big market where we could get something to eat and ply our trade."

Miriam raised an accusing eyebrow. "You mean steal?"

Obadiah grinned magnanimously. "After such a long journey and a welcome like that, we had to amuse ourselves. But I didn't go. I found a way to get Joachim's message to the old man."

His face lit up with pride, softening the strangeness of his features. His dark eyes glowed like coals.

"For three day and three nights," he said, "I didn't move from

outside that farmhouse or whatever it is, where he lives with his followers. All of them in the same white tunics, beards so long they
could walk on them. Always looking furious, as if they were going to
cut you in pieces. Always washing themselves and praying. Constantly praying! I've never seen people pray so much. But for those
three days, they kept seeing me, which really got on their nerves.
Then on the fourth day, surprise! I wasn't there. No more *am ha'aretz*
to sully their eyes. They ran to tell Giora the good news. But that
night, another surprise! When Giora walks into his bedchamber,
what does he see? Me, sitting on his bed! You should have seen the
way he jumped, heard the way he screamed, that wise old Essene. . . ."

Obadiah laughed heartily at the memory.

"You should have heard him, waking up the whole pack of them.
And me, sitting there as calm as anything while they all shouted at
me. I had to wait for them to tire themselves out before I could tell
them why I was there. Then the old man took another two or three
days to make up his mind. Anyway, here we are. It took time to get
back because we had to stop twenty times a day for prayers. . . . If
we're going to have Giora with us for this rebellion, it won't be fun,
I can tell you."

When Miriam finally met Giora, she realized that Obadiah had
been telling the truth. She, too, was very struck by his appearance
and character.

He was so small and had such a long beard that it was impossible
to guess his age. He looked frail, but he possessed enormous energy.
His voice was shaky but solemn, and he underlined every one of his
sentences with a sharp movement of his hands. If he caught your
eye, he wouldn't let go of you, forcing you in the end to look down
as if to shield yourself from a blinding light.

The evening that he arrived, he demanded that neither she nor
Halva nor Obadiah share his meal. That would have been impure, he
explained: Women and children were by nature bearers of weakness
and infidelity. Only Yossef and Joachim could break bread at his

table—apart from the other newcomer, of course. This other man's name was Joseph of Arimathea, and he had come all the way from Damascus, where he, too, led a community of Essenes. But even though he wore the same immaculately white tunic as Giora, he was quite different.

He was tall and well built, with a short beard, a bald head, kindly features, and a friendly manner. He was perfectly civil toward Obadiah. Miriam felt immediately drawn to him, if for no other reason than the serenity that emanated from him. His calm presence seemed, as if by magic, to temper Giora's aggressiveness.

All the same, the meal was somewhat out of the ordinary. Giora demanded absolute silence. When Joseph of Arimathea suggested that words could be tolerated while they were on their travels, he replied, his bread quivering, "Would you sully our Law?"

Joseph of Arimathea did not take offense, but yielded to his wishes. A strange silence filled the house. All that could be heard was the noise of the wooden spoons in the bowls and the chomping of jaws.

Disgusted, perhaps even somewhat alarmed, Obadiah grabbed a lump of buckwheat and some figs and went and ate them under the trees in the yard, surrounded by the nocturnal chirping of the crickets and the rustling of leaves.

Fortunately, the dinner did not go on for too long. Giora announced that Yossef and Joachim were to join him in a long prayer. Joseph of Arimathea, who was tired after his journey, skillfully managed to spare them this chore. He convinced Giora that praying in solitude would be more pleasing to the Lord.

THE following day was no less full of surprises. At first light, Barabbas arrived, pushing his flock ahead of him. With him were three men covered in dust.

"I found them at nightfall, lost on the path," Barabbas said to Joachim, with a hint of mockery.

Joachim smiled as he and Yossef greeted the newcomers. One of them, a stocky man with a dark complexion, had a large dagger thrust through the belt of his tunic. "I'm Levi the Sicarion," he announced in a loud voice.

Behind him, Joachim recognized Jonathan of Capernaum. The young rabbi timidly bowed his head. The oldest of the three, Eleazar, the Zealot from Jotapata, rushed to Joachim and hugged him, babbling about how glad he was to see him alive and well.

"God is great not to have called you to him too early!" he cried in delight. "Blessed be the Lord!"

The other two men noisily echoed his words. Barabbas explained, with the same mocking tone as before, how he had discovered them in the forest, heading wearily away from Nazareth, in the direction of Samaria, for fear of finding mercenaries in the village.

"I let them sleep a few hours before we set off, guiding ourselves by the stars. Not bad training for future fighters."

Joseph of Arimathea, drawn by the noise, appeared in the yard. His reputation for wisdom and great medical knowledge, and the renown of the Essenes of Damascus, preceded him, but none of the newcomers had ever had the opportunity to meet him.

Joachim introduced them. Joseph of Arimathea took their hands in his with a simplicity that put them immediately at their ease.

"Peace be with you," he said to Levi, Eleazar, and Jonathan in turn. "And blessed be Joachim for having brought about this meeting."

Yossef invited them to sit down around the big table beneath the plane trees. Then each man spoke at length, presenting his life story and detailing the misfortunes that had befallen his region, misfortunes for which, in each case, Herod was to blame.

Meanwhile, Halva and Miriam were busy laying the tables, putting out fruit, cups of curdled milk, and biscuits, which Obadiah, his cheeks red with the heat, had skillfully removed from the oven.

"I was apprenticed to a baker for half a year," he said proudly to Halva when she expressed surprise at this dexterity. "I liked it a lot."

"So why didn't you also become a baker?"

Obadiah's laugh was more mocking than bitter. "Have you ever seen an *am ha'aretz* as a baker?"

Miriam had heard this exchange. She looked at Halva. Neither could stop herself blushing. Halva was about to say something kind to Obadaiah, when the sound of raised of voices in the yard made her turn. Giora had come out and was standing before the newcomers, so stiff and tense that his small stature was forgotten.

"What's all this noise?" he exclaimed, gesticulating. "I can hear your voices from the other side of the house, and I can't study anymore!"

They all stared at him in surprise. Joseph of Arimathea stood up and went close enough to Giora for the physical difference between them to be particularly striking. He smiled. It was an amiable, amused, but curiously glacial smile. There was a strength in his features that would not easily be shaken, it seemed to Miriam.

"We were making so much noise, my dear Giora, to express our joy at being here together. These companions have just arrived here after a difficult trek through the forest. God guided them to our friend, who led them here by trusting in the stars."

"Trusting in the stars!" Giora's beard quivered, and his shoulders shook with rage. "Absurd! You, a follower of the sages, dare to repeat such nonsense?"

Joseph of Arimathea's smile was broader than ever now, but just as glacial as before.

Obadiah had left the oven and was standing beside Miriam. She sensed that he was having to stop himself from jeering. Out in the yard, the newcomers had risen, embarrassed by Giora's anger. While Joachim appeared to be amused by the situation, Yossef was watching the two Essenes anxiously. Without responding to Giora's belligerence, Joseph of Arimathea pointed to a free place on the bench.

"Giora, my friend," he said calmly, "do join us. Sit down and drink some milk. It'll be good for us to get to know one another."

"There's no point. We don't need to know one another, we only need to know Yahweh. I am going back to my prayers in order to cultivate that knowledge."

He turned abruptly, glared at Miriam, Halva, and Obadiah, who were in his way, then turned again, just as abruptly.

"Unless we start the meeting we've come here for, and get it over with?"

Joachim shook his head. "Nicodemus isn't here yet. We ought to wait for him."

"Nicodemus from the Sanhedrin?" Giora said disgustedly.

Joachim nodded. "He's coming all the way from Jerusalem. It's a long journey, he has to be careful."

"That's the Pharisees for you! They'd keep God himself waiting!"

"Let's give him another day," Joseph of Arimathea intervened, ignoring Giora's invectives as usual. "Besides, our friends need to rest. The mind is clear only when the body is at peace."

Giora laughed. "Rest! A body at peace! Damascus nonsense! Study and pray if you want to have a clear mind. That's what you need. Anything else is folly and weakness!"

This time he disappeared behind the house without turning back.

Obadiah gave a stifled groan and touched Miriam's hand. "I may have judged him badly, this Giora. There's no need for battles or rebellions. Just put him in front of Herod. In less than a day, the king would be even sicker and more insane than he is now. 'Giora our secret weapon,' that's what we should call him!"

He had said this in a loud voice, with such comical seriousness that Halva and Miriam burst out laughing.

From the table in the yard, the men looked at them and frowned. Barabbas gave Obadiah a scathing look. But Joseph of Arimathea, who like the others, had heard what Obadiah had said, responded with laughter, although in moderation. That set the others giggling, which did them all a lot of good.

———

I n the middle of the afternoon, while the late spring sun was still hot, Obadiah's comrades, who were keeping watch, came running into the yard.

"Someone's coming along the Tabor road!"

"The wise man from the Sanhedrin?"

"Doesn't look like it. Unless he's in disguise. He looks more like a ghost."

Accompanied by Barabbas and Yossef's children, Joachim again went to greet the newcomer. As soon as he saw the figure, he realized that the boys were right. It wasn't Nicodemus. Dressed in a brown linen cloak, his face hidden by a hood, the man was advancing quickly, and his shadow seemed to run behind him like an apparition.

"Who can this fellow be?" Joachim muttered. "Do you think we invited him?"

Barabbas kept watching the newcomer. When the man pushed back his hood, he cried, "Mathias of Ginchala!"

The man let out a cry like a horse's whinny and waved a hand sparkling with silver rings. Barabbas grasped him by the shoulders, and they embraced with a great show of friendship.

"Joachim, let me introduce my friend. More than a friend, a brother. Mathias led the rebellion in Ginchala last year. If there's one person in Galilee with the fighting spirit to stand up to Herod's mercenaries, here he is."

That fighting spirit had left its mark on his face, Joachim thought, as he greeted him. There were two wide scars on Mathias's forehead, which ran back across his head, leaving two pale, ugly furrows in his hair. Behind his graying beard, his lips were scarred. When he opened his mouth, he revealed gums from which most of the teeth had been knocked out. A terrifying face, all in all; it was obvious why Mathias preferred to hide it under a hood.

"I heard you were in the area," he said to Barabbas, "so I thought I'd come and congratulate you on your exploit in Tarichea! And talk about your rebellion. . . ."

Barabbas laughed exaggeratedly to hide his embarrassment.

"You knew?" Joachim asked in surprise. "How?"

Mathias laughed. "I know everything that happens in Galilee." He seized Barabbas's wrist in his ringed fingers. "You could have sent me a proper invitation, like the others."

"You know about the invitations, too?" Joachim said, coldly. "You're right, we can't hide anything from you."

"You grabbed one of the boys, is that it?" Barabbas said, pretending, unconvincingly, to be offended.

"The one who was supposed to take your message to Levi the Sicarion," Mathias said with a wink. "You mustn't be angry at the kid. When he saw me, he got scared. If it had been anyone else, I'm sure he'd have held his tongue. Anyway, I gave him a nice purse to reward him for his dedication. I wanted to surprise you."

Joachim was watching them, torn between irony and anger. The act the two bandits were putting on did not deceive him. He did not doubt for a moment that Barabbas had managed somehow to inform Mathias. . . . And without telling anyone, for fear that he, Joachim, would be against the idea. Not that he would have been, because in fact it wasn't a bad idea at all.

"A surprise that ought to please our friends," he said, in a sardonic tone that made it clear to the two robbers that he had not been taken in.

M ATHIAS'S arrival certainly created a stir. Obadiah made no secret of his enthusiasm.

"Now, there's a real warrior," he whispered excitedly to Miriam. "They say he once fought thirty-two mercenaries single-handed. They all died and he . . . Did you see his face? That's what I call a scar!"

Yossef, Eleazar, and Levi greeted Mathias in an unbiased manner. Joseph of Arimathea was pleasant toward him and showed particular interest in his scars. Jonathan seemed disconcerted to be in the company of two actual brigands about whom some not very flattering rumors circulated. All of them, however, were waiting with some anxiety for Giora's reaction. Joachim and Barabbas both warned Mathias about the Essene's prickly character. But when the old man appeared, Mathias bowed to him with what seemed like genuine respect.

Giora looked at him for a moment, then merely shrugged his shoulders and let out a sigh of impatience between his dry lips.

"Here's another one," he grunted, addressing Joachim and Joseph of Arimathea. "But your Pharisee from Jerusalem still isn't here. What's the point in waiting any longer? He won't come. You must never trust those snakes in the Sanhedrin, you ought to know that."

Barabbas agreed, with a fervor that impressed Giora. But Joachim, supported by Joseph of Arimathea, asked that they wait a little while longer.

At last, as twilight was approaching, one of the young *am ha'aretz* on watch announced that a small team was approaching.

"A team?" Barabbas said in surprise.

"A big man on a light-colored mule with a Persian slave running behind him. Gold in the tunic and necklaces that could probably buy us a dozen fine horses."

Nicodemus, the Pharisee from the Sanhedrin, was finally arriving. There were smiles, but no one made any comment.

When Nicodemus entered the yard, everyone, even Giora, was waiting for him. He was a stout man, attractive and ageless. He wore his silk embroidered tunic with unaffected ease. He had as many gold rings on his fingers as Mathias had silver ones on his.

There was nothing arrogant in his manner, and his voice had a comfortable charm that made him pleasant to listen to. He received with modesty the respect that was due to him. Before Giora had even had time to utter a word, Nicodemus praised him for his virtue.

Clearly, he was as shrewd as he was wise. Next, he told them all how he had had to stop at a large number of the many synagogues along the way.

"In every one, I made the point that we members of the Sanhedrin don't visit the villages of Israel often enough to meet the people." He smiled. "That way, everyone can see I have a perfectly normal reason for coming to Galilee. That's also the reason, my friends, why I have to travel with a slave and a mule. Otherwise, it would arouse suspicion. In any case, I'm not going to stay here long this evening, Yossef. I've promised the rabbi of Nazareth that I'll spend the night at his house. I'll be back tomorrow morning, and then we can talk for as long as you wish."

He took the time to drink a cup of milk before continuing on his way to the village. Deep down, everyone was relieved—especially Halva and Miriam, who, apart from the growing number of mouths to feed, had been worried that they would not know to behave in front of such an important figure.

But once Nicodemus, his mule, and his slave had left the yard, an embarrassed silence fell over the company. Mathias broke it with an amused little snort. "If the mercenaries come for us tomorrow, we'll know why."

The others stared at him in alarm.

"I was always opposed to his coming," Barabbas said, with a reproachful glance at Joachim.

"You're wrong to say that," young Rabbi Jonathan protested. "I know Nicodemus. He's an honest man, and a lot braver than you might think to look at him. Besides, it can't be a bad idea to hear the opinion of a man who knows the Sanhedrin from the inside."

Barabbas sighed. "If you think so. . . ."

W H E N the night was well advanced and she and Halva were dropping with exhaustion after tidying and cleaning the house in the dim lamplight, Miriam, unable to explain her intuition, even to her-self, had the sudden conviction that all the words that would be spoken the next day would lead nowhere.

Lying in the darkness near the children, their regular breathing like a caress, she reproached herself for this thought. Her father, Joa-chim, had been right to invite these men. Joseph of Arimathea was right to support the presence of Nicodemus. Even the presence of "that Giora man," as Obadiah called him, was a good thing. The more different the men were, the more important it was that they speak to one another.

But what would they do with all those words?

Oh, why all these questions? she wondered. It was too soon to form an opinion.

It was quite presumptuous of her, she thought, to make the least judgment on things—power, politics, justice—that had always been the preserve of men. Where did she get her self-confidence? Cer-tainly, she could think as well as her father or Barabbas. But in a dif-ferent way. They had experience. She had nothing but her intuition.

She ought to show more modesty. Besides, doubting at such a moment was tantamount to a betrayal of Barabbas and Joachim.

She fell asleep promising herself that she would keep her place from now on, and smiling in the darkness at the thought that Giora of Gamala would surely be unable to force her to do so.

CHAPTER 7

O N C E the morning ablutions and prayers were over, Joachim
looked at the faces raised to him.

"Praise be to the Lord God, king of the world, who has given us
life, kept us in good health, and allowed us to reach this day." His
voice throbbed with emotion.

"Amen!" the others responded.

"We know why we're here," Joachim went on, but Nicodemus,
raising his gold-ringed hand, interrupted him.

"I'm not so certain, friend Joachim. Your letter was not very
clear. All it said was that you wanted to bring together a few wise
men to consider the future of Israel. That's quite vague. I recognize
some of the faces around this table; others are unfamiliar to me. As
far as my Essene brothers are concerned, I know a little of what they
think, and even the things they reproach me for."

He bowed with an amused smile toward Giora and Joseph of Arimathea. His voice was starting to cast a spell. They all realized that
the reason Nicodemus had been able to carve out a reputation among
the Sadducees of Jerusalem was that he knew how to handle words.

Joachim had difficulty hiding his embarrassment and instinctively looked for help from Joseph of Arimathea. But Barabbas, whose eyes were bright with anger, was quicker than him.

"I can tell you the reason for this meeting, because it was my idea," he said. "It's simple. We, the people of Galilee, can no longer bear the hold that Herod has on our lives. We can no longer bear the injustices that he and his mercenaries inflict on Israel. We can no longer bear the fact that Rome is his master, and therefore ours. All this has been going on for too long. We have to put an end to it, and we have to do it now."

The only sound disturbing the perfect silence that followed Barabbas's words was a sarcastic chuckle from Giora. Now everyone was waiting for Nicodemus's reaction.

The Pharisee nodded and put his fingers together under his chin. "And how do you propose to put an end to it, my dear Barabbas?" he asked.

"By force of arms. By the death of Herod. By the rising of a suffering people. By a rebellion that sweeps away everything. That's how. I was not in favor of your coming. But now you know everything. You can denounce us, or you can join us."

As he spoke these last words, Barabbas placed his hand on Joachim's shoulder. Joachim looked embarrassed. Not because of this demonstration of friendship, but because Barabbas seemed to him to be going too fast and too far. Bluntness was a bad strategy. It was surely not the way to go about convincing Nicodemus, or even the others, perhaps.

In fact, he could already see the result. Although Levi the Sicarion and Mathias greeted Barabbas's words with enthusiasm, the others cautiously lowered their eyes—all except Joseph of Arimathea, who remained calm and attentive.

As for Giora and Nicodemus, they both made disdainful faces.

Joachim feared the effect on Barabbas and hastened to intervene. "Barabbas has his own way of saying and doing things. It's quite genuine. I owe a lot to his way of doing things. I owe it my life—"

He was interrupted by a shrill squeal, which made young Rabbi Jonathan jump. It came from Giora, who was pointing his finger at Joachim's chest.

"Certainly not! You owe your life to the will of Yahweh and nothing else. I know what happened in Tarichea. I know about your act of violence here in Nazareth, and about your being put on the cross. You came down from that cross not because a boy took you down, but because it was Yahweh's will! If it hadn't been, you would still be rotting there."

Giora's pointed finger and fiery gaze came to rest on Barabbas, like a threat. "No reason to be proud of your exploits, brigand that you are. You were merely the instrument of the Lord! All our destinies are subject to the will of God!"

Turning red, Barabbas rose to his feet. "Do you mean to say that God has willed the madness of Herod and his hold over Galilee? Over Israel? That he has willed Herod's mercenaries to humiliate and kill us? That he has willed the Temple's tax collectors to rob us and drag us through the mud? That he has willed all the crosses on which Jews just like you rot? If that's the case, Giora, I tell you this to your face: You can keep your Yahweh. And that I'll fight him just as hard as I fight Herod and the Romans!"

The cries his words provoked shook the leaves on the plane trees above their heads.

"Don't blaspheme!" Nicodemus cut in. "Or else I'll have to leave. Giora is exaggerating. His words go farther than his thoughts. God is not to blame for our misfortunes—"

"Yes, he is!" Giora screamed. "I meant what I said, and you understood me perfectly well, Pharisee! You all keep moaning, Herod, Herod! It's all Herod's fault! But it isn't. It's all the fault of this stiff-necked people. That's what Moses said, and he was right. A stiff-necked people roaming the desert because it doesn't deserve Canaan. Suffering and shame. That's what we've come to!"

Again there were cries of protest, but Giora was unimpressed. His sharp voice rose above the commotion.

"Who, in this country, follows the laws of Moses, as the Book demands? Who prays and purifies himself as the Law prescribes? Who reads and learns the word of the Book to build the Temple in his heart, as the prophet Ezra ordered? No one. The Jews of today pretend to love God. What they really love is to be present at horse races, like the Romans, to go and see plays in the theater, like the Greeks! They cover the walls of their houses in images. And sacrilege of sacrileges, they even work on the Sabbath! Even in the heart of the Sanhedrin, where trade is more important than faith. This nation is ungodly. It deserves its punishment a hundredfold. Herod is not the cause of your misfortunes; he is the consequence of your sins!"

There followed a brief, stunned silence, broken by a deep voice: the voice of Eleazar, the Zealot from Jotapata.

"I tell you this, Giora, from the bottom of my heart: You are mistaken. God desires what is good for his people. He chose us in his heart. Us, and no one else. I respect your prayers, but I am as pious as any Essene. If there is someone blaspheming here, I fear it is you."

"You're just a Pharisee, like this other one!" Giora retorted, his beard bristling with rage. "You Zealots think you're so superior because you kill Romans. But in your ideas, you're nothing but Pharisees."

"Is it an insult to be a Pharisee?" Nicodemus said, taking offense.

Before Giora could respond, Joseph of Arimathea, who had not yet said anything, placed a firm hand on his arm and declared, with an authority that surprised everyone, "This argument is pointless. We know what our differences are. What's the point in making them worse? Let's try at least to be civil to one another."

The Zealot thanked him with a nod of the head. "No one submits more to the laws of Moses than a Zealot. We also regard Herod's conduct as a blemish on the land. The Romans' gold eagle he has allowed to be raised over the Temple in Jerusalem burns our eyes with shame. We, too, reproach the people for being neither as wise nor as pious as Yahweh wishes. But I repeat to you, Giora: The Almighty cannot wish for the suffering of his people. Barabbas and Joachim are right: The people are suffering and cannot endure any more. That is the truth. Our sons are crucified, our brothers sent into the arena, our sisters sold as slaves. How much longer are we going to tolerate this?"

"My own thoughts are not so far from yours, friend Eleazar," Nicodemus said, ignoring Giora's protests. "But does that mean that we must respond with arms and bloodshed? How often have you Zealots confronted the Romans or Herod's mercenaries?"

"A good thousand times, you can be sure of that!" Levi the Sicarion laughed, raising his dagger. "We really made them suffer!"

"So you say!" Nicodemus retorted coldly. "But it doesn't seem that way to me. The Romans are still Herod's masters. Come on, let's use a little common sense. A rebellion will get you nowhere. Even supposing you're capable of leading it!" He shook his head to show that he doubted this.

"And what makes you so sure of yourself?" Mathias asked, with a hint of contempt. "The Sanhedrin's no place to judge what can be done with spears and swords." He pushed back his hood, uncovering his face, which was made all the more terrifying by his smile. "You don't see faces like mine there. But look at this face well, because it says we can fight the Romans and the mercenaries and . . . defeat them."

He looked at each of them in turn, savoring the effect he was having.

"For me, it's fine," he resumed. "If Barabbas goes to war against Herod, we're ready."

"Ready to get yourselves cut to shreds," Rabbi Jonathan said. "Just as you did last year, when you tried to take Tarichea."

"That was then, Rabbi, this is now. We didn't have enough weapons at that time. It was a useful lesson. Just one moon ago, in the bay of Carmel, near Ptolemaïs, we seized two Roman boats loaded with spears, knives, and even a siege machine. Now, if the people are brave enough, we can arm twelve thousand men."

"There's a time for peace and a time for war," Barabbas said in a determined tone. "The time for war has come."

"You mean, the time for you to die?" Nicodemus insisted, and Giora made a noisy squeal in support.

Mathias and Barabbas both made the same gesture of exasperation. "If we have to die, we'll die! It's better than living on our knees."

"Utter nonsense!" Levi the Sicarion muttered. "The question is not whether we live or die. I'm not afraid to die in the name of the Lord, *al kiddush ha-Shem*. The question is, can we bring down Herod, then defeat the Romans? Because this is what's going to happen: If we weaken that madman, he'll ask the emperor Augustus for help. And that, you have to agree, will be a whole other story."

"Augustus doesn't give a damn about Herod!" Barabbas said, becoming heated. "According to the merchants, all the legions in the empire are massing on the northern frontiers to fend off the Barbarians. They even say that Varron, the governor of Damascus, has had to part with a legion. . . ."

Barabbas waited for Joseph of Arimathea to confirm this, which he did, however reluctantly. "That's what they say, yes."

Barabbas banged the table with his fist. "Then I say to all of you: There's never been a better moment to bring down Herod. He's old and ill. His sons, daughters, wife, the whole of his family, are at each other's throats, thinking only of betraying him and seizing power! As soon as his illness abates a little, he poisons a few of them to feel safer. Everyone in the palace is afraid. From the cooks to the prostitutes. Even the Roman officers don't know who they're supposed to take their orders from anymore. The mercenaries are afraid they won't get paid . . . I repeat: Herod's house is in chaos, and it's for us to take advantage of it. The opportunity won't arise again any time soon. The people of Galilee have nothing to lose but their fear and timidity. Mathias and I can bring thousands of *am ha'aretz* along with us. You Zealots have a lot of influence in the villages of Galilee. They admire you for the blows you've struck against the tyrant. If you say the word, they'll follow you. And you, Nicodemus, you could bring together people favorable to our cause in Jerusalem. If Judea rises at the same time as us, everything's possible. The people of Israel are waiting. They just need to see that we're determined, and they'll summon their courage and follow us—"

"Is that what you believe?" Nicodemus interrupted, all amiability gone from his voice now. "Then you believe in something insane. You can't just conjure up an army or a war. You can't turn a band of paupers into soldiers capable of defeating mercenaries hardened by years of combat. Your rebellion will result in lots of bloodshed, and all for nothing."

"You're saying that because you hate the *am ha'aretz!*" Barabbas exploded. "Like all the Pharisees, like all the rich people in Jerusalem and the Temple, you have nothing but contempt in your hearts for the poor. You are traitors to your people."

"What do you suggest we do, Nicodemus?" Joachim asked, trying to temper Barabbas's anger.

"I suggest we wait."

The angry cries of Mathias and Barabbas, Levi and Eleazar, shattered the warm, still air.

Nicodemus raised his hands authoritatively. "You asked for my opinion. I came all the way here to give it. You could at least hear me out."

Reluctantly, the others granted him the silence he was demanding.

"You're right, Barabbas, Herod's house is in chaos. In which case, why anticipate God's work? Why shed blood and heap suffering on suffering, when the Almighty is already punishing Herod and his family? You should believe in the Lord's foresight. It is he who decides on matters of good and evil. As far as Herod and his ungodly family are concerned, his justice is already at work. Soon, they will be gone. Then it will be time to bring pressure to bear on the Sanhedrin."

"I understand what you're saying, Nicodemus," Joachim said. "But I fear it's only a dream. All that will happen is that Herod will die and another madman will take his place—"

"How ignorant you all are!" Giora yelled, a wild look in his eyes, unable to contain himself any longer. "And what bad Jews! Don't you know that there is only one person who can save us? Have you forgotten the word of Yahweh? The one you are waiting for to save you, you band of ignoramuses, is the Messiah! He alone, do you hear me? He alone will save the people of Israel from the mire into which it has sunk. You're so stupid, Barabbas. Don't you know that the Messiah cares nothing for your swords? All he wants is your obedience and your prayers. If you desire the end of the tyrant, come with us to the desert and follow the teachings of the Master of Justice. Come and add your prayers to ours in order to hasten the coming of the Messiah. That is your duty."

"The Messiah, the Messiah! That's all you and your kind ever talk about! You're like babies longing for their mother's breast. The Messiah! You don't even know if he exists, your Messiah! Or if you'll ever see him. On every road in this land, you see fools crying out that they're the Messiah! The Messiah! It's only a word you use to disguise your fear and cowardice."

"Barabbas, this time you've gone too far!" Nicodemus cried, his cheeks scarlet.

"Nicodemus is right," Rabbi Jonathan said, already on his feet. "I didn't come here to listen to your ungodliness."

"God has promised the coming of the Messiah," Eleazar the Zealot said, pointing an accusing finger at Barabbas. "Giora is right. Our purity will hasten his coming."

"But so will our swords, for they come down on the ungodly like a prayer," Levi the Sicarion said.

The cries subsided.

"All right, I understand," Mathias sighed, putting his hood back over his head and standing up.

Everyone looked at him, suddenly anxious.

He gave Barabbas's shoulder a friendly pat. "You gathered an assembly of crybabies, my friend. Herod is right to despise them. With these people around, he can still reign for a long time. There's nothing more for me to do here."

He turned on his heel. The crickets and cicadas were chirping, but the only sound anyone heard was the rubbing of his sandals on the ground as he left Yossef's yard without another word.

I N the coolness of the kitchen, Miriam and Halva were listening out for the slightest noises coming from outside. After the departure of Mathias and the long silence that ensued, the men resumed their discussion—this time so quietly, it was as if they were afraid of their own voices.

Miriam approached the door. She could hear Joseph of Arimathea speaking calmly, but so low that she had to make an effort to understand him. He, too, believed in the coming of the Messiah, he was saying. Barabbas was wrong to see this belief as a weakness. The Messiah was a promise of life, and only life could give rise to life, quite unlike Herod, who gave rise to death and suffering.

"To believe in the coming of the Messiah is to be certain that God hasn't abandoned us. That we deserve his attention and are strong enough to bear and defend his word. Why do you want to deprive our people of this hope and strength, Barabbas?"

Barabbas made a face, but Joseph of Arimathea's words struck home, and the others around the table agreed.

"However, you are right about one thing," Joseph of Arimathea went on. "We can't simply fold our arms when confronted with suffering. We must reject the evil that Herod spreads. We must act in such a way that goodness becomes our Law; we must do all we can, we men, to make life more just. It is that, and not only prayer, as Giora believes, which will make the coming of the Messiah possible. Yes, we must unite against evil. . . ."

"He speaks well," Halva whispered, squeezing Miriam's arm. "Even better than your Barabbas."

Miriam was about to reply that Barabbas was not "her" Barabbas, but when she turned to Halva, she saw that there were tears in her eyes.

"My Yossef hasn't opened his mouth, poor man." She smiled sadly. "But perhaps he's the one who's right. None of these fine phrases lead anywhere, do they?"

Anguish took hold of Miriam. Halva was right. A thousand times right. And it was terrifying. She was witnessing the despicable folly of men.

Her father and Barabbas, she knew, were both good, strong men. Barabbas spoke well and knew how to persuade and lead others. Joseph of Arimathea was surely the wisest of all, and the others, even Giora, had no other desire than to do good and behave honestly. They flaunted their knowledge and power, but it was their powerlessness that made them clash so intolerably.

"He's gone for good!"

It was Obadiah, returning out of breath from having run after Mathias.

"I called to him and asked him to come back, but he just raised his arm and waved good-bye."

He, too, had a lump in his throat and tears in his eyes. He, too, was discovering that the men he most admired were powerless, and the shame of it gripped his heart.

Outside, Nicodemus was asking Joseph of Arimathea, with a touch of bitterness, if he had lost his head. Did he, too, want to take up arms? No, Joseph answered, violence wasn't the solution. This drew another ferocious retort from Barabbas. Giora intervened, repeating in his shrill voice his usual litany on prayer and purity, and crying that violence was only valid if it was the will of God.

Halva sighed. "Are they starting again?"

"If they keep quarreling," Obadiah said gloomily, "Barabbas will leave. I know him. I wonder how he's managed to stand Giora and the fat man from the Sanhedrin all this time."

Meanwhile, Joachim was trying to calm everyone down. This meeting had failed, he said, with bitterness in his voice. They might as well admit it. Quarreling as they were doing only demonstrated how weak they were and how strong Herod and the Romans were. He was angry with himself for having forced them to make such a long, pointless journey.

"It's never pointless to search for the truth," Joseph of Arimathea said calmly, "even if the truth we discover is an unpleasant one. And there is one point about which we are all in agreement: The worst enemy of the people of Israel isn't Herod, it's our own lack of unity. That's why Herod and the Romans are strong. We have to unite!"

"But how?" Joachim cried. "Judea, Samaria, and Galilee are divided, just as we are divided in the Temple and in our interpretation of the Book. We may be sincere, but we quarrel. You've just seen it for yourself."

Was it the sadness in her father's voice? Halva's tears of discouragement? Obadiah's disappointment? Or Yossef's stubborn silence? Miriam was never to know.

Whatever the cause, she could not help herself. She grabbed a large basket of apricots that she had just made ready, hurried out into the yard, and walked right up to the men, her chest and face burning. They fell silent, their faces hardening in surprise and reproach. Ignoring that, she placed the basket on the table and turned to her father. "Will you allow me to say what I think?" she asked.

Joachim did not know what to reply and looked questioningly at the others. Giora was already raising his hand to dismiss her, but Nicodemus took an apricot from the basket with a condescending smile and made a sign of approval. "Why not? Go ahead and tell us what you think."

"No, no, no!" Giora protested. "I don't want to hear anything from this girl!"

Joachim took offense at this. "This girl is my daughter, Giora," he said, turning red. "She and I both know the respect we owe you, but I haven't brought her up to be ignorant and submissive."

"No, no!" Giora repeated, getting to his feet. "I don't want to hear anything from unbelievers. . . ."

"Speak," Joseph of Arimathea said in a kindly tone, ignoring Giora's anger. "We're listening."

Miriam's throat was dry. She felt as though her body was hot and cold at the same time. Embarrassed and yet unable to hold back the words she was burning to speak, she gave her beloved father a look that seemed to be asking him to forgive her.

"You all love words," she began, "but you don't know how to use them. You can't stop speaking. Yet your words are as sterile as stones. You fling them in other people's faces in order not to hear what's being said. Nothing can unite you, since each of you considers himself the wisest. . . ."

Giora, who had already walked away, now spun around, sending his long beard swaying. "Are you forgetting Yahweh, girl?" he thundered. "Are you forgetting that every word comes from him?"

Painfully but bravely, Miriam shook her head. "No, Giora, I haven't forgotten. But the word of God that you love is the one you study in the Book. It makes you a learned man, but it does not help to unite us." The confidence of her tone astonished them.

She looked at their stunned faces, saw their anger and incomprehension. She feared she had offended them, when all she had wanted to do was help them. Speaking more softly now, she went on. "You are all learned men, and I am nothing but an ignorant girl, but I have listened to you and I see that your knowledge leads only to argument. Who among you could be the one everyone listens to?

And if you managed to defeat Herod, what would happen? Would you argue like before and fight each other? The Pharisees against the Essenes? Everyone against the Sadducees?"

Barabbas laughed. "So you, too, are waiting for the Messiah!"

"No . . . I don't know . . . You're right: There are many who stand up and cry, 'I am the Messiah.' But they achieve nothing. They have dreams, but those dreams are sterile. What's the point of urging the people to rise against Herod if none of you knows what you're leading them to? Herod is certainly a bad king; he brings us nothing but misfortune. But who among you could be our king of justice and goodness?"

She lowered her voice, as though she were about to tell them a secret.

"Only a woman who knows the price of life can give life to that person. Didn't the prophet Isaiah say that the Messiah will be born to a young woman?"

They stared silently at her, their faces frozen in amazement.

Now Giora laughed. "I think we understand. You want to be the mother of the Liberator. But who will be the father?"

"The father doesn't matter. . . ." Miriam stared into the distance, and her tone became incantatory. "Yahweh, holy, holy, holy is his name, will decide."

No one said a word, until Barabbas leaped to his feet, his face distorted with rage. He walked up to Miriam so abruptly that she stepped back.

"I thought you were with me. You said you wanted this rebellion, that there was no point in waiting! But you're like all girls: One day you say one thing and the next day another!"

Giora laughed again. Joachim placed his hand on Barabbas's wrist. "Please," he said, forcing himself to lower his voice.

Barabbas pulled his arm free and beat his chest, grimacing in disgust. "If you're so intelligent," he cried to Miriam, "you ought to know this: I'm the one, I, Barabbas, who will be king of Israel!"

"No, Barabbas, no. Only the man who knows no other father, no other authority than the Lord, our father who is in heaven, will have the courage to confront the order brought about by the wickedness of men and change it."

"You're mad! I'm the one, I, Barabbas. I'm the only one here who has never known a father. Barabbas, the king of Israel! You'll see. . . ."

He turned on his heel and strode off toward the path leading out of the yard, still crying, "Barabbas, the king of Israel! You'll see. . . ."

Obadiah ran after him, making a distressed grimace at Miriam as he left.

Barabbas's cries had dispelled the others' astonishment. Nicodemus and Giora both laughed scornfully.

"The boy's mad. He'd be quite capable of plunging the whole country into bloodshed."

"He's a good boy, a brave boy," Joachim retorted. "And he's young. He can keep alive a hope we're no longer capable of sustaining."

He looked at his daughter and gave her a sad, gentle smile in which Miriam thought she saw a reproach.

The other men's silence condemned her more surely than words. She ran off to the kitchen, numb with shame.

CHAPTER 8

IT was the dead of night. Only the regular chirping of a tireless cricket broke the silence around Yossef's house. Dawn could not be far off.

Unable to sleep, Miriam had left her bed near the children. She was waiting for the light of dawn while all the while dreading it, wishing that the darkness around her would never end.

She could not help reliving the madness that had come over her and compelled her to speak out in front of the men. Nor could she forget the shame she had brought on her father. And Barabbas! She would have liked to run after him and beg his forgiveness.

Why was he so full of pride? She admired him and would always be grateful to him for what he had done. She had certainly not wanted to hurt him! And yet he had left convinced that she had betrayed him. And Obadiah has gone with him. . . .

The grimace Obadiah had given her as he followed Barabbas still brought a pang to her heart.

The others had left Yossef's house with the same distress on their faces. Eleazar the Zealot, Rabbi Jonathan, Levi the Sicarion . . . Nicodemus and Giora had been in a particularly bad mood.

Only Joseph of Arimathea had not fled. He had politely asked Halva for a bed for the night. The road to Damascus was a long one, and he preferred to rest before going back.

Miriam had not had the courage to apologize to them. Suddenly, words had failed her. Most of all, she had not wanted to open her mouth for fear of saying something else that would hurt them.

She had not even had the courage to appear at the evening meal, although Halva had kissed her with all the tenderness of which she was capable and assured her that she had been right, a thousand times right, to tell them the truth, even if they had not wanted to hear it.

But Halva spoke with a heart overflowing with friendship, and her trust in Miriam blinded her to the point of madness.

No! It was Giora who had told the truth: She was only a girl full of pride who interfered in things that did not concern her. She had sown discord among them as if casting a stone into their gathering. How stupid she had been! When all she had wanted was to unite them!

Why, oh, why wasn't it possible to go back in time and put right what you had done wrong?

N o w the sky over Nazareth was growing pale. The early morning cold, damp with dew, had numbed Miriam without her being aware of it, absorbed as she was in her own thoughts, reproaches, and doubts.

It was only at the last moment that she heard footsteps behind her. Yossef was approaching, a large blanket in his hands and a smile on his lips.

"I was getting ready to go and take care of the animals, since Barabbas seems to have given up being a shepherd."

He looked at her—her red eyes, her trembling lips, the gooseflesh on her bare arms—and frowned. "I hope you're not mad enough to have spent the night here?" He put the blanket over her. "Warm yourself, or you'll catch cold," he said, tenderly. "The dawn is deceptive."

"Yossef, I'm so angry with myself," Miriam murmured, the words rasping her throat, and seized his hand.

"Why, dear Lord?" Yossef asked, keeping her hand in his.

"I'm so ashamed . . . I should never have spoken the way I did to all of you yesterday. I shamed not only myself, but you and my father, too."

"Are you mad? Shamed? Quite the contrary. I didn't say a word because I'm not very good at expressing myself, especially with someone like Giora around, but I was so happy to hear you! It was like honey flowing into my ears. Oh yes! At last, someone was saying what we needed to hear."

"Yossef! You're not thinking about what you're saying!"

"What do you mean? It's what we all think. Your father, Halva, even Joseph of Arimathea. He said that to us last night. If you hadn't hidden yourself away, you'd have heard."

"But the others fled. . . ."

"With shame, yes. They definitely felt ashamed. They knew that what you said was right. They had nothing to add. You are right. We're unable to join together in a single will. Messiah or no Messiah, the man who is capable of uniting us and leading us has not been born yet. For people like Giora or Nicodemus, that isn't an easy truth to admit." He sighed and shook his head. "Yes . . . we all have a lot of soul-searching to do."

"Barabbas clearly doesn't think so," Miriam murmured, shaken.

"Barabbas!" Yossef exclaimed mockingly. "You know him better than we do. He's spoiling for a fight! He's so impatient. And most of all, he wants to dazzle you. Who knows? He might even become king of Israel just to conquer you!" Yossef's irony turned to laughter.

Miriam lowered her eyes, swaying with exhaustion and stunned by what she had just heard. Was Yossef telling the truth? Could she have been wrong about everyone's reaction?

"You wasted a good night's sleep for nothing," Yossef said in conclusion. "Come inside the house. Halva will take care of you."

YOSSEF was telling the truth.

As she was finishing drinking a bowl of hot milk, Joachim came looking for her. His eyes bright, he whispered in her ear, "I'm proud of you."

Joseph of Arimathea appeared, smiling. Beneath his kindliness, there was a genuine concern. "Joachim told me his daughter was no ordinary girl. I don't think he's wrong, and I don't think it's just his father's pride."

Miriam looked away in embarrassment. "I'm a girl like any other. I simply have more of a temper. You mustn't take what I said last night seriously. I'd have done better to keep quiet. I don't know what came over me. Perhaps it was because I was annoyed by Giora, or because Barabbas . . ."

She did not finish her sentence. The three men and Halva all laughed.

"Your father told me that you learned to read and write here in Nazareth," Joseph of Arimathea said.

"Very little . . ."

"Would you like to spend some time with some female friends in Magdala? You could learn more there."

"Learn? Learn what?"

"To read Greek and Roman books. Books that make you think, like the Torah, but in a different way."

"I'm a girl!" Miriam exclaimed, hardly able to believe her ears. "A girl doesn't learn from books."

Her reply amused Joseph, but not Joachim, who muttered that if she started talking like her mother, Hannah, she really would make him feel ashamed.

"It sometimes happens that a woman's brain is worth more than most men's," Joseph of Arimathea declared. "The women in Magdala are like you. It's not so much that they want to be scholars, more that they're eager to understand and to do something useful with their minds."

"And besides, you have to think about the days to come," Joachim said. "We won't be able to go back home to Nazareth for a long time."

Miriam hesitated, and looked at the children clinging to her friend's tunic. "Precisely. Halva needs me here. This is not the moment to leave her alone."

Halva was about to protest when cries came from outside. They recognized Obadiah's voice before he burst in through the doorway.

"That's it!" he cried, trying to catch his breath. "They're in Nazareth!"

"Who?"

"The mercenaries, damn it! Barabbas was right. This time they've come for you, Joachim!"

For a moment, they were thrown into disarray. They urged Obadiah to tell them what he knew. He had been sleeping under the low branches of an acacia on the road to Sepphoris, in the company of Barabbas and his companions, when he had been woken by the noise of marching soldiers. It was a Roman cohort, followed by at least a century of mercenaries, heading in the direction of Nazareth. They were marching quickly in the dawn light, still carrying the torches they had used to light their way in the dark. Behind them came mule-drawn carts filled with firewood and jars of oil.

"Firewood and oil?" Joseph of Arimathea said in surprise. "To do what?"

"To set fire to the village," Joachim replied in a toneless voice.

Obadiah shook his head. "Not to the village. To your house and workshop."

"Are you sure of that?"

"Barabbas asked us to go and wake everyone and warn them that the Romans were coming. But when the mercenaries arrived, they went straight to your house."

"Lord God!"

Yossef squeezed his friend's shoulder. Joachim broke away and rushed to the door, but Obadiah stopped him from going out.

"Wait! Don't be a fool, Joachim, or they'll take you."

"My wife is there!" Joachim cried, pushing him away. "They're going to hurt her!"

"I keep telling you, don't do anything stupid," Obadiah said, pressing his small hands to Joachim's chest.

"I'll go," Yossef said. "I'll be quite safe."

"Will you all just shut up and listen to me!" Obadiah cried. "Nothing will happen to your wife, Joachim, she's on the way here with some of my friends! We got her out of the house and I ran ahead to tell you. And to get away from her. My God, that woman can really scream!" Obadiah smiled to overcome his annoyance.

"Where's Barabbas?" Miriam asked. "If he stays in the village, he could get arrested."

Obadiah shook his head, avoiding her eyes. "No, no . . . He . . . He didn't come back with us. He said you didn't need him anymore. He must be nearly in Sepphoris by now."

There was a brief silence. Joachim, pale-faced, whispered, "This time, it's over. My house is gone. My tools are gone. . . ."

"We couldn't do anything," Obadiah said softly. "Barabbas was right: The mercenaries were bound to come back sooner or later."

"What about Lysanias?" Yossef asked suddenly.

"The old madman who was working with you? He almost got himself killed. He didn't want to leave the workshop. He screamed even louder than Joachim's wife. The neighbors almost had to knock him out to keep him quiet."

"It isn't wise to stay here," Joseph of Arimathea said.

"That's for sure," Obadiah agreed. "The mercenaries will stick their noses in every corner, just to scare the whole village."

"You can hide in my workshop," Yossef suggested.

"No, you've taken enough risks," Joachim declared firmly, going to the door. "Joseph of Arimathea is right. As soon as Hannah gets here, we'll leave for Jotapata. My cousin Zechariah the priest will take us in."

"My friends and I will go with you, Joachim."

By way of reply, Joachim, who was standing waiting for Hannah to come along the path, put his hand on the back of Obadiah's neck in a fatherly gesture.

Miriam's eyes clouded over. Standing beside her, Joseph of Arimathea said gently, "Your parents are in good hands, Miriam. I think it would be best if you came with me to Magdala."

PART TWO

MIRIAM'S CHOICE

CHAPTER 9

"MARIAMNE!" Miriam cried. "Don't swim too far out. . . ."

It was a pointless warning, and she knew it. Rachel's daughter Mariamne's joy in living was contagious. She was also beautiful to watch, swimming with all the vigor, all the carefree eagerness, of youth. The water slid over her slender body like transparent oil, and each time she moved, there were flashes of copper in her long hair, which spread around her like living seaweed.

It was two years since Joseph of Arimathea had brought Miriam to Rachel's house in Magdala. Immediately on her arrival, Rachel had declared that the newcomer was so like her daughter Mariamne, they might almost be sisters. The women in the house had agreed. "It's really amazing," they had cried. "You're as alike as your names: Mariamne and Miriam!"

It was meant kindly, but it wasn't true.

Of course, the two girls had certain characteristics in common, quite apart from their physical appearance. Yet Miriam could see only the differences between them: differences that were not due only to age, even though Mariamne, the younger of the two by two years, still had all the passion and fickleness of childhood.

There was nothing, not even the difficult initiation in languages and other knowledge, that Mariamne was unable to transform into pure enjoyment. This hunger for pleasure could not have been a greater contrast with Miriam's austerity. Rachel's daughter was born to love everything about the world, and Miriam envied her this power of wonderment.

When she looked back over her own life, she could find nothing similar. During the first months she had spent in the shadow of her young companion's exuberance, she had often felt her own common sense, determination, and stubbornness weighing heavily on her. But Mariamne had demonstrated that she had enough joy in her for the two of them, which had only made Miriam love her even more. A friendship had soon sprung up, which even now helped Miriam to support the somewhat prickly character the Almighty had bestowed on her.

And so the happy, peaceful, studious days had flown by on this beautiful estate whose courtyards and gardens stretched as far as the shore of the Lake of Gennesaret.

Rachel and her friends were no ordinary women. They had none of the reserve usually demanded of daughters and wives. They talked about everything, laughed over everything. Much of their time was devoted to reading and conversations that would have horrified the rabbis, convinced as they were that women were only meant for maintaining the home, weaving, or, when they were well-to-do, like Rachel, an idleness as arrogant as it was senseless.

Ten years previously, her husband, a merchant who had owned a fleet of ships plying between the great ports of the Mediterranean, had been stupidly knocked down and killed in a street in Tyre by a Roman officer's wagon. Since then, Rachel had used her considerable fortune in an unexpected way.

Refusing to live in either of the luxurious houses she had inherited from her husband, in Jerusalem and Caesarea, she had settled in Magdala, a town in Galilee two days' walk from Tarichea. Here, it was easy to forget the hustle and bustle of the great cities and ports. Even on the hottest days, a gentle breeze blew in from the lake, and all day long you could hear, through the constant birdsong, the water lapping on the shore. Depending on the season, the almond trees, the myrtles, and the caper bushes were a riot of color. At the foot of the hills, the peasants of Magdala assiduously cultivated long strips of wild mustard seed and rich vineyards lined with sycamore hedges.

Built around three courtyards, Rachel's house had the sobriety and simplicity of the Jewish buildings of bygone days. Cleared of the opulent clutter usually found in Roman-style houses, several rooms had been transformed into study rooms, their bookcases bulging with works by Greek philosophers and Roman thinkers from the time of the Republic, manuscript scrolls of the Torah in Aramaic and Greek, and texts of the prophets dating back to the Babylonian exile.

As soon as she was able to, Rachel invited the authors she admired to the lake. They would stay in Magdala for a whole season, working, teaching, and exchanging ideas.

Joseph of Arimathea, defying the traditional Essene mistrust of women, was a frequent visitor. Rachel greatly appreciated his company and always gave him a warm welcome. Miriam had learned she secretly gave financial support to the Essene community in Damascus, where Joseph not only shared his wisdom and his knowledge of the Torah, but also taught the science of medicine and relieved the sufferings of ordinary people as best he could.

Above all, though, Rachel had opened her doors to those women in Galilee who desired to educate themselves. She had to do so with a great deal of discretion; if the suspicions of Herod and the Romans— as well as their spies—were to be feared, the narrow minds of rabbis and husbands were a no less formidable threat. Many of those who crossed the threshold of the house in Magdala, mostly wives of merchants or rich landowners, did so on the sly. Sheltered from the disgust that men felt for educated women, they threw themselves with abandon into learning to read and write, very often passing on their own taste for knowledge and passion for thought to their daughters.

And so Miriam had learned the kinds of things that in Israel were normally reserved for a few men: the Greek language, political philosophy. With her fellow students, she had read and discussed the laws and rules governing justice in a republic or power in a kingdom, and had pondered the strengths and weaknesses of tyrants and sages.

Rachel and her friends suffered just as much as she did from the yoke of Herod. The moral and material humiliation, as well as the spiritual decay, of the people of Israel were growing worse every day. These misfortunes were a constant subject for debate—debate that all too often ended with the terrible admission that they were powerless. They had no weapons against the tyrant but their own intelligence and stubbornness.

If the rumors were to be believed, Herod was becoming ever more dangerously insane and seemed determined to drag the people of Israel down with him into his personal hell. Every day, his mercenaries were crueler, the Romans more contemptuous, and the Sadducees of the Sanhedrin greedier. Yet Rachel and her friends dreaded Herod's death. What was there to stop another madman, a younger one from the same degenerate line, from seizing power?

True, Herod seemed to be trying to assassinate his entire family. Already, his wife's relatives had been decimated. But the king had distributed his seed generously throughout his life, and there were many who could lay claim to his lineage. So there was a strong likelihood that even when the tyrant finally got his just deserts, the people of Israel would not be delivered from his evil.

Miriam had recounted how Barabbas had hoped, but failed, to start a rebellion that would not only overthrow the tyrant, but also liberate Israel from the Romans and wipe the Temple clean of Sadducee corruption.

Even though the stupid quarrels among the Zealots, the Pharisees, and the Essenes saddened the women of Magdala, they still could not resign themselves to the idea of violence as a means to attain peace. Did not Socrates and Plato, whom they admired, teach that wars led to more injustice, more suffering for nations, and the ephemeral rise of conquerors blinded by their own strength?

But did that mean that they simply had to wait for God to intervene? If the men and women of Israel could not deliver themselves from misfortune, did they have to bide their time until the Lord, through the intermediary of the Messiah, was able to free them?

Most of the women thought so. Others, including Rachel, believed that only a new justice, born of the human mind and the human will, a justice founded on love and respect, could save them.

"The justice taught by the law of Moses is great and even admirable," Rachel would say, provocatively. "But we women are well placed to see its weaknesses. Why does it lay down that men and women are unequal? How could Abraham have given his wife Sarah to Pharaoh without being condemned for such a sin? Why is a wife always dust in her husband's hands? Why do we women count for less than men? There are as many of us as there are of them, and we work as hard. Moses chose a black woman to be the mother of his children. So why does his justice not treat all men and women on earth as equals?"

To those who objected that this was an ungodly idea, that the justice of Moses could only apply to the nation chosen by Yahweh in his covenant, Rachel would reply, "Do you think the Almighty wants happiness and justice for one nation only? No! That's impossible. That would reduce him to the level of those grotesque divinities worshipped by the Romans or those perverse idols venerated by the Egyptians, the Persians, and the northern barbarians."

This would be greeted with protests. How could Rachel dare to think such a thing? Had not the history of Israel, from its beginnings, demonstrated the bond between God Almighty and his people? Had not Yahweh said to Abraham, "I have chosen you and I will establish a Covenant with your descendants . . ."?

"But did Yahweh say that he would grant his justice, his strength, and his love to no other nation?"

"Do you want us to stop being Jews?" a woman from Tarichea said, in a shocked voice. "I'd never be able to follow you. It's inconceivable. . . ."

Rachel shook her head. "Has it never occurred to you that the Lord might have made a covenant with us only as a first stage? So that we could then reach out our hands to all men and women? That's what I think. Yes, I believe Yahweh expects us to love all the men and women in this world, without exception."

Arguing long into the night, until there was no more oil in the lamps, Rachel would try to demonstrate that the obsession of the rabbis and the prophets with preserving their wisdom and justice purely for the benefit of the people of Israel might well be the reason for their misfortunes.

"So what you want," another woman mocked, "is for the whole universe to become Jewish?"

"Why not?" Rachel retorted. "When a few sheep break away from the flock, they become weaker and risk being devoured by wild beasts. It's the same with us. The Romans have understood that. They want to impose their laws on all the nations of the world in order to remain strong. Our ambition, too, should be to convince the world that our laws are more just than those of Rome."

"That's quite a contradiction! Didn't you just say that our justice is not just enough, since it leaves aside us women? If that's the case, why should we want to impose it on the rest of the world?"

"You're right," Rachel admitted. "Before anything else, we need to change our laws. . . ."

"Well, you certainly don't lack imagination!" a laughing woman cried, easing the tension. "Changing the brains of our husbands and our rabbis, now that's something harder to bring about than the fall of Herod, I can tell you."

———

For days, Miriam had listened to them debate like this, their moods alternating between the greatest seriousness and riotous laughter. She rarely intervened, preferring to leave to other, more-experienced women the pleasure of confronting Rachel's sharp mind.

But the debates never deteriorated into quarrels or sterile squabbles. On the contrary, the clash of opposing views was a lesson in freedom and tolerance. Rachel, modeling herself on the practice of the Greek schools, had decreed that no woman was to suppress her opinions, nor to condemn the words, the ideas, or even the silence of her companions.

Nevertheless, having first filled Miriam with enthusiasm, these lively exchanges had been saddening her irreparably. The more passionate and brilliant they were, the less they could conceal an insistent, nagging truth: Neither Rachel nor her friends had a solution to the problem of Herod's tyranny. They did not know any way to unite the people of Israel into a single force. On the contrary, month after month, the news that reached Magdala indicated that the most defenseless—the peasants, the fishermen, those whose work barely ensured their survival—were the most apprehensive about the future.

Without any other way out, despised by the rich people of Jerusalem and the priests of the Temple, they put their faith in orators and false prophets, who proliferated in the towns and villages. Bellowing their alarming speeches, in which threats alternated with the promise of supernatural happenings, these men claimed to be the prophets of a new era. Alas, there was little to choose among their prophecies. They all consisted of hate-filled harangues against humanity and unrestrained, apocalyptic visions full of the most hideous punishments. It seemed as if the only thing these prophets, with their pretensions to being pure, pious, and exemplary, really wanted was to add terror to the despair already felt by the people. They all

denounced the ills afflicting Israel, but they appeared to have no interest in suggesting any remedies for those ills.

In spite of the sweetness of life in Magdala, in spite of Mariamne's infectious joy and Rachel's tenderness, the more time passed,
the more Miriam's thoughts dwelled on the chaos and destruction
abroad in the land. Her silences grew longer, and her nights were
restless, spent endlessly going over the same ideas. The debates led by
Rachel began to seem pointless to her, and her companions' laughter
unthinking.

But wasn't her own powerlessness a sin? Hadn't she made a mistake? Instead of leading a life of luxury in this house, shouldn't she
have joined Barabbas and Mathias in a fight that was about something
more than words? Each time she thought this, however, her reason
retorted that she was just replacing one illusion with another. The
choice of violence was, more than any other, the choice of the powerless. It meant behaving like the false prophets: adding pain to pain.

But she couldn't simply stay here and do nothing.

A decision had lately been growing within her: to leave Magdala.

She ought to rejoin her father, and make herself useful to her
cousin Elisheba, in whose house Joachim and Hannah had found
refuge. Or else go to Halva, on whom time and children must be a
heavy burden indeed. Yes, that was what she ought to do: help life
grow, instead of remaining here, where all this learning, fine as it was,
faded under the impact of reality like smoke scattered on the wind.

She had not yet dared tell Rachel or Mariamne that she was planning to leave. Rachel was away in the port of Caesarea, welcoming
the arrival of her ships before they sailed off again to Antioch and
Athens. Apart from the fabrics, the Persian spices, and the Cappado-
cian wood in which she traded, as had her late husband, this fleet was
also supposed to be bringing back some books she had long been
waiting for. In addition, today was Mariamne's fifteenth birthday, and
Miriam did not want to spoil her young friend's celebrations. But
from now on, she would be counting the days to her departure.

———

"MIRIAM! Miriam!"

Mariamne's calls jolted her from her thoughts.

"Come in! The water's so gentle!"

She refused with a gesture of her hand.

"Don't be so serious," Mariamne insisted. "Today isn't just any day."

"I can't swim. . . ."

"Don't be afraid. I'll teach you . . . Come on! It's my birthday. Do it as a gift to me. Come in and swim with me."

Miriam had lost count of the number of times Mariamne had tried to persuade her to join her in the lake.

"You already have my gift," she replied, laughing.

Mariamne snorted. "A piece of the Torah! I suppose you think that's funny. . . ."

"It's not just a 'piece of the Torah,' you silly thing. It's a beautiful story, the story of Judith, who saved her people thanks to her courage and purity. I'm surprised you didn't know it before. And I copied it out myself. You should be grateful."

Mariamne's only response was to slip back into the water. With the ease of a naiad, she swam along the shore. Her naked body rippled gracefully against the green background of the lake.

Mariamne's very impudence was beautiful. Judith might well have been the same, Judith who had declared in front of everyone, "Listen to me! I am going to do something the memory of which will be handed down from generation to generation among our people." And she had done it so well that God had saved the people of Israel from the tyranny of Holofernes the Babylonian.

But who could be Judith today? A woman's beauty, however extraordinary, would not assuage the demons at work in Herod's palaces!

Mariamne's head suddenly broke the surface. She emerged from the water and leaped onto the shore. Before Miriam could react, she threw herself on her, growling like a wild animal.

Yelling and laughing, they rolled on the grass, clasped together, fighting. With all her strength, Mariamne was trying to drag Miriam into the water, her naked body soaking her friend's tunic.

Out of breath, shaking with laughter, their fingers intertwined, they collapsed onto their backs. Miriam pulled Mariamne's hand to her lips and kissed it. "You're completely mad! Look at the state of my tunic!"

"Serves you right. All you had to do was swim. . . ."

"I don't like the water as much as you do. You know that."

"You're too serious, that's your trouble."

"It isn't hard to be more serious than you!"

"Come on! Nobody's forcing you to be so silent. Or so sad. Always thinking about God knows what. You've been worse than ever lately. We used to have fun together. . . . You could be as cheerful as me, but you don't want to. . . ."

Mariamne lifted herself on one elbow and placed her index finger on Miriam's forehead.

"You have a line forming between your eyebrows. Here! Some days I can see it first thing in the morning. Carry on like this, and you'll soon have wrinkles, like an old woman."

Miriam did not reply. They were both silent for a moment. Mariamne grimaced and asked in an anxious whisper, "Are you angry?"

"Of course not."

"You know how much I love you. I don't want you to be sad because of my stupidity."

"I'm not sad," Miriam replied, lowering her eyes. "What you're saying is true. I am 'Miriam the serious.' Everyone knows that."

Mariamne rolled over onto her side, shivering in the breeze. With the suppleness of a young animal, she huddled in Miriam's arms to warm herself up. "Yes, my mother's friends do call you that. They're wrong. They don't know you the way I do. You are serious, but in a funny way. In fact, you don't do anything like other people.

Everything matters so much to you. You don't even sleep and breathe like the rest of us."

Her eyes closed, happy to feel their bodies warming each other, Miriam did not reply.

"And you don't love me as much as I love you, I know that, too," Mariamne went on. "When you leave, because you *will* leave this house, I'll still love you. But I don't know about you."

Miriam was startled. Had Mariamne guessed what she was thinking? But before she could reply, Mariamne sat up suddenly and squeezed her hand hard. "Listen!"

The rumble of a wagon's wheels could be heard from the vicinity of the house.

"My mother's back!"

Mariamne leaped to her feet. Without worrying that she was still wet, she grabbed her tunic from where it was hanging on the branches of a tamarisk tree, slipped it on, and ran to meet her mother.

T H E handmaids were already helping Rachel down from the wagon. Covered with a thick green canvas roof, it required a team of four mules, which only the coachman Rekab, the only manservant in the house, could drive.

Mariamne rushed to her mother and kissed her effusively. "I knew you'd be back for my birthday!"

Rachel was a little taller than her daughter. With age, her figure had become a little fuller, but this was concealed beneath a simple, elegant tunic with embroidered fringes. She responded tenderly to Mariamne's greeting, but Miriam sensed that Rachel was troubled about something. She did not seem to be as happy to be back as she claimed she was.

It was only later, after she had given her daughter a necklace of coral and glass beads from beyond Persia, and had made sure that the precious cases of books taken down from the wagon had been opened correctly, that she made a discreet sign to Miriam. She led her out onto a terrace overlooking the orchards that descended toward the lake. Protected from the wind, the balsam trees, apple trees from Sodom, and fig trees gave gentle shade. Rachel loved to relax here. She often chose this place for private conversations.

"I didn't want to spoil Mariamne's pleasure. She's such a child sometimes!"

"It's good that she's so determined to keep the innocence of youth."

Rachel nodded and looked out, beyond the fragrant rushes and papyrus on the edges of the water, to where the smooth surface of the lake was dotted with the sails of fishing boats. Her face had clouded over.

"Everything's going badly, even more than we imagine here. Caesarea is buzzing with rumors. It's said that Herod has had his two sons, Alexander and Aristobulus, murdered." She hesitated, then lowered her voice. "Everyone in the place is scared. He's so afraid of being poisoned that he kills and imprisons people on the slightest suspicions. His best servants and his commanding officers have been tortured. They confess to all kinds of things to save their lives, but their lies just make the king even madder."

She recounted how the king's sister, Salome, and his brother, Pheroas, suspected by many of wanting to seize power, had gone to earth in one of the fortresses of Judea. Filled with hatred for his family and the Jewish people, Herod had taken up with a Lacedaemonian named Eurycles. A man of prodigious deceit and limitless greed, Eurycles had insinuated himself into the court by presenting Herod with luxurious gifts, all of which he had stolen in Greece. With a mixture of craven flattery and vicious slander, he'd laid the trap that led the king to murder his sons.

"I caught a glimpse of him in the harbor, where he was flaunting

himself in a chariot that glittered with gold," Rachel went on, disgustedly. "He's servile arrogance personified. It's easy to imagine the
kind of vile acts he gets up to. But that's not the worst of it. No one
would care if the king and his family killed each other, if the whole
arrogant bunch weren't dragging us down with them. Herod and all
those swarming around him are human only in appearance. The
vices of power have made them rotten to the core."

She sighed wearily.

"I no longer know what the Lord wants of us . . . Even what we're
doing here seems pointless to me! What's the use of the books I've
brought with me? All those bookcases in the house? The things we
learn, the things we discuss? Not so long ago, I was convinced that
cultivating our minds would help us change the course of this world.
I told myself, We women should change. Then we might be able to
curb the folly of men. I don't believe that now. As soon as I leave Magdala, as soon as I spend a day in the streets of Tarichea, I get the feeling
we're becoming more and more learned and more and more useless."

"You can't say that, Mother!" Mariamne cried, behind her. "Not
you. . . ."

"Oh, were you there?"

"Yes, and I heard everything. Though I notice you always reserve
these serious conversations for Miriam."

She came closer, eyes full of reproach, and lifted the necklace
that hung on her chest. "I was coming to show you how well it
suited me. But I suppose that seems quite futile to you."

"On the contrary, Mariamne. Why else would I have given it to
you? And it's true, it suits you perfectly. . . ."

Mariamne dismissed the compliment with an aggressive gesture
of her hand. "You're becoming like Miriam. Austere, obsessed with
Herod. But you're not entitled to have doubts. Didn't you used to tell
the women who came here, 'As long as a single man or woman can
be found who defends knowledge and reason, and remembers the

wisdom of the ancients, he or she would save the world and the souls of humans before the judgment of God'?"

"You have a good memory," Rachel said, smiling.

"I have an excellent memory. And contrary to what you think, I always listen to you carefully."

Rachel reached out her hand to stroke her cheek, but Mariamne pulled her head away. Rachel grimaced and lowered her eyes wearily.

"You speak with all the passion of youth. But everything around us seems so ugly to me."

"You're completely wrong," Mariamne said, becoming heated. "First of all, age has nothing to do with it. Miriam is only two years older than me. Both of you have forgotten how to look at beauty. And yet it exists."

Angrily, Mariamne pointed out the splendor surrounding them.

"What could be more beautiful than this lake, these hills, the flowers on the apple tree? Galilee is beautiful. We are beautiful. You, Miriam, our friends. . . . The Almighty has given us this beauty. Why would he want us to ignore it? On the contrary, we should feed on the joy and happiness he gives us, not just the horrors of Herod! He's only a king, and he'll die soon. One day, he'll be forgotten. But the things the books in this house say will only disappear if we no longer want to keep them alive."

The smile had returned to Rachel's face. A tender, slightly mocking smile, but one that revealed her pleasure and surprise. "Well, I see my daughter has been growing in reason and wisdom, and I didn't even realize it."

"Of course not, since you still think of me as a child!"

Again, Rachel reached out her hand to stroke her daughter's face. This time, Mariamne did not evade her. In fact, she even slipped into her mother's arms.

"I promise I shan't treat you as a child ever again," Rachel said.

With an impish laugh, Mariamne freed herself. "But don't expect

me to become serious like Miriam. That's something I'll never be."
She turned and announced, as if to underline what she had just said,
"I'm going to change my tunic. This one doesn't match this necklace
at all."

She walked quickly away. When she had disappeared inside the
house, Rachel shook her head. "That's how daughters get older and
become strangers to you. But who knows? She may be right."

"She is right," Miriam said. "Beauty does exist, and God certainly doesn't want us to forget it. It's a good thing, a wonderful
thing, that creatures like Mariamne exist. And she's also right when
she says I'm too serious! I'd like to—"

She broke off. She was trying to find a way to tell Rachel that she
wanted to leave her house and either go back to Nazareth or join her
father. Birds passed above their heads, chirping noisily, and she
looked up to watch their flight. From the other side of the house
came the sound of Mariamne laughing with the handmaids, the rolling of the wagon being put away. Before Miriam could resume
speaking, Rachel took her by the wrist and led her down below the
terrace and into the orchards.

"There's something else I wanted to tell you before Mariamne interrupted us," she said in an urgent voice. She took a sheet of parchment from the little pouch in the belt of her tunic. "I've had a letter
from Joseph of Arimathea. He won't be able to come here anymore
because these visits are causing a scandal in his community. The new
brothers who've joined recently to study medicine with him are demanding that he distance himself from us 'women.'. . . He doesn't
say it, but I think we can see Giora's hand in this. He's probably
afraid of Joseph's influence over the Essenes. He and his disciples in
Gamala have an intense hatred of women."

"Not only women," Miriam said indignantly. "The *am ha'aretz*,
foreigners, and the sick, too! The fact is, Giora hates the weak and
only respects force and violence. He isn't a pleasant man, and in my

opinion, he isn't even a wise man. I met him in Nazareth, with my father, Joseph of Arimathea, and Barabbas. He didn't agree with anyone except himself. . . ."

Rachel nodded, amused. "That's another thing I wanted to talk to you about: Barabbas. His name was on everyone's lips in Caesarea and Tarichea, and on the road coming back."

Miriam felt a shiver down her back, and she stiffened.

Sensing her anxiety, Rachel shook her head. "No, I'm not bringing bad news—on the contrary. They say he's raised a band of more than five or six hundred brigands. And that he's formed an alliance with another bandit—"

"Mathias, I'm sure," Miriam said.

"I didn't find out his name, but the two of them have gathered about a thousand fighters. It's said they've routed the cavalry two or three times, taking advantage of the fact that Herod, in his madness, has imprisoned his own generals."

Miriam smiled. More than she would have liked to admit, she was relieved, happy, and even envious.

"Yes," Rachel said, responding to her smile, "it's nice to hear that. Of course, there are people in Caesarea and Tarichea, and even in Sepphoris, who fear for their own riches. They bandy words like 'brigand' and 'ruffian,' and call Barabbas 'the henchman of terror.' But I was told that the good villagers of Galilee pray for him. And that he always finds a hiding place among them when he needs to. That's good. . . ." She fell silent, staring into the distance.

"I'm leaving," Miriam declared suddenly.

"Are you going to join him?" Rachel immediately asked. "Yes, of course. I suspected as much as soon as I heard the news."

"I'd already decided to leave before I heard any of this. I wanted to wait for your return, and for Mariamne's birthday."

"She'll be sad without you."

"We'll see each other again."

"Of course." Rachel's eyes had misted over.

"I love both of you with all my heart," Miriam went on, with a quiver in her voice. "I've had times in this house that I'll never forget. I've learned so much from you."

"But it's time for you to go," Rachel said without bitterness. "Yes, I understand."

"My mind is no longer at peace. I wake up at night and tell myself I shouldn't be sleeping. It's true, I'm fine, I learn so much, receive so much, your love and Mariamne's . . . but I give so little in return!"

Shaking her head, Rachel tenderly put her arm around Miriam's shoulders. "You mustn't think that. Your presence is a gift, and that's enough for Mariamne and me. But I understand how you feel."

They were both silent for a moment, united by the same sadness and the same fondness.

"It's time something happened, but what?" Rachel said. "We don't know what we want. Sometimes it seems to me there's a wall in front of us, which keeps getting higher and harder to get over every day. Words, books, even our most just thoughts seem to make the wall thicker. You're right to go back to the world. Are you going to join Barabbas?"

"No. I doubt he needs me for his fight."

"Perhaps we're wrong and he's right. Perhaps the hour for rebellion really has come."

Miriam hesitated for a moment, then said, "I haven't had any news of my father or mother for a long time. I'm going to look for them. Then . . ."

"At least stay until tomorrow. Then Mariamne can say good-bye to you properly. You can borrow my traveling wagon. . . ."

Miriam tried to protest, but Rachel placed her fingertips on her lips. "No, let me at least help you with this. The roads are not so safe that a young girl can venture out on them alone."

CHAPTER 10

T H A T night, as on so many other nights, Miriam woke up when
it was still pitch black outside. She opened her eyes. Mariamne was
sleeping nearby, breathing regularly. Once again, she envied her
friend's calm sleep.

Why was it that every time she opened her eyes, she had the
guilty feeling that she was not entitled to sleep? Anxiety seemed to
be suffocating her, as though a wet cloth had been stuffed down her
throat. She regretted having promised Rachel that she would stay in
Magdala for an extra day. It would have been better to set off for
Nazareth or Jotapata at the first light of dawn.

Silently, she got out of bed. In the adjoining room, she walked
around the bed where two handmaids were asleep and came out into
the large vestibule.

Barefoot, a thick shawl thrown over her tunic, she left the house,
treading without hesitation on the damp grass. On the shore of the
lake, vague shapes could be made out in the light of the quarter
moon. She advanced cautiously. She had so often walked here at
night during these last few weeks that she could find her way guided
only by the rustle of leaves in the breeze and the lapping of waves.

She headed for the low wall that served as a landing stage, where the boats belonging to the house were moored. She trailed her hand over the stones until she found one that was wider than the others and sat down on it. Before her, the rushes rose in opaque walls, leading into the lake like a corridor. The sky, by contrast, appeared clear. On the other shore, the darkness was tinged with blue, announcing that dawn was near.

As she sat there, she started to feel calmer. It was as though the immensity of the sky relieved her of the weight that had been pressing on her chest. There was as yet no birdsong. The only sound was the water subsiding on the shingle or breaking up among the rushes.

She sat like this for a long while. Motionless. A shadow among the shadows. Her anxieties, her doubts, even her reproaches, all vanished. She thought of Mariamne. She felt happy now that she was going to spend the day with her. Their farewells would be full of tenderness. Rachel had been right to stop her leaving too quickly.

She gave a start. There was a regular noise coming from the surface of the lake. The dull thud of wood on wood. The knocking of an oar against the gunwale of a boat, she realized. A regular, powerful but unobtrusive movement. She peered out at the waters.

Worried, she wondered if she should go and wake the handmaids. Could a jealous husband have sent some ruffians to do something nasty? That had happened before. Several threats had been made against Rachel and her "house of lies" by men who had discovered her influence over their wives.

Cautiously, Miriam backed away along the wall and hid beneath the branches of a tamarisk. She did not have long to wait. The sky in the east was clear now, and where it was reflected on the surface of the lake, a narrow boat appeared.

It was gliding smoothly toward the shore. A man stood in the prow, plying the long oar. When he reached the middle of the corridor of rushes, he stopped. Miriam guessed that he was trying to make out the landing stage.

With a skillful stroke, longer and more forceful than the others, he turned the boat, and headed it straight toward Miriam.

Once again, she thought to flee, but she was rooted to the spot with fear. As she peered at him, something in his figure, in his hair, in his way of throwing his head back, struck her as familiar. No, it wasn't possible. . . .

Soon, the man stopped pushing the boat, merely guiding it with the oar. There came a thump; the prow had hit the wall. For a moment, the man vanished in the shadow, then he suddenly reappeared, bending to tie a rope to the ring on the landing stage. The boat swayed, and he moved quickly to avoid falling. There was more light now, and his profile appeared clearly. Miriam knew she had not been mistaken.

How was it possible?

She emerged from her hiding place and walked forward.

He heard her light footsteps and leaped onto the wall. A metal blade flashed in the half-light. Taking fright, she stifled a scream; perhaps she had been wrong after all. For a moment, they both stood motionless, mistrustful.

"Barabbas?" she said in a barely audible voice.

He did not move. He was so close, she could hear his breathing.

"It's me, Miriam," she said, trying to sound at least a little assured.

He did not reply. He turned back toward the boat, and crouched to make sure that the rope was securely tied. Again, his profile appeared clearly in the wan light. There could be no doubt now.

She walked toward him, hands held out. "Barabbas! Is it really you?"

This time, he turned to face her. When she was close enough to touch him, he exclaimed absurdly, in a hoarse, weary voice, "What are you doing here in the middle of the night?"

That made her laugh. It was a nervous but happy laugh. Carried away by a joy she had long thought dead, she drew him to her and kissed his cheek and neck.

She felt him tremble shyly in her arms. He stiffened, pushed her away and, before she could ask him any questions, said, "I need your help. Obadiah is with me."

"Obadiah?"

He pointed to the boat. She made out a dark shape in the bottom of the boat, beneath a sheepskin.

"He's asleep," she said smiling.

Barabbas slid down into the boat. "He isn't asleep. He's wounded. Badly wounded."

The joy that had overcome Miriam faded abruptly. Barabbas lifted Obadiah's inert body.

"What happened?" she asked. "Is it very serious?"

Barabbas dismissed the question with an irritated gesture. "Help me."

She crouched and slid her hands under Obadiah's back. It felt hot and damp to the touch.

"Sweet Lord! He's covered in blood."

"We have to save him. That's why I came."

IT did not take long for the house to awake. Lamps and torches were brought to light the room where Barabbas had laid Obadiah.

Rachel, Mariamne, the handmaids, even the coachman Rekab, all crowded around the bed. Obadiah's pale body seemed as frail as that of a child of ten, but his strange face, rigid with unconsciousness or pain, looked older and harder than before. A makeshift bandage, black with blood and dirty with solidified dust, had been wound tightly around his chest.

"We did what we could to stop him bleeding to death like a sheep," Barabbas said. "But his wound keeps opening. I don't know anything about plasters. No one could help us in the place where we were. It wasn't so far from here, so . . ." He didn't finish the sentence, just waved vaguely in the air.

Rachel nodded, then assured him that he had done the right thing. She roused the handmaids, who were staring at the bandit they had heard so much about. In the lamplight, Barabbas's face looked gray with exhaustion, tortured with sorrow. There was no longer any of the fire and rage that Miriam had so often seen in his eyes. His arms were covered in big crusts where his wounds had not healed properly, and he kept shifting his weight from one leg to another.

"You're wounded, too," Rachel said, worried.

"It's nothing."

The handmaids brought hot water and clean linen. Miriam hesitated to take off the bandage. Her hands were shaking. Rachel kneeled and slid the blade of a knife underneath the dirty cloth. Little by little, she cut through the bandage, and Miriam moved it aside, revealing the wound.

The wound was beneath the rib cage, right at the top of the stomach. It was so large, you could see the innards. It had been caused by a spear, which the mercenary had twisted in the wound to make it even worse. Some of the handmaids groaned and covered their eyes and mouths. Rachel shooed them away. Bravely, Mariamne sat down next to Miriam, her lips quivering. She dipped a cloth in the water and handed it to her friend. Hard-faced and dry-eyed, Miriam started to clean the outside of the wound.

Once she had taken off the soiled bandage, Rachel turned to Barabbas. "It's worse than I thought. There's no one here skillful enough to treat such a deep wound."

Barabbas let out a wild moan. "We have to save him! We must close the wound, put on plasters . . ."

"How long has he been like this?"

"Two nights. He wasn't so bad at the beginning. The pain kept him awake. I should have come before. But I was afraid of making the wound bigger. We have to save him. I've seen men survive worse. . . ."

The words came out mechanically, as if he had repeated them to himself a thousand times, at every stroke of the oar bringing him closer to Magdala.

Rachel saw him start to reach out to touch Miriam's shoulder as she silently washed Obadiah's face. But then he let his arm fall, a bitter look on his face.

"Go and rest," she said to him gently. "You need care, too. At least eat something and get some sleep. You're no use to us in here."

Barabbas turned to Rachel as if he had not understood. She looked into his eyes: eyes haunted by the slaughter they had witnessed. She felt a shudder go down her back. Bringing it under control, she forced herself to smile.

"Go," she insisted. "Go and rest. We'll take care of Obadiah."

He hesitated, glanced again at Miriam, and left the room. Miriam seemed not to notice.

IN all the time they tended him, Obadiah did not regain consciousness. There was no sign of suffering on his face, only a sense of abandonment. Several times, Miriam moved her cheek close to his mouth to make sure he was still breathing. Whenever she washed the sweat-congealed grime from him, her gestures were more and more like caresses.

Obadiah's body was covered in wounds. His thighs were black with bruises, and the skin on his hips was torn. It looked as if he had been tied to a horse and dragged along the ground for a great distance.

Without admitting it to herself, Miriam was afraid that his bones were broken. Rachel came to the same conclusion. In silence, she gently felt Obadiah's arms and legs. Then she looked at Miriam, and shook her head. Nothing seemed broken, although it was hard to be sure about the hip.

The handmaids returned with a large quantity of clean linen. The coachman had gone to fetch the local midwife, who was well known for her knowledge of plants.

When she saw Obadiah, she retched and started to moan. Curtly, Rachel silenced her and asked her if she would make some plasters to treat the wound, especially to prevent hemorrhaging.

The woman calmed down. Mariamne handed her a lamp. She moved it close to the wound and examined the boy carefully, all fear gone now.

She straightened up. "I can certainly make a plaster," she said. "And even a bandage to stop the wound rotting too quickly. I can also make a potion to sustain the poor boy, if you can get him to drink it. But I can't guarantee any of this will help him, let alone cure him."

With the help of Mariamne and the handmaids, the midwife prepared a plaster made from clay and wild mustard seed ground together with peppers and powder of cloves. She sent the handmaids to gather downy leaves from the comfreys and plantains lining the garden paths, which she added to the mixture. Then she kneaded everything together until she obtained a sticky paste.

Meanwhile, on her instructions, Mariamne had boiled some garlic, root of wild thyme, and cardamom grains in goat's milk with added vinegar: a concoction used to help old people with weak hearts.

The midwife covered Obadiah's wounds with the plaster and put a new bandage around it. Then Miriam and Rachel gave him the concoction Mariamne had prepared. It was not easy; in his unconscious state, he kept regurgitating the liquid. They had to be patient and make him swallow it drop by drop.

It seemed to have an effect. As they turned him over to tighten his bandage, Obadiah gave a loud moan, which took them by surprise. They stood looking at him, not daring to move, and saw his fingers wriggling, as if he were trying to grab hold of something. Then, as they gently eased him onto his back, his breathing quickened and his eyes opened. At first he seemed to see nothing. Then it became clear that he was regaining consciousness.

He looked at Mariamne and Rachel, both unknown to him, and the expression on his gaunt, prematurely aged face was a mixture of surprise, pain, and fear. Then he saw Miriam, and he let out a faint sigh and relaxed, although he was still breathing with difficulty.

Moving her face close to his, Miriam gently squeezed his hand. "It's me, Miriam," she whispered. "Do you recognize me?"

He blinked. There was a hint of a smile in his eyes. He seemed so weak that she feared that he would lose consciousness again. But he struggled and found the strength to murmur, "Barabbas promised me . . . I'd see you before . . ."

The words seemed to crumble on his lips. He could not finish the sentence. But his eyes said what his mouth could not utter.

"Don't tire yourself out," Miriam said, pressing her fingers to his mouth. "There's no point in speaking. Keep your strength; we're going to cure you."

Obadiah made a gesture of denial. "Not possible . . . I know . . ."

"Don't talk nonsense."

"Not possible . . . The hole is too big . . . I saw . . ."

Sobbing, Mariamne stood up and left the room. Miriam picked up the pitcher containing the potion. "You must drink."

Obadiah did not object. Miriam first moistened his cracked lips with a cloth, then delicately inserted the edge of a cup between his teeth. He drank a little, shaking with the effort. But he had no sooner absorbed a little of the mixture than he had to catch his breath.

After a few mouthfuls, Miriam moved the cup away and tenderly stroked his cheek. Obadiah groped for her hand and clutched it in his dry fingers. "I promised Joachim . . . I promised"—strangely enough, there was a hint of irony in his eyes—"I'd be your husband. . . ."

"Yes!" Miriam cried passionately. "Live, Obadiah! Live, and you'll be my husband!"

This time, Obadiah really smiled. He blinked again, and squeezed Miriam's fingers slightly. Then his eyes closed, and only a grimace remained on his lips.

"Obadiah?" Miriam said softly, but could obtain no reply.

"Is he still alive?"

It was Barabbas, standing in the doorway, who had asked the question. Miriam, huddled at the foot of the bed and pressing Obadiah's fingers to her lips, did not reply. By her side, Rachel leaned over and placed her palm on the boy's chest.

"Yes," she said. "He's alive. His heart is beating like a hammer. May the Almighty have mercy on him."

IT was noon, and Obadiah was still alive. But his body was burning with fever, and he had not regained consciousness for a moment. Miriam never left his bedside.

The midwife prepared more plasters and another potion, had some cloths boiled in an infusion of mint and cloves—in order to stop the bandage rotting the wound, she explained. But when Mariamne asked her if Obadiah was going to survive, she merely sighed. She pointed to Barabbas with a haughty air and said, "We have to take care of that one too."

Barabbas objected scornfully, but the woman would not let herself be intimidated by him.

"You can hide it from the others, but I see it: You have a fever. You're badly wounded, and it's eating away at you. In a day or two, you'll be as bad as this poor boy."

Stubbornly, Barabbas called her a madwoman. Rachel forced them both out of the room, saying, "I don't want all this noise near Obadiah." But then she insisted that Barabbas agree to be treated by the midwife's care. "We're going to need your help in saving your companion. So I don't want to see you in the same state as he's in."

Reluctantly, Barabbas lifted his tunic. There was a torn, bloody piece of cloth around his right leg. The midwife pulled it away and grimaced with disgust when she saw the wound. The tip of an arrow had gone through the fleshy part of his thigh. It was only a minor wound, but it had not been looked after, and was now oozing with yellow, foul-smelling pus.

The midwife sighed. "You're filthier than a louse, you are!"

With an abrupt movement that took him by surprise, she tore off Barabbas's tunic, revealing a torso covered in scars and scabs.

"Look at this! Gashes, wounds, bumps . . . When was the last time you washed yourself?"

Barabbas cursed her and pushed her away angrily. But the woman grabbed the back of his neck and forced him to listen to her, their faces so close that it looked as if they were about to kiss.

"Shut up, Barabbas. I know who you are; your name has come as far as here. I know what you do and why you fight; you don't have to prove you're a brave man. And you don't have to die pointlessly because you're so sad about your young companion being at death's door. Use your head. Let us look after you, rest for a few hours, and then you'll be able to help him."

The tension in Barabbas's muscles relaxed all at once. He glanced toward the room where Miriam and Obadiah were. His shoulders sagged. Even though no tears came, his lips quivered. Rachel and the midwife both knew what that meant, and they discreetly looked away.

A little later, he slid into the bath the handmaids had prepared and fell asleep, weary to his very soul. The midwife smiled and whispered in Rachel's ear that his medicine could wait.

If Miriam had heard the argument, or Barabbas's protests, she did not show it any more than she inquired about his condition.

Beside her, Mariamne observed her face and did not recognize it. The serious but welcoming features had turned harsh and fierce, gaunt with anger as much as with sadness. Her fixed stare seemed not to see Obadiah's body. Beneath the folds of her tunic, the extreme tension of her back was evident. Her breathing was as faint as Obadiah's.

Disconcerted, Mariamne did not dare utter a word. Nevertheless, she was dying to know the identity of this young *am ha'aretz* who had so distressed her friend. Miriam had never spoken of him, whereas they had often joked together about Barabbas, whose courage, determination, and pride Miriam loved to describe.

Hesitantly, she touched her hand. "You need rest too. You hardly slept last night. I'll stay with him. You have nothing to fear. If he opens his eyes, I'll call you right away."

Miriam did not react immediately, and Mariamne thought that perhaps she had not heard. She was about to repeat her words when Miriam raised her head and looked at her. Strangely enough, she smiled. A joyless but tender smile, which broke up the harshness of her features like a fragile piece of pottery cracking.

"No," she said, with some effort. "Obadiah needs me. He knows I'm here, and he needs me. He draws his strength from my heart."

T H E sun was not yet high when Barabbas awoke. His first concern was to know if Obadiah had regained consciousness. The midwife shook her head, but she did not give him time to ask any other questions before tending to him. When she had finished putting a thick bandage around his thigh, stiffening his leg, he approached Miriam.

She did not even seem to notice his presence. With a gesture that was never mechanical, she would sponge Obadiah's forehead from time to time or place a few drops of potion on his lips. At other times, she would stroke his hands, cheek, or neck. Her lips would move as if she were uttering words that neither Rachel nor Mariamne, crouching on the other side of the bed, could understand.

Suddenly, Barabbas's harsh, abrupt voice broke the silence. Facing Miriam, as if addressing only her, he started to tell the story.

"Mathias, my friend who joined us in Nazareth, at Yossef's house, came one day to the place where we were hiding from the mercenaries, near Gabara. 'How long do you plan to hide like a rat?' he asked me. 'We need men to fight Herod and really hurt him. You have a thousand men ready to follow you. I have only half that, but I have a lot of weapons. I haven't changed my mind, you know. We have to fight. And if we have to die, at least let's die planting our swords in the bellies of those pigs!' He was right, and I was tired of hiding.

And also of constantly remembering your reproaches, Miriam. You may be right; perhaps we do need a new king. But he won't come just because you wish it. So I shook Mathias's hand and said yes. That's how it all started."

At first, their best weapon had been surprise. There were enough of them to organize attacks in several places simultaneously: on passing columns of soldiers, on camps or small forts built on the edges of villages . . . Herod's mercenaries, not expecting their attacks, made little attempt to defend themselves and fled, leaving many dead. Or if they resisted, being superior in numbers, Mathias and Barabbas would retreat so quickly the enemy was unable to pursue them. Most often, it was an easy task to plunder or burn the reserves.

Within a few months, anxiety had spread through Herod's troops. The mercenaries were afraid of moving around in small numbers. No camp in Galilee was safe enough for them anymore. The thefts and burning of the storehouses disrupted supplies to the legions. Even the Roman officers commanding the forts, usually so sure of themselves, started to get worried.

"But in Herod's house, madness reigned," Barabbas went on. "The Romans feared him and didn't dare tell him the truth. In the palaces, no one could tell the difference anymore between truth and lies. Everything was happening exactly as I'd predicted. There was no better time for a rebellion."

Every day, men came to them to join the fight. In the villages of Galilee and the north of Samaria, they were welcomed with open arms. The peasants were only too happy to give them food and, if necessary, hide them. In return, when their sorties against the tyrant and his supporters brought in sufficient booty, they were pleased to share it out among everyone, fighters and villagers alike.

Encouraged by their newfound strength, Barabbas and Mathias had decided to launch attacks farther afield, outside Galilee. Never big battles, but rapid, deadly fights. In Samaria at first, then in the port of Dora, in Phoenician territory, where they had captured a fine cargo of weapons forged on the other side of the sea. On that same occasion, they had freed a thousand slaves: barbarians from the North, some of whom had stayed with them. They had attacked Shechem and Acrabeta, at the gates of Judea, thumbing their noses at the surviving sons of Herod, who had taken refuge in the fortress of Alexandrion.

"We didn't need to fight them, since at the last moon, Herod murdered them himself!"

After each victory, enthusiasm grew in the villages.

"Even the rabbis stopped denouncing us in the synagogues," Barabbas said in a toneless voice. "And when we entered towns not watched over by the mercenaries, the inhabitants would greet us with singing and dancing. That may have been what brought about our downfall."

He was talking and talking, as if to clear his mind of all the intense, extraordinary things he had lived through in the course of the last few months. Meanwhile, Miriam had not taken her eyes off Obadiah. She showed no sign that she was listening, unlike Rachel and Mariamne, who were looking up at Barabbas, hanging on his every word.

He pointed to Obadiah with a painful, almost caressing gesture.

"He liked it too. He's always liked fighting. In close combat, when we're there with our swords in our hands, everyone cutting and slashing and yelling, he's in his element. He takes advantage of his size. Of the fact that he looks like a child. But he's not to be trusted. He's cleverer than a monkey and braver than all of us. Yes, he really likes to fight. It's his revenge. . . ."

Barabbas broke off for a moment and watched as Miriam stroked Obadiah's arm and dabbed his temples. He shook his head.

"It was his idea to come back to Galilee and attack the fortress of Tarichea. He wanted to pull off a major feat. Not out of pride, but as a final demonstration to everyone that both the Roman legionnaires and Herod's mercenaries were at our mercy. Even where they thought they were at their strongest.

"We had to find a place with the reputation of being impregnable. We thought of the fortresses of Jerusalem and Caesarea. But Obadiah said, 'It's Tarichea we have to take. We nearly did it once already.' "

It was true. The attack during which they had freed Joachim had exposed the weaknesses of the fortress. The Romans were too stupid and too sure of themselves to have remedied them. Stupidly, they had rebuilt the market stalls and the wooden buildings surrounding the stone walls. Just as they had done the first time, all they had to do was set fire to them.

But this time, instead of taking advantage of the confusion caused by the fire to escape, they would storm the gates. They were sure they had enough men to overrun the place.

In addition, Barabbas and Mathias were convinced that once battle was joined and it was clear that the mercenaries and legionnaires were weakening, the people of Tarichea would take up sledgehammers, scythes, and axes and join in the fight.

"The hard part of it," Barabbas went on, "was trying not to arouse suspicion. Herod's spies were everywhere. More than a thousand people couldn't just turn up in the town overnight."

So the two bands had divided into small groups of three or four. Disguised as merchants, peasants, artisans, and even beggars, they had found refuge in the hill hamlets and fishermen's villages between Tarichea and Magdala. That took time: almost an entire month.

"Of course, some guessed," Barabbas sighed. "But we thought . . ."

He made a weary gesture.

Who had allowed himself to be bribed? Was the traitor from Mathias's band or from his? A fisherman? A scared peasant or just someone who wanted to make a few denarii at the cost of other people's lives?

"We'll never know, but I think it was one of us. Otherwise, how would they have known where Mathias and I were staying? Obadiah was with us. That's what the traitor must have told them: that Mathias and I were in that village. That all they'd have to do would be to take us and the others wouldn't dare to fight."

Two nights before the attack, in the first light of dawn, while the village was still asleep, a deluge of fire had descended on the thatched cottages. During the night, a large fighting boat had taken up position on the lake, close to the little harbor. The catapults on board had hurled dozens of burning javelins onto the roofs. As the families fled in panic, a cohort of Roman horsemen had entered the village from the north and the south. Children, women, old men, fighters—the horsemen had cut them down indiscriminately.

"It was an easy job for them," Barabbas went on. "There was so much panic. The women and children were screaming and running in all directions, and the horses' hoofs just knocked them down. The Romans were jubilant. We were barely able to fight. There were only five of us: Mathias, two of his men, Obadiah, and me. Mathias died immediately. Obadiah helped me to escape. . . ."

Barabbas could not say anything more. He rubbed his face, in a vain attempt to wipe out what he could still see.

The silence that followed was so intense, so terrible, that Obadiah's harsh breathing could clearly be heard.

Without realizing it, Mariamne had been clutching her mother's hand. Now, weeping noiselessly, she slid down the wall into a crouching position.

Miriam had still not moved. It was as if she had turned to stone. Rachel knew that Barabbas was waiting for her to say something, anything, to him. But nothing came. All she said, in a curt voice, was, "If Obadiah stays here, he won't live."

Rachel shuddered. "What can we do? The midwife says she's done all she can. And she's the best healer there is, here in Magdala."

"There's only one person who can bring him back to life, and that's Joseph. In Beth Zabdai, near Damascus. He knows how to treat the sick."

"Damascus is much too far! Three days at least. Don't even think about it."

"We can do it. We'd only need a day and a half at most, if we don't stop at night and we have good mules."

Miriam's voice was sharp and cold. It was clear that during the whole of Barabbas's account, she had been thinking about one thing, and one thing only: how to get to Damascus as quickly as possible. She looked up at Rachel.

"Will you help me?"

"Of course, but . . ."

There was no point in vacillating. It was obvious that, if need be, Miriam would carry Obadiah in her arms all the way to Beth Zabdai. Rachel got to her feet, ignoring Barabbas's stunned look.

"Yes . . . You can take my wagon. I'll ask Rekab to get it ready."

"He needs to make it more comfortable," Miriam said. "We must have a supply of bandages, water, and plasters. And also a second person to drive the mules. They can take turns. We have to leave right away."

The words rang out like commands, but Rachel did not take offense, merely nodded.

Mariamne stood up, wiping her eyes with a pleat of her tunic. "Yes, we must hurry. I'll help you. I'm going with you."

"No," Barabbas said. "I'm the one who should go with her. We need a man to drive the mules."

Miriam did not even glance at him, any more than she had before, nor did she either accept or reject his help.

CHAPTER 11

Leaving Magdala not long before the sun reached its zenith, they did not allow themselves any rest. The team had been doubled, and Rekab, Rachel's coachman, had sat down beside Barabbas on the driver's bench. Taking turns at the reins, they had to keep the fastest pace the mules could bear.

Jars of water and nourishing potions, pots of ointments and a flask of citron vinegar were ready to hand, in large baskets tied to the benches. Mariamne and Rachel had added clean bandages and spare linen. The speed made for a bumpy ride, even though the handmaids had lined the interior of the wagon with thick woolen mattresses, as Miriam had demanded. Obadiah lay on one of these mattresses, still unconscious, his body tossed about between the cushions.

Miriam watched over him and checked his breathing. Regularly, she would dip a cloth in water and wipe his face, hoping to cool him down.

Not a word was spoken. The dull rumble of the wheels covered every other sound, except for the occasional yell from Barabbas or Rekab ordering people out of the way.

On the road, or in the hamlets and villages they passed through, the fishermen, the peasants, and the women returning from the wells would stop dead for a moment, then quickly move aside and watch with a mixture of surprise and suspicion as the mules and the wagon sped past, raising as much dust as a storm.

In this way they passed through Tabgha, Capernaum, and Coro-zain. By nightfall, they had reached the southern tip of Lake Merom, from where the Jordan could be crossed.

There, in the dim twilight, Barabbas had to argue with the boat-men to persuade them to take the wagon and the animals on board. One after the other, the men came and raised the jute curtains that hid the interior of the wagon. Glimpsing Miriam's leaning figure and Obadiah's shapeless mass among the cushions, they recoiled, horri-fied, at the odor of sickness. The handful of denarii that Barabbas took from a purse—a contribution from Rachel—made up their minds for them. They demanded three times the usual price and pre-pared their oars and their rigging.

It was almost completely dark by the time they reached the shore of Trachonitis. There, Arab horsemen from the kingdom of Hauran subjected them to a torchlit inspection. They, too, demanded a fee to let them pass.

Once again, time was wasted in haggling. When the horsemen took the covers off and shone their torches into the wagon, Miriam turned to them, lifted the blanket off Obadiah, and said, "He'll die if we don't get to Beth Zabdai soon."

They saw her bright eyes and Obadiah's bandaged body and pale face, and immediately drew back.

They turned to Barabbas and Rekab. "Your mules are exhausted. You'll never get to Damascus, especially at night. There's a farm two miles from here, where they hire out animals. You'll be able to change your team there. If you have enough denarii."

Relieved, Barabbas agreed. The horsemen took up position on ei-ther side of the wagon, brandished their torches, and escorted them between the shadows of the agave and prickly pear that lined the road.

They had to wake the farmers, overcome their surprise, and count out a generous number of denarii. When, at last, the yokes were placed on the necks of the new animals, Rekab put torches on the harnesses and lanterns all around the wagon, plus one inside.

When it was done, he said to Miriam, "Now that it's dark, we won't be able to go as fast as before. The mules could fall in a rut and hurt themselves."

Miriam merely replied, "Go as fast as you can. And don't make any more stops."

B y the time the horizon, on the edge of the desert, was pink with dawn, they were only fifty miles from Damascus. The lanterns and torches had long since gone out. Beneath the leather harnesses, the mules were white with sweat.

Barabbas and Rekab were struggling to keep their eyes open, even though they had changed places a dozen times. Inside the wagon, Miriam was still sitting, her muscles stiff, her head nodding with every jolt.

When the lamp had gone out, plunging her into darkness and making it impossible to see Obadiah's face, she had taken his hand and pressed it to her chest. Since then, she had not let go of it for a moment. Her numbed fingers no longer even felt the pressure Obadiah sometimes exerted in his coma.

As soon as she sensed that day was breaking, she lifted the curtain. The cool night air struck her face and chased away both her torpor and the mustiness of the interior, of which she was no longer aware.

Gently, she prized Obadiah's fingers from her hand, dipped a cloth in water, and wet her face. Her mind clearer now, she again moistened the cloth and was about to wipe Obadiah's face with it when she stopped in midgesture and stifled a scream.

Obadiah's eyes were wide open. He was looking at her. For a

brief moment, she wondered if he was still alive. But there could be no doubt. Within the dark rings of pain and illness, Obadiah's eyes were smiling at her.

"Obadiah! God Almighty, you're alive! You're alive. . . ."

She stroked his gaunt face and kissed him on the temple. He responded with a shudder that went all through his body. He did not have the strength to speak or even raise his hand.

Miriam moistened his lips, then gave him a little to drink, struggling to keep the cup close to his mouth in spite of the jolts. Obadiah did not take his eyes off her. His pupils appeared immense, darker and deeper than night. You could drown in them. They seemed to offer a softness, a tenderness without limits.

Miriam looked at him, spellbound. It seemed to her that Obadiah was strangely happy. His heart and soul spoke neither of pain nor reproach, neither of struggle or regret. On the contrary, he was offering her a kind of peace.

She did not know long they remained like this, bound together. Perhaps only until the wagon jolted again or day rose completely.

Obadiah was speaking to her of his love and his joy at being in her hands. Together, they remembered their encounter in Sepphoris, how he had led her to Barabbas and how he had saved Joachim. She thought she heard him laugh. He was telling her things she did not know. The shame you felt if you were an *am ha'aretz* and you saw a girl like her. He was telling her about happiness and the hope of happiness. He had wanted to fight so that she would be proud of him.

She mustn't be sad, because thanks to her he had done something that made him happy: He had fought so that life could be more just and evil weaker. And she was so close to him, so close that he could melt into her and never leave her. He would be her angel, such as Almighty Yahweh, it was said, sometimes sent humans.

Without even realizing it, she was smiling at him, even as a howl of terror swelled in her breast. Obadiah's eyes stared into hers, burning her heart with a possible and impossible love, radiant with hope. She responded with all the promises of life of which she was capable.

Then a more sudden jolt than the others tilted Obadiah's head to the side, and the light went from his eyes like a wire being cut, and Miriam knew he was dead.

She screamed his name at the top of her voice. In a frozen trance, she threw herself on him.

Rekab pulled so violently on the reins that one of the mules jerked sideways, almost breaking its harness. The wagon came to a halt. Miriam was screaming herself hoarse. Barabbas jumped down from the bench. One glance inside the wagon was enough.

He clambered in, seized Miriam by the shoulders, and pulled her off Obadiah's body, which she had been shaking as if it were a sack. She pushed him away with astonishing force. He toppled over the handrail and fell heavily in the road, among the dust and stones.

Miriam stood up, screaming more loudly, lifting Obadiah's corpse as if wanting to show heaven the immensity of the injustice and grief that was overwhelming her. But her legs, numbed by the long hours of stillness, could not carry her. Under Obadiah's weight, she in turn toppled over into the dust. She lay there motionless, Obadiah's body rolled into a shapeless ball beside her.

Barabbas ran to her, stomach tight with fear. But Miriam was not even unconscious. Not a single bone in her body was broken. When he touched her, she pushed him away again. She was crying with great wrenching sobs, the tears turning the dust on her cheeks to mud.

Barabbas moved back, terrified, at a loss what to do. The wound in his thigh had reopened, and he was limping. Rekab went to give him support. Both men were stunned to see Miriam get to her feet and threaten Barabbas with her fist. "Don't touch me!" she cried like a madwoman. "Never touch me again! You're nothing. You're not even capable of bringing Obadiah back to life!"

———

THE cries were followed by a surprising silence, broken only by the wind sighing across the sand and in the prickly shrub.

Rekab waited a moment, then went to Obadiah's body and took it in his arms. The flies were already swarming, attracted by the smell of death. As Miriam watched icily, he placed the body in the wagon and carefully covered it, his gestures as tender as a father's.

Barabbas made no attempt to help him. He was dry-eyed, but his lips were trembling, as if he were searching for the words of some long-forgotten prayer.

When Rekab climbed down again from the wagon, Barabbas went to Miriam and made a gesture of powerlessness, of inevitability. She was crouching on the ground, huddled as if she had been hit. He might have tried to lift her, but he did not dare.

"I know what you think," he said angrily. "That it's my fault. That he died because of me."

His voice was loud in the surrounding silence. Miriam, though, did not flinch. It was as if she had not even heard him. Barabbas grew agitated and turned to Rekab for support. But the coachman, standing motionless by the mules with the reins in his hands, bowed his head. Barabbas limped to one of the wheels and leaned on it. "You condemn me, but it was a mercenary's spear that killed him!" He waved his fists, his muscles taut. "Obadiah loved fighting. He loved it. And he loved me, too, as much as I loved him. Without me, he wouldn't have survived. When I took him in my arms, he was only a child. A little brat no bigger than this."

He struck his chest violently.

"I was the one who saved him from the clutches of those traitors in the Sanhedrin, after respectable people like you had let his parents die of starvation! I gave him everything. Food and drink and a roof to protect him from the rain and cold. I taught him how to live by stealing, I taught him how to hide. Every time we went into combat, I feared for him, the way a brother fears for his brother. But we are warriors. We know the risks we take! And why we do it!"

He gave an unpleasant, anguished laugh.

"I haven't changed my mind. I'm not afraid. I don't need to stick my nose in books to know if I'm doing something good or bad. Who will save Israel, if we don't fight? Your women friends in Magdala?"

Miriam had still not moved. She seemed impervious to the words he flung at her like stones.

Incredulous, powerless, his face racked with pain, he confronted this indifference. Taking a few unsteady steps, he cast his eyes up to heaven.

"Obadiah! Obadiah!"

Around them, the crickets fell silent. Again, the only sound was the wind in the thorns.

"There is no more God for us!" Barabbas screamed. "It's over. There's no more Messiah to wait for. We must fight, fight, fight! We must strike the Romans or be slaughtered by them. . . ."

At last, Miriam raised her head and looked at him, coldly, calmly. With an almost mechanical gesture, she picked up a handful of dust and scattered it over her hair, as a sign of mourning. Then she gathered the tails of her tunic and got unsteadily to her feet.

Rekab took a step forward, fearing that she might collapse again. But she walked all the way to the wagon. Before climbing in, she turned to Barabbas and, without raising her voice, declared, "You're stupid and narrow-minded. It isn't only Obadiah who died because of you. Women and children died too. A whole village. And your companions and those of Mathias. For what? For what victory? There was none. They died because of your stubbornness. Your pride. They died because Barabbas wanted to be what he will never be: the king of Israel. . . ."

At these words, he swayed. But what most overcame him was the glacial contempt on Miriam's face.

"It's easy to condemn me, but at least I dare."

"You'll never be the strongest. You'll only bring blood and suffering where there is already blood and suffering."

"Didn't you come to find me to help save your father? You weren't too bothered then if people killed or got killed! You're quick to forget that you, too, were in favor of a rebellion!"

She nodded. "Yes. I'm at fault too. But now I know. It's not the way. This is not how we will impose life and justice."

"How, then?"

She did not reply. She climbed into the wagon and lay down next to Obadiah's body, placed her head against the blanket covering him, and embraced him.

Barabbas and Rekab stood there, stunned. At last, Rekab asked, "What shall we do? Go back to Magdala?"

"No," Miriam murmured, her eyes closed. "We must go to Beth Zabdai, to Joseph's house. To the Essenes. They can cure the sick, and bring them back to life."

Rekab thought he had misheard her. Or else Miriam was a little mad with the exhaustion. He threw a glance at Barabbas, ready to ask him a question. But tears were streaming down the cheeks of this brigand admired by everyone in Galilee.

Rekab lowered his eyes and took his seat on the bench. He waited a moment for Barabbas to join him.

As Barabbas did not move, Rakab cracked the reins on the mules' rumps and set off.

THEY entered Damascus just before nightfall. Several times, Rekab had stopped to let the mules rest, taking advantage of these brief halts to check on Miriam's condition.

She seemed to be asleep, although her eyes were open. Her arms were still wrapped around Obadiah's body. Rekab had filled a cup with water from one of the jars.

"You must drink, or you'll get ill."

Miriam had looked at him as if she barely saw him. Because she did not take the cup, he had dared to put his hand behind her neck and force her to drink, as she had done to Obadiah during the previous night and the days before that. She had not protested. On the contrary, she had let him do it with surprising docility, closing her eyes and thanking him with a vague smile. Rekab had been surprised by the way she looked. For the first time, Miriam's face was that of a girl, not an austere, intimidating young woman.

At the entrance to the opulent gardens that surrounded Damascus and enclosed it in a splendid casket of greenery filled with bustling crowds from the poorer parts of the city, Rekab stopped again. This time, he carefully closed the curtains.

"There's no point in them seeing you," he said by way of explanation.

But he was mainly thinking of Obadiah's corpse. If one of the peasants noticed it, a crowd might gather, and it would not have been easy to explain away.

But Miriam seemed not to hear him. Some time later, he inquired after the village of Beth Zabdai. Directions were soon forthcoming: The village was two leagues from the outskirts of Damascus, and was known to everyone as the village where people were healed. And, fortunately, the path that led to it was wide enough for Rekab to drive the wagon along it without too much difficulty. Situated to the west of Damascus, and surrounded by fields and orchards, the village consisted merely of a few whitewashed buildings. The flat roofs were covered in creepers. The walls had no windows on the outside, but enclosed inner courtyards. The house before which they stopped had only one large wooden door, painted blue. A smaller door set in it, just big enough for a child, made it possible to enter without it being necessary to open the main door. There was a bronze knocker.

Rekab brought the team to a halt, got down, and went and knocked at the door. He waited and, because no one came, knocked again, more loudly. Still no response. He did not think they would open. As the sky was already red and night quite close, this was not very surprising.

He turned back to the wagon, anxious to announce the news to Miriam, when the smaller door half opened. A shaven-headed young Essene in a white tunic put his head through and looked at Rekab suspiciously. This was the hour for prayers, he said, not for visitors. They would have to wait for the next day if they wanted medical care.

Rekab ran to the door and held it before the Essene could close it. The young man started to protest. Rekab grabbed him roughly by the tunic and pulled him to the wagon. He lifted the curtain. The young Essene, who was crying insults and struggling furiously, breathed in the smell of death. He froze, opened his eyes wide, and saw Miriam in the darkness of the wagon's interior.

"Open the door," Rekab growled, letting go of him at last.

The boy straightened his tunic. Uncomfortable at the sight of Miriam, he lowered his eyes. "It's not the rule," he said stubbornly. "At this hour, the masters forbid us to open."

Before Rekab could react, Miriam spoke.

"Give my name to Joseph of Arimathea. Tell him I'm here and can't go any farther. I am Miriam of Nazareth."

She had sat up a little. Her voice was gentle, which embarrassed the young Essene even more than what he saw. He did not reply, but ran back inside the house—without even closing the small door behind him, Rekab noticed.

They did not have long to wait. Joseph of Arimathea came running, accompanied by a few of the brothers.

He did not bother to greet Rekab, but jumped into the wagon. Before he could question Miriam, she uncovered Obadiah's face. He immediately recognized the young *am ha'aretz* and let out a moan. Miriam murmured a few barely comprehensible words. Rekab realized that she was asking Joseph to bring the boy back to life.

"You can do it, I know you can," she muttered, as if she had lost her reason.

Joseph did not waste time in replying to her. He seized her under the arms and called to his companions to help him get her down from the wagon. She protested, but she was too weak to struggle. She held out her hands to Joseph, imploring him in a voice that gave him gooseflesh, "I beg you, Joseph, perform this miracle . . . Obadiah didn't deserve to die. He has to live again."

With a tense, grave face, Joseph stroked her cheek without a word. Then he made a sign for her to be taken inside the house.

LATER, when Rekab had parked the wagon in the courtyard, and Obadiah's body had been taken out of it, Joseph joined him. Gently, he placed a hand on the coachman's shoulder.

"We're going to take good care of her," he said, pointing to the women's quarters, where Miriam had been taken. "Thank you for what you did. The journey must have been rough. You must eat and get some rest."

Rekab pointed to the mules, which he had just freed from the yoke. "They have to be looked after and fed, too. I'm leaving again tomorrow. The wagon belongs to Rachel of Magdala. I have to get it back to her as soon as possible."

"My companions will look after the animals," Joseph said. "You've done enough for today. Don't worry about your mistress. She can wait a few more days for her wagon. Then you'll be able to give her good news about Miriam."

Rekab hesitated, torn between protesting and accepting. Joseph impressed him. His benevolence, his calm, his bald skull, his gentle blue eyes, the great respect shown him by the young Essenes bustling around the house—everything about this man intimidated him. At the same time, his heart was bleeding. He could not stop thinking about what he had just lived through, so far beyond anything he could ever have imagined.

Joseph squeezed his shoulder affectionately, then led him to the main room of the house.

"I didn't know this young man Obadiah very well," he said. "But Miriam's father, Joachim, said a lot of good things about him. This death is a sad one. But then all deaths are sad and unjust."

They entered a long, white, vaulted room, furnished only with a huge table and benches.

"You mustn't worry about Miriam," Joseph said. "She's strong. She'll feel better tomorrow."

Again Rekab was impressed by the attentiveness shown him by the master of the Essenes. Even in Rachel's house, he wasn't treated with such consideration. He looked into Joseph's blue eyes and said, "Barabbas the brigand was with us last night. He was the one who brought the boy to Magdala. . . ."

Joseph nodded. He invited Rekab to sit and sat down next to him. A young brother put a platter of semolina and a cup of water in front of them on the table.

His hand trembling a little, Rekab raised a first spoonful to his mouth. Then he put the spoon down, turned to Joseph, and started to tell him all about the horrors he had seen on the journey.

CHAPTER 12

MIRIAM took longer to recover than Joseph had foreseen.

She had been put in one of the small rooms in the woman's quarters, in the north of the house. At first, she had protested. She wanted to be near Obadiah. She refused to rest, to calm down, to be reasonable as she was asked. Every time one of the handmaids told her she had to take care of her own health, not Obadiah's, since he was dead, Miriam would insult her without restraint.

Nevertheless, after a difficult day during which she struggled and screamed constantly, the handmaids managed to get her to take a bath, eat three spoonfuls of semolina in milk, and drink some herb tea that put her to sleep without her even being aware of it.

This went on for three days. As soon as she opened her eyes, she would be fed and given a narcotic herb tea to drink. When she woke again, she would find Joseph beside her.

In fact, he came to visit her as often as he could. While she slept, he would watch her, anxiously. But when she opened her eyes, he would smile and utter calming words.

She barely listened to him. Tirelessly, she would ask him the same questions. Couldn't he treat Obadiah? Wasn't it possible to bring him back from the land of the dead? Why couldn't Joseph perform this miracle? Wasn't he the most learned of doctors?

Joseph would merely shake his head. Avoiding giving cut-and-dried answers, he would try to divert Miriam from her anxieties and her obsession. He never mentioned the name Obadiah. His main concern was to get her to eat and, as soon as possible, to drink the potion that would put her to sleep.

Joseph never came alone to see Miriam. Within the community, the rules did not allow a brother to remain alone in the company of a woman. So he was always accompanied by the most brilliant of his disciples, a man named Geouel, from Gadra, in Perea. He was barely twenty, with a thin, rather bony face, and eyes that were constantly judging everything and everyone he saw.

Geouel admired Joseph greatly. But his uncompromising attitude often concealed his real qualities and irritated his companions. Joseph tolerated this prickly character, although he sometimes mocked him affectionately. Most often, he used him to keep his mind alert, like a man putting cold water on the back of his neck early in the morning to wake himself up.

When Miriam, stubbornly ignoring Joseph's replies, repeated her questions for the fourth time, Geouel declared, "She's losing her mind."

Joseph did not agree. "She's refusing to accept something that makes her suffer. That doesn't mean she's losing her mind. We all do it."

"Which is why we can no longer tell the difference between God and Evil, Darkness and Light. . . ."

"We Essenes," Joseph remarked with a smile, "believe that he who has died may live again."

"Yes, but only by the will of God Almighty. Not through our own powers. And only if the man who will live again has lived a life of perfect goodness . . . which is certainly not the case with this *am ha'aretz!*"

Joseph nodded mechanically. He often had this debate with his brothers. Everyone in this house knew his point of view: Life deserved to be sustained, even in darkness and death, for it was a light given by God to man. It was a precious gift, the very sign of Yahweh's power. Everything had to be done to sustain it. That certainly did not rule out the possibility that if one day man attained supreme purity, he might be able to rekindle life even when it seemed to have gone. The fact that Joseph had professed this opinion many times did not prevent Geouel from arguing.

"None of us has yet seen the miracle of resurrection with his own eyes," he said now. "Those we care for and bring back to life haven't died. We are only healers. We dispense love and compassion, within the narrow limits of the human heart and mind. Only Yahweh can perform miracles. This girl is mistaken. In her grief, she thinks you're as powerful as the Lord. That's blasphemy."

This time, Joseph nodded with more conviction. Looking at Miriam's face as she slept, he let a few moments pass, then said, "Yes, only God can perform miracles. But consider this, Brother Geouel. Why are we living in Beth Zabdai and not in the world, among other men? Why do we sustain life here, inside, and not outside, if not to make it stronger and richer? Deep in our hearts, we hope that we can become pure enough, loved enough by Yahweh, for the covenant he made with the descendants of Abraham to be completely fulfilled. Isn't that why we observe Moses' laws so strictly?"

"Yes, Master Joseph, but—"

"Which means, Geouel, that we hope, with all our souls, that one day Yahweh will use us to realize his miracles. Otherwise, we will have failed at being his choice and his joy. We will be a race that has disappointed him."

Geouel tried to reply, but Joseph raised his hand commandingly. "You're right about one thing, Geouel," he went on. "It would be wrong to encourage Miriam's illusions. She mustn't believe that we can perform such miracles. But as a doctor, you're wrong: She isn't losing her mind. She's suffering from an invisible wound that has left a gash as deep as a sword thrust. You shouldn't think of the words she utters, the hopes she entertains, as insane, but wise; they soothe her wound as surely as any plaster and make it possible for her to expel the corruption from her body."

W H E N Miriam awoke, she again started begging Joseph to bring Obadiah back to life.

This time, his answer was different.

"After you arrived, we said farewell to Obadiah's body, according to custom. We wrapped it in the cloth of the dead and commended it to the light of Yahweh. His flesh is in the earth, where it will return to dust as the Lord intended when he made us mortal by the grace of his breath. He will still be among us in spirit. That is as it should be. Now you must think about your own health."

Joseph's voice was cold, with none of its usual gentleness. His face was inscrutable, and even his mouth appeared hard. Miriam stiffened. Geouel was watching her closely. Their eyes met and she sustained his gaze, before again looking to Joseph for help.

"In Magdala," she said, her voice throbbing with anger, "you taught us that justice is the supreme good, the way to the light of goodness that Yahweh holds out to us. But where is justice when Obadiah dies and Barabbas doesn't? He could easily have died, determined as he is to challenge Herod through bloodshed."

Geouel emitted a groan. Joseph wondered, a little embarrassed, if his young companion was reacting to Miriam's condemnation of Barabbas or to the mention of his own "teaching" among the women of Magdala.

With an authority that did not exclude the wish to provoke Geouel, he took Miriam's hand.

"God decides," he declared, regaining his customary gentleness. "No one else but God decides our destinies. Neither you, nor I, nor any other human. God decides miracles, punishments, and rewards.

He decides on the life of Barabbas, and it is he who recalls Obadiah. Such is his will. We can treat the sick, relieve pain, cure illness. We can make life strong, beautiful, and powerful. We can make justice the rule that unites men. We can avoid using evil as our weapon. But death and the origin of life belong only to the Almighty. If you haven't understood that from what you call my teaching, then my words must be clumsy and of little weight."

These last words were spoken with an irony that was lost on Miriam. She had closed her eyes again while Joseph spoke. When he stopped, she took her hand from his and, without a word, turned in her bed and faced the wall.

Joseph looked at her, reached out his arm and stroked her shoulder. Then, with a fatherly gesture, he pulled the thick woolen blanket up over her. Geouel watched him as he did so.

He forced himself to be silent and still. He did not think that Miriam would speak to him again, but he wanted to make sure that she was breathing more easily.

When he was satisfied, he stood up and gestured to Geouel to follow him out of the room.

In the vestibule, as they were going back to the courtyard, they were suddenly surrounded by a group of handmaids on their way back from the washroom, laden with baskets of linen. Joseph stepped back into a recess, but Geouel kept straight on, forcing the handmaids to move aside with their heavy burdens. Despite the effort they had to make to give way to him, they made not the slightest protest, but instead avoided his eyes and bowed their heads respectfully.

Reaching the courtyard, Geouel turned to wait for Joseph, eyebrows raised in surprise. He pointed to the handmaids. "Couldn't they have let you pass? They're getting more and more insolent."

Joseph concealed his irritation behind a smile. "The fact is, there are fewer and fewer of them, which means they're overworked. And if they weren't there, would you be prepared to wash our dirty linen at the time when you should be studying and praying?"

Geouel dismissed this thought with a grimace. When they had almost crossed the courtyard, he remarked, in a tone that was meant to be conciliatory, "Sometimes, listening to you, anyone would think you wouldn't mind if women became rabbis!" He paused to give an amused little chuckle. "Such is God's will. It'll never be possible, and it's mere pride to think otherwise and to expect of women that they will ever be able to rid themselves of what makes them women."

Joseph hesitated before replying. He was worried about Miriam, and was not in the mood to smile at Geouel's obstinacy.

"It is God's will that we are born from both a man and woman. We emerge from a woman's belly, don't we? Why would the Lord want us to emerge from a cesspool?"

"That's not what concerns me. Women are what they are: driven by the flesh, the absence of reason, and the weakness of pleasure. All of which makes them unsuited to attain the light of Yahweh. Isn't that what is written in the Book?"

"I know, Geouel, that you and many of our brothers condemn my opinion. But neither you nor the others have yet answered my questions. Why should evil inhabit the container and not the seed? Why should we be more inclined to purity than those who give us life? When have you ever seen a source purer than the cave from which it springs?"

"We have answered you, with the words of the Book. They constantly divide woman from man and judge her unsuited for knowledge."

They had gone over these arguments a thousand times. This kind of conversation led nowhere. Joseph made an irritable gesture, as if swatting a fly, and abstained from replying.

"I had the *am ha'aretz*'s body taken out of our graveyard," Geouel said, through pursed lips. "They must have misunderstood your instructions. You know his grave can't be with ours. The *am ha'aretz* aren't entitled to be buried in consecrated ground."

Joseph stopped dead and a shudder of revulsion went through

his body. "You took him out of the ground?" he asked in a toneless voice. "You want to deny him a burial?"

Geouel shook his head. "Oh no!" he said, with an unpleasantly victorious smile. "Without a burial, he'd be damned. I don't suppose he deserved that, did he? Even though the fact that he died while not much more than a child must mean that God had no great plans for him. No, don't worry. We put him back in the ground beside the road to Damascus. Where foreigners and thieves have their graves."

Joseph could not say a word in reply. He was thinking of Miriam. It seemed suddenly as though everything he had said to her was a lie.

Geouel was perceptive enough to guess what he was thinking. "It might be better if you didn't see that girl again," he said. "Her health is not in danger, only her mind. She doesn't need you anymore, and our brothers wouldn't look too kindly on any further visits to the women's quarters."

CHAPTER 13

MIRIAM was listening to the comings and goings in the house, the murmurs of the women, sometimes even their laughter. The regular blows of the pestle reducing the grains of rye and barley to flour echoed through the walls, like the beating of a peaceful but powerful heart.

She wanted to get up, join the handmaids, and help them with their work. She did not feel tired anymore. She was weak, of course, but only because she had eaten very little in the last few days. Her anger, though, had not abated.

She refused to accept the words Joseph had spoken. The mere thought of Obadiah's body in the ground brought a pang to her heart, and she had to clench her fists not to cry out.

In addition, her mind was still clear enough for her to know that she was not welcome in this community. She had seen it in the eyes of the brother who always came with Joseph. The sensible thing to do would be to gather her strength and willpower, leave Beth Zabdai, and do what she had already decided to do back in Magdala: join her father.

But this thought rekindled her anger. To leave this house and

Damascus meant abandoning Obadiah for good, bidding his soul farewell, perhaps even starting to forget him.

"Are you really awake this time?"

Startled, Miriam turned. A woman of indeterminate age was standing near her bed. Her hair was as white as snow, and there were hundreds of fine wrinkles around her lips and eyelids. But her skin looked as fresh as a young woman's, and her very clear eyes sparkled with intelligence—and perhaps a touch of cunning.

"Awake and very angry, I see," she continued, coming closer.

Miriam sat up in bed, speechless with surprise. She was not sure if the unknown woman was mocking her or being kind.

The woman also seemed uncertain. She looked at Miriam, her eyebrows arched, her lips rounded in a pout. "Being angry on an empty stomach isn't a good idea."

Miriam stood up too quickly. She felt dizzy, and had to sit down again and put both hands on the bed to stop herself from falling.

"Just as I was saying," the woman said. "It's time you stopped sleeping and started eating."

Behind her, the handmaids were crowding into the doorway, burning with curiosity. Drawing on her reserves of pride, Miriam jutted out her chin and forced a smile. "I feel fine. I'm getting up. I'd like to thank you all for—"

"I should think so too! As if we didn't already have enough to do without having a stuck-up little thing like you moaning in our ears."

Miriam opened her mouth to apologize, but the tenderness on the unknown woman's face made it clear there was no point.

"My name's Ruth," the woman said. "And you don't feel fine, not yet anyway."

She took her under the arms and helped her to her feet. In spite of this support, Miriam swayed.

"Well, it really is time we got you better, my girl," Ruth said.

"I just have to get used to—"

Ruth signaled with her eyes for one of the handmaids to come and help. "Stop talking nonsense. I'm going to feed you, and you'll like it. No one turns her nose up at our cooking, it's far too good!"

LATER, as Miriam was nibbling at a buckwheat pancake filled with goat's cheese, which she dipped in a platter of barley boiled in vegetable juice, Ruth said, "This house isn't like other houses. You have to learn the rules."

"There's no point. I'm leaving tomorrow. I'm going to see my father."

Frowning, Ruth asked Miriam where her father lived. When Miriam told her that she was from Nazareth, in the mountains of Galilee, Ruth pulled a face. "That's a long way for a girl on her own. . . ."

She stroked Miriam's forehead and ran her worn fingers through her hair. Moved by this unexpected gesture, Miriam quivered with pleasure. It was a long time since a woman had last stroked her with such motherly tenderness.

"Get that idea out of your head, my girl," Ruth resumed, gently. "You're not leaving here tomorrow. The master has ordered that you stay here. We all obey him and you must obey him too."

"The master?"

"Master Joseph of Arimathea. Who else would be the master here?"

Miriam did not reply. She knew that was what they called Joseph. Even in Magdala, some of the women had used that title for him as a mark of respect. But obviously here, in Beth Zabdai, Joseph was a different man than the one she had met in Nazareth, the one who had taken her to Rachel's house.

"I have to go to the graveyard, to see where Obadiah is buried," she said. "I have to say prayers for him and bid him farewell."

Ruth looked surprised, and then worried. "No, you can't. You're in no fit state to fast. You have to eat . . . the master says so!" She spoke quickly, her cheeks flushed.

"Are there brothers watching over his grave?" Miriam said. "If not, I have to go myself. I'm the only person Obadiah has to see him on his way."

"Don't worry. The men of this house do their duty. It is not for us women to do it in their place. You must eat."

The noise of the pestles echoed behind her, silencing them for a moment. The women's refectory was a long room with a low ceiling. Sacks and baskets of fruit and dried vegetables were lined up along the sides, as well as what looked like benches with holes in them to support jars of oil. The door at the far end, which was wide open, led to the kitchen, where the oven was kept constantly stoked.

A few handmaids were grinding grain for flour on a stone with the help of an olive-wood mallet, while four women were kneading and stretching pastry for biscuits. From time to time, they raised their heads and glanced curiously at Miriam.

Mournful but satisfied, Miriam had nearly finished her platter. Ruth hastened to refill it. "You're much too thin. We have to fill you out again if you want men to like you."

It was said affectionately, the way such things were always said by an older to a younger woman. Ruth was taken aback by Miriam's reaction: the stiffening of her body, the glaring look, the ferocity of her tone.

"How can we want men to look at us when we know how much the men who live here hate us?"

Ruth threw a cautious glance toward the kitchen. "The Essene brothers don't hate us. They fear us."

"Fear us? Why?"

"They fear what makes us women. Our wombs and our blood."

This was something that Miriam knew only too well. She had had the opportunity to discuss it many times in Magdala, with Rachel's companions.

"We are the way God wanted us to be, and that should be enough."

"I'm sure you're right," Ruth said. "But for the men in this house, it takes us away from the path that leads to reach the Island of the Blessed. That's what matters more than anything else in the world to them: reaching the Island of the Blessed."

Miriam looked at her, uncomprehending. She had never heard of this island.

"It's not for me to explain," Ruth said, embarrassed. "It's too complicated, and I'd only say something stupid. We don't receive any teaching here. We sometimes hear the brothers talking among themselves, we pick up a few words here and there, and that's it. The one thing we know is that we have to follow the rules of the house. That's all that matters. Thanks to the rules, the brothers purify themselves so that they can gain admittance to the island. The first rule is to stay in the part of the house reserved for us. We can go into the courtyards, but the rest of the house is out of bounds. Then, it's forbidden to speak to a brother if he hasn't spoken to us first. We have to bathe before baking bread, which happens every day before dawn. . . ."

The chores consisted of preparing semolina soup and making biscuits filled with cheese twice a day, washing the brothers' clothes, and making sure their linen loincloths and tunics were immaculately white.

"Another thing: we mustn't spoil anything. Not the food, not the clothes. As far as the food is concerned, we must cook only what's needed, neither too much nor too little. The ordinary clothes, the brown work tunics, the brothers don't throw away, even if they're full of holes. They only part with them when they're in tatters. Which is not too bad, because it means less work for us."

The advice continued. The most important thing of all was that they were not allowed to go near the brothers' refectory. It was a sacred place, reserved for men. To the Essenes, meals were like prayers. Eating and drinking were a gift of the Almighty, and in return for this gift they had to love him. So, before each meal, the brothers took off their coarse brown tunics, put on white linen loincloths, and bathed in absolutely pure water to wash away the stains of life.

"Of course, I've never seen them do that," Ruth whispered, with a wink. "But you can't be here as long as I have without picking up a few things. The bathing is really important. After they've bathed, the master blesses the food, and they eat, all sitting at the same table. Then they put on their ordinary clothes again, and we have to wash the tunics they've been wearing for the meal. When it snows, the water in their bath may be freezing, but they don't care. The well they draw it from is in the house itself. Our well, where we get the water for cooking and washing, is outside. As you see, there's plenty of work to do. You'll soon fit in."

Miriam silently pushed away her platter.

"Eat!" Ruth said immediately. "Eat more, even if you don't feel like it. You have to get your strength back."

But Miriam did not even lift the spoon.

"You are staying, aren't you?" Ruth asked, her voice as anxious as her face.

Miriam looked at her in surprise. "Why are you so determined that I stay? There's nothing for me here. That's obvious."

Ruth sighed. "You're a stubborn one. Master Joseph says so, that's why. He asked me personally. He said, 'She won't want to stay, but you have to persuade her.' You see, he loves you and wants only what's best for you. There's no one better than him!"

"I came here so that he could treat Obadiah, and he did nothing."

"You really are mad, aren't you? You know perfectly well the boy was dead! In fact, he'd been dead for a while. What could the master have done?"

Miriam seemed not to hear this reproach. She had closed her eyes, and her lips were quivering again. "I don't like this house," she murmured. "I don't like these men, and I don't like these rules. I thought Joseph could teach me how to fight evil and suffering, but I won't learn anything here because I'm a woman."

Ruth sighed and shook her head in disappointment.

"Obadiah was an angel from heaven," Miriam went on, in a voice that was both subdued and intense. "He should have been saved. There's no justice, none at all! Barabbas shouldn't have let him fight. I should have known how to look after him, and Joseph should have known how to bring him back to life. We're all at fault. We don't know how to bring about goodness and justice."

Ruth was starting to wonder if the master was wrong and Brother Geouel, alas, was right. This girl from Nazareth had not recovered. On the contrary, she had well and truly lost her mind.

Miriam saw the doubt on Ruth's face. The anger that had overwhelmed her in the last few hours came back, throbbing in her temples and throat. She stood up abruptly and stepped over the bench as if about to go.

In the kitchen, the handmaids had stopped work and were watching them, on the lookout for a quarrel. Miriam had second thoughts. She bent toward Ruth and said, "You think I'm mad, don't you?"

Ruth blushed and looked away. "There's no point in coming to a decision now. You can make up your mind tomorrow. Rest a while longer, and in the morning—"

"In the morning, it'll be another day, exactly the same as today. I'm not mad, and you're too pleased with your own ignorance. I'm going to tell you who Obadiah was."

In a toneless voice, she recounted how she had met the young *am ha'aretz* in Sepphoris, how he had saved her father, Joachim, from the cross in Tarichea, and how Herod's mercenaries had killed him and spared Barabbas.

"Obviously, it was a mercenary who planted a spear in his chest. And, of course, it's Herod who pays the mercenaries to bring suffering to the people. But we were the ones, all of us, who thrust Obadiah in front of that spear. Through our weakness. We tolerate those who humiliate us and don't react. We've grown accustomed to living without justice, without love or respect for the weak. We do not refuse the burden of the evil that weighs on our necks. When an *am ha'aretz* dies for us, the evil is all the greater, the sin all the graver. Because no one thinks about him, no one cries vengeance. On the contrary, we all stoop a little lower in our indifference."

Miriam had raised her voice. Ruth had not expected this flood of words and looked at her openmouthed, as did the handmaids in the kitchen.

"Where is goodness?" Miriam roared. "Here? In this house? No, I don't see it anywhere. Am I blind? Where is the goodness generated by these men who are trying to be pure so that they can get onto the Island of the Blessed? The goodness they're offering all of Yahweh's people, where is it? I don't see it."

Ruth stared at her in horror, with tears in her eyes. "You mustn't talk like that! Not here, where they come in their hundreds to be relieved of pain by the master. Oh no, you mustn't! There they are with their children, their old relatives, and every day the master has the door opened and lets them in. He does all he can for them. Often, he cures them. Sometimes, they die in his arms, but that's how it is. The Almighty decides."

Miriam had heard this argument once too often. "The Almighty decides! But I say that what is unjust is unjust, and we shouldn't simply bow our heads and accept it." With an angry snort, she walked away.

"Wait! Where are you going?"

Ruth had grabbed her tunic and was holding her back. Miriam tried to break free, but the old woman's grip was firm.

"I'm going to the graveyard, to see Obadiah! I'm sure no one has gone there to mourn him!"

"Wait, please wait!"

Miriam was puzzled by the supplication in Ruth's voice. She stopped struggling, and let Ruth take her hands in her own rough, worn fingers.

"The boy isn't in the graveyard."

"What do you mean?"

"The brothers wouldn't allow it. The *am ha'aretz* aren't—"

"God Almighty! It's not possible."

"Have no fear. He's in the ground, but—"

"Joseph would never have allowed that!"

"It's not him. I swear it! It isn't him, don't think that! He didn't know . . ."

With a yell, Miriam broke free from Ruth's grip. "Obadiah is dead, but he's only an *am ha'aretz*! Who cares whether he lived or not? May God curse you all!"

Miriam rushed out, leaving the words echoing beneath the vaults.

Ruth closed her eyes and hit the table with the flat of her hand. She began weeping: hot, scalding tears. She should have run after Miriam. The girl may have been full of anger, but she was right, and Ruth knew it. She had seen it in Master Joseph's eyes when he had asked for her help. He, too, knew Miriam was right. He, too, feared her anger.

B Y nightfall, it was the one topic of conversation among the handmaids. They asked a thousand questions of Ruth, who became more and more sullen and refused to answer. The girl from Nazareth, they said, had taken advantage of the comings and goings of the sick in the main courtyard to leave the house and go to the little burial ground, a mere two or three hundred paces away. There, she had asked where the body of the young *am ha'aretz* had been laid to rest. She had found the place, and now she was mourning him, tearing her tunic and covering her hair with ashes and earth.

Returning from the fields, the inhabitants of Beth Zabdai, surprised by the violent fervor of these laments and prayers over a grave that was not even in sacred ground, had stopped some distance away to watch her. They, too, were probably wondering if she was mad.

All she was doing was performing the prescribed rituals for the seven days of mourning. But she was doing it with such devotion that all those who saw her and listened to her felt shivers down their backs, as if the pain of death had gotten into their bones.

No one stayed long. Many lowered their eyes and discreetly moved away. Some came up to her and joined her in a short prayer. Then they shook their heads sadly and left, silent and abashed.

THEIR work over, Ruth and a few of the handmaids climbed up onto the roof as night was falling.

Miriam was some distance from the house, but she could still be seen by the grave. It did not take a lot of imagination to think of her there, silent, prostrate, dirty, and alone.

When she had heard what was happening outside, Ruth had asked if the master had tried to bring Miriam back to the house. The handmaids had looked at her in surprise. Why would the master have contravened the rules? The door would stay closed. A woman in mourning, sullied in body and mind, could hardly be admitted when the brothers were already purified after their baths and their evening meal.

Yes, Ruth knew that. All the same, she kept thinking of how insistent Joseph had been when he had asked her to keep an eye on Miriam. It had been such an unusual request that she could not help remembering the exact words he had used. "Don't let her get away. She'll be in a terrible rage, and she's very strong. She's no ordinary girl and she can turn her strength against herself. Keep a close watch on her, if you can. . . ."

He had not needed to add, "*Because I can't.*" There was no point. Ruth had understood.

For some reason she did not know, and which she would make no attempt to discover, this girl from Nazareth was dear to the master's heart. That was something the brothers would never accept. They condemned him in advance. Geouel, who considered himself the wisest and most inflexible of the brothers, and the most beloved by God, would use it as the opportunity for a scene or even an expulsion. He did not like the master. Everyone knew it, felt it, and Ruth had sometimes seen Joseph fear it.

But Joseph of Arimathea had already given her, Ruth, so much, it was right that she should give something in return. He had turned to her, hinting at how worried he was and how much he needed her support.

Now, standing on the roof of the house in the deepening twilight, Ruth could not escape the feeling that she had failed.

"She's going to spend the night outside," she murmured, her fists pressed to her chest.

Those around her shrugged. Although they did not dare say it out loud, they were all thinking that it might do the girl some good, calm her down. A night in the open air had never killed anyone. The people who brought the sick to the house often slept in the surrounding area. Some had carpets or blankets that they stretched over poles to make a kind of tent. Others were content with a tree or a low wall as shelter from the wind. The girl from Nazareth could do the same. Even though it was sad to see her in such exaggerated mourning for an *am ha'aretz* boy.

But Ruth knew that nothing was simple with this Miriam. The other handmaids had not seen her eyes, her anger, up close. They had not had her rebellious words addressed directly to them. Words more wounding than blows.

You just had to look at her, there by the grave, a small, prostrate figure, to know that she would do nothing to protect herself in the night from the cold, or the dogs that wandered in the darkness in search of carrion, or even evil men prowling for prey.

She might even be insane enough to set off for Galilee, with nothing but the moon to light her way. At the risk of becoming even more lost than she already was, her stomach half empty, her brain on fire.

———

————

Ruth told no one of these thoughts. But her mind was made up. She could do nothing, though, until the women had finished their meal and retired to their bedchambers.

She endured this wait impatiently, barely touching her own platter. She prayed in silence, without moving her lips, but appealing to the Almighty from the bottom of her heart for his indulgence, his understanding, his blessing. As long as Miriam didn't leave the burial ground!

She pretended to go to bed like her companions. Once in her bedchamber, she quickly tied her blanket around her waist. Without a sound, she walked back along the pitch-black corridors to the kitchen. Earlier, she had discreetly prepared a bundle containing a few biscuits and a gourd of goat's milk. She knew the place so well that she did not waste too much time in finding it.

Groping her way along the walls with her fingertips, she reached the large storeroom behind the kitchen. There was a hatch in the storeroom wall, through which grain was unloaded from outside into a large tub. That avoided a lot of to-and-froing in the courtyard and preserved the tranquil atmosphere of the house.

Stumbling a little as she went, she finally found the low wall surrounding the tub. Awkwardly, she climbed over it, and her feet sank into the grain. She panicked, feeling as though it might bury her, and searched desperately for the hatch. At last, her fingers found the wooden shutter and the metal lock, which could only be worked from the inside.

She sighed with relief, then fumbled a little while opening the lock, which had not even been touched in months. It seemed to her that she was making so much noise, she could easily wake everyone in the women's quarters.

The hinges creaked at last, and the hatch was open. Her heart beating fit to burst, Ruth breathed in a lungful of air. She must have been mad, she thought. What would happen to her when they found out what she had done? Because they would find out. Nothing in this house ever remained a secret. And never, in all the years she had lived here, had she been so disobedient.

Horrified at her own daring, she slid her torso through the hatch. The opening was just big enough for her. After the absolute darkness, the light of the half-moon seemed almost unreal, but so harsh that she could make out the smallest details of her surroundings.

The hatch proved to be farther from the ground than Ruth had anticipated. She was no longer as supple or agile as she had once been. Clenching her jaws, short of breath, she grasped the edge of the wall and tipped forward. The hatch snapped shut and she collapsed on the ground, letting out a little cry as she did so.

She had fallen in a position so grotesque that, at any another time, she would have laughed about it. Luckily, the blanket firmly tied around her waist had cushioned the impact, and the path was deserted.

She got to her feet, cursing. The bundle had rolled under her; the biscuits had broken and scattered on the ground. She gathered a few pieces that did not seem soiled, then moved away from the house toward the path leading to the village.

She was surrounded by shadows and strange noises. As if they were alive, the things around her—the trees, the stones on the path—subtly changed shape as she advanced. Ruth knew that it was the effect of the moonlight, but she was no longer accustomed to the illusions of the night. She had lost count of the years since she had last walked like this, at the hour when the demons played with you.

She murmured the name of the Almighty, called for his forgiveness and begged him once again to keep the girl from Nazareth by the grave of the *am ha'aretz*.

She was there.

Ruth did not see her at first. She was indistinguishable from the bushes that dotted the burial ground between meager graves devoid of stones or any sign indicating the name of the dead person they housed. Then Miriam swayed slightly, and the moon illumined her torn tunic and loose hair heavy with earth.

Ruth waited until her breath had resumed its normal rhythm before approaching her. Her heart was beating so loudly, she felt sure that Miriam was going to hear her.

But Miriam did not seem to realize that there was someone near her. Ruth held back her desire to take her in her arms.

"It's me, Ruth," she murmured.

"If you've come here to ask me to go inside, you'd do better to go back to bed."

Miriam's tone was so sharp that Ruth took a step back. "I didn't think you'd heard me," she whispered.

"If you've come to mourn Obadiah with me, you're very welcome. Otherwise, you can leave."

Ruth untied the blanket from around her waist, laid it down on the ground, took off the gourd of milk, and crouched. "No, I haven't come to make you go back inside. Even if I wanted to, it wouldn't be possible. The door is closed for the night. I also have to wait until tomorrow. If they let me in again."

She waited for Miriam to react, but as not a word passed her lips, she went on, "I've brought some milk and a blanket. Dawn's going to be cold. I also had some biscuits, but I fell and they broke."

She could smile about it now. But Miriam said, without turning her head, "I don't need your food. I'm fasting."

"Drinking milk isn't forbidden when you're in mourning. Nor is having a blanket. And in your state, it's stupid to fast."

Again, Miriam did not reply. The silence around them was full of chattering and scraping, the rustle of the wind and the chirring of insects. Ruth sat down on the ground and tried to find a reasonably comfortable position.

She was afraid. She couldn't help it. Knowing that there were all these graves around her, all these dead people who had not been blessed by the rabbis, terrified her. She hardly dared turn her head, for fear of seeing a monster loom over her. The very thought of it gave her gooseflesh. You had to be Miriam not to tremble with fear in the midst of this silence filled with noise.

"I don't know if I've come to mourn with you," she sighed. "I don't like mourning. But I couldn't leave you all on your own outside."

She hoped that Miriam was going to ask her why, but no question came. To break the silence, she said, almost mechanically, "At least drink a little milk. It'll give you the strength to wait for morning. And also to fight the cold . . ."

She did not finish her sentence. Now that she had heard the clear, harsh voice of Miriam, her advice seemed pointless and even slightly ridiculous. This girl knew what she wanted, and did it. She didn't need any sermons.

Ruth clenched her teeth and her fists, listening for sounds within the silence. Time passed. Neither of them moved, and the muscles of their thighs and lower back went numb. Every now and again, Miriam's lips moved, as if she were murmuring a prayer. Or words. Unless it was an effect of the moonlight through the leaves of the big acacia that stood over them.

Suddenly, Ruth seized the corners of the blanket, opened it out, and spread it over Miriam's legs and her own. Miriam did not protest, did not remove it. That persuaded Ruth to speak.

"I came because I had to. Because of Master Joseph. To tell you something. You say the master is unjust, but it isn't true."

She looked at her hands lying quite flat on the coarse wool over her legs. On either side of her face, her white hair shone like silver in the moonlight.

"I had a husband. He worked in leather. With a single goatskin, he was capable of making a two-bushel gourd so perfect not a single drop of water leaked in the summer sun. He was a simple, gentle man. His name was Joshua. My mother chose him for me without my knowledge. I'd just reached the marriageable age. Fourteen, perhaps fifteen. When I saw Joshua for the first time, I knew I could love him the way a woman is supposed to love her husband. For eighteen years, we were happy and unhappy. We had three daughters. Two died before they were four months old. The third one grew tall and beautiful. Then she died too. That's when I started hating mourning. But I still had my Joshua, and I thought we would have another child. We were still young enough, and we knew what to do."

She tried to laugh at her own joke. The laugh did not come. Barely a smile.

"One day, Joshua decided that he loved the Lord more than he loved me. It took him like a wind that rises and lays low a field of barley. He came to live in this house. The brothers took a long time to accept him. They don't easily accept newcomers. They're suspicious. They fear they may not have the strength to become pure enough. . . . But I took even longer to accept losing him. Every day I'd sit outside the door of the house. I couldn't believe he'd stay. I was sure he'd change his mind. The Almighty had taken my daughters from me. He couldn't take my Joshua, too. What was my sin? Where was his justice?"

Ruth's voice was barely audible. Despite herself, tears started to form. It had been such a long time since she had last dredged this story from her heart.

"He never came back to me."

Through the thick blanket, she struck her thigh with the palm of her hand and took a deep breath to dispel the lump in her throat.

"One day, Master Joseph came out to speak to me. I was in the shade of the large fig tree to the left of the house. I was watching the door, but I'd been watching it so long, I'd stopped seeing it. When he opened his mouth, I was as scared as if a scorpion had stung my backside."

She smiled again. She was exaggerating a little, but not much, and thinking about it gave her the chance to dry her eyes. Miriam must have been interested, for she asked, in her curt voice, "What did he say to you?"

"That my Joshua would never come back to me because he had chosen the way of the Essenes. That this way forbade him to be with his wife as before. That the Lord would forgive me if I wanted to consider myself a woman without a husband. That I was still young and beautiful and could easily find a man who'd be happy to love me."

How strange it was to utter such words today!

"If I'd had a big enough stone to hand, I'd have smashed his skull. Change husbands without it being a sin! You have to be a man, wise or not—may the Almighty forgive me!—to have ideas like that. One moon later, I was still outside the house. Winter had just started. It was raining all the time. The villagers would give me food, but they couldn't do anything against the cold and rain. Master Joseph came to me again. This time, he said, 'You'll catch your death of cold if you stay here. Joshua isn't coming back.' 'In that case,' I replied, 'I'm the one who'll come back here, every day. If the Lord wants me to die, I'll die, and so much the better.' He wasn't pleased about that. He stayed there for a long time in the rain beside me, without saying a word. Then suddenly he said, 'You can come in and consider this house as your own. But you'll have to respect our rules, and you might not like them. You'll have to become our handmaid.' That wasn't so bad! It took my breath away. Master Joseph said, 'Sometimes, during your work, you'll see your husband coming and going, but he won't see you. It'll be as if you weren't there. And you won't be able to speak to him or do anything to make him come back to you. That could cause you more pain than the one you feel today.' So what? I thought. I was prepared for anything, just to be under the same roof as Joshua. But the master insisted. 'If the pain is too great, you will have to leave. Neither God nor I wish you any harm.' He was right. It was terrible to see my husband and be nothing but a shadow. Like a wound that opens again every day. And yet I stayed."

She fell silent, and waited for the fire that still burned in her breast to die down.

"It was a long time ago. Twenty years, perhaps. I was in a bad way. I begged the Almighty to let me die. Sometimes, the pain was so great, I couldn't move. The master would come to see me. Mostly, he didn't speak. He'd take my hand and sit down beside me for a moment. Which is against the rules. But this was before Geouel's time. One day he said to me, 'Your Joshua is dead. His body is dust, but all our bodies will be dust. His soul is eternal. It lives with Yahweh, and I know it lives with you. Your home is here. You can live here as long as you wish, like a sister living in her brother's house.' I didn't weep. I couldn't. But I knew my love for Joshua was as strong as ever. One day, much later, Master Joseph said to me, 'The goodness and love we have in our hearts don't always need to see a face in order to exist and even to receive love in return. You women have bigger and simpler hearts than ours. You have to make less effort to want what's best for those you love. You are great because of that, and although you are our handmaids, I envy you. As long as you live, your Joshua will be with you.'"

Miriam's expression changed, but Ruth had no idea what to make of that. There seemed to be anger, sadness, and even a kind of disgust in it. Or perhaps that was the effect of the moonlight.

Ruth felt the need to add, "It was only later that I understood the meaning of Master Joseph's words. At that moment, all that mattered was that he said, 'Your Joshua.'"

She fell silent. Miriam had turned to look at her, but was still silent. Ruth felt strangely embarrassed to be looked at like that. You could never guess what was happening in this girl's brain, let alone understand it.

"I told you my story so that you wouldn't be angry with the master. He's the best man who's ever lived on this earth. Everything he does, everything he says, is good for us. It isn't his fault that your friend isn't in a proper graveyard. He's the master, but he doesn't make the decisions on his own. He can do a lot, but he can't perform miracles. I'd have liked him to bring my Joshua back to life too. But it's the Almighty who performs miracles. That's how it is. What's certain is that the master knows what we women feel. He doesn't despise us. And he loves you very much. He can't say it or show it in the house. Because of the rules. But he wishes you well. And he even expects something of you."

Ruth was surprised by her own words. It was not like her to talk this way. But tonight, the words just came to her. And she needed to say them. And not only because she wanted to be fair to Master Joseph.

She was startled by the question Miriam now asked. "Have you seen your Joshua since he died?"

Ruth hesitated. "In dreams, often. But not for years now."

"I see Obadiah. But I'm not asleep, and my eyes are open. I see him, and he speaks to me."

A shiver went down Ruth's spine. She peered into the darkness around them. In the course of her long life, she had heard many stories of this kind. Dead people who left their graves and went wandering. Whether they were true or false, she hated them. Especially hearing them sitting on a grave, in the dark, on ground that wasn't blessed by the rabbis!

"Hunger is playing tricks on you," she said, trying to make her voice sound as firm as possible.

"No, I don't think so," Miriam replied calmly.

Ruth closed her eyes. But when she opened them, everything looked exactly the same as before. "What does he say to you?" she asked in a low voice.

Miriam did not reply, but she was smiling—a smile as difficult to understand as her anger.

"Don't scare me," Ruth begged. "I'm not a brave woman. I hate darkness and shadows. I hate you seeing things I can't see."

She let out a little cry of terror when Miriam's hand touched her arm. Miriam was looking for her hand. She took it and held it. "There's no reason to be scared. You were right to come. And I'm sure you're right about Joseph, too."

"So you're staying?"

"It's not yet time for me to leave."

CHAPTER 14

MIRIAM was determined to observe the full seven days of mourning, as custom demanded.

The inhabitants of Beth Zabdai, leaving for the fields in the morning or coming back in the evening, would often join Miriam and pray with her, just as if Obadiah's grave were on sacred ground. Sometimes, they were also joined by those bringing the sick to be healed, who would add prayers for the health of their loved ones to the prayers of mourning.

This unaccustomed activity soon attracted the attention of the Essene brothers. At twilight, the chanting of prayers over Obadiah's grave even penetrated the walls of the house. That disturbed some of them, who wondered if it might not be a good idea to go and join the villagers in prayer.

Was not prayer the first principle of their retreat from the world? Was it not prayer that would ensure the reign of the light of Yahweh after centuries of darkness?

The ensuing debate was a heated one. Geouel and a few others were strongly opposed to the idea. The brothers were being led astray, they said, blinding themselves to the consequences. The pray-

ers of the Essenes were not the same as the routine chanting of ignorant peasants who could not read a single line of the Torah! And
anyway, how could they even think of praying for an *am ha'aretz* who
had been refused burial because of his impurity? Had they forgotten
the teachings of the wise men and rabbis who had often declared
that the *am ha'aretz* had no souls and so were unworthy of the covenant between Yahweh and his people?

Not all the brothers were convinced by these arguments. Prayer
was something unique and irreplaceable. The more prayers there
were, the purer the world would become. And the closer the day
would come when the Messiah appeared. Had Geouel and the others
forgotten that this was their one aim? Every prayer brought them a
step closer to Yahweh. It was for him, and him alone, to decide who
was worthy and who unworthy; men were too shortsighted to do
that for themselves. If this girl from Nazareth, the peasants, and the
sick joined their prayers in a chorus of love for the Almighty, where
was the harm in that?

At this, Geouel flew into a temper. "Are we going to start praying for dogs and scorpions next? Are they the pure you want to lead
to the Island of the Blessed? Is that your only ambition—to populate
it with the dregs of the earth?"

During this debate, Joseph of Arimathea remained silent. But
the last word fell to him. Although he refused to rule on whether the
am ha'aretz had souls, he declared that whoever went and prayed over
the boy's grave with Miriam would not be committing a sin.

In the end, none of the Essenes ventured out to the graveyard.
The arguments of Geouel and his supporters were too wearying, too
unsettling. Not one of the brothers was prepared to do something
that might disrupt the harmony of the community. But when Ruth
met Joseph's eyes after the debate, she saw that they were bright with
satisfaction.

———

W H E N the seven days of mourning were over, Miriam entered the house without any opposition.

She made her ablutions in the kitchen of the women's quarter, where Ruth and two other handmaids had filled a large tub with pure water.

Miriam was a painful sight to behold. She had grown thinner than was advisable. Her face had not only become gaunt, it had also hardened. In a few days, she seemed to have aged several years. Her eyes had dark rings under them, but they also had a strange radiance that was hard to look at. Her muscles seemed as taut as ropes. Beneath the mask of exhaustion and willpower, there was, if not beauty, a kind of wild charm, as disturbing as it was attractive, and unlike anything else. It was surely this strangeness, as well as her obstinacy, which had won over the villagers and drawn them to join her in prayer.

Ruth knew now what Joseph had known from the beginning: that Miriam's apparent fragility concealed an inflexible strength. And that this strength made Miriam different, and hard to understand. To be convinced of this, you only had to hear her laughing and joking as the handmaids poured water over her back.

Where did she find the capacity for laughter, when only yesterday she had been cursing injustice and the horror of death?

S T A R T I N G the following day, Miriam came to the courtyard to welcome the sick, who were visited twice a day by Joseph and the brothers.

There were many old people among them, and many women with young children. They would crouch in the shade and wait. The handmaids would give them something to drink, and sometimes distribute food to the hungriest children.

They also brought linen and other things needed for the treatments. Some of the commonest potions and ointments were prepared in advance in the kitchen, to Joseph's recipes.

It was here that he and Miriam met again and exchanged a few words.

Miriam was carrying a large pitcher of milk, which she poured into wooden platters held out by the mothers of the sick children. Geouel was with Joseph, his eyes and ears alert as usual.

On seeing Miriam, Joseph went up to her and greeted her with a friendly smile. "I'm happy you're still in the house."

"I've stayed in order to learn."

"To learn?" Geouel said in surprise. "What could a woman possibly learn?"

Miriam did not reply. Nor did Joseph react in any way. It seemed to those around them that Geouel had wasted his breath.

This went on for several days. Following Ruth's instructions, Miriam gave the sick all the help she could. She would talk to them gently, listen to them for as long as they wanted, and prepare the potions and the plasters, which she gradually learned to apply properly.

She always stayed close to Joseph when he made his visits, but he never spoke a word to her or tried to look at her. But in dealing with the patients, especially those whose ailments were particularly mysterious, he always spoke loudly enough for her to hear. He would ask a lot of questions, palpate, examine, and reflect aloud as he did so.

In this way, Miriam gradually began to understand that a stomachache could derive from something eaten or drunk, or that a pain in the chest might be caused by a damp house or by grain dust after the harvest. An old childhood wound in the feet, which a person had learned to tolerate, might lead to the adult's putting his back permanently out of joint.

The eyes and the mouth were the seat of all suffering. Every day, the latter had to be purified with citrus or cloves, the former with kohl. The women often had infections they did not dare talk about, even though the pain was as strong as if someone had thrust a dagger into their stomachs. This was the surest indication that they would die in childbirth.

ONE day, when Miriam had been in the house for nearly a month, a man arrived carrying a boy in his arms. The boy, who was seven or eight, had broken his leg falling from a tree. He was screaming with pain, and his father was yelling just as loudly with fear.

Although it was late, nearly time for evening prayers, Joseph went out to meet them. He spoke to them, trying to calm both of them down. He assured them that the fracture would heal well and that the boy would be running again before the end of the year. He asked for wooden boards and linen to make a splint.

With his delicate fingers, he palpated the already swollen flesh. The boy cried out. Without warning, Joseph suddenly pulled on the leg to reset the broken bones, and the boy fainted. Now came the moment to put on the splint. Joseph held the leg and asked Miriam to massage it gently with ointments, while Geouel made the wooden boards ready.

As Miriam bent over their work, the comb holding her thick hair in place fell out, and in coming loose the hair brushed against Geouel's face. He let out an angry cry and jumped.

If it had not been for the quick reflexes of Joseph and one of the handmaids, the boy would have fallen from the table where he had been laid. Joseph, fearing that the fracture might have been aggravated by the sudden movement, reprimanded Geouel in no uncertain terms.

"I'm not here to put up with this woman's flesh," Geouel retorted threateningly. "The obscenity of her hair is a corruption you've imposed on us. How are we supposed to cure with goodness when evil slaps us in the face?"

Everyone looked at him in amazement. Joseph's embarrassment

was clear to see, as was Miriam's. Undaunted, Geouel added, with a malicious smile, "I hope, Master, that you're not planning to have another Potiphar's wife with you in the house, like the other Joseph!"

Her face smarting with humiliation, Miriam gave the pot of ointment to one of the handmaids and ran off into the women's quarters.

Fearing the worst, Ruth ran after her to dissuade her from taking Geouel's words too much to heart.

"You know what he's like. A goatskin filled with gall! A man twisted with envy! Nobody in the house likes him. The brothers are no fonder of him than we are. Some say he'll never attain the wisdom of the Essenes because he's too eaten up with jealousy. Unfortunately, as long as he doesn't break any rules, the master has nothing to reproach him with. . . ."

Once again, Miriam astonished Ruth.

She took her hand and drew her into the kitchen. There, she held out to her the knife used for cutting leather straps.

"Cut my hair."

Ruth stared at her, dumbfounded.

"Go on, cut my hair! Leave it no thicker than my finger."

No, Ruth cried, it couldn't be done. A woman had a duty to be a woman, which meant she had to have long hair. "And besides, it's so beautiful! What will you look like?"

"I don't care what I look like. It's just hair. It'll grow back."

As Ruth was still hesitating, Miriam grabbed a handful of her own hair, held it away from her temple, and sliced it off without hesitation.

"If I do it myself, it'll be worse," she declared, holding out the cut hair to Ruth.

Ruth let out a cry of horror, at which Miriam laughed merrily.

So it was that she appeared to everyone the following day with her hair so short that she was unrecognizable. It made her look like a boy and a girl at the same time, and also made her eyes look bigger and more vivid. Her prominent nose and cheekbones had a virility about them that was belied by her tender, feminine mouth. She was wearing her tunic pulled in at the waist in the manner of a man, and hid her chest beneath a short caftan, creating an unsettling illusion.

Joseph did not recognize her immediately. When he did realize who she was, he raised his eyebrows, while Geouel frowned. Breaking the rule that a woman should not speak before being spoken to, Miriam turned to Geouel and said, "I hope I never again impose my womanly corruption on you, Brother Geouel. No one can undo what the Almighty has made. A woman I was born, and a woman I shall die. But while I am here, I can conceal the appearance of womanliness so that your eyes no longer suffer corruption."

She said this with a smile devoid of the slightest irony.

There was a brief silence. Then Joseph burst out laughing, and the other brothers did the same. Their laughter rang out so loudly in the courtyard that even the patients joined in.

For weeks, then months, there were no other incidents. Brothers, handmaids, and patients all grew accustomed to Miriam's face.

There was hardly a day when she did not learn more about how to tend the sick and relieve pain, although there existed many ailments whose cure remained an enigma, even for Joseph.

From time to time, and always briefly, taking advantage of the rare moments when they were thrown together, Joseph would exchange a few words with her.

Once he said to her, "We each have to fight the demons that are determined to lead us from the path before us. Some carry these demons with them, clinging to their tunics on the sly. They have little chance to escape them. Some healers think that the diseases we cannot understand or cure are their work. I don't believe that. For me, the demons are a perfectly visible bunch. And when I see you, daughter of Joachim, I know that you are fighting only one demon, but a very powerful one. The demon of anger."

He said this in his usual calm, persuasive tone, his eyes full of kindness.

Miriam did not reply, but simply nodded in agreement.

"We have many reasons to feel anger," Joseph went on. "More than we can bear. That's why anger can never give rise to anything good. Over time, it works like a poison, stopping us from accepting Yahweh's help."

On another occasion, he laughed and said, "I hear the handmaids are all thinking of imitating you. Geouel is getting worried. He thinks he's going to see all of you with short hair one of these mornings. I told him he was much more likely to wake up one fine morning without a single handmaid in the house, because you'd have taken them a long way away to start a house for women. . . ."

Miriam laughed with him.

Joseph passed his palm over his bald cranium. It was clear that although he was joking, he was profoundly serious. "It wouldn't be impossible. You already know a lot."

"No, I still have too much to learn," Miriam replied, with the same half-serene, half-severe expression. "And I wouldn't open a house for women, but a house for everyone. Men and women, *am ha'aretz* and Sadducees, rich, poor, Samaritans, Galileans, Jews and non-Jews. A house for people to join together, the way that life joins us together and jumbles us up. We shouldn't cut ourselves off from other people behind walls."

Joseph was taken aback by this. He remained lost in thought and did not reply.

THE first rains of winter shook the leaves from the trees, making the paths impassable. Fewer sick people came for treatment. The air smelled of fire from the hearths. The brothers began going out into the countryside around the house, because this was one of the best times to gather the herbs needed for ointments and potions. Miriam got into the habit of following them at a distance to see what they were gathering.

One morning, walking ahead of the others, Joseph found Miriam waiting at the side of the path, sitting on a rock.

"Do you know Obadiah often pays me a visit?" she said. "Not in a dream, but in broad daylight, when my eyes are wide open. He talks to me, he's happy to see me. And I'm even happier than he is." She laughed. "I call him my little husband!"

Joseph frowned. "And what does he say to you?" he asked in an even gentler voice than usual.

Miriam put a finger on his lips and shook her head. "Do you think I'm mad?" she asked, amused by the anxiety she sensed in Joseph. "Ruth's positive I am!"

Joseph did not have the chance to reply. The brothers had just come into view and were staring at them.

Subsequently, Joseph never displayed any curiosity about these visits from Obadiah. Perhaps he was waiting in his own way for Miriam herself to talk about it again. But she never did. Any more than she answered Ruth when, from time to time, unable to hold her tongue, she asked her, a touch sardonically, for news of her *am ha'aretz*.

O N E snowy morning, a group of people arrived at the house yelling at the tops of their voices. They had brought a very old woman with them. The roof of her house, rotten with damp, had collapsed on her.

Joseph was out gathering herbs, in spite of the bad weather, and it was Geouel who came into the courtyard to examine the woman. Miriam was already bending over her.

Sensing Geouel behind her, she quickly stepped aside. Geouel looked at the woman's face and the many superficial wounds on her legs and hands.

After a moment, he rose to his full height and declared that the woman was dead and that nothing more could be done. But Miriam startled him with the cry, "No! Of course she isn't dead!"

Geouel glared at her.

"She isn't dead," Miriam insisted.

"Do you know these things better than I do?"

"I can feel her breath! Her heart is still beating! Her body is warm!"

Geouel made a great effort to control his anger. He took the old woman's hands, crossed them over her torn, dusty tunic, turned to those around them, and said, "This woman is dead. You can prepare her grave."

"No!"

This time, Miriam pushed him aside unceremoniously, dipped a cloth into a pitcher of vinegar, and started rubbing the old woman's cheeks.

Geouel laughed. "Ah, you're determined to have your miracle!"

Taking no notice of him, Miriam demanded more cloths to clean the old woman's body, and asked for water to be heated so that she could be bathed.

"Don't you see that Yahweh has taken her life from her?" Geouel cried indignantly. "What you're doing to the body of a dead woman is a sacrilege! And if any of you help her, you'll be committing sacrilege too!"

After a brief moment of hesitation, everyone set about following Miriam's orders. Cursing, Geouel disappeared inside the house.

The old woman was immersed in a tub of hot water in the kitchen of the women's quarters. Miriam kept rubbing her throat and cheeks with vinegar thinned down with camphor. But there were no signs of life now, and everyone was starting to have doubts.

In the middle of the day, Joseph returned. When he heard about what was happening, he came running. Miriam explained to him what she had done. He lifted the old woman's eyelids and looked for a pulse in her neck.

It took him a little time to find it. He got to his feet with a smile.

"You're right, she's alive. But now we need more hot water. We also need to make a drink for her that could just as easily kill her as wake her."

He went into the house and came back with an oily black potion made from ginger root and various snake poisons.

Very carefully, a few drops were poured into the old woman's toothless mouth.

They had to wait until nightfall, constantly replenishing the scalding water in the bath, before they finally heard her let out a distinct groan.

The handmaids and the people who had brought the woman stepped back, more in terror than in joy. When she had looked like a corpse, they had clung to the thought that she was alive. Now that they had the proof that she was really alive, they were terrified. One of them cried, "It's a miracle!"

Some of the handmaids started weeping, others repeated, "It's a miracle. A miracle!"

They praised the Lord, rushed outside, and shouted themselves hoarse announcing the miracle.

Joseph, as irritated as he was amused, looked at Miriam. "Geouel's going to like this! In a little while, everyone in the village will be outside the door, calling it a miracle. I'd be surprised if one of them didn't come up with a prophecy to go with it."

Miriam appeared not to hear him. She was holding the old woman's hands, looking at her closely. She could see her eyes moving now beneath her wrinkled eyelids. From her throat came the spasmodic purr of her breathing.

Miriam looked at Joseph. "Geouel is right. This isn't a miracle. It's your skill and your potion that gave her back her life, isn't it?"

CHAPTER 15

JOSEPH'S prediction came true.

In almost no time at all, the path leading to the house in Beth Zabdai was filled with a motley crowd muttering prayers from morning to night. Among them were a few men in rags who chanted and shouted more loudly than the rest and unhesitatingly proclaimed themselves prophets of the days to come. The most eccentric of them assured the crowd that they were about to perform genuine miracles. Others harangued the gathering with descriptions of hell so terrible and so precise that anyone would have thought they had just come back from there. Still others stirred up the sick, assuring them that the hand of God was on the Essenes, who now had the power not only to heal wounds and soothe pain, but also to bring the dead back to life.

Furious at this growing chaos, the brothers decided to safeguard their prayers and studies. They sealed the door and stopped admitting patients. Joseph did not agree with this decision, but since he felt embarrassed to be the cause of this disorder, he made no objection. He let Geouel deal with this unexpected closure.

When Ruth told Miriam what was happening, Miriam gave a pout of indifference. The only thing that interested her was the treatment of the old woman, who was making good progress every day, breathing more easily, eating, and gradually returning to consciousness.

Discreetly, Joseph of Arimathea came to examine her every day. His visits were like a ritual. First, he would observe the old woman in silence. Then, bending his head, he would listen to her chest through a cloth. Then he would inquire about what she had eaten and drunk, and whether she had emptied her bowels. Finally, he would ask Miriam to palpate her limbs, pelvis, and ribs. As he guided Miriam's fingers, he watched for any reaction of pain on the old woman's face. In this way, Miriam learned how to recognize any possible fractures and contusions beneath the skin, bones, and muscles.

Five days after death had loosened its grip on the old woman thanks to him, Joseph said, "It's too early to know whether or not the bones in the back and hips are intact, or if she'll be able to walk again. But I doubt that the bones have been affected. For the moment, judging by what you can feel with your fingers, it looks as if only one rib is broken. It'll hurt her for a long time, but she can live with it. The worst thing is when the bones in the chest break and tear the lungs. Then we can't do anything except watch while the patient dies an excruciating death."

Miriam asked him how he could be certain this wasn't the case with this woman.

"When it happens, you'll know! The patient can't breathe. Bubbles of blood form on the lips. And when the patient breathes out or in, the chest makes a roaring noise like a heavy rainstorm!"

"But if nothing was broken," Miriam said, surprised, "why did this woman appear to be dead?"

"Because when she was buried under the rubble, she didn't have any air. The effort she had to make to survive weakened her heart. It didn't really stop beating, but the beats slowed down, and there was only just enough blood flowing to keep her alive. That, more than anything else, is what life is: a beating heart that sends the blood all over the body."

"So your potions made her heart stronger?"

Joseph nodded with a satisfied air. "That's all it was. I just gave God's will a little nudge. Of course, in the end he decides, but that's been our covenant since the days of Abraham: We can do our share to sustain life on this earth."

There was a hint of irony in his tone; Joseph hated to appear presumptuous. But Miriam knew he was sincere. Man was not born into the world like a stone suspended above a well. He had his own destiny in his hands.

They were both silent for a moment, looking at the old woman. Just as the indelible circles of the seasons accumulate in the trunks of trees, so the whole of this woman's life was etched in the lines of her face: the innocence of the child, the beauty of the young girl, maturity, children, joys and sorrows, the years of hardship and labor that had eroded it to produce, finally, the chaotic mask of old age. This face celebrated life, the power of it, the human craving for it.

In spite of the thick walls, the silence was broken by the cries of one or other of the "prophets" haranguing the crowd. From one man's strident sermon, they made out a certain number of words—*promises, lightning, great uprising, savior, ice, fire*—being screamed now in Aramaic, now in Hebrew, now in Greek.

Joseph sighed. "There's someone who wants to show how learned he is! They must like it."

As if in answer, there was a sudden clamor outside: two or three hundred voices shouting the words of a psalm of David.

O God, look at the face of your Messiah
One single day in your courts is worth more than a thousand
*   elsewhere*
My God, I have chosen to remain on the threshold of Your house. . . .

Immediately, the prophet resumed his resonant diatribe.

"If the Lord hasn't made him a true prophet," Joseph said, amused, "at least he's given him a voice that could announce good news in the desert."

"Brother Geouel won't feel any happier when he hears him," Miriam remarked, half smiling.

"Geouel is a proud and presumptuous man," Joseph muttered.

Miriam nodded. "If he were humbler, he'd know that those he despises, the women and the weak, are like the people shouting out there. Only our cries make less noise. In my opinion, those people are as much to be pitied as this old woman before us. They're suffering as much as she is. Their pain comes from not knowing where life is leading them. Not understanding why they're here. They see themselves walking without any aim in the days to come, expecting the earth to open beneath their feet and drag them down into the abyss. I feel sad to hear them shouting themselves hoarse like that. They're so afraid that God will turn his face from them that it drives them mad. They no longer feel his hand guiding them to joy and goodness."

Joseph stared at her intensely, completely stunned. Ruth, who was standing some distance from them, also looked at Miriam as if the words she had just uttered were totally extraordinary.

With a gesture he often made when he felt embarrassed or puzzled, Joseph passed his hand over his bald cranium. "I understand you, but I don't share your feeling, any more than I feel the fear of those who are outside. An Essene, if he conducts himself with justice and purity, and for the good of mankind, knows where life will lead him: to Yahweh. Isn't that the meaning of our prayers, the reason why we choose poverty and communal life in this house?"

Miriam looked him in the eyes. "I'm not an Essene, and I can't be one, since I am a woman. I'm like those people: waiting impatiently for God to spare us those misfortunes tomorrow which overwhelm us today. It's my only hope. And this better future mustn't be only for a handful of us. It must be for all people in the world."

Joseph did not reply. He gave the old woman something to drink, and then Miriam and Ruth washed her face.

The next day, when Joseph came back to examine the old woman, the commotion was still at its height outside. It was slightly different, though, as a new "prophet" had arrived during the night. This one, who had come with about twenty of his followers, spoke of the joy of martyrdom and expressed hatred for the human body, which was weak and corruptible. Since dawn, his followers had been taking turns to whip themselves until the blood ran, chanting their praises of Yahweh and their contempt for life.

When Joseph entered the bedchamber where the old woman lay, Miriam and Ruth saw that his face, usually so serene and welcoming, was as closed and hard as a stone. He said nothing until the sound of weeping and strident cries from outside made him shudder.

"Those who claim to be prophets are more arrogant than us Essenes, more arrogant even than Geouel himself," he muttered. "They think they can reach God by getting themselves all burned up in the desert. They spend months standing on columns, eating nothing but dust and drinking very little, until their skin is as tough as old leather. They're drunk on their own supposed virtue. By claiming to love God, they question his will to make us creatures in his image. And the reason they scream and whip themselves to hasten the coming of the Messiah is that they hope the Messiah will free us of our bodies, which are open to temptation. What an aberration! They forget that the Almighty wants us to be healthy, happy men and women, not cankered worms at the mercy of demons."

Joseph's voice, full of suppressed anger, echoed in the silence. Miriam looked at him and gave him a smile he found astonishing.

"If there are men who hate human beings to that extent, then God must make them a sign. He is responsible for them. And if he wants us to be happy men and women, as you say, then he mustn't send us strange messengers we can't recognize. His envoy must be a man who resembles both us and him. A son of man who would share our fate

and help us in our weakness. He would bring love, a love like yours, ·
Joseph, you who give life back to the old and the infirm of body and
say that the harmony of words and deeds creates good health."

Joseph raised his eyebrows. His anger subsided all at once, and
he calmed down. "Well," he said, "you certainly didn't waste your
time with Rachel! You've become quite a thinker." Then, realizing
that this was not quite the compliment Miriam had expected, he
added, in a conciliatory tone, "You may be right. The man you describe would be the finest of all kings of Israel. Alas, Herod is still
our king. And where would your king come from?"

I T was seven days later. The uproar around Beth Zabdai had not
subsided. The rumor of a miraculous resurrection had spread well beyond Damascus. From dawn to dusk, more sick people arrived to join
those who came daily to hear the sermons of the so-called prophets.

The Essene brothers feared that the crowd, inflamed to the point
of madness by the promises of miraculous cures, would overrun the
house. They barricaded the door, and ten of the brothers took turns
in mounting guard. Unable to go out into the fields, refusing admission to anyone, the community was soon forced to ration its food. It
was like being under siege.

Alas, these measures succeeding only in exciting the false prophets
even more, who took them as an excuse to deliver a mysterious and
threatening message from God. The agitation did not die down—
quite the contrary, in fact.

One stormy day, a large wagon made its way through the crowd
and stopped outside the door.

The coachman got down and knocked on the door, demanding to
be admitted. As had become their custom during this difficult time,
the brothers guarding the door paid no attention to his appeals. For a
good hour, he shouted himself hoarse, but to no avail. The cries of
the young girl who was with him had no greater success.

But the next day, before dawn prayers, and as an icy rain fell on the village, the voice of Rekab, Rachel's coachman, somehow penetrated the courtyard and reached the ears of Ruth, who, as luck would have it, was just then on her way to draw water. Putting down her wooden pails, she ran to tell Miriam.

"The man who brought you here is outside the door!"

Miriam looked at her, uncomprehending.

"The man with the wagon!" Ruth went on, in an urgent voice. "The man who brought you with poor Obadiah . . ."

"Rekab? Here?"

"He's calling your name desperately from the other side of the wall."

"We must let him in at once."

"How can we? The brothers certainly won't open the door to him. If only we could get out of the house. . . ."

But Miriam was already running into the main courtyard. She made such a commotion in front of the brothers guarding the door that Geouel appeared. He refused point-blank to open the door.

"You don't know what you're saying, girl! Open the door a little way and all those mad people will come flooding in!"

The dispute became so heated that one of the brothers ran to fetch Joseph.

"Rekab is outside!" was all Miriam said by way of explanation.

Joseph understood immediately. "There must be a reason he's here. We can't leave him out in the rain and cold."

"There are hundreds out there in the cold and rain, and it doesn't seem to discourage them!" Geouel said sourly. "The sick even seem to thrive on it, as far as I can see. Perhaps that's the real miracle!"

"That's enough, Geouel!" Joseph roared with unaccustomed vehemence.

Startled by this outburst, the brothers stood there, numb with cold, and looked at Joseph and Geouel, who were like two wild beasts ready to tear each other to pieces.

"We're trapped here like rats," Joseph went on in a cutting tone. "That's not the vocation of this house. This closure has no purpose. Or, if it has, it's a bad one. Haven't we gathered in a community in order to find the way of goodness and assuage the suffering of this world? Are we not healers?"

His cheeks were quivering with rage, and his face was red all the way to the top of his bald cranium. Before Geouel or anyone else could retort, he pointed his index finger at the brothers guarding the door and commanded, in a tone that brooked no reply, "Open the door! Open it wide!"

As soon as the hinges creaked, the commotion on the other side ceased. There was a moment of stunned silence. Their feet in the mud, their faces hollow with weariness, all the people who had been waiting outside for days froze, like a collection of clay statues, streaming with rain and with stunned expressions on their faces.

Then a cry burst out, the first of many. In an instant, the chaos was overwhelming. Men, women, children, old and young, sick and healthy, rushed into the courtyard to kneel at the feet of Joseph of Arimathea.

Miriam then saw Rekab, standing in the wagon, firmly holding the reins of the terrified mules. She immediately recognized the figure beside him.

"Mariamne!"

"Your hair!" Mariamne cried. "Why did you cut it?"

Rekab, his eyes bright, looked at Miriam with emotion and astonishment, while, behind them, Joseph and the brothers tried to calm the crowd, assuring them over and over that the treatments would be resumed.

"How thin you are!" Mariamne said in surprise, hugging Miriam to her. "I can feel your bones through the tunic . . . What's happening here? Don't they feed you?"

Miriam laughed. She quickly drew them both into the women's courtyard, where Ruth was waiting, with a frown on her face and her fists on her hips. She made a sign to Rekab to come into the handmaids' kitchen and have something to eat.

"Take advantage before these madmen steal all our reserves," she said, grouchily.

In the main courtyard, the crowd had not yet calmed down. The brothers relayed Geouel's orders for them to be patient and orderly.

"The real miracle would be if God could put a bit of common sense in the brains of all these men," Ruth snorted. "But that's probably a bit of a tall order. The Lord's been putting it off since the days of Adam!"

She abruptly turned on her heels and went inside the house. Taken aback, Rekab turned to Miriam. She signaled to him to follow Ruth and not take any notice of her moods.

"You should eat and drink something, too," Miriam said to Mariámne. "And change your tunic, if you've spent all night in the rain. Come and warm yourself. . . ."

Mariamne followed her, but accepted only a bowl of hot broth.

"The wagon's so comfortable, you forget the cold and rain. And my tunic's made of wool. What I want to know is why you cut your hair so horribly, and what's going on in this house. Where have all these people come from who are out there with Joseph? Did you notice he didn't even seem to recognize me? Even though he came all those times to Magdala. . . ."

"Don't be upset with him. He'll see you this evening."

In a few words, Miriam told Mariamne how the Essene brothers lived, how they treated the sick, and how the survival of the old woman, which had happened quite recently, had been taken as a miracle, attracting a crowd of the desperate to Beth Zabdai.

"These poor people think Joseph possesses the gift of resurrection. Just thinking it is enough to make them lose their minds."

Mariamne had regained her mocking smile. "Which is quite

strange and contradictory, when you think about it," she said. "None of them like the life they lead, and yet they all hope that thanks to the miracle of resurrection, they'll live forever."

"You're wrong," Miriam said confidently. "What they hope for is a sign from God. The assurance that the Almighty is with them. And that he'll still be with them after they die. Aren't we all like that? Alas, Joseph doesn't possess the gift of resurrection. He wasn't able to save Obadiah."

Mariamne nodded. "I know he's dead. Rekab told us when he got back."

There were many other questions that Mariamne was burning to ask, but did not dare. Miriam did not yield to her friend's silent requests.

Rekab must have mentioned the state she had been in and the care Joseph of Arimathea had taken to keep her in sound mind. But she did not want to talk to Mariamne about that. Not yet. Mariamne and she had not spoken in months. Many things had happened that had made them rather like strangers to one another, as witness this short hair that so shocked Mariamne.

But Miriam did not want to hurt her young friend. "You're more beautiful than ever. It's as if the Almighty granted you all the beauty he could gather together in one woman!"

Mariamne blushed. She clasped Miriam's hands and kissed her fingers: a tender gesture she had so often made in Magdala. Here, in the house in Beth Zabdai, Miriam thought it excessive. But she did not say anything. She had to get used once again to Mariamne's carefree enthusiasm.

"I missed you!" Mariamne said. "A lot, a lot! I thought about you every day. I was worried. But my mother wouldn't let me come here. You know how she is. She told me you were being taught how to heal by Joseph of Arimathea and weren't to be disturbed."

"Rachel's always right. That is what I've been doing."

"Of course she's always right. That's what's so annoying. She told me I'd love learning Greek. And now guess what? I speak better than her. And I really enjoy it!"

They both laughed. Then Mariamne suddenly broke off. She hesitated for a moment, glanced toward the kitchen, where Rekab and Ruth were watching them, and looked at Miriam again.

"The reason my mother let me come here now was to bring you some bad news."

From the folds of the tunic, she took a small cylindrical leather case, the kind used for carrying letters, and handed it to Miriam.

"It's about your father."

H E R stomach in knots, Miriam took the scroll from its case. The long sheet, thicker in one half than in the other because of the irregularity of the fibers, was almost entirely covered with a tangled mass of writing, the brown ink smudged in places, where it had been absorbed by the papyrus.

Miriam recognized her father's plain handwriting. At least, she thought with relief, whatever had happened, he was still alive.

She had to make an effort to decipher the words. But it did not take her long to know. Hannah, her mother, had been killed by a mercenary.

Since leaving Nazareth, Joachim wrote, they had been living in peace in the north of Judea, where they had taken refuge with his cousin, the priest Zechariah, and his wife, Elisheba. With the passing of time, their yearning to see the mountains of Galilee again had grown ever more insistent. Besides, Joachim admitted, he was missing his workshop, missing the smell of wood and the noise of gouge and mallet on cedar and oak. In Judea, where the houses had flat roofs of cob and sunbaked bricks, a carpenter's skills were useless.

So, thinking that it was time to forget the past, and accompanied by Zechariah and Elisheba, who were also eager for a change,

Hannah and he had set off for Nazareth before the worst of the winter made the roads impassable.

The first week of the journey had passed happily. As they approached Mount Tabor, their joy grew. Even Hannah, who was always so ready to fear the worst, had a smile on her lips and a carefree feeling in her soul.

It had happened as they were nearing Nazareth.

Why had the Lord felt the need to strike at them yet again? For what sin was he constantly punishing them?

They had come across a column of mercenaries. Joachim had hidden his face, and the mercenaries had not paid him any particular attention. In any case, his beard was so long now that he was certain no one would recognize him, not even a friend. But as always, Herod's soldiers could not let the opportunity pass. They had decided to search the wagon. As usual, they did it in the roughest and most humiliating way possible. Hannah had panicked. In her ridiculous and unfortunate haste to be compliant, she had accidentally knocked over a jar of water. It had hit an officer's leg, nearly breaking his foot. Miriam could picture what had followed: the angry reaction, the sword plunged into Hannah's frail chest.

And that was it.

Except that Hannah had not died immediately. She was still in agony when they reached first Nazareth, then Yossef's house. It had taken her one long night before she joined the Almighty, a night spent in pain and anguish, without a moment's respite—just like the rest of her life.

Perhaps, Joachim wrote, rather bitterly, perhaps Joseph of Arimathea might have been able to treat the wound and save his faithful Hannah.

But Joseph is a long way from here, and so are you, my beloved daughter. For a long time I made an effort to be satisfied with the thought of you to fill your absence. Today I would like you near me. I miss your presence, your spirit and all the new blood that has flowed into you, which makes me hope for a less somber future. You are the one good thing I still have left in this world.

"I'LL take you to Nazareth as soon as you like," Rekab the coachman said. "My mistress Rachel has ordered me to serve you for as long as you wish."

"And I'll go with you," Mariamne said. "I'm not leaving you."

Miriam responded to both with silence. It was as if an icy wind had penetrated her chest. She was suffering for the pain endured by her mother before dying, but she was suffering even more for her father, whose words echoed within her.

At last she said, "Yes, we have to leave as soon as possible."

"We could do it today," Rekab said. "It's a long time to nightfall. But perhaps it's best if the mules can rest until tomorrow. It's a long way to Nazareth. At least five days."

"Tomorrow at dawn, then."

That was what she announced to Joseph of Arimathea when he finally got away from the crowd, which had been monopolizing his attention. He was exhausted, his mouth was dry from having talked too much, and he had rings around his eyes. But when Miriam told him about Joachim's letter, he put his hand on her shoulder, in a gesture filled with tenderness.

"We are mortal. It is as Yahweh wished. So that we can live a true life."

"My mother died at the hands of two men. Herod, and a mercenary paid to kill. How can Yahweh allow such a thing? Is it he who wishes us to be humiliated? Prayer isn't enough. We need to shatter the air around us, the air we breathe."

Wearily, Joseph passed his hand over his face, rubbed his eyes, and said, "Don't give in to anger. It doesn't lead anywhere."

"I'm not angry," Miriam replied firmly. "But I know now that patience is not the sister of wisdom. Not anymore."

"War won't help us, either," Joseph said. "You know that."

"Who said anything about war?"

Joseph looked at her without a word, waiting for her to say more. She merely smiled. Seeing him like that, weighed down with fatigue, she felt remorse. She leaned toward him and kissed his cheek with an unaccustomed tenderness that made him quiver.

"I owe you more than I could ever repay," she murmured. "And I'm abandoning you just when you need me to deal with all these people who'll be coming to see you."

"No, please don't think you owe me anything," Joseph said, fervently. "What I've been able to give you, you've already given back without even realizing it. And it's best if you leave. We both know this house is not for you. We'll meet again soon, I have no doubt of that."

THAT evening, when the lamps were already lit, Ruth came to see Miriam. "I've been thinking," she said in a firm voice. "If you'll have me, I'd like to go with you. Who knows? I could be useful to you in that Galilee of yours."

"You'll be welcome in Galilee. I have a friend who'll need you. Her name is Halva, and she's the best of women. She's not in terribly good health, and she already has five children clinging to her tunic. She may even have another one by now. Your help will a great relief to her, especially if I have to stay with my father, who's alone now."

The next day, in the gray and still rainy dawn, Rekab had the wagon brought out of the house. The crowd, calmer now, stood aside. For the first time in weeks, people were waiting patiently, and paid little attention to yet another prophet announcing that soon the fields would turn to ice, then into a fire writhing with tongues of poison.

Joseph walked with Miriam to Obadiah's grave. She was anxious to bid him farewell before joining Ruth and Mariamne. She knelt in the mud. Joseph, who had been expecting to hear her pray, was surprised to see her lips moving without any sound emerging. When he helped her back on her feet, she said, with a contentment she could not conceal, "Obadiah still talks to me. He comes to me and I see him. It's like a dream, but I'm not asleep and my eyes are wide open."

"And what does he say to you?" Joseph asked, without hiding his unease.

Miriam blushed. "That he hasn't abandoned me. That he'll go wherever I go, and that he's still my little husband."

CHAPTER 16

THEY were within sight of the roofs of Nazareth. It was two days to the beginning of the month of Nisan. The sky was suffused with that beautiful light that heralded spring and helped you to forget the harshness of winter. Since they had left Sepphoris, the sunlight had danced between the clusters of cedar and larch, and, as they approached Nazareth, the shade was deep beneath the hedges lining the path. To Ruth and Mariamne, who had never before seen these hills, Miriam pointed out the paths and fields that had been the scene of her childhood joys. She was so impatient to see her father, Halva, and Yossef again that the thought of her mother receded.

When they were within sight of Yossef's house, she could no longer contain herself. The weary mules were pulling the wagon too slowly. She jumped down onto the path and rushed toward the big, shaded yard.

Joachim, who had obviously been watching for her arrival, was the first to appear. He opened his arms to her, and they embraced, tears in their eyes, lips quivering, joy and sadness intermingled.

"You're here . . . you're here . . . ," Joachim kept repeating.

Miriam stroked his cheek and the back of his neck. She noticed that his face was more deeply furrowed with lines and his hair was whiter. "I came as soon as I got your letter!"

"But your hair! What have you done to your beautiful hair? What happened on the journey? It's such a long way, for a girl. . . ."

She pointed to the wagon coming into the yard. "Oh, don't worry. I didn't make the journey alone."

There was a moment of confusion when, as she was introducing him to Rekab, Mariamne, and Ruth, a middle-aged couple came out of Yossef's house.

The man had the kind of long beard worn by priests and intense, somewhat staring eyes, and the woman was about forty, short, plump, and amiable. She was hugging a baby, only a few days old, to her breast. A whole cluster of little faces peered out from the shadows behind her. Miriam recognized Halva's children: Yakov, Yossef, Shimon, Libna, and her little sister.

She called to them and held out her arms. But only Libna approached, smiling timidly. Miriam caught her and lifted her up. "Don't you recognize me?" she asked the others. "It's me, Miriam."

Before the children could reply, Joachim, still overcome with the emotion of this reunion, pointed to the plump woman and the priest, and said, a trifle abruptly, "This is my cousin Zechariah. Your poor mother, God rest her soul, and I stayed in his house. And this is his wife, Elisheba, holding Yossef's new baby, Yehuda, may the Lord protect him. . . ."

Miriam laughed. "So that's it! Frail as she is, Halva couldn't stop herself from having another child. But where is she? Still in bed? And Yossef?"

There was a brief silence. Joseph opened his mouth, but he was unable to utter a word. Zechariah, the priest, looked at his wife, who was fervently kissing the sleeping baby's forehead.

"Well, what's going on?" Miriam insisted, less confidently now. "Where are they?"

"I'm here."

Yossef's voice, coming from the workshop behind her, surprised her. She turned quickly, let out a cry of joy, put Libna down, and opened her arms for him to come to her. He walked toward her, passing Ruth and Mariamne without paying any attention to them. That was when Miriam saw that his eyes were red, and she felt a tightness in her chest.

"Yossef . . . Where's Halva?" she stammered, already half knowing the answer.

Yossef swayed as he took the last steps. He gripped Miriam by the shoulders and held her to him to stifle the sobs that shook his chest.

"Yossef . . . ," Miriam said again.

"She died giving birth to the baby."

"Oh no!"

"Seven days ago."

"No! No! No!"

Miriam's cries were so intense that they all bowed their heads, as if they had been hit.

"She was so happy when she knew you were coming," Yossef said, shaking his head. "Lord Almighty, how excited she was! She kept repeating your name at every opportunity. 'Miriam's like a sister to me . . . I miss Miriam . . . At last Miriam's coming back.' And then . . ."

"No!" Miriam cried, stepping back, face raised to heaven. "Oh, God, no! Why Halva? Why my mother? You can't do that." She waved her fists and struck her stomach as if to rip out the pain that was gripping it. Then, suddenly, she beat Yossef on the chest. "And you!" she cried. "Why did you make her bear another child? You knew she wasn't strong enough! You knew!"

Yossef did not even try to dodge the blows. He nodded, tears rolling down his cheeks. Mariamne and Ruth both rushed to pull Miriam off him, and Zechariah and Joachim grabbed Yossef by the arms.

"Come, girl, that's enough!" Zechariah said, shocked.

"She's right," Yossef said. "She's only saying the same things I keep telling myself."

Elisheba had moved back to protect the children from Miriam's rage. The baby had woken in her arms. "No one's to blame," she said, with a touch of reproach in her voice. "You know women always pay more than their due. It's God's will!"

"No!" Miriam cried, pulling herself free from Ruth's grip. "It shouldn't be that way! We shouldn't accept a single death, especially not the death of a woman giving life!"

This time, the baby started crying. Elisheba, cradling him to her breast, went and took refuge on the steps of the house. Libna and Shimon were crying and clutching her tunic. Yakov, the eldest, held the young ones firmly by the hand and looked wide-eyed at Miriam. Shaken by choking sobs, Yossef crouched, his head between his arms.

Zechariah placed a hand on his shoulder and turned to Miriam. "Your words are meaningless, girl," he said, making no attempt to conceal the reproach in his voice. "Yahweh knows what he's doing. He judges, he gives, he takes away. He is the Almighty, Creator of all things. All we can do is obey."

Miriam seemed not to hear him. "Where is she? Where is Halva?"

"Beside your mother," Joachim said in a low voice. "Almost in the same plot."

WHEN Miriam rushed to the graveyard in Nazareth, no one made any move to follow her. His face drawn with grief, Yossef watched her go until she was swallowed up in the shadows along the path, then, without a word, went and shut himself up in his workshop. At the same time, Elisheba pushed the children inside the house, trying to calm little Yehuda.

At last, Joachim could contain himself no longer. He followed his daughter at a distance, and the others went with him. But at the entrance to the graveyard, Ruth gripped Mariamne's wrist to hold her back. Rekab came to a halt behind them. Zechariah was advancing determinedly behind Joachim. But they, too, stopped dead a dozen paces from the loose earth that covered Hannah and Halva.

Miriam remained in the graveyard until twilight. According to tradition, anyone who visited a grave was supposed to place a small white stone on it as a mark of his visit. Miriam, though, took dozens of stones from the sack placed for that purpose a few paces away and covered the grave with them until it was a blinding white in the winter sun. When she had none left, she went back to the sack and started over again.

Zechariah tried to protest, but Joachim silenced him with a glance. Zechariah shook his head and sighed.

During all this time, Miriam kept speaking, or rather, her lips kept moving, although no one could hear a word. Later, Ruth told them that Miriam was not really saying anything. She had done the same over Obadiah's grave in Beth Zabdai, she said.

"It's her way of conversing with the dead. We others aren't capable." Casting a glance at Zechariah, who was rolling his eyes with disgust, she added, a little testily, "In Beth Zabdai, Master Joseph of Arimathea never expressed any surprise and never reproached her. Nor did he ever say she was mad. And when it comes to madness, you wouldn't believe the things he's seen! If there's anyone who knows about sickness, of the mind as well as the body, it's him! And I can tell you this, too: If there's a woman he admires and considers the equal of a man, young as she is, it's Miriam. He said it often enough to the brothers, who were as surprised as you are, Zechariah: She's different than the others, he'd say, and we mustn't expect her to behave like everyone else."

"She's right to rebel against so many deaths," Mariamne said softly. "Since Obadiah died, she's done a lot of mourning! So have all of you. I wish I could say something to tell you all how sorry I am."

But to their surprise, when Miriam returned to Yossef's house that evening, she appeared to have calmed down. "I asked Mother to forgive me for all the pain I caused her," she said to Joachim. "I know she missed me and would have liked me to be with her. I told her why I hadn't been able to give her that joy. Perhaps where she is, under the eternal wing of the Almighty, she'll understand."

"You have nothing to blame yourself for," Joachim said, his eyes bright with emotion. "None of this is your fault; it's all mine. If I'd been able to control myself, if I hadn't gone mad, killed a mercenary and wounded a tax collector, your mother would be here now, alive and well, and our life would be quite different."

Miriam stroked his beard and kissed him. "If I have nothing to blame myself for, then you are even purer than me," she said tenderly. "You have always acted in the name of justice. That day was no different than any other day of your life."

They all bowed their heads again when they heard these words. This time it was not Miriam's anger that impressed them, but her confidence. Even Zechariah made no objection and bowed his head. But they would have been hard put to explain where she got this newfound strength from.

THAT evening, immediately after kissing her father good night, Miriam went to see Yossef in the workshop. He looked frightened when she appeared in the doorway.

She walked up to him, took his hands, and bowed. "Please forgive me. I'm sorry about what I said earlier. I was unfair. I know how much Halva loved being your wife and how much she liked having children."

Yossef shook his head, unable to make a single sound.

Miriam smiled gently. "My master, Joseph of Arimathea, often reproached me for these fits of anger. He was right."

The lightness of her tone calmed Yossef. He got his breath back and wiped his eyes with a cloth that was lying on the workbench.

"You didn't say anything that was untrue. We both knew that another birth could kill her. Why couldn't we have abstained?"

Miriam's smile widened. "For the best of reasons, Yossef. Because you loved each other. And because that love had to create a life as beautiful and good as itself."

Yossef looked at her with a mixture of gratitude and surprise, as if this idea had never crossed his mind.

"When I stood over Halva's grave," Miriam went on, "I promised her I wouldn't abandon her children. Starting today, if you want me to, I'll take care of them as if they were my own."

"No, that's not a good decision! You're young, you'll be starting a family of your own soon."

"Don't speak for me. I know what I'm saying and what I'm committing myself to."

"No," Yossef said again. "You don't realize. Four sons and two daughters! That's a lot of work! You're not used to it. It cost Halva her health. I don't want you to ruin yours."

"Nonsense! Do you think you can manage on your own?"

"Elisheba is helping me."

"She's not a young woman. She won't be able to do it for much longer. And she was never Halva's friend."

"One day, when the time is right, I'll find a widow in Nazareth."

"If it's a wife you want, that's another matter," Miriam said, a little curtly. "But in the meantime, let me help you. I'm not alone: I have Ruth with me. She can do the work of two. I even told her we'd be helping Halva before we came here."

This time, Yossef agreed. "Yes," he said, closing his eyes shyly, "she would have liked you to take care of the children."

When she learned about it, Ruth approved Miriam's proposition unreservedly. "As long as you and Yossef want me, I'll help you."

Joachim seemed content, his mind at rest for the first time in days. He would work with Yossef in the workshop. Together, they would get enough work to feed this large family.

"This is life as Yahweh wills it," Zechariah said, sententiously. "He leads us between death and birth to make us more humble and more just."

But Joachim would not let him continue in this tone. Overjoyed at Miriam's decision, he said, "Zechariah has some good news to announce. His modesty prevented him from doing so during these days of mourning. So, I'll be the one to tell you: On the way to Nazareth, Elisheba discovered that she was pregnant. Who would have believed it?"

"I certainly wouldn't," Elisheba said pleasantly. "Yes, by the will of Yahweh, I am with child. May the Almighty be blessed a thousand times for this gift! At my age!"

Elisheba, who must have been twice the age of Mariamne and Miriam, looked radiant and unable to conceal her pride. The young girls looked at her in astonishment.

"You have good reason to be surprised. Who would have thought it possible?"

"Everything is possible if God extends his hand over us. Praise be to the Lord a thousand times!"

"Yes, everything's possible. I have been as sterile as a field of stones during all these years when a woman should be having children. . . ." She chuckled, and winked at Ruth. "And it all came to us in a dream."

"It's true," Zechariah said, with the greatest seriousness. "It was an angel from God who urged me to make this child. An angel who declared: 'It's the will of God, you will be a father.' I was full of pride, and protested that it was impossible. 'You're not so old, Zechariah. And your Elisheba is almost young compared with Abraham's Sarah. They were older than you two, much older.'"

"Actually, I made fun of his dream," Elisheba said. "I didn't believe it at all! 'Look at us, my poor old Zechariah,' I said. 'It was a nice dream, but now that your eyes are wide open, you're going to forget it.' I mean, how could I ever have imagined he was still capable of such a fine performance?"

Elisheba's laugher rang out loud and clear. Then she thought better of it, and peered at Yossef and Joachim to make sure they were not shocked by this irrepressible gaiety of hers.

But Joachim was encouraging. "You're right to be jolly. At sad times, an event like this gladdens the heart."

Elisheba stroked her belly as if it were already swollen.

Ruth, who had remained distant during all this excitement, asked dubiously, "Are you sure?"

"Shouldn't a woman know when she's expecting a child?"

"A woman can sometimes be wrong, and take her dreams for reality. Especially when it comes to things like that."

"I know what God has commanded me!" Zechariah said indignantly.

Miriam, gently intervening, put her hand on Ruth's shoulder. "Of course she's pregnant."

Ruth blushed in embarrassment. "I'm stupid, forgive me. I come from a place where people are often ill or mad. If you listen to them, heaven is overcrowded with angels, and the land of Israel is swarming with genuine prophets. It's probably made me a bit too suspicious about everything."

At any other time, Joachim and Yossef would have smiled at this.

LATER, Mariamne asked Miriam, "Do you want me to stay with you for a while? I don't know anything about children, but I can still make myself useful. I know my mother wouldn't refuse. We'll send Rekab back with a message for her. She'll understand."

"I don't need you to help with the children. But for the sake of my morale, and to be able to talk about things I can only talk about with you, yes, I would like you to stay. You have some books from Rachel's library with you. You can read them to me."

Mariamne blushed with pleasure. "Your friend Halva was like a sister to you. But we're like sisters too, aren't we? Even if we're not as alike as we used to be, now that your hair is short."

So it was that Yossef's house came back to life. The multitude of daily chores kept all of them busy, and distracted them from their grief. Zechariah and Elisheba's joy in their imminent parenthood helped to lighten the mood. It was like a new start, a convalescence.

After one moon, it was confirmed that Elisheba was indeed pregnant. She often went up to Miriam and said, "You know something? The child in my belly already loves you! I can feel him moving about whenever I'm close to you. It's as if he's clapping his hands."

This greatly irritated Ruth, who still found it hard to accept this miraculous birth. Elisheba's belly had hardly grown, she pointed out. For the moment, the child was probably nothing but a little ball no bigger than a fist.

"That's what I think too," Elisheba would reply with satisfaction. "A little fist that punches when I least expect it."

"Well," Ruth would sigh, raising her eyes to heaven, "if he's like this after one or two moons, what will he be like when he's standing upright?"

N O T long after this, Miriam got into the habit of leaving the house at dawn, before the children were up. In the half-light between night and day, she would take the descending path that led through the forest to Sepphoris and wander aimlessly.

By the time the sun started to appear, she would be back, and would cross the courtyard lost in thought.

Mariamne and Ruth noticed that she was becoming more and more silent, and even a little distant. It was only once the day's work was done that she listened to the others' chatter. Mariamne still read to Miriam while the children were taking their nap, but she gradually seemed to lose interest, even though it was something she herself had asked for.

One evening, as they were finishing the kneading of the dough for the next day's bread, Mariamne asked, "Don't you feel exhausted, always going out for a walk in the morning the way you do? You get up so early, you're going to tire yourself out."

Miriam smiled. The question seemed to amuse her. "No, I don't feel exhausted. But I can see you're intrigued. You'd really like to know why I go off like that almost every morning."

Mariamne blushed and lowered her eyes.

"Don't be embarrassed. It's quite normal to be curious."

"Yes, I am curious. Especially about you."

They cut the dough in silence and rolled it into balls. As they shaped the last one, Miriam stopped.

"When I'm out walking like that," she said in a low voice, "I feel Obadiah's presence. He's as close to me as if he were still alive. I need his visits the way I need to breathe and eat. Thanks to him, everything becomes lighter. Life isn't so painful anymore. . . ."

Mariamne stared at her in silence.

"Do you think I'm a little mad?"

"No."

"That's because you love me. Ruth also hates me to talk about Obadiah. She's convinced I'm going out of my mind. But because she loves me, she won't say it."

"No, I assure you. I don't think you're mad."

"Then how do you explain the fact that I still feel Obadiah's presence?"

"I can't explain it," Mariamne said, frankly. "I don't understand it. And what you don't understand you can't explain. But just because you don't understand something doesn't mean it doesn't exist. Isn't that what we learned in Magdala from reading those Greeks my mother likes so much?"

Miriam reached out her flour-stained hands and lightly touched Mariamne's cheek. "Do you see why I need you to stay with me? So that you can tell me such things, which calm me down. Because I do often wonder if I'm going mad."

"When Zechariah claimed he'd seen an angel, no one wondered if he was mad!" Mariamne protested. Then she added, mischievously, "But perhaps without that angel, no one would have believed he'd made a child with Elisheba."

"Mariamne!" In spite of her scolding tone, Miriam was amused.

Covering her mouth with her flour-whitened hands, Mariamne started to giggle, and this time her impish laughter set Miriam laughing too.

Ruth appeared in the doorway, with little Yehuda in her arms. "At last!" she exclaimed. "A little laughter in this house where even the children are serious! It's good to hear."

A FEW days later, as Miriam was out walking less than a mile from Nazareth, Barabbas suddenly appeared beneath a big sycamore.

The sun was barely up. Miriam recognized his slender body, his thick goatskin tunic, his hair. Nothing about him had changed. She would have picked him out among a thousand men. She slowed down and stopped some distance from him. In the uncertain light of dawn, she could barely make out his features.

He did not move. He must have seen her coming from a distance. Perhaps he had been intrigued by this woman with her short hair, and had not recognized her immediately.

Neither said a word. They stood looking at each other, at a distance of more than thirty paces, both unsure how to make the first move or what to say.

Suddenly, unable to sustain her gaze a moment longer, Barabbas turned away. He went around the sycamore, climbed over a small stone wall, and walked away. He had a pronounced limp and kept his hand flat on his left thigh to steady himself.

Miriam remembered the wound he had received on the shore of the Lake of Gennesaret. She remembered him in the boat, carrying Obadiah in his arms. She remembered their violent quarrel in the desert on the road to Damascus. She remembered him with his leg bleeding, screaming in rage against her and against everything, as the daylight revealed Obadiah's lifeless body.

That day, after she had abandoned him, Barabbas must have walked for hours with that bleeding wound before getting any care.

She had wiped these memories from her mind, as she had almost wiped Barabbas from her mind. Now she felt both compassion and remorse.

All the same, she was starting to feel sorry that she had met him again. She hated the fact that he had appeared to her, so close to Nazareth and to Yossef's house. Without knowing why, she was afraid that seeing him and talking to him would mean she would no longer have Obadiah's presence near her.

These thoughts were absurd, inexplicable. Just as inexplicable as the fact that she had been hearing Obadiah's voice whispering to her for months now. All the same, Mariamne was right. It didn't really matter if you understood. The soul saw what the eyes were unable to. And wasn't Barabbas one of those people who only wanted to see with their eyes?

She turned around and went back to the house much earlier than usual.

Toward midday, she went to Joachim and said, "Barabbas is here. I saw him this morning."

Joachim looked closely at her, but her face seemed expressionless. "I know," he said. "He was here some time ago. He helped me a lot after your mother died, may God rest her soul. He had to leave Nazareth for a while, but he was planning to return. He has some things to tell you."

Two days passed. Miriam avoided any mention of Barabbas. Neither Joachim nor Yossef spoke his name.

At dawn on the third day, he appeared to her as she was walking away from the house. He was standing on the path, waiting for her. This time, she understood from his bearing that he wanted to talk to her. She stopped a few paces from him and looked into his eyes.

The day had only just risen. The dim light made his face look hollow, without in any way altering the gentleness of his expression. He made an embarrassed gesture with his hand. "It's me," he said, awkwardly. "You should recognize me. I've changed less than you have."

She could not help smiling.

Encouraged by her smile, he went on, "It's not only your hair that's changed, it's the whole of you. That's obvious straightaway. I've been wanting to talk to you for a long time."

Still she said nothing, but she did nothing to discourage him either. In spite of everything she had thought about him, she was happy to see him, to know that he was alive, and he could see that in her face.

"I've changed too," he said. "I know now that you were right."

She nodded.

"You're not very talkative," he said anxiously. "Are you still angry with me?"

"No. I'm happy to see that you're alive."

He massaged his leg. "I've never forgotten him. Not a day goes by that I don't think of him. I was nearly crippled."

She slowly bowed her head. "That wound is there to remind you of Obadiah. He made sure that I don't spend a day without him either."

Barabbas frowned. He was about to ask her what she meant by that, but in the end he did not dare.

"I was sorry to hear about your mother," he said. "I suggested to Joachim that we should punish the mercenaries who killed her, but he refused."

"He was right."

Barabbas shrugged his shoulders. "It's true we can't kill them all. There's only one man we must have done with, and that's Herod. The others can find their way to hell all by themselves. . . ."

She neither objected nor agreed.

"I've changed," he said again, his voice harder now. "But I haven't forgotten that Israel still has to be freed. I'm still the same when it comes to that, and will be for as long as I live. I'll never change."

"I thought as much. That's good."

He seemed relieved at these words.

"We and the Zealots pulled off a few things together. Herod keeps putting up Roman eagles on the Temple and the synagogues, and we pull them down. Or when there are too many hungry people in a village, we plunder the legions' reserves. But we don't go in for big battles anymore! Which doesn't mean I've changed my mind. We really have to resolve what to do. Before Israel is entirely destroyed."

"I haven't forgotten anything either. But from Joseph of Arimathea I learned the power of life. Only life can generate life. We have to hold life in one hand and justice in the other. That's what will save us. It's more difficult than fighting with spears and swords, but it's the only way there will ever be justice in our land."

She spoke very calmly, in a low voice. In the rising light, Barabbas looked closely at her. Perhaps he was more impressed by her determination than he would have liked to admit.

They fell silent for a moment. Then Barabbas smiled broadly, and his teeth flashed. "I've also been thinking about life," he said in a rush, his voice quavering a little. "I've been to see Joachim and told him I want you as my wife."

Miriam gave a start of surprise.

"I've been thinking about it for a long time," Barabbas went on hurriedly. "I know we don't always see eye to eye. But no other woman in the world is your equal, and I don't want anyone else."

Miriam lowered her eyes, suddenly intimidated. "And what did my father say?"

Barabbas gave a tense little laugh. "That he consents. And that you should too."

She looked up, gave Barabbas the tenderest look that she could, and shook her head. "No, I can't."

Barabbas stiffened, then nervously rubbed his thigh. "You can't?" he whispered, barely knowing what he was saying.

"If I had to take a man as a husband, yes, it would be you. I've known that for a long time. Since the day I found you on the terrace of our house trying to get away from the mercenaries."

"Well, then?"

"I'll never be the wife of any man. That, too, I've known for a long time."

"Why? That's stupid. You can't say something like that. All women have husbands!"

"Not me, Barabbas."

"I don't understand what you're saying. It doesn't make any sense."

"Don't be angry. Don't think I don't love you. . . ."

"It's because of Obadiah! I knew it. You're still angry at me!"

"Barabbas!"

"You say you love life, you want justice! But you can't forgive. Do you think I've stopped grieving? I miss Obadiah as much as you do. . . . No, you still want revenge!"

"No! No, you're wrong. . . ."

He did not want to hear anything more. He turned his back on her and walked quickly away, anger and pain accentuating his limp. The sun had risen now over the hills. Barabbas was like a shadow fleeing from the light.

Miriam shook her head, a lump in her throat. She knew how angry and upset he must be feeling. And how humiliated. But how could it have been otherwise?

CHAPTER 17

"I DON'T understand. You don't want a husband? Why not?"

It had not taken long for Joachim to find out about Miriam's rejection of Barabbas. In spite of the rain teeming down on Galilee, Barabbas had come to him in the night, soaked to the skin and as pale as a corpse, and opened his heart to him.

Now, after prayers, everyone was sitting around the big table for the morning meal. It might have been better to wait for a more appropriate moment, but Joachim could not contain his anger. Pointing his wooden spoon at Miriam, he went on. "I don't understand you, any more than Barabbas does! If you don't like him, then say so. But don't tell me that you don't want a husband."

His voice shook and his eyes were wide with incomprehension.

"That's the way it is," Miriam replied, in a humble but firm tone. "I have other things to do in this world than be a man's wife."

Joachim struck the table with the palm of his hand. They all jumped. Yossef, Zechariah, Elisheba, Ruth—all of them avoided looking at him. It was the first time they had ever seen him angry at his beloved daughter.

But Miriam's words, her refusal, embarrassed them even more. Who was she to dare oppose her father's choice, whatever it might be?

Only Mariamne was prepared to leap to Miriam's defense. She was not surprised. How many times had her mother, Rachel, repeated that the aim of a woman's life didn't have to be to end up in the arms of a man?

"Solitude isn't a sin or a misfortune," Rachel would say. "On the contrary, it's when she's able to live alone that a woman can give the world what it lacks. That's what men deny by forcing her into the role of a wife. We must learn to be ourselves."

As if these very words had been spoken now, Joachim again hit the table, making the platters and the bread shake. "And if you're alone, without a husband, who will help you, who will provide for you and make sure you have a roof over your head when I'm not here anymore?"

Miriam looked at him sadly. She reached out her arm across the table and tried to take his hand. But he pulled it away, as if trying to put his heart and his anger out of reach of his daughter's tenderness.

"I know my decision hurts you, Father. But for the love of God, don't be so impatient to give me to a man. Don't be in a hurry to judge me. You know I want what's best, just as you do."

"Does that mean you'll change your mind?"

Miriam sustained his gaze, then shook her head without replying.

"So, what am I supposed to wait for?" Joachim growled. "The Messiah?"

Yossef put a hand on his friend's shoulder. "Don't let yourself be ruled by your anger, Joachim. You've always trusted Miriam. Why doubt her now? Can't you give her time to explain?"

"Oh, you think there's something to explain, do you? Barabbas is the best young man in the world. I know how much he cares for her. And he's felt this way for a long time."

"Oh, Joachim," Elisheba said, with an affectionate glance at Miriam. "Saying that Barabbas is the best young man in the world is a bit of an exaggeration. Don't forget he's a thief. I know what Miriam must be going through. Becoming the wife of a thief—"

Zechariah interrupted her. "A girl must marry the man her father has chosen for her. Otherwise, what would happen to the order of things?"

"If that's really the order of things," Mariamne cut in, in as peremptory a tone as Zechariah, "then there must be something wrong with it."

Miriam put her hand on Mariamne's wrist to silence her.

Joachim gave Elisheba a withering look and pointed to the slopes above Nazareth, where Barabbas might well be wandering at this moment, in spite of the rain that was transforming the paths into muddy streams. "This thief, as you call him, risked his life to save mine! Why did he do that? Because this girl, my daughter, asked him to. I still remember that. I don't have a short memory. My gratitude doesn't vanish in the gray light of dawn."

He turned to Miriam, and again pointed at her with his spoon.

"I, too, am sad about Obadiah's death," he said, his voice breaking. "I, too, will always remember the boy who took me down from the cross. But I tell you this, my girl: You've been wrong from the start in blaming Barabbas for his death. It was the mercenaries who killed him. The same people who killed your mother. No one else. Except that Obadiah was fighting. Because he was a brave boy. A fine death, if you want my opinion. For the freedom of Israel, for us! I wish I could die like him. There was a time when you would have said the same, Miriam."

He paused for breath, and once again brought his fist down on the table.

"And I tell all of you this, once and for all," he went on, head held high, a severe look in his eyes. "I don't want anyone to call Barabbas a thief in front of me! Call him a rebel, a fighter, a resister, whatever you like, but not a thief. He's head and shoulders above most of us. He has the courage to do what other people don't dare, and he's loyal to those he loves. And when he asks me for my daughter, I'm proud to say yes. No one else deserves her, only this thief."

This powerful speech was followed by a glacial silence.

Miriam, who had not taken her eyes off Joachim, nodded. "What you say is right, Father. Please don't think my refusal is due to resentment. I know that Obadiah, wherever he is, loves Barabbas, just as Barabbas loved him. I also think Barabbas is a courageous man, and he should be admired for that. I know as you do that beneath his fierce exterior he's a good, gentle, tender man. As I said to him, 'If I had to marry a man, it would be you.'"

"So do it!"

"I can't."

"You can't? Why not, damn it?"

"Because I am me, and that's how it is." Calmly, unhurriedly, confidently, she stood up, and said to her father, as gently as she could, "I, too, am a rebel; you've always known that. We won't achieve a better tomorrow through Herod's death and the slaughter of his mercenaries. We'll only achieve it through the light of life, through a love for mankind such as Barabbas will never be able to bring about."

She turned, left the table and, without another word, went inside the house to join the children, leaving everyone dumbfounded.

Ruth was the first to break the embarrassing silence that had settled over them. "I haven't known your daughter for very long," she said to Joachim. "But what I do know of her, from having seen her at Beth Zabdai, is that she never yields. Whatever it costs her. Even Master Joseph of Arimathea had to admit it. But make no mistake: She loves and respects you as much as a girl can love her father."

Overcome with emotion, Joachim nodded his head.

"If you're worried about it," Yossef said suddenly, "Miriam will always have a roof here. You have my promise, Joachim."

Joachim stiffened, and his eyes narrowed suspiciously. "You'd let her stay with you, even if she wasn't your wife?"

Yossef blushed to the roots of his hair. "I think you understand what I'm saying. This is Miriam's home. She knows that."

For the next few days, not only did Joachim's mood not improve, but it also infected everyone. Mealtimes passed in heavy silence. Joachim tried as far as possible to avoid Miriam, and he was distant toward Yossef while they worked together.

Yossef did not take offense at this. The depression into which he had fallen after Halva's death seemed to have lifted, to be replaced by a serenity, a peace that was not shared by the others.

Barabbas did not reappear. No one dared ask Joachim if he was still in the vicinity.

Then time did its work. Spring arrived, and the fields and groves burst into bloom. The children were the first to respond by leaving the house and running into the countryside to play.

There was a more forgiving expression now in Joachim's eyes. More than once, he was heard joking with Yossef in the workshop. One day, at the end of a meal, he took Miriam's hand. The others looked at each other and smiled with relief. Joachim kept Miriam's hand in his while Ruth and Mariamne recounted, with much laughter, how young Yakov had started acting the prophet to his brothers and sister.

Ruth found this very amusing. "Your son has a real aptitude for it," she said to Yossef. "He was better than all those people in Beth Zabdai. I wonder where he got it from."

"A man was holding forth in the synagogue when I went there with Yakov the other day," Zechariah said, only half laughing. "Yakov liked it a lot. You joke about it, woman, but he may have an aptitude."

Ruth gave a sardonic chuckle and glanced at Miriam. She and her father, still holding hands, both laughed.

On another occasion, Elisheba took their hands and joined them on her belly. She still loved getting other people to feel the child inside her. "This boy moves as soon as he senses Miriam's hand," she said. "Don't you feel it?"

Joachim laughed. "He runs about just as much when other people put their hands on your belly. All babies do that."

"He's different. He's telling me something. Perhaps the day is not far off"—and here she winked at Joachim—"when you, too, will become a grandfather. It'll happen, I'm sure of it."

Joachim raised Miriam's hand, then let go of it, and feigned a gloomy expression. "You're very clever if you can tell me what's in store for me, with a daughter like this one."

In his voice, though, there was obvious tenderness and even amusement.

M ARIAMNE was the only one to notice it: Although Joachim's bad mood had abated, Miriam remained distant. Her nights were restless, and full of dreams that she refused to talk about the following day. At other times, she would wake very early. No longer at the crack of dawn, as before, but well before anyone in the house had woken. Mariamne decided to keep an eye on her. She lay in the darkness, eyes wide open, listening to her slip out of their bedchamber and waiting for her to return. Because it was still so dark, she knew that dawn was a long way away.

The third time it happened, she said to her, "Isn't it dangerous to go out the way you do, in the middle of the night? You don't know who might be lurking out there. Or you could easily hurt yourself in the dark."

Miriam smiled and stroked Mariamne's cheek. "Go to sleep and don't worry about me. I'm in no danger."

That merely stoked Mariamne's curiosity. The next time it happened, she decided to follow her. But the moon was nothing but a thin sliver of silver, and the stars gave barely enough light to illu-

mine a single stone. By the time Mariamne got to the yard, she could
see only shadows, and none of them stirred. She stopped dead and
peered into the darkness, listening. She heard the crickets chirping,
and sensed an owl flying overhead, but that was all.

Anxious and disconcerted, she resolved to confide in Ruth.

Ruth took her time before replying. "It's Miriam, so what do you
expect? All the same, it's best if the others don't notice she spends
half the night outside. Keep all this to yourself."

Ruth waited until a moment when she was certain that she and
Miriam were out of earshot of the others, then said reproachfully,
"I hope you know what you're doing."

"What are you talking about?"

"The nights you spend away from your bed."

Miriam looked at her wide-eyed, then burst out laughing. "Not
whole nights. Only dawns."

"Dawn is when it starts to get light," Ruth snorted. "Not when
it's pitch dark. When you go out, no one can see a thing."

Miriam was still smiling, but the amusement had gone from her
eyes. "What is it you're thinking?"

"Nothing! Where you're concerned, I don't think anything at all.
But take my advice. Make sure your father, Elisheba, and Zechariah
don't find out about your escapades."

"No, Ruth! You must be imagining something."

Ruth went red with embarrassment and waved her hands. "I
don't want to know what's making you so strange lately and drawing
you outside like this, let alone imagine it. The best thing you can do
is take my advice."

Some time later, Miriam sat down next to Mariamne. "Don't
worry," she said. "Have no fear. Sleep all night, and don't try to spy
on me. There's no point. You'll know when you have to."

Mariamne was burning with curiosity. She was tempted to visit
Yossef's workshop in the middle of the night, but she resisted the
temptation. Although Miriam had not said it in so many words,

Mariamne knew that if she wanted to keep her friendship, she had better avoid letting her suspicions get the better of her. But sometimes, in the morning, she and Ruth exchanged knowing glances.

Almost an entire moon went by. And then, as they were entering the month of Sivan, the blow fell, as sudden as lightning.

MIRIAM came to see her father when he was alone and said, with a happy, confident look on her face, "I'm pregnant. A child is growing inside me."

Joachim's face went as white as a block of chalk.

"What Elisheba said was true," Miriam went on, gaily. "You're going to be a grandfather."

Joachim tried to stand, without success. "Who with?" he breathed.

Miriam shook her head. "Don't worry."

There was a curious rumbling in Joachim's chest. His lips curled, as if he were trying to chew the hairs of his beard. "That's enough. Answer me. Who with?"

"No, Father. I swear to you, may the Lord strike me down."

Joachim closed his eyes and struck his chest. When he opened his eyes again, the whites had turned red. "Is it Yossef?" he asked. "If it's Yossef, tell me. I'll talk to him."

"No one. That's how it is."

"If it's Barabbas, tell me."

"No, Father. It isn't Barabbas, either."

"If he took you by force and doesn't dare admit it, I'll kill him with my own hands, Barabbas or no Barabbas."

"Listen to me. It wasn't Barabbas, it wasn't anyone."

Joachim finally grasped what Miriam was saying, and her words chilled him. He let out a little groan, and for the first time looked at his daughter as if she were a stranger.

"You're lying."

"Why should I lie? We'll see this child born. We'll see him grow up. We'll see him become king of Israel."

"What are you talking about? That's not possible."

"Yes. It's possible. Because it's what I've wanted more than anything. Because I asked Yahweh, blessed be his name forever."

Again, Joachim closed his eyes. His hands were shaking. He touched his chest, then rubbed his face as if in doing so he could wipe away the words Miriam had spoken.

"It isn't possible," he said. "It's blasphemy. You're mad. Zechariah's angel is one thing, but this, no."

"But it is possible. You'll see."

His eyes still closed, Joachim shook his head vehemently.

"Why make yourself suffer when this is such good news?" Miriam asked, as calm as ever. "Isn't it something we all know—you and I, and Joseph of Arimathea, and a few others? It isn't death or hate that changes the face of the world. It's the life of men. The only things that will bring down Herod are life and love. The very things the Romans and the tyrants belittle."

Joachim waved his arms vigorously as if trying to dismiss Miriam's words the way a man chases away troublesome flies. "This is not about Herod and Israel!" he cried. "This is about my daughter, who's been defiled! Don't tell me it's good news."

"Father, I haven't been defiled. Believe me."

He looked at her now as if she were his enemy.

Miriam knelt before him and took his hands in hers. "Father, please try to understand. What can a woman do to free Israel from the Roman yoke, except give birth to its liberator? Remember the meeting Barabbas called to decide on the best time to start a rebellion? Even then, I talked about the Liberator. The man who will know no other authority than that of Yahweh, the Master of the Universe. The man who will revive his word and establish his law.

"I've thought a lot about it since then, Father. I've seen prophets.

All men tarnished by blood and lies. There wasn't a single one among them who talked about love. Yet our holy Torah says, *Love your neighbor as yourself.*

"All of you think women are only there to give birth. Give birth to submissive men or rebellious men. But what if one of them gave birth to the man we have all been waiting for all these years—all of us, you and I and all the people of Israel?

"To give birth to the Liberator. No one ever thought of that. But I did. And it's what I'm going to do. I told you it would be like this. So why worry, why torture yourself, why ask all these questions?"

Joachim's lips moved, tears clinging to his beard. "What have I done for the Almighty to keep striking me down?" he moaned. "What have I done that's so unforgivable?"

He looked down at Miriam's hands holding his and grimaced, as if at the sight of some disgusting animal. He pulled his hands free and got unsteadily to his feet, making a huge effort not to scream out the words crowding into his mouth.

I T took him half the day to gather his courage and go to confront Yossef. He looked closely at his friend's face, determined to study his reactions as he questioned him.

"Did you take my daughter?"

Yossef looked at him dumfounded, as if he had no idea what Joachim was talking about. "Your daughter?"

"I have only one. Miriam."

"What are you asking me, Joachim?"

"You know what I'm asking. Miriam says she is with child. She also says no man has touched her."

Yossef was speechless.

"It's impossible, of course," Joachim growled. "She's either mad or lying. Which it is depends on your answer."

Yossef did not seem to be angered by Joachim's insistence. But what his face expressed was a lot worse: the immense sadness and pain of a man betrayed by his friend's mistrust.

"If I wanted to take Miriam as my wife, I wouldn't have to hide. I'd come straight to you and ask your blessing."

"I'm not talking about taking her as a wife. I'm talking about sleeping with her and making a child."

"Joachim—"

"Damn it, Yossef! You're not saying the words I'm waiting for! I'm her father. You just have to say yes or no."

Yossef's face grew harder suddenly. His cheeks and temples turned gaunt, and his mouth narrowed. Joachim had never seen him like this before.

Yossef's hostile attitude shook Joachim. For a moment, he turned his eyes away. Then he asked, "So, do *you* believe she's pregnant?"

"If she says she is, I believe her. I believe what Miriam says and I always will, for as long as I live."

"What do you mean?"

"I think you know what I mean," Yossef said, withdrawing into an attitude of wounded pride.

Joachim passed his gnarled fingers over his face. "I don't!" he moaned. "I don't know! I don't know anything anymore."

Yossef did nothing to help him, but turned his back on him and busied himself tidying the tools left lying on the workbench.

Joachim walked up to him and seized him by the shoulder. "Don't be angry at me, Yossef. I had to ask you."

Yossef turned and looked him up and down with an expression that seemed to say that instead of asking, he should have trusted him.

"Yossef, Yossef!" Joachim cried, tears rolling down his cheeks. He put his arms around his friend. "Yossef, you're like a son to me. Everything I have now, I owe to you. If you wanted Miriam, I would give her to you in preference to Barabbas. . . ."

He broke off with a moan, moved away from Yossef, and looked at him. Yossef looked back, stone-faced.

"But now that she's pregnant," Joachim said, "that's not possible anymore, is it? For either of us."

"Listen to what your daughter is saying. Listen to her, instead of always suspecting her, which you've been doing ever since she came back."

It might have been Yossef's tone or his words, but Joachim's suspicions suddenly returned. "You're hiding something."

Yossef shrugged and was about to turn away, but he forced himself to sustain the look Joachim gave him through narrowed eyes. He blushed, as he often did at emotional moments. "I have nothing more to add. But I love Miriam, and I will do whatever she asks."

AFTER Miriam had announced her condition to them, Ruth wandered through the house, distraught, unable even to look after the children, who chose to go and play far from the cries and the joyless faces.

"Stop walking around and around like that," Mariamne finally muttered. "It's annoying."

Obediently, Ruth sat down, and stared into the distance.

"Come on," Mariamne grumbled. "Tell me what's on your mind."

"I said it. I said it would happen."

"What's 'it'?"

Ruth merely pouted in reply.

But Mariamne stood over her, eyes flashing. "I'll tell you what 'it' isn't," she said. "It isn't what's happening to Miriam! Don't you understand?"

"We know what's happening to her."

"Lord God Almighty! How stupid they all are! They don't want to hear! And you claim to be her loyal friend. It's disgraceful!"

"I *am* loyal to her. Just as loyal as you. Have you heard me utter a word of reproach? All I'm saying is that instead of admiring her, people are going to be pointing the finger at her. Am I supposed to rejoice?"

"Yes, precisely! You should forget your sorrow and rejoice at the good news."

"Stop saying it's good news!"

"Listen to what Miriam keeps saying. Not a man has touched her."

"Don't talk nonsense! I'm old enough, experienced enough, to know how a woman becomes pregnant. Why did she come out with that ridiculous story, that's what I keep wondering."

"If you loved her, you wouldn't wonder!" Mariamne cried, striking her own thigh in anger. "All you have to do is believe her. The son of light is coming, he is in her belly, and she is still pure."

"I can't believe her," Ruth said, also angry now. "I heard all sorts of crazy notions in Beth Zabdai. But the idea that a woman can make a child without opening her thighs and taking a man inside her—that's the most absurd thing I've ever heard in my life!"

"If that's the case, you don't deserve to stay with her."

THAT evening, Elisheba announced, in tears, "Zechariah has decided to stop speaking. He's so ashamed, he won't utter another word in this house."

"Then let him take his shame elsewhere!" Mariamne cried. And in response to the mournful looks that Elisheba and Ruth gave her, she pointed her finger at Elisheba's belly and added cruelly, "You've been telling everyone an angel came and announced to your Zechariah that he'd be a man again, even though a puff of wind could knock him over. And here you are, with child, even though you haven't given birth for more than twenty years! Why is that less of a miracle than what happened to Miriam?"

Unexpectedly, Elisheba nodded, although her tears still flowed. "Yes, I'd like to believe that. But Zechariah . . . Zechariah is a man. And a priest. And he's just as skeptical as Joachim. . . ."

The three women all fell silent, calmer now, and each lost in her own thoughts.

"Where is she?" Ruth breathed. "We haven't seen her since this morning."

"We won't see her again," Mariamne said, "as long as Joachim blames her for her condition every time she sets foot in the house."

B UT Joachim would not budge.

When Barabbas came to see him, he asked him the same questions he had asked Yossef.

Barabbas's first reaction was to say sourly, "Why should I take a girl who won't have anything to do with me?"

"That's exactly what happens sometimes. Disappointment causes anger, and anger makes us lose our heads."

"I haven't lost my head, and I've never been so short of women that I would lose it. The only fights I like are against the Romans and the mercenaries. What pleasure would I have in assaulting Miriam?"

Joachim knew he was telling the truth. The astonishment on his face said as much as his words.

Barabbas found the news just as hard to take as Joachim had. Both men wished they could wipe Miriam's words from their minds.

Suddenly, Barabbas said, "It's Yossef!"

"How do you know?"

"I feel it."

"He swore to me it wasn't him."

"What do you think that's worth? No one admits to something like that."

"Miriam swears on her mother's head that it was neither him nor you."

Barabbas dismissed Joachim's assurances with a gesture.

Joachim lowered his voice. "She also claims that no man has touched her. Why would she say such a thing?"

"She's ashamed, that's why. It's Yossef. I could see it coming. Halva's death stirred his blood, and he can't endure loneliness. He's been hovering around Miriam like a fly around an open fruit. He'd wash her feet with his tongue if he could."

"So why has Yossef never asked me for Miriam's hand? He could have. I wouldn't have refused him, any more than I refused you."

"He wants to, but he's afraid she'll refuse him. He's a sly one."

"That's ridiculous!" Joachim protested. "It's your jealousy speaking!"

"I have eyes and a brain, and I see what I see," Barabbas replied, unable to resign himself to being in such a powerless position, and blinded by what he could not understand. "When the child is born, you'll see I was right. It'll look like Yossef."

He was so insistent that Joachim started to have his doubts.

"Put the two of them face-to-face, Miriam and him," Barabbas said. "Then you'll see they're lying."

So it was that the next day Miriam appeared before them, as if before a court. Seven people had gathered in the main room, and were standing in front of the dining table: Joachim and Barabbas, Zechariah and Elisheba, Ruth, Mariamne, and Yossef.

Joachim had demanded her presence without even knowing where to find her. He had gone to the far end of the yard and had called out her name, without success. Mariamne had just declared that no one knew where she was, when young Yakov, the eldest of Yossef's children, had said, "I know where she is. We've been playing together all day. Right now, she's bathing in the river with Libna and Shimon."

He rushed off, and came back hand in hand with Miriam. As soon as they saw her face, they all felt ill at ease.

Never had she looked so beautiful, never had her eyes been so clear and so serene. Her copper-colored hair had grown again as far down as the back of her neck, and a few untidy curls were strewn across her cheeks.

She kissed Yakov on the forehead and sent him back to join the

other children. When she turned to them, she immediately understood what they wanted. She smiled at them. There was no trace of
mockery in this smile, only tenderness.

There was tenderness too in the first words she spoke. "So you
don't believe me."

They would have lowered their eyes if Barabbas had not retorted, "Even a child wouldn't believe you."

"I believe you!" Mariamne immediately protested.

"You'd say anything to defend her," Barabbas muttered.

"Don't argue over me," Miriam said in a firm voice. She came
and stood before Barabbas. "I know you're hurt, I know my refusal
to be your wife has been a blow to your heart and your pride. And I
also know that you love me as I love you. But I told you: I can't be
your wife. The decision is mine and the Almighty's."

"You keep contradicting yourself!" Barabbas cried. "How can
anyone believe you?"

Miriam smiled and put the tip of her fingers to his lips to silence
him. "Because that's how it is. If you love me, you'll believe me."

Ignoring Barabbas's protests, she turned to Joachim. "You also
doubt me, Father. And yet you love me more than all the people
here put together. You must accept things as they are. There is a
child in my belly. But I have not been defiled."

Joachim shook his head and sighed. The others did not dare
speak. A harder expression came into Miriam's. She took a few steps
back, her eyes fixed on Joachim, and suddenly grabbed the bottom
of her tunic with both hands and raised it to her knees.

"There is one proof, the simplest of all. Make sure that I'm still
a maiden."

Joachim opened his eyes wide and muttered something incom-
prehensible. By his side, Zechariah moaned. For the first time, Barabbas lowered his head.

"Do it," Miriam insisted, "and then your minds will be at rest.
I'm ready."

It was as if they had all been slapped in the face.

"Of course, you can't do it yourself," Miriam said, her voice glacial. "But Elisheba can. . . ."

"No, no!"

"Ruth, then."

Ruth turned away and took refuge at the far end of the room.

"It can't be Mariamne. Barabbas will say she's lying to protect me. Go to Nazareth and find a midwife. She'll certainly be able to tell you."

She stopped, and in the silence the buzzing of flies was like the distant rumble of a storm.

"There's no shame in it, since you all doubt me."

Joachim moved back, leaning on Zechariah's arm, and sat down on the bench that ran alongside the table.

"Let's suppose you are telling the truth," he said, in a weary voice, looking at his daughter with a hint of compassion, as if looking at a sick person. "Do you know what happens to pregnant women without husbands?" He forced himself to say the words. "They're stoned to death. That's the law." He placed his callused hands on the table. "First comes the rumor. It'll start in Nazareth and quickly spread through Galilee. People will say, 'The daughter of Joachim the carpenter is carrying a stranger's child.' The shame of it will lead to the judgment. And the child you are expecting will never see the light of day." Joachim looked around at the gathering. "And because we wanted to protect you, we'll all be cursed forever."

"Are you afraid?" Miriam asked, her voice still glacial. "You could always denounce me."

They all lowered their eyes, self-contempt bringing lumps to their throats. And in the strange silence that descended on the gathering like a curtain, Miriam went up to her father, kissed him on the forehead, as she had done earlier to young Yakov, and walked out of the room as calmly as she had come, leaving them all distraught.

———

———

ALL day, they avoided each other, fearing their own thoughts and one another's.

At twilight, Yossef broke the silence and unleashed the storm they had all been dreading. He came to Joachim and said, "Don't condemn your daughter. I told you my roof will always be her roof, my family her family. Miriam is at home here, and her child will live with my children, as my child. And if the day comes, after she has given birth, when the people of Nazareth ask her the name of her child's father, she will be able to say that we are betrothed and give mine."

"Ah!" Barabbas cried. "So now it comes out!"

Yossef turned to him, his fist already raised. "Stop insulting her! She is greater than you!"

"A liar and a coward, that's what you are. Miriam is making it all up in order to protect you!"

Yossef leaped on Barabbas, and they both fell to the ground and rolled in the dust, roaring like wild animals. With some difficulty, Joachim managed to prize Barabbas's fingers from around Yossef's throat.

"No! No!"

Ruth and Mariamne ran to them and helped Joachim to separate them, while Zechariah and Elisheba looked on in horror.

On their feet again, wiping the dust from their torn tunics, Yossef and Barabbas stood looking at each other, shaking and breathless. Joachim seized their hands, but was unable to utter a word.

Yossef tore himself free and walked away, head bowed, trying to catch his breath. When he looked up again, he said, "My house is open to everyone. But not to those who refuse to hear the truth from Miriam's lips."

———

Full of anger and doubt, Barabbas left Nazareth within the hour.

The next day, Zechariah tied his mule to the uncomfortable wagon that had brought them from Judea to Galilee, the wagon in which Hannah had been killed by the mercenaries. Elisheba climbed into it, weeping and protesting that there was no need for them to leave so soon. But Zechariah, who was still observing his vow of silence, ignored her complaints. Bridles and whip in hand, he waited for Joachim to make up his mind.

Joachim took three steps in one direction, two in another, his throat so tight that he felt as though he were breathing sand. He went up to Yossef, hit his chest with the flat of his hand, and said in a low voice, "Either you are guilty and God will forgive you, or you are a good, generous man and God will bless you."

Yossef put his hand on Joachim's arm. "Come back, Joachim! Come back whenever you want."

Joachim nodded. He walked past Miriam without looking at her and gripped the side of the wagon. Unnecessarily, he checked that the bench had been wiped clean of Hannah's blood, and finally climbed in and sat down. For the first time in his life, he looked like an old man.

He gave a start when he realized that Miriam had followed him and was standing quite close to him, beside the wagon. She took his hand, kissed it fervently, and buried her face in his callused palms.

"I love you. No daughter has ever had a better father than you."

At that moment, Joachim, who had sat up, with his back straight and his chest out, hesitated, as if he might even be about to climb out of the wagon. But Zechariah whipped the mules' rumps, Elisheba wept loudly, and the wagon set off, the big wooden wheels rolling along the stony path with a rumbling sound that gradually faded.

Shyly and tenderly, Yossef put his hand on Miriam's shoulder. "I know Joachim. One day he'll come and play with his grandson."

Miriam smiled at him gratefully, standing amid the children.

Ruth had come to her during the night. "Keep me with you, Miriam," she had begged, the lines on her face accentuated by the flickering of the oil lamp. "Don't ask me to believe what I can't believe. Ask me only to love and support you. That's something I'll do as long as I have breath in my body, even if I don't understand."

Now Miriam made a sign with her hand in the direction of her two friends. It was a strange, rather slow gesture, as if she had come back from a journey and was waving to them from a distance. For the first time, Ruth and Mariamne had a feeling they would often have in the long years to come: the sense that this young woman they thought they knew so well was a stranger to them.

CHAPTER 18

Spring passed, and summer came and went. Miriam's belly grew round, and the people of Nazareth started to say that Yossef had such a big appetite that he was living with three women.

It was also said that he had thrown Joachim out of his house.

Poor Joachim, bless him! His life had been nothing but a series of misfortunes since the day he had defended old Houlda against the greed of the tax collectors.

In the synagogue, they whispered the word *thief*. They wondered why Yossef and Miriam needed two handmaids, one old and one young—and put the worst complexion on it.

A few women shrugged and said to the men, "Don't ask such stupid questions. Yossef has four sons and two daughters. That's why Miriam has two handmaids."

But that did not convince anyone.

People recalled that Yossef was living in the house where Joachim had been born, and that Joachim had given it to him two decades earlier. Joachim, who was a generous man, had also taught him everything he knew, and passed on his own customers to him. But he had not given him his daughter. If he had known that she was expecting a child with Yossef, he would never have left Nazareth, where his Hannah was buried. Was that proof that Yossef had forced Miriam?

Perhaps.

Other tongues started wagging, saying that Barabbas had been seen fleeing the village one day in spring, his face bathed in tears. Could he have been Miriam's partner in sin?

Some asked, "And what about Miriam? Why do we never see her here?"

The answer was simple. She was hiding because she was guilty.

Soon, when Ruth came to buy cheese or milk, when Mariamne came for wool or bread, they were made to feel less and less welcome. By the end of summer, they were given only what they needed and no more.

Yossef went so far as to complain in the courtyard of the synagogue.

"Put your house in order," he was told.

"What do you mean?"

The looks he was given in reply were more eloquent than all the words in the language of Israel.

"If we don't marry," he said to Miriam on his return, "the day is not far off when they come here and stone us to death."

"Are you afraid?" Miriam asked.

"Not for myself. But for you and the child. And for Ruth and Mariamne."

They were not stoned to death, but he was given less and less work. By the first cold autumn days, his workshop was strangely empty.

It was then that the news reached them, carried from village to village by Herod's mercenaries. They would enter yards, knock at doors, and cry to all and sundry that Caesar Augustus, master of Rome and Israel, wanted to know the name of everyone who lived in his kingdom.

"Go to the village of your birth and register. You'll be given a leather token. By the first day of the month of Adar, whoever cannot show his token when he is asked to do so will be imprisoned."

The news aroused both anger and confusion.

"I don't even know where I was born," Ruth said.

"I was born in Bethlehem," Yossef said. "A tiny village in Judea where King David was born. No one there even knows me!"

"And I'd have to go back to Magdala," Mariamne said irritably. "This is one more measure by the Romans and Herod to keep their eyes on us. But they're so stupid. What's to stop people from forging the leather tokens? What's to stop people from registering in two or three villages, one after the other, if they want to?"

"It could be a trick," Yossef said, cautiously. "There may be something else behind it that we don't know."

Miriam placed her palms on her belly, which was already slowing her down. "Since we're no longer welcome here in Nazareth," she said to Yossef, "why don't we go to your village while I can still travel? The child would be born there, and no one would take any notice. I'd say I'm your wife, and they'd think it was perfectly normal that I registered there."

They thought it over for a day or two.

Ruth said eagerly, "There's no point in discussing this: I'm going with you. You'll need someone to take care of Yossef's children. And of you, too, when the time comes for you to give birth. And if they don't remember Yossef in Bethlehem, who can say I wasn't born there?"

Miriam agreed. "We'll say you're my aunt."

Mariamne also wanted to stay with them until the child was born. On the other hand, if she did not go back to Magdala, where they must be expecting her for the census, she would put her mother in a difficult position: The Romans did not like her, and had their eyes on her.

"You'll be more useful to me if you go back to Magdala than if you come with me to Judea," Miriam said. "In the spring, when the roads become practicable again, I'll join you with the child, if Rachel doesn't mind. Her house would be the perfect place for him to grow up in and learn what a new king needs to know."

Reluctantly, Mariamne yielded. Several times, she asked Miriam to assure her that they would meet again in Magdala.

"You mustn't doubt it," Miriam said. "Any more than you should doubt the rest of it."

I T was snowing when they came in sight of Bethlehem. A bitingly cold wind was blowing, but Yossef had made a tarpaulin and even a stand for a brazier, which turned the wagon into a comfortable mobile tent. They huddled there with the children, like a little pack in its lair. Sometimes, the roads were so bumpy that they were sent rolling, one on top of the other. The children laughed until they cried, especially the youngest, Yehuda, who saw it as a wonderful game.

Miriam was close to her labor. Occasionally, she would clench her teeth and grip Ruth's wrist. Whenever that happened, Ruth would call out to Yossef to stop the mules. But as she had not yet given birth by the time they entered the curved main street of Bethlehem, Miriam said, "Let's go straight to the census, before the child is born."

Ruth and Yossef protested. It was dangerous for her and the child. They could easily wait a week or two, until he was born. The Romans would still be there.

"No," Miriam said. "When he's born, I don't want him to have anything to do with the Romans or the mercenaries. I don't even want them to lay eyes on him."

T H E census was taking place in front of a big square house that the Roman officers had requisitioned, having thrown out the owners.

The decurions sat outside at tables, in the heat of two big fires. Other officers, their spears in their hands, watched over the line of people waiting in the wind.

When the people of Bethlehem saw Miriam standing there with her big belly, leaning on Yossef and Ruth, and the children shivering behind them, they said, "Don't stay here. Go in front, we're in no hurry."

When they reached the table, one of the decurions looked them up and down. He saw Miriam's big belly beneath her thick cloak, grimaced, and jutted his chin out at Yossef. "Name and age?"

"Yossef. I'd say I'm about thirty-five. Perhaps forty."

The decurion wrote it down on the papyrus scroll. His fingers were numb from the cold, and the ink did not flow freely. He had to write in large letters.

Miriam saw that he was using the Latin language, translating the name Yossef as Joseph.

"What about you?" the decurion asked. "Name and father's name?"

"Miriam, daughter of Joachim. I'm twenty years old. Perhaps more, perhaps less."

"Miriam," the decurion said. "That doesn't exist in the language of Rome. As of today, your name is Mary."

He wrote it down, then pointed his stylus at Miriam's belly. "And what are you going to call that one?"

"Yeshua."

The decurion looked at her, uncomprehending.

"Yeshua," she repeated.

"That name doesn't exist!" he grunted, blowing on his fingers.

Miriam leaned over and said in Greek, "Iesous. That means the man who saves."

The man laughed nervously. "So you speak Greek, do you?"

He wrote: *Jesus, son of Joseph and Mary. Age: zero.*

He looked at Ruth. "What about you?"

"Ruth. I have no idea of my age. You decide for yourself."

That made the decurion smile. "I'll write that you're a hundred, but you don't look it."

Then it was the turn of the children.

"My name is Yakov," Yossef's eldest child said proudly. "He's my father, my mother's name was Halva, and I'm nearly ten."

The decurion sighed, no longer smiling. "Your name is James."

And so it was that in those days they all changed names for the future.

Mariamne became Mary—Mary Magdalene.

Hannah became Anne.

Halva became Alba.

Elisheba became Elizabeth.

Yakov became James.

Shimon became Simon.

Yehuda became Judas.

Zechariah became Zachary.

Geouel became George.

Rekab became Roland.

And so on for all the names used by the people of Israel.

Only Barabbas's name was not changed. First, because he refused to present himself before the Romans. And second, because, in the Aramaic language that everyone spoke in those days in the kingdom of Israel, Barabbas meant "son of the father." That was the name given to children whose mothers could not name the fathers. It was the name of those who had no name.

But the Romans did not know that.

Nor did they know that the name of Mary's son, to whom she gave birth eleven days later in an abandoned farm near Bethlehem, this Yeshua whom the decurion had named Jesus because that was the closest to it in sound, meant "savior."

AND THAT WAS WHERE I BELIEVED MY BOOK ENDED.

What happened next is the best-known story in the world, I thought. Quite apart from the Gospels, countless painters, writers and, in our own day, filmmakers have told it in a thousand different ways over the centuries.

During the several years it took me to research and write this novel, this portrait of "my" Mary, I had made an effort to imagine what this Miriam of Nazareth, born in Galilee, was like, to imagine her as a real woman, living in the troubled kingdom of Israel in the year 3760 after the creation of the world by the Almighty, according to Jewish tradition, the year that was to become the first year of the Christian era.

What the Gospels have to say about the mother of Jesus could be written on a pocket handkerchief. A few vague, contradictory sentences. This void was filled by the imaginations of the novelists of their time, the authors of the apocrypha that flourished up until the Renaissance. These had given rise to a none-too-convincing image of Mary, tailored to suit the tastes of the Roman Catholic Church, and showing a complete ignorance of the history of Israel, of which Miriam was a part.

But the destiny of a book is not sealed in advance. The wind of chance blows over the pages, scattering them, disrupting their carefully planned order, challenging what has long seemed obvious. The fact is that the characters do not exist only on paper. They demand their own lives, their share of surprises. And those surprises disturb the sentences and change their meaning.

As chance would have it, then, I found myself, just a few days after finishing a first draft of my novel, on my way to Warsaw, the city of my birth. I was going there to finish *The Righteous Among Nations*, a film about those people—some Christians, some not—who saved Jews during the Second World War, often at great risk to themselves.

I had never been back to Poland since arriving in France as a very young man. I had conflicting emotions about this return: not only the nostalgic but ambivalent pleasure we all feel in returning to the scenes of our childhood, but also an old anger that could never quite be wiped out.

The Warsaw I discovered was quite different from the Warsaw of my memories. That febrile, turbulent world, suffused with the voluble, colorful Yiddish of my grandfather Abraham, a printer by trade, who died in the Warsaw ghetto uprising, had vanished. It had been wiped out as thoroughly as if it had never existed.

As Joseph of Arimathea said to Miriam of Nazareth, anger blinds us even when our cause is just.

No sooner had I arrived in Warsaw than my one desire was to leave as soon as possible. To escape the past and those who prefer to ignore it, who have nothing more to teach me. The only reason I stayed was an appointment that had been arranged some weeks in advance with a woman who, I had been told, had saved two thousand Jewish children from the ghetto. Canceling the appointment would have been an unforgivable insult.

And so I went to see her, reluctantly. How wrong I was: Destiny was lying in wait for me.

I climbed three rickety flights of stairs and found myself face-to-face with an old Polish woman with finely drawn features and a youthful expression. When she smiled, her eyes creased and she looked as mischievous as a child. She wore her white hair short, in the style of a schoolgirl in the 1930s, held in place by a barrette just above the forehead. She moved cautiously, with the help of a walking frame.

We exchanged small talk for a while, trying to break the ice. As her name was Maria, I told her that I was writing a book about Mary, the mother of Jesus.

Her face lit up. "You've come to the right place," she said. "I also had a son named Jesus, Yeshua."

I stiffened. She took no notice of my unease and started talking about the ghetto. When I asked her how she had managed to save nearly two thousand Jewish children, to my surprise she started to cry.

"We should have saved more. We were young, we didn't know what we were doing. . . ."

She dabbed her temple with a tiny lace handkerchief, and opened her mouth as if about to say more. Then she thought better of it, and silence fell between us.

Over the last twenty or thirty months, I had lived very little in the present day. I had been like an addict, intoxicated with visions of an imaginary Galilee, its infinite plains and dark wooded slopes. I had sailed across the dazzling surface of the Lake of Gennesaret, trod the dusty paths of the white, fragrant villages that had long been swallowed up in the mists of time. Now all of a sudden, those dreams had faded, and in front of me there was a square table covered with a plastic tablecloth, surrounded by three plywood chairs whose blue paint was flaking.

Disconcerted, I forced myself to carry on. I remarked that she had not answered my question.

She looked at me with a kindly, somewhat amused expression. She had no intention of answering me. She now asked a question herself.

"Do you know why so much of Warsaw is raised above street level? You must have noticed that to get to most streets, you have to climb up a few steps."

I nodded. Yes, I had noticed, but I had no idea of the reason.

"After the war, the survivors didn't have either the money or the time to clear away the ruins of the Jewish houses. Nor did they have time to take away the bodies that were still buried beneath them. So they just bulldozed it all flat, sweeping away what was left of the courtyards, the alleys, the washhouses, the wells, the fountains, the schools. . . . Once they'd razed everything to the ground, they built houses for the living over the houses of the dead. When you climb those steps, you're treading on the largest Jewish cemetery in the world."

We fell silent again, both embarrassed. There always comes a moment when the horrors committed by men leave you speechless.

Involuntarily, I found myself staring at the number tattooed on her forearm. She noticed, and covered it with her withered hand.

There were two windows in the room, looking out on one of those communal courtyards so frequently found in prewar buildings in Warsaw. In a corner of the room, there was a tiny white pasteboard chapel, adorned with a picture of the Virgin Mary by Leonardo da Vinci. Between the two windows, behind a sheet of glass speckled with dirt, I saw a photograph of two men side by side, one young, the other old.

Noticing that I was looking at the photograph, she smiled and said, "My husband and my son."

Then, seeing that I was fascinated by her son's face, she added, "You can see it, can't you, even though the photo's not very good? In him, there was only mercy."

I studied the photograph more closely. It was true. I noticed that he had that curious look men have when they know what is in store for them. His long hair gave his face an air of fragility, at odds with those strong hands folded over his stomach.

"I used to love his hair," Maria said. "As silky as a girl's. Of course, they cut it off. Incredible, isn't it, that obsession they had with hair? Like the Philistines terrified of Samson's hair." She shook her head, lifted her walking frame, and brought it down on the floor in an angry little gesture. "That mountain of hair they had at the entrances to the camps!"

Again, all I could do was remain silent.

I thought to get up and leave with those all-too-familiar images in my head.

She must have read my thoughts. She threw me a mischievous look and said, "Before you go, I'd like to give you something."

She stood up with the help of her frame. With small cautious steps, she walked to the one closet in the room. Turning her back on me, she rummaged in a drawer and took out a tube-shaped object wrapped in an old Yiddish newspaper. She half turned to me, one hand gripping the aluminum support of her frame, and with the other handed me the object.

"Take it."

"What is it?"

Beneath the partly torn newspaper, I could feel something hard. I took it out. It was a cylinder made of very thin wood and covered in leather as transparent as skin that had grown darker with time, and as hard as horn. I had only ever seen this kind of object behind glass in museums, but I recognized it. It was one of those tubes used in the Middle Ages to protect writings of some importance: letters, official documents, even books.

"But this is valuable!" I cried in astonishment. "I can't possibly—"

She swept aside my protests. "Take it away and read it," she said, and closed her eyes.

"I can't take something as valuable as this! You must—"

"It's all there. You'll recognize the words of a woman who wasn't much listened to in her time."

"Mary? Miriam of Nazareth?"

"Just read it," she repeated, walking over to the door with little jerks of her frame, this time dismissing me in a way that brooded no reply.

The newspaper protecting the case came away by itself, burned as it was by time. I had to struggle a bit to take off the cap. The wood and the brittle leather threatened to break beneath my shaking fingers.

Inside, I found a strip of rolled parchment, which had been carefully wrapped in a sheet of crystal paper.

The parchment, already crumbling at the edges, stuck to the pads of my fingers as soon as I touched it. I rolled it out on my hotel bed, inch by inch, afraid it would disintegrate at any moment.

The parchment had been awkwardly folded. Fragments of text had come away where the folds were. The brown ink had faded and was blurred in places by damp stains. The handwriting was small and regular. My first thought was that the script was Cyrillic, but that was only my ignorance.

To my surprise, as I unrolled the parchment, I found a number of small sheets of squared paper. They, too, were yellowed by time, but they were only a few decades old. This time, I immediately recognized the language: Yiddish.

I sat down on the edge of the bed to read them. As soon as I started, my eyes misted over, and I found it impossible to go on.

I stood up, went to the minibar, took out the few small bottles of vodka that were there, and poured them all into a glass. It was a mediocre vodka, which burned my throat. I waited for it to take effect and for my heart to stop pounding.

January 27, the year 5703 after the creation of the world by the Lord, blessed be He.

"You, You, holy one, whose throne is surrounded by the praises of Israel, it was in You that our fathers trusted. They believed in You and You saved them. Why not us? Why not us, Lord?"

My name is Abraham Prochownik. I have been living in a cellar on Kanonia Street for months. I may well be the only surviving member of the Prochownik family. Thanks be to our neighbor Maria.

I hope the day will come when the Christians revere her as a saint. I, a Jew, can only hope that she will remain in the memory of men as one of the Righteous among nations. May the Almighty, the God of love and mercy, protect her.

If anyone finds these papers, I want it to be known: Maria saved hundreds of Jewish children. She was deported by the Nazis—may their name be cursed for all eternity—as a Jew, with her son Jesus, whom she called Yeshua, and her husband, her son's father. Father and son both perished in the camps, but Maria escaped with the help of the Catholic Zegota network.

It took ten generations from Adam to Noah, says the Treatise of the Fathers, for the long patience of God to be revealed,

even though the generations did all that they could to provoke Him, before He swallowed them up in the Flood.

How long do I still have to live? Only the Lord, the Master
of the Universe, knows that.

And only the Lord knows, as written above, if there are
any other Prochowniks left apart from me. We were once an
illustrious family. According to the legend handed down by
my father and grandfather, our ancestor Abraham (whose
name I bear) was crowned king in the year 936 of the current era by Slavic tribes who had converted from Paganism
to Christianity. The most important tribe was that of the
Polanes and our family had been living among them for several generations.

The Lord God of Wisdom no doubt inspired Abraham,
and he refused the honor of being king. He told the Polanes
that it was not right for a Jew to rule over Christians, that
they should find a leader among the members of their own
families. He suggested that he appoint one of their peasants
who produced the most corn. The man's name was Mieszko,
from the Piast family. The Polanes followed his advice and
the peasant became Mieszko I.

The Piast dynasty was a long one and always behaved well
toward the Jews.

At least if you believe our family legend.

Grandfather Solomon never doubted it. He took it all as
absolute truth. The only time he ever raised his hand to me
was when I made fun of him one day by claiming that our
ancestor Abraham had been nothing but a poor penniless
boot maker.

For grandfather Solomon, the one irrefutable piece of evidence that our family had once been great was our family heir-
loom: the scroll which Abraham Prochownik was supposed to
have received from the Piasts to show their gratitude.

On the day of his bar mitzvah, every boy in our family had the right to open the case, unroll the scroll a little and contemplate the writing.

According to grandfather Solomon, this scroll was given to the Piasts by none other than Saint Cyril himself when they were converted. It is only a copy. The original scroll was written in Hebrew and Greek. But both the copy and the original contain the same thing: the Gospel of Miriam of Nazareth, Mary, the mother of Jesus.

Grandfather Solomon used to tell us that Helena, the mother of Constantine the First, the Roman Emperor who converted to Christianity, brought it back from Jerusalem. She claimed that the original scroll, made of papyrus as was the custom at the time, was given to her by a group of Christian women when she visited Jerusalem in the year 326 of the current era to build the Church of the Holy Sepulchre, on the very spot where Jesus was crucified.

Some centuries later, under the Byzantine emperor Michael the Third, the great evangelist Cyril is said to have taken a copy of the scroll with him when he went to Khazaria with his brother Methodius in the year 861 on a mission to convert the Khazar Jews to Christianity. He hoped the fact that the scroll was the testimony of a Jewish mother would help him in his task.

Fortunately, the Holy God of Israel protected the king of the Khazars against temptation.

Cyril then decided to convert the pagan peoples who led a nomadic existence in the Caucasus and around the Black Sea. The contents of the scroll proved the existence of Jesus, which was something the pagans still doubted. Cyril translated the text into several languages: Adzhar, which was spoken in the mountains; Georgian, which was written using the Phoenician alphabet; and Slavonic.

It was because of this story that Solomon's son, my father Yakob, became a great professor of ancient languages. The best known and most respected at the universities of Vienna, Moscow, Budapest, and Warsaw, where he taught. He was still there when the Germans entered Poland.

It was he who recognized the language in the scroll our ancestor Abraham had handed down. It is Adzhar. No one should waste their time searching for another language.

My father could have become incredibly famous if he had revealed the existence of the scroll. Why did he not do so?

The only time I ever asked him the question, he replied that he had no need to be famous. Later, he added that what the text contained could give rise to pointless disputes. "There are enough conflicts in this world without adding to them. Especially for us, at the moment." That was seven years ago, when Hitler was already stirring up the crowds. My father was always a very farsighted man. That was why he did not leave behind any translation of the scroll, even though he was the only one among us who had ever read it.

Nobody knows what became of the original scroll, the one that Helena brought back from Jerusalem. Destroyed in the sacking of Byzantium, my father assumed.

Warsaw, February 2, the year 5703 after the creation of the world by the Everlasting, blessed be He.

The organization of Jewish fighters is urging us to resist. Maria, may the angels of heaven protect her, brought me their pamphlet in Yiddish. "Jews! The occupier is speeding up our extermination! Don't go passively to your deaths! Defend yourselves! Take up axes, iron bars, knives! Barricade your houses to save your children, but let adult men fight by any means possible!"

They are right. We must fight. But with what? We don't

have anything to fight with. We don't even have the axes and iron bars mentioned in the pamphlet, let alone real weapons and ammunition. . . .

I beg you, O Almighty! May our persecutors be punished, may those who are causing us to perish end up in hell! Amen.

Warsaw, February 17, the year 5703 after the creation of the world by the Lord, blessed be He.

Maria came again, even though it is dangerous and difficult to move around. She brought me two lumps of sugar, four walnuts and seven potatoes. I have no idea how she got hold of them. May God Almighty bless her! May He always protect her.

Yesterday, the Germans entered the hospital, shot those patients who could not stand, and dragged away the others through the snow to Umschlagsplatz, from where they were sent off to Auschwitz.

We fought, we resisted as no one had ever resisted before. Through the word that the Lord gave us so that it may enter the hearts of our tormentors; through the testimony which, if such is the wish of the Lord of Hosts, will preserve our breath among the nations. And now—Holy, Holy, Holy is Your name!—death is the only weapon we still have against those who bring death, so that Your name, Lord, and the name of Your people, may be glorified forever! Amen.

Tomorrow, I will no longer be here. The scroll of the Gospel of Mary, which the Prochowniks have handed down from generation to generation for more than a thousand years, is now in Maria's hands. She is free to do with it whatever she wishes. No one has better judgment than she does.

It is thanks to her, the most Righteous of the Righteous, that the name of the Prochowniks will remain. Amen.

THE GOSPEL OF MARY

I Miriam of Nazareth, known as Mary in the language of Rome, daughter of Joachim and Anne, address this to Mariamne of Magdala, also known as Mary in the language of Rome, daughter of Rachel.

In the beginning the word,
God is Word, God, word that engenders the word.
In the beginning, without the word nothing has been of what was.
Word, the light of men, without any darkness.
The word of the beginning, the night never grasps it.

I address this to Mariamne of Magdala, the sister of my heart, faith and soul. I address this to all those women who are following her teaching on the banks of the Lake of Gennesaret.

In the year 3792 after the Lord, blessed be He, created the world, in the month of Nisan, in the thirty-third year of the reign of Antipas, son of Herod.

For those women who worry and who fear his death, I testify for my son, Yeshua, so that they are not deceived by the rumors spread as far as Damascus by the corrupt ones of the Temple of Jerusalem. This is my testimony.

He is among you, and you do not know him.

This is what happened in the days when Antipas cut off the head of John the Baptist. Thirty years had passed since the birth of my son, and for thirty years, since the death of his father Herod, Antipas had ruled over Galilee. He did not have power over the whole kingdom of Israel, because the Romans mistrusted him.

I knew John the Baptist, son of Zechariah and Elisheba, when he was still in his mother's womb. And Mariamne, the sister of my heart, also knew him, may she remember. According to the will of God, children came to us, first to Elisheba, and then to me. For both of us, it happened in Nazareth, in Galilee.

When he became a man, John went out on the roads. Wherever he went, he took the word and baptized those who came to him. That is why he was called the Baptist.

His reputation grew.

From Jerusalem, the priests of the Sanhedrin and the Levites came to him and asked him, Who are you?

He answered humbly and said, I am not the one you are waiting for. I come before. I am not he who opens the gates of heaven. I am the word before the word, crying in the desert.

That happened in Bethany near the Jordan.

For ten years, John the Baptist's fame grew.

For ten years, my son, Yeshua, studied and listened. He heard the word of John and approved of it. When he himself spoke, his word was heard only by a small number.

For ten years, the gates of heaven remained closed and did not open to him whom Israel awaited.

One day, John the Baptist said to me, Let your son come to be baptized. And I replied, You know better than anyone who he is. Why do you want to baptize him? When you put men and women in the water, it is to purify them. Of what do you want to purify my son, Yeshua?

My answer did not please him. And John the Baptist said to whoever would listen to him, We would like to hear Yeshua, the son of Miriam of Nazareth, but we do not hear him. We would like to see if he is as miraculous as his birth and can open the gates of heaven. But we do not see him. He speaks, but all that comes out are the words of man, not the breath of Yahweh.

Thus spoke John the Baptist. Let Mariamne, the sister of my heart, testify to that, for she was present. It happened in Magdala.

From that day, my son Yeshua was at Capernaum, on the shores of the Lake of Gennesaret. He no longer saw John the Baptist. The fame of the word of John the Baptist continued to grow. It even reached Antipas, who took fright and said, The man they call the Baptist pours out words against me. He wants the end of my house.

Everyone listens to him, in Galilee and beyond. He has more influence than the Zealots, the Essenes, and the thieves.

Antipas made up his mind to have John the Baptist arrested. Sharing the vice of his family, which had run in his blood since his father, Herod, Antipas offered the head of John the Baptist to his wife, Herodias, who was also his niece and his sister-in-law.

On the eve of the day when they were due to bury John, son of Zechariah and Elisheba, Joseph of Arimathea, the holiest of men and the most loyal of my friends, came to me and said, We must go to the tomb of John the Baptist. Your friend Mariamne is with your son, Yeshua, in Capernaum. They are too far and cannot come back in time for the burial. It is for you to be at the grave of him whom Antipas killed because he was afraid of him.

This happened in Magdala.

I answered Joseph of Arimathea and said, I did not like it when John the Baptist spoke against my son, Yeshua. But you are right: We must hold hands before the grave where Antipas wishes to bury the word of the Almighty beneath his vice.

At night, by boat, we went from Magdala to Tiberias.

In the morning, not many of us assembled before the open grave. Barabbas the thief was there. Since the first day he had loved me, just as I loved him. The Almighty had never wanted us to be separated by tribulations. Let my sister Mariamne testify, she who saw us as both friends and enemies.

Barabbas complained that we were few. He said, Yesterday, they ran to John the Baptist to wash themselves of their sins. Today, when we have to stand before his grave, watched by Antipas's mercenaries, they are nowhere to be seen.

He was wrong. When the earth covered the headless body of John the Baptist, thousand and thousands arrived to mourn him. The roads of Tiberias were full of people. No one could move. Everyone wanted to put a white stone on the grave and sing the greatness of the Almighty. It lasted until evening. By the end of the day, the grave of John the Baptist was a white mound that could be seen from afar.

Joseph of Arimathea and Barabbas took me aside for fear that I might suffocate in the multitude. Joseph of Arimathea said, The word of John the Baptist is gone. The people who are here today are lost again, like children in the dark. They thought they had found the one who would open the gates of heaven to them. They do not yet know that the one they must follow now is in Capernaum. They do not know it and again they doubt.

Barabbas agreed and said, Antipas kills, he cuts the head of the Baptist, and the anger of God is nowhere to be seen. And Barabbas turned to me and said, Joseph is right. How can we believe that your son is he who was announced by John if he does not give a sign? They will not rally behind Yeshua only by listening to him.

Hearing these words, I became angry and said, I am like them. My son was born thirty years ago, and for thirty years I have been waiting. I was a girl in the flower of her youth, now I am a woman who looks at the darkness of her time. Patience has an end. John the Baptist mocked Yeshua and me. Zechariah and Elisheba said to me before they died, We thought your son was like ours, but he is not. I listened to them and was humiliated. I was ashamed. I said, What is happening? Does God not know what he wants? Did God make me mother of Yeshua in vain? When will he give the sign, through the hand of my son, to open the gates of heaven? When will he give the sign that brings down Antipas and frees Israel? Is that not what we are living for? And have we not lived long enough in purity to deserve it?

From Joseph of Arimathea and Barabbas I hid nothing. I said to them, Today, I have no more patience. Seeing these thousands at the grave of John the Baptist does not comfort me. It is not a grave we should be celebrating, it is the light of life. That is why Yeshua was born.

My anger did not subside before I returned to Magdala. Joseph of Arimathea did not try to assuage it. He was like me, and even further on in years. His days were numbered, his patience had worn thinner than his tunic.

Two days passed, and Mariamne, the sister of my heart, returned from Capernaum. May she remember. She announced with great joy, I have wonderful news. Yeshua preached at Capernaum. Those who heard him said, Here is John the Baptist reborn. The rumor of his word reached the ears of a Roman centurion. He came to hear him, and everyone feared his presence. But Yeshua said to him, I know that your daughter is between life and death. Tomorrow, she will be on her feet. The centurion ran home. The next day, he returned and bowed down before Yeshua and said, My name is Longinus, and I must recognize before you that you spoke the truth. My daughter is on her feet.

And Mariamne also announced, Next week, there will be a big wedding at Cana, in Galilee. The bridegroom's father is rich and respected. He heard Yeshua and invited him.

Then Joseph of Arimathea looked at me. I knew he was thinking the same as me. I said, Let us go to Cana too. It is [. . .]*

[. . .] named Claudia, wife of Pilate, governor of Judea. She said to me, I heard your son speak at Capernaum and I am here. I am a daughter of Rome, and my birth places me above the people, but please do not think that this makes me blind and deaf. I know what Antipas is doing in this country. I also know what his father did.

To the sister of my heart, Claudia the Roman said, I admire the wise teaching that you give in Magdala. They say you are the one who exalts the word of Yeshua among women. And Mariamne answered and said, Come to Magdala to be with me. There will be a place for you there, even though you are a daughter of Rome.

This is what happened at the wedding feast at Cana. Yeshua said to the bride and bridegroom, Let no one light a lamp and then bury it in a hole. The joy of marriage makes of the body a light that chases away all darkness. The flesh of the bride and groom is radiant and reveals how much my father loves the life that is in you.

---

*At this point in the scroll, part of the text is missing, where a damp patch has caused the material to tear.

A disciple of my son came to me, a small man, with thin cheeks and a direct look. His name was John in the language of Rome. His greeting surprised me, since the disciples of Yeshua do not like to show themselves to me. But he was friendly to me and said, At last, you have come to hear the word of your son. It is a long time since I last saw you with him. And I answered, How could I follow him when he chases me away? He keeps saying that he has no family, not even a mother. And John shook his head and said, No! Do not be offended. It is not a word against you but against those who doubt him. That will soon change.

The day was hot in Cana. Everyone drank for pleasure and to quench their thirst. The end of the wedding feast was approaching. There were many people. Some had come from Samaria, from Bethsaida. Geouel, who did not like me when I was in their house with Ruth, blessed be she, was present among the others. He came to me with respect and said, The time when I was against you has long gone. I was young and ignorant. Today, I know who you are.

When the sun began to set, Barabbas said to me, You brought us here, but nothing has changed. Your son speaks, and the others are thirsty from listening to him.

At that moment, Joseph of Arimathea came to me and said, There will soon be no more wine. The feast will be spoiled.

I understood what he meant. I stood up, with fear in my heart. It could be seen on my face. May my sister Mariamne remember. I went to my son and said, They have no more wine. You must do what is expected of you. It is time.

John the disciple was close to me. Yeshua looked me up and down as if I was a stranger and said, Woman, do not meddle in what I must do or not do. My hour has not yet come.

Then I, his mother, said, You are wrong, Yeshua. The sign is in your hands. You cannot hold back any longer. We are all waiting.

He again looked me up and down. He was not like a son looking at his mother. He turned to the bride and bridegroom, to John his disciple, to Joseph of Arimathea and Barabbas, and also to Mariamne, may she remember. He was silent. Then I asked the people serving at the wedding to approach, and said to them, Yeshua will speak to you. Whatever he orders you to do, do it.

Everyone looked at me in surprise, without understanding. There was silence at the wedding feast. Yeshua finally commanded the servants and said, Go to the jars intended for the purification and fill them. They said, We have only water to fill them, Rabbi, and this is a wedding day. He replied, Do as I say and fill the jars with water.

Once the jars were full, Yeshua ordered, Dip a cup in it and take it to the bridegroom's father. They did so, and the bridegroom's father exclaimed, This is wine! From the water has come wine, the best I have ever drunk.

Everyone wanted to see and to drink. They were given cups and they exclaimed, This is the wine of the Almighty! He is blessing our wedding! He is making Yeshua his son and his word!

Mariamne, the sister of my heart, was in tears. She went to Yeshua and kissed his hands, and he embraced her. She came to my arms and laughed through her tears, may she remember. Joseph of Arimathea embraced me and said, This is the first sign, God Almighty. Are you at last opening the gates of heaven?

John the disciple came to me and said, You are his mother, no one can doubt that.

All the wedding guests came to Yeshua and knelt before him and drank the wine. Claudia the Roman, the wife of Pilate, was in the front row, as humble before the Lord as a Jewess.

As for myself, I thought and I trembled. I prayed and said, It has happened. May the Almighty forgive me, I had no more patience, and I hurried up time. I pushed the word into the mouth of my son. But, Lord Everlasting, is it not for this that he was born: for the love of men to be revealed and to speak? God of Heaven, protect him. Follow him. Stretch your hand over him. Your breath.

Barabbas said to me, You were right, he may be our king. This time, I must believe it, or else I can no longer believe the evidence of my own eyes! From now on, Yeshua must take to the roads and give more signs like this one. The whole people of Israel will come to him.

That is what he did. For more than a year, the signs were plentiful. First in Galilee, then in Judea. Among the people, they were beginning to say, Here is Yeshua the Nazarene, he gives signs, he is in the hands of God. That was why one day he came to Jerusalem.

Thanks to the intercession of John, the disciples did not prevent me from following him. With me came Joseph of Arimathea, Barabbas, and Mariamne of Magdala, may she remember. In Jerusalem, we were joined by Yakov, known as James in the language of Rome, the son of Joseph, who was my husband at the time of the birth of Yeshua. He went to Yeshua and kissed him, and Yeshua said, Stay with me, you are my brother and I love you. It does not matter that we have neither the same mother nor the same father, we are brothers and sons of the Same Father.

Passover came.

You all know the story of what happened at Passover. How Yeshua took us to the Temple and there found the crowd that had come to purify itself. How the courtyard of the Temple was filled with those who transformed the sanctuary into a place of trade. The money changers had their tables there. The merchants of oxen and [. . .]* night, Barabbas held out the whip of rope and knots, and Yeshua took it. He cracked the whip before him. He drove the oxen out of the Temple. He drove out the sheep. The cages of doves broke on the ground, and the birds flew away. The coins of the money changers rolled on the flagstones. Yeshua overturned the tables, and chased everyone out of the courtyard.

This all happened before the eyes of those who had come to purify themselves, and they looked at each other and said, This is Yeshua of Nazareth. He has been all over Galilee, Samaria, and Judea giving signs through his word. He transformed water into wine at a wedding feast. Those who could not walk he made to walk. Nobody gives signs like this if the Lord is not with him. Now he is rising up against the corruptions of the Sanhedrin. Blessed be he!

---

*Here, three lines of text are missing because of a tear. Only a few words remain on the left-hand side of the scroll, which do not by themselves allow for a viable reconstruction.

This happened while he was emptying the courtyard of the Temple. To those who protest, Yeshua replied, Take this away! Never show yourself any more in my father's house as in a house of trade.

The priests of the Sanhedrin arrived, the Pharisees and the Sadducees, and cried, Who do you think you are to behave like this? And Yeshua replied, Do you not know, you who teach Israel?

Caiaphas, the high priest who had his power from the will of the Romans and his father-in-law, Annas, was drawn by the noise of the crowd. He feared what he saw. He stood up before Yeshua and said, Prove by a sign that Yahweh is with you. Prove to us that he has given you the right to oppose our decisions!

Yeshua replied, Tear down this temple, and I will rebuild it in three days.

May Mariamne, the sister of my heart, remember, those were his words. The words the crowd heard. The words the corrupt priests heard. For when Yeshua spoke, they all fell silent. They looked at the walls of the Temple and trembled. Their eyes were ready to see the sanctuary collapse by the will of the Almighty.

Nothing happened. Caiaphas mocked and said, Herod took forty-six years to build this temple, and you would raise it again in three days? You lie. Yeshua said, Lying is at the root of your thoughts. How could this temple be the sanctuary of God, since it is Herod who built it and your rotten hands that maintain it?

The crowd made a great noise. In the tumult, there was the threat of rebellion. Cries were heard announcing, The Messiah is in the courtyard of the Temple. He is confronting Caiaphas and the priests who are in the pay of the Romans.

Barabbas came to my side and said, The city is seething with anger. The streets are full. The people are arriving from everywhere for Passover. This is the moment we have been waiting for for so long, you and I. A sign from your son, and we will overturn the Sanhedrin. We will run to the Roman garrison and take it. Hurry.

Before doing anything, I took counsel with Joseph of Arimathea and Mariamne, may she remember. Both answered and said, This depends on Yeshua. To which I said, Barabbas is right. Never has there been a better moment to free the people of Jerusalem from the Roman yoke.

To my son, Yeshua, I said, Give the crowd a sign so that it will follow you. It will not wait. It is seething to follow you against the Sanhedrin and the Romans. Do not hesitate any longer.

Yeshua looked at me as he looked at me at Cana. His mouth remained closed. His eyes said to me, Who is this woman who thinks she can ask me to obey as a son should obey his mother?

This was the moment that Caiaphas chose to stir up his guard of mercenaries. He cried that the Nazarene was a usurper, a false prophet, a false Messiah. He pointed a finger at us, at the disciples, at me, at Joseph of Arimathea and Mariamne, and said, Those are they who want to destroy the Temple. Those are the ungodly! The mercenaries lowered their spears and drew their swords. Barabbas made the crowd surround us in order to save our lives.

May Mariamne remember. Everything that happened later, we were side by side to live it.

Yeshua and his disciples were welcomed in the house of a man named Shimon, on the Bethany road, less than an hour's walk from Jerusalem. I, his mother, Mariamne, and Joseph of Arimathea were placed in the neighboring house. Barabbas said to me, I am going back to Jerusalem. The people are too febrile for me to remain with my arms folded. It is no longer possible to hold them back. My place is there, at the head of those who want to fight. Let your son make up his mind. He has thrown a stone; it is for him to know whom it will strike.

I kissed him with all the love in my heart. I knew he might die in this combat, if Yeshua did not make up his mind.

Mariamne was at my side, and we tried to convince Yeshua. We said, You spoke before the people and said that the Temple could be destroyed and you would rebuild it in three days. The people will destroy it to put you to the test. They want to see the power of God act through your words. They want a pure sanctuary. They want you before them. They want to see the man you are. The people of Israel can wait no longer. They want the heavens to open.

Yeshua did not look at us. He said to his disciples, Why are they in a hurry? Moses wandered a long time in the desert and did not even reach Canaan. Nevertheless, he performed wonders under the palm of Yahweh. And now the stiff-necked people have demands?

After these words, the disciples chased us from the house.

John came to me with a sad face and said, Do not be offended. We understand the words of your son, Yeshua, but we do not yet understand him. He is right, though: Yahweh alone decides on the time of men.

Before night, the news arrived. The streets of Jerusalem were red with blood. The horsemen of Pilate the governor charged, with their spears pointed. At night, we learned that Barabbas had killed a priest of the Temple. I was told, He is a prisoner. He has been taken to Pilate's jail. I turned angrily to John and said, Has this not opened my son's mouth?

Above Bethany, the night sky was red with the fires burning in Jerusalem. Mariamne, the sister of my heart, wept and said, It is the blood of the people rising to heaven. As the gates of heaven were still closed, it covered heaven with our grief.

An old man joined us. He could hardly walk, and was brought in a cart. He spoke to me and said, I am Nicodemus, the Pharisee of the Sanhedrin, who came to Nazareth, to the house of Yossef the carpenter, more than twenty years ago, at the request of your father, Joachim.

I recognized him in spite of his age. He said, I am here because of you, Miriam of Nazareth. I am here because of your son, Yeshua. Take me to him. What I have to tell him is as important as his life.

John the disciple took him to Yeshua.

Nicodemus said to Yeshua, I am from the Sanhedrin, but my heart tells me that you are he who can teach us about the will of the Almighty. I prayed for God to enlighten me, and I saw your face. That is why I am here, and I say to you, Tonight, you must do something to show everyone who you are. Yeshua answered, What do you want of me? And Nicomedus said, A sign. The sign you announced. Go to the people who are destroying the Temple and raise it again in three days. And Yeshua said, How do you know that the hour has come? You know nothing, not even if you are in the hands of my Father! But Nicodemus insisted, You must give this sign, or the Romans will seize you at dawn. Caiaphas and his father-in-law, Annas, have condemned you on behalf of the Sanhedrin. They want you dead for what you did today. The people have revolted against them. At this hour of the night, they are tamed and Barabbas is in prison. Act in the hands of Yahweh or their blood will have been spilled for nothing. I say to you, the people of Jerusalem are waiting for a sign.

My son said nothing. We waited for him to give an answer to Nicodemus. Finally, he said, All of you want to hurry up time. It is all right for an impatient mother who has forgotten her place. But you, Pharisee, do you not know who decides? Your impatience is making you a slave of the world. Yet I say to you, In the world, you will have nothing but distress.

Nicodemus was disconcerted by what he heard. Even the disciples had been hoping for different words. I said to Mariamne, My son condemns me in public. Have I committed a sin? Have I committed an irreparable sin? May she remember, for it was the first time I had thought about it.

Nicodemus left as he had came. All night, Jerusalem held its breath. Thousands waited for a sign from my son.

None came. The gates of heaven were still closed.

At dawn, a Roman cohort, its tribune, and the Temple guard came to Bethany. Yeshua went with them like a lamb going to the slaughter. They led him to Caiaphas, who handed him over to Pilate the Roman. In the streets of Jerusalem, anger grew. This time, against Yeshua. We heard people say, Where has he led us? He announces that he will rebuild the Temple in three days, but he is not even capable of pushing Caiaphas from his seat! Our blood is on the streets, and for what purpose?

Claudia the Roman, who had been following Mariamne's teaching ever since Cana, came running to me in tears and said, Pilate is my husband. He is not a bad man. I shall go and ask him for clemency for your son, Yeshua. He must not die, he must not go on the cross. I answered her, Do not forget Barabbas. He is in [. . .]*

[. . .] crowd. Him! Him! He fought for us. The other one [. . .] sentence of Pilate owed to the vicious influence of Annas over [. . .]

[. . .] knees before me and said, What shame to have been chosen by the people in place of your son! What good is this to me? This life they have given back to me, what shall I do with it? I would have preferred to die.

It was the first time I had seen tears in Barabbas's eyes. His white head was heavy in my hands, his tears wet my palms. I raised him up. I was torn apart by his words. I embraced him and said, I am happy that you are alive, Barabbas. I am happy that the people chose you for Pilate's clemency. I do not want to lose you as well as my son. You know as I do that our lives [. . .]

[. . .] not to agree for him to be harmed. I, Claudia, had a terrifying dream last night. The fire of heaven flowed over us after his torture. Everyone assured you, Yeshua of Nazareth is a good man. If the crowd chose Barabbas, that does not mean that Yeshua's death will not give rise to a new rebellion. And my husband answered me and said, You speak thus of this Nazarene because you have become his disciple. I, Pilate, governor of Judea, listen to what the high priest Caiaphas tells me. He knows what is good and what is bad among the Jews.

At these words, everyone sighed. The disciples protested and moaned. Claudia the Roman continued, The truth is that Pilate, my husband, is afraid of Caesar. If he shows himself to be magnanimous, in Rome they will say that he is a weak, useless governor.

After these words, we knew that there would be no pardon. Everyone went away in tears and sadness. Mariamne, the sister of my heart, asked me, Why do your eyes remain dry? Everyone is weeping except you.

---

*This part of the scroll is badly deteriorated, presumably because it has been handled more than the others. Damp and wear have made about twenty lines illegible. For a further twenty lines, only a few fragments are decipherable.

May she remember my answer. I said to her, Tears are for weeping only when everything is over. For my son, Yeshua, nothing is over. And I may well be the reason for his torments of today. My heart tells me, Lacerate your face and ask the Lord to forgive you. Your son is going to die because of you. Yeshua told you, My time has not yet come, but you carried on regardless. At Cana, I forced him to give us a sign. I forced him to reveal the face of the Almighty in himself. The water of Cana became the wine of Yahweh. I had the pride of impatience. That is the sword that now pierces my soul and makes me see my sin.

And I said to Mariamne, There is no hour of the day or the night in which I do not beg the Lord God to punish me for having wanted to hurry up time. I wanted deliverance here and now. I am like the people, I want light, the love of men, and I can no longer bear the fact that heaven is closed. But what will the death of Yeshua bring? His word has not yet changed the face of the world. The Romans are still in Jerusalem. Vice is in the Temple, it reigns over the throne of Israel. Nothing is yet accomplished. And yet did I not give birth to this Yeshua so that the light of the days to come and the liberation of the people of Israel should arrive?

May Mariamne remember, these were the words I spoke. I said, I shall do what a mother must do to prevent her son from dying on the cross. Did I not prevent Herod from letting my father, Joachim, die there? I shall do it again. God may punish me. Pilate may punish me. I committed a sin, and I am ready to be punished. Let them crucify me in my son's place. Let them nail my hands and feet.

And Mariamne answered and said, That will never be. You cannot replace Yeshua in his torment. Women have no rights here, not even the right to die on the cross.

I knew she was right. I went to Joseph of Arimathea and said, Who can come to my aid? This time, I do not want to ask anything of Barabbas. The disciples of Yeshua are pointing the finger at him. He is hiding his shame at being freed instead of my son. He suffers so much that he is losing his reason, and I can no longer rely on him. And Joseph answered me and said, I will come to your aid. I will be the one to save your son. God will decide. If it is the will of the Almighty that your son die on the cross, then Yeshua will die. If the decision belongs only to Pilate, then Yeshua will live.

We gathered together in a very small number. Joseph of Arimathea assigned roles to those who could be useful without betraying us: Nicodemus the Pharisee from the Sanhedrin, Claudia the Roman, the Essene disciples who had come from Beth Zabdai at her request [. . .]*

[. . .] raised, as Claudia the Roman had announced. To the left of his cross, the man being crucified was Gestas of Jericho. A panel said that he was a murderer. To the right, the man was older than many. His name was Dismas, and he was from Galilee. Below him, his family wept and cried that he was not a thief, but a tavern keeper who did nothing but good to those around him.

On Yeshua's cross, these words were written on a board: Yeshua, king of the Jews. In Hebrew, in Aramaic, in Greek, and in the language of Rome—all the languages of Israel. The Romans knew that the people of Jerusalem had called Yeshua this before the Temple. They wanted to humiliate all those who had believed in him.

May Mariamne remember, the mercenaries kept us, the women, at a distance, with their spears lowered. Mariamne begged and became angry, but to no avail. They would not even listen to Claudia, the wife of Pilate.

When the sun was high, the onlookers came in large numbers. Some cried, Is it there, on your cross, that you will rebuild the Temple? Others felt pity and remained silent.

Joseph of Arimathea and the disciples from Beth Zabdai arrived. They went and stood beneath the cross and chased away the people who had been shouting. Nicodemus arrived on a chair carried by his servants. His body suspended on the cross, Yeshua spoke. We women could not hear the words he was saying. I said to Mariamne, Look, he is alive. As long as his lips move, I know he is alive. And I, seeing him like this, it was as if I were dead.

---

*Here, the scroll has been torn, perhaps deliberately. The missing part is large, and the two torn edges are held together by a thread of red silk.

The sun was higher and higher. The heat increased, and there was almost no shade. The centurion Longinus, he whose daughter Yeshua brought out of illness in Capernaum, arrived. Longinus made a sign to Claudia. He ignored Joseph of Arimathea and Nicodemus. He ignored us who were being kept at a distance. He talked to the soldiers at the foot of the cross, and they laughed. Their laughter went right through me. Longinus was playing the role assigned him by Joseph of Arimathea, but this laughter was unbearable.

Mariamne, the sister of my heart, exclaimed, What shame! This Roman whose daughter was saved by Yeshua, and now here he is mocking. Infamy on him! The mercenaries silenced her. May she remember and forgive me. I who knew, I did not soothe her pain. I remained silent. It was the price I had to pay for the life of my son.

Joseph of Arimathea pointed to Yeshua and said, His lips are cracked with thirst. Nicodemus said, Let him drink. The disciples from Beth Zabdai cried, We must give him to drink. The centurion Longinus said, That is good. He gave the order to the mercenaries.

A soldier went to dip a cloth in a jar. Longinus had warned us, They are filled with vinegar. Thus Rome quenches the thirst of the condemned men by adding suffering to suffering. Longinus stopped the mercenary's hand. He handed him another jug, which Nicodemus had brought in his cart without anyone noticing. Longinus said to the soldier, Use this vinegar instead. It is stronger, more suited to the king of the Jews. He laughed when the soldier dipped the cloth.

Mariamne cried out by my side. The mercenaries pushed us back harshly. I had no more breath in me. I feared everything. With the point of his spear, the mercenary stuffed the cloth into Yeshua's mouth. I knew what was to happen, and yet my heart stopped beating.

Yeshua's head tipped onto his chest. His eyes were closed. He might have been dead.

Mariamne fell to the ground. May she forgive my silence. I, too, did not know if my son was alive or dead. I did not know the will of the Almighty.

Large numbers were drawn by our cries and tears. The crowd pressed around Yeshua's cross. We heard the words, There is the

Nazarene. He died like a man without strength, he who was supposed to be our Messiah. Even the thieves around him are still alive.

The end of the day was approaching. The next day was the Sabbath. Most people were returning to the city. The centurion Longinus announced, He is dead, there is no point in staying here. He walked away without looking back. The mercenaries followed him.

The disciples from Beth Zabdai formed a circle around the cross and forbade anyone from approaching. The others kept their distance. They prayed and wept. And we, too, the women, were left alone. I ran to see the face of my son. It was a face without life, burned by the sun.

Joseph said to Nicodemus, It is time. Let us go to Pilate, quickly. Claudia the Roman said, I will take you. Through her tears, Mariamne was surprised and said, Why go to the Roman? I answered, To ask for my son's body so that we can give him a dignified burial. From my face, Mariamne guessed that I was between terror and joy. She asked, What is being hidden from me?

The walls of Jerusalem were red from the twilight, but Joseph and Nicodemus had not yet returned. A cohort of mercenaries arrived. The officer ordered the soldiers, Finish off the condemned men! With a sledgehammer on a long handle, they broke the legs and ribs of the thieves. The disciples from Beth Zabdai stayed at the foot of Yeshua's cross, ready to fight. We were petrified with fear.

The officer looked at us. He looked at my son. He mocked, This one is already dead. No point tiring yourselves out with the sledgehammers. All the same, whether for viciousness or hatred, a soldier aimed his spear. The head of it entered my son's body. Blood flowed. Water, too. It was a good sign. I knew it. Joseph of Arimathea had told me. Yeshua my beloved was showing no sign of life. The officer said to the mercenary, You see, soon the birds will deal with him.

I fell to the ground, as if my consciousness had abandoned me. Mariamne, the sister of my heart, took me in her arms. She wept into my neck and said, He is dead! He is dead! How can God let such a thing happen? May she remember and forgive me. I did not tell her what I knew. I did not say, He is still alive. Joseph of Arimathea put him to sleep with a drug that made him appear dead. I said nothing, and I was afraid.

Joseph and Nicodemus returned with a letter from Pilate, and said, Yeshua's body is ours. They saw the wound and said, Quick, quick.

The disciples from Beth Zabdai untied Yeshua and took him down from the cross. I thought of Obadiah, my beloved, who brought down my father in the same way from the field of crosses in Tarichea. I felt his protective wing, he was with me, my little husband. He reassured me.

I kissed my son's brow. Joseph asked for help. A plaster was placed on the wound. His body was entirely wrapped in strips of byssus coated with ointments, and he was carried in Nicodemus's wagon to the cave we had bought five days previously.

We women remained outside.

Joseph of Arimathea and the disciples from Beth Zabdai closed up the entrance to the cave by rolling a large stone called a gotal in front of it. Before going in, Joseph had shown me the phial, the one he had used in Beth Zabdai to bring back the old woman from death. The one that made the crowd cry out and believe in miracles.

The priests of the Sanhedrin came and asked questions before Sabbath began. The disciples, in white tunics such as are worn in the houses of the Essenes, pushed them back, saying, The Sanhedrin has no power here. Here, we come to bless, not to curse. They asked us, the women, to pray, so that our voices might be heard from afar.

In the night, Joseph came to us and said, We must go now. The disciples are guarding the cave. Let us go to the house of Nicodemus, near the pool of Siloe.

I was alone with Joseph, and I asked him, Is he alive? I want to see him. He answered, He is alive. You will not see him until Pilate's spies are sure that the cave is his tomb.

I saw him in the night after the Sabbath. We entered the cave through a fault concealed behind a terebinth bush. My son was wrapped in linen, on a bed of moss covered with a sheet. There was myrtle in the oil of the lamps, so that there might not be a bad smell.

Joseph said to me, Put your hand on him. Beneath my palm, I could feel his heart beating. Joseph said, If God wishes it, it will not be any more difficult than it was for the old woman you saved at Beth Zabdai. And God wishes it, otherwise he would not have let him survive until now.

We watched over him for three days. After three days, he opened his eyes and saw me, but the light from the lamps was dim, and he did not recognize me.

When he was able to speak, he asked Joseph, How long is it since you took me down from the cross? And Joseph said, Three days. And Yeshua smiled happily and said, Did I not say that it would take me only three days to rebuild the ruined Temple?

After another night, he announced that he wanted to leave. I protested and said, You are not strong enough! For the first time in a long time, he gave me a tender look and said, What does a mother know of her son's strength? And Nicodemus said to him, You are not safe in this land. They will be looking for you. Do not show yourself to the people. Your word will survive you. Your disciples will spread it. And Joseph of Arimathea said to him, Wait a few days, and my brothers from Beth Zabdai will take you to our house near Damascus. You will be safe there.

But he did not listen. He went away saying, I am going back whence I came. This is a road I will travel alone. Joseph of Arimathea and I understood that he intended to go all the way to Galilee. We protested again, but to no avail. Yeshua left.

When he was out of sight, when he had waved us away, we returned to the house of Nicodemus.

Mariamne, the sister of my heart, saw my distress and questioned me. I was ashamed of the secret that had closed my mouth, and I confessed to her, Yeshua is alive. Joseph of Arimathea saved him from the cross. I have done what I said. The cave was not his tomb. Mariamne cried, Where is he now? On the road to Galilee. On the road to Damascus. She ran to catch him up. I know he did not wave her away.

Barabbas joined us in the house of Nicodemus. He told us about what was happening in the city. A woman had discovered the cave open, the stone of the entrance rolled away. The crowd came to see. They called it a miracle. They cried, Yeshua was indeed what he said he was. The priests of the Sanhedrin came out on the square in front of the Temple. They said, The demons rolled the stone from before the Nazarene's tomb. They took away his body to feed the underworld!

There were fights. Barabbas predicted, They will not fight for long. Pilate has made it known that the disciples of Yeshua will be crucified. Tomorrow, they will be as meek as lambs.

Claudia the Roman agreed and said, I have never seen my husband so afraid. If I go to him today, he will not recognize me and will throw me in jail.

Barabbas was proved right. Three months have gone by, and already the disciples who were with my son on the first day have scattered. Only John is still with me. The others fish in the Lake of Gennesaret. To salve their consciences, some say I am mad.

In Jerusalem, the Sanhedrin teaches that Yeshua was not born the way he was in fact born. They say, His mother, Miriam of Nazareth, is a madwoman who slept with demons. She did not want anyone to know. She invented a story to conceal the facts of her son's birth.

You, my sisters, who are now following the teachings of Mariamne, say, If Miriam had not done what she did, Yeshua would be great today. They would not have forgotten him. You say, Miriam, his mother, refused her son's death, but the Almighty wanted him to die in order to provoke a rebellion. Now, nothing will happen.

But I answer, You are mistaken. The Almighty does not care about our rebellion; he cares about our faith. Rebellion is in our hands as long as we support life against death and light against darkness. I wanted my son, Yeshua, to remain alive as long as nothing has been accomplished of what gave birth to him. The Romans are still in Jerusalem, injustice reigns over Israel, the strong slaughter the weak, men despise women . . .

You say, Yeshua is alive today, but no one cares to listen to him, except his three remaining disciples. You say, On the cross, he made us ashamed, and out of his suffering revenge could have been born.

I answer, Revenge is as worthless as death. Leave it to the Lord, the Almighty, the Master of the Universe. That is a word of Yeshua. Put me on trial, for I committed the sin of impatience at Cana. God is angry. I did not let my son die. God is angry. But how could the Almighty, God of Mercy, be angry to see Yeshua alive? How could he choose grief and curses instead of joy and blessings? How could he want tomorrow to be only darkness in which humiliation and mutual hatred reign? May the Everlasting Lord forgive a mother's pride. A mother who gave birth to Yeshua, revealed him to the world, and kept him alive. For ever and ever. Amen.

This is the word of Miriam of Nazareth, daughter of Joachim and Hannah, known as Mary in the language of Rome.

MONTHS LATER, I RETURNED TO WARSAW. ONCE AGAIN, I found myself outside the door of the dilapidated apartment on Kanonia Street, in the old town. Maria recognized me, and understood immediately why I was there.

She did not need to ask me any questions. Her smile and the look in her eyes were eloquent enough. She seemed more tired than before. But the light in her eyes was as fresh and eternal as a child's.

"I had the text translated and read it," I said.

She nodded, smiling even more.

"What about you? Did you read it? Do you have a translation?"

"Abraham Prochownik told me the story."

"If he didn't die on the cross," I asked, "how did he die?"

She shrugged, irritated at having to say something so obvious.

"Who are you talking about? My Jesus? My Yeshua? I told you. He died in Auschwitz."